PRAISE FOR PHIL]

In The Way of Edan, Philip Chase has written a highly accomplished first novel. The storytelling is top-notch. There's a gravitas in the writing that put me in mind of Tolkien, with definite shades of Katherine Kerr, along with John Gwynne. This is a novel born of love for the story.

— MARK LAWRENCE

What a wonderful read! Prose that is smooth and accessible, a world with a weight and depth to it, and a gripping and emotional story. There's a lot to love here. Lovely to see the Anglo-Saxon influences that gave me a real sense of time and place, and the storytelling was done with a deft, assured hand.

— JOHN GWYNNE

The Way of Edan encompasses an expanding war driven by voracious religious fanaticism. Young heroes emerge, bonded by loyalty, in an age of ripening prophecy. Traditional fantasy readers will find elves with a fresh spin expanding the familiar bounds of individuality, and women, old and young, who wield magic in positions of power.

— JANNY WURTS

PRAISE FOR PHILIP CHASE (CONTINUED)

An impressive debut novel. Chase deftly weaves mystery and action with profound world-building. Deeply realized and compelling.

— IAN C. ESSLEMONT

Gemmell's characters have invaded the landscape of Tolkien in this immersive, addictive, poetic read. An instant classic that will have fantasy and historical fiction fans desperate for more.

— ED FROM THE BROTHERS GWYNNE

Every element of storytelling comes together to weave an engaging and immersive story that is an absolute joy to follow.

— WILL FROM THE BROTHERS GWYNNE

THE WAY OF EDAN

Book One of The Edan Trilogy

PHILIP CHASE

❀ Created with Vellum

ACKNOWLEDGMENTS

Many people — family, friends, and students — have helped me in the crafting of this story by reading it and offering their encouragement, without which I would have found it far more difficult to persevere. The numerous friends I have made on "BookTube" in recent years have aided me in ways they will never know to get this book to the finish line. I am more grateful for their kindness than I can express.

Special thanks to Simon Lipskar, who helped me believe I am a writer.

I could not be happier with the beautiful cover that Kyra Gregory and Jack Shepherd created, and Jack brought Eormenlond to life with his fantastic map. Jimmy Nutts is a hero for helping me with my author website, and what an honor for The Edan Trilogy to be Allen Walker's first (but surely not last) undertaking as an audiobook narrator! My thanks to Dan Koontz for his keen-eyed proofreading. Also vital was Vaughn Roycroft, Thiago Abdalla, and Ryan Cahill's helpful advice for navigating the self-publishing seas.

There can be few feelings to compare with having people whose writing one admires say kind things about one's book; my gratitude to those authors who have shown such generosity to me is immense.

Finally, while many authors mention friends on pages like this, few have the opportunity to bring up their very own Nemesis. Thank you, A.P. Canavan, from the bottom of my nefarious heart for the uncountable and illuminating critical insights that I could only refer to as fireballs.

For Rama

Outer Isles
Hemeldowns
Frost Bay
North Downs
Hrones Sea
mjothelf
The Mark
hwitwater
Beoroth
Farwick
Northweald (Ilcharwyn)
Norfast
Rimdale
Wolvendon
withweald
Kinsford
folkwater
folkmere
Birch Bay
Southweald (Ilcharwyn)
DWEORG BARROWS
anrod
theodamar
The Dweorgblithes
Etinstone
Woodburg
Torrlond
ORMETBERG
Bar of Harlon
Hasumere
Gorifaen Hills
Torrhelm
ea
Belzlam
Sundring Sea
Derwyn
Caltrilion
glas
BALNOR PASS
Gadomiel
Harith
gilion
Iarraen
Marar Mtns
Culvor Sound
maranant
Adanon
Asdralad
Bar of Frradan
Palahon
Dirgal
Dwarioth
Isles of Yaladir
Gulf of Gath
Kiriath
Halion Sound
Firdal
Ermenlond
or
Andumedan
Isthmus of Lod
Yalawyn
25 50 75 100 150 200 300
scale in miles

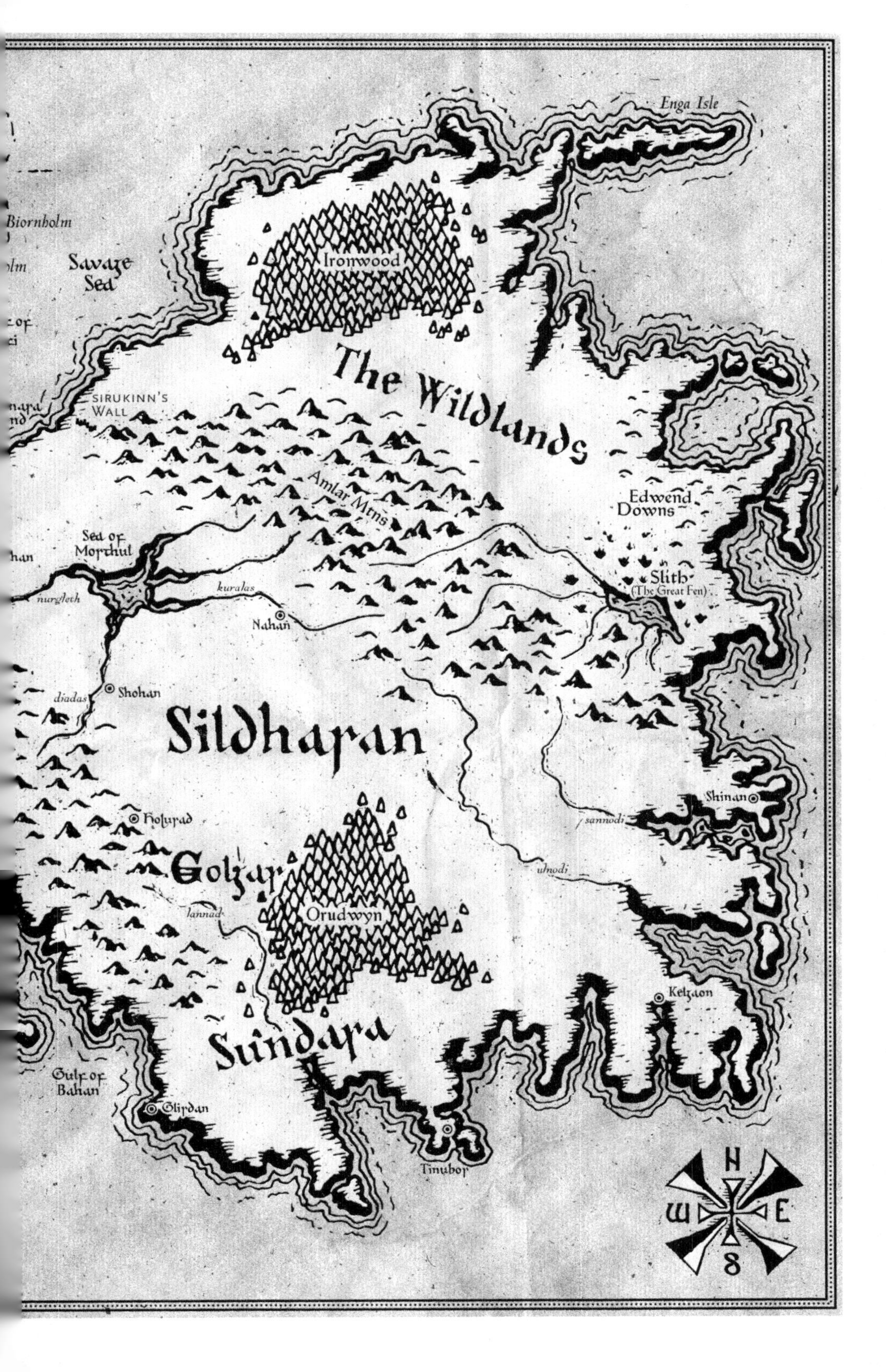

Enga Isle
Biornholm
Savage Sea
Ironwood
The Wildlands
Sirukinn's Wall
Amlar Mtns
Edwend Downs
Sea of Morthul
nurgleth
kuralas
Nahan
Slith
(The Great Fen)
Shohan
diadas
Sildharan
Shinan
sannodi
Holurad
Golzar
ulnodi
lannad
Orudwyn
Kelzaon
Sundara
Gulf of Bahan
Slipdan
Tinubor
N
W
E
S

CONTENTS

PROLOGUE

Deathlike silence descended upon the temple. It began with a hush when Finan and his two companions approached the steps leading up to the columned building. With each marble step they trod, the merchants and citizens behind them in the courtyard quieted more and more, their loud bargaining and conversing of moments before cut off and forgotten. By the time the three priests reached the top step, an eerie stillness had seized everything. Each of Finan's labored breaths seemed drawn out to an eternity, each intake laden with the scent of smoke and spices from the food stalls behind him mixed with the stench of what he carried. Beneath his white woolen robe, sweat trickled down his back. He tried to steady his breathing and calm his trembling body, and then, in unison with his companions, he turned around.

A crowd had formed within moments while Egbert, Deda, and he climbed the steps up to the temple, and more onlookers were arriving. Dozens of pairs of dark eyes gazed up at Finan and his two companions, squinting with curiosity, surprise, and hostility. For a generation, the Caergilese had grown accustomed to missionary priests from Torrlond preaching on the street corners of Iarfaen, but the sight of three of them before the doorway of the temple dedicated to their goddess was another matter.

Egbert shattered the silence, crying out his sermon.

"Edan sends us to bring His light to your darkness, His truth to your ignorance!" The Caergilese frowned at the three of them in confusion and rising anger, the murmurs in their tongue growing louder until they vied with Egbert's impassioned words, which washed over Finan almost without comprehension.

His senses were alert and numb all at once, as if he were not part of the scene but an observer hovering over it. Some distant instinct of self-preservation screamed at him that he should not be doing this, that he should abandon his two companions and flee this place. Such thoughts were unworthy. They had begun the thing, and it would run its course. Feeling like a rider on a galloping horse with no reins, Finan gritted his teeth and reminded himself that they were doing Edan's will. *Give me strength, Almighty One.*

The three priests of the Way from Torrlond stood in their white robes beneath the portico screening the entrance to the temple of Anghara, one of the two heathen gods the Caergilese worshipped in their ignorance. They faced the throng gathering before them in the cobbled courtyard without the temple. Opposite them on the other side of the courtyard, beyond all the merchants' stalls and carts, loomed the columned temple of Oruma. Together, the two structures formed one of the holiest sites in Iarfaen, Caergilion's chief city. Finan and his companions had come there in dedicated service to Edan, in accordance with the Supreme Priest Bledla's instructions.

The heavy wooden bucket's handle dug into Finan's clammy palm, and the tired muscles in his forearm began to ache and quiver. He wrinkled his nose as he shifted the bucket to his other hand, swallowing and blinking while studying the Caergilese in their queer, colorful tunics and dresses. There was Torrlonder blood in some of these folk if the tales told true, but Finan would not have guessed it from their brown skin and dark hair. Nevertheless, he had come to do his part in saving them. *Your will be done, Edan.*

A few in the crowd directed their glares at him, but most scowled at Egbert while the old priest thundered words that perhaps one in ten of the Caergilese understood. On Egbert's other side, his face near as pale as his robe, Deda prayed aloud for Edan to give them courage, his words gathering speed as the throng grew noisier and some of the Caergilese began cursing them and hurling insults.

Spittle flew from Egbert's lips while he imparted Edan's truth to the unbelievers. "When the Kingdom of the Eternal takes hold over Eormenlond, only those who follow Edan, only the righteous, will dwell with Him in bliss! All others, believers in false gods and worshippers of demons, will gnash their teeth and wail in torment. Abandon your false gods, and embrace the truth. The time is nigh! So says the Supreme Priest Bledla, Edan's chosen."

Finan closed his eyes and, even as his body continued to tremble, a sense of acceptance and peace welled inside him with the memory of the supreme priest's words when he sent them forth from Torrhelm. *He entrusted this mission to me. To us. We will not fail him. We will not fail Edan.*

How proud he had been that day! It had been a trial to maintain his humility afterward, but he knew why Bledla had selected him and the others. The gift was not strong in any of them, but they were all firm in their faith. This was how he could best serve Edan. Not only that, but, in obeying, he was doing what was best for the Caergilese, though they could not have known that. What they were committing was an act of love, but the Caergilese present this day would never understand. *All that matters is that Edan knows.*

He opened his eyes and smiled. Egbert ceased speaking and glanced at him, nodding at the bucket. The crowd below them had become a furious, boiling mob, with many screaming and raising their fists. A small group of Caergilese soldiers in their red tunics had arrived and were barking commands while pushing their way to the front of the crowd, no doubt to arrest the three trespassing priests. No matter. Edan would deliver them.

It was time.

Finan's smile broadened as he returned Egbert's nod, and then he took up the heavy bucket with both hands. The putrid reek of it wafted up his nose as he raised it level with his face. With all his might, and perhaps with the strength Edan lent him, he cried out and heaved the contents of the bucket toward the temple of Anghara.

Brownish clumps and ropes hung in the air before spattering on one of the columns and the marble floor near the doorway to the temple. Some chunks clung to the column while dark yellow rivulets trickled down the white marble. Finan had been sure to scoop up the runniest dung in the stables by the inn, and he had pissed in it himself to give it the right consistency.

A collective gasp preceded a long moment of silence. Finan dropped the bucket, which made a hollow thunk when it hit the marble and clattered onto its side before rolling to a stop. He turned toward the crowd, where every face gawked at him in wide-eyed, slack-jawed shock. He raised his trembling arms toward the heavens. "Your will be done, mighty Edan."

Screams of rage twisted the features of the Caergilese as they sprinted toward the three priests in a mad stampede. Deda and Egbert held up their arms like Finan, and they awaited their attackers with beatific grins.

Women, men, and even children surged up the steps, but the first to reach the priests were the Caergilese soldiers with their swords out. A bright rush of steel swept toward Egbert, and wet warmth pattered on Finan's face. He glanced down at his white robe covered with bright crimson spatters. Deda screamed, but Finan could not see him as so many hands seized him at once and threw him onto the hard marble, driving the wind out of him with a grunt.

Pain battered him from many places at once as his bones splintered and shattered under blows and kicks, but the worst was the searing agony that cleaved his chest when a sword thrust through him, forcing the remaining air from his lungs with a final gasp. In spite of the hot agony, he continued to smile. His martyrdom accomplished, he had fulfilled the supreme priest's bidding and Edan's will, and his reward would be in accordance with his suffering. A white flash accompanied a loud crack that split his skull, and his vision reddened for a brief moment before fading to black.

I

TROUBLES FROM OUTSIDE

Light crept on the land. A swollen red crescent bled over green hills to the east and bathed them in dawn's golden hues. On a grassy slope, Oswy squinted at the rising sun and walked with his family's sheepdog.

The solitude this time of morning was an old friend, and the stocky lad grinned at the landscape growing more vivid with each step he took. He raised the cloth bag he held in one hand to his nose and breathed in the scent of the fresh-baked bread his mother gave him before he set out that morning, when the predawn sky was still a deep dark blue surrounding their little farmstead on the outskirts of Kinsford. The dog padded along beside him. His tongue lolled out, and he sniffed at the bag in his master's hand.

"You and I are of one mind, Kip," said Oswy with a laugh. "But not just yet. If you're quick with the sheep today, might be I'll spare a morsel for you."

He would wait until he reached the sheepfold for the pleasure of tearing open the fresh loaf and eating some of it, and he knew he would share some with the dog no matter what. The strap of a calfskin flask of water dug into his shoulder, and in his breeches he had tucked his sling, which pressed against his stomach under his white kirtle. An ash staff in his right hand completed his gear. It was the staff his father Oslaf had used for years, and the smooth wood fit right in his hand. Sometimes Oswy liked to reflect that his son would one day hold the same staff.

For the present, his thoughts turned to the loaf of bread he would soon devour. The boy made his way across the undulating meadows towards the fold between two hills wherein his family's sheep pen nestled. As he and Kip approached the last hill lying between them and the little valley, the dog let out a low growl.

"What's the matter, boy?"

Kip's ears went flat against his head. His neck extended forward as he tensed and sniffed. He growled again. It was then that Oswy noticed something odd. *Should hear the sheep bleating by now,* he thought. Instead, all he heard was the cawing of crows.

"Wolves? Go get 'em, boy."

Like an arrow released from a taut bowstring, Kip streaked up the hill. After the dog passed over the crest, his distant bark came several times. Oswy hurried up the hill, but speed had never been his greatest asset. His cheeks puffed out as he struggled up, and his heart hammered and squirmed in his chest. His father would not be pleased if wolves had gotten into the pen and eaten one of their sheep.

When Oswy crested the hill, he bent over to catch his breath. Wincing from a cramp in his side, he looked up. "Regnor, Hruga, and all the gods," he swore between heavy gasps.

Forgetting the pain in his side, the boy ran down the hill toward the four stone walls enclosing his family's sheepfold. He darted toward the wooden gate, which was still tied closed with a rope. When he untied the rope and ran inside the pen, a flock of crows beat their wings and took to the air, cawing in raucous protest against the interruption. A cloud of flies buzzed and danced up with the crows but circled back to their feast.

"Shit. What in all of Eormenlond?"

The sheep were dead. All forty-two. It was a bizarre scene of carnage. Only something possessed by a demon could have produced such a frenzied slaughter, leaving the stench of blood and shit heavy in the air. Slick, shiny innards lay strewn everywhere and crimsoned the earth. Whatever attacked the sheep had torn off their legs and heads and scattered them in every direction. Blood stained their wooly bodies so that they were more red than white. One head at Oswy's feet stared up at him with blank eyes. Its tongue sagged out between its teeth. No wolves he had ever heard of would do something like this.

Oswy bent over to look at the head. Teeth marks left seeping holes all over it. *Too small for a wolf. But what else could do this?*

He remembered Kip. Where was the dog? *Must've caught their scent and run after 'em. Better call him back.* "Here, boy! Kip! Come 'ere, boy!" He whistled.

Something stirred behind the stone wall. A sound like raw meat tearing and then a gristly pop. Oswy walked toward the noise. "Kip. Here, boy."

A flash of movement. Had something just looked over the wall at him? "Kip?" He could not be sure, but he thought the flesh of the head that peeked over the wall was green. The eyes were yellow. It came to him at once. "Nightganger."

Oswy dropped the cloth bag with the bread in it and fumbled his leather sling out of his breeches. His other hand, all white-knuckled, clutched his staff. Staring at the spot where the creature's head had poked up from behind the wall, he glanced down for a rock to fit in his sling. A likely candidate lay just off to his right. He eased down, all the while keeping his eyes on the wall, and extended the hand that held the sling toward the rock.

One had to be careful with nightgangers, or pucas, as most folk called them. Everyone knew pucas were cunning. But what was this creature doing here in the daytime? And why had it killed all the sheep? *Wait*, thought Oswy with a sudden chill. *Pucas never hunt alone*.

Before his trembling fingers grasped the rock, before he turned his head, something slammed into him from behind. Oswy grunted and crashed to the ground, which knocked the wind out of him. His face and palms scraped on the earth, and his staff clattered beside him.

Clammy, calloused hands gripped his head with wiry strength like tree roots. The world went black when something dagger sharp plunged into his eyes with sudden, searing pain. Oswy screamed. His blood sprayed onto his face, and his bowels released their warm contents all over his thighs. Sharp teeth pierced soft flesh and ripped a gobbet out of his neck. The boy's terrified scream turned into a gurgle. Wet warmth seeped down his chest. As he lay writhing on the ground, a deep purring from dozens of throats surrounded him, and then it turned into a cackling kind of laughter. Teeth tore into his body from everywhere at once.

AFTER THE SUN HAD RISEN A LITTLE HIGHER, THREE MEN STOOD over what was left of Oswy's body. Two wore leather armor, vambraces, greaves, and heavy boots. Under their armor they were clad in grey kirtles and dark breeches. They carried short swords and bows, and each had a quiver full of arrows on his back. Their beards were thick and scraggly, their faces smudged with dirt.

The third man bore no weapons. He wore a hooded robe of white wool.

"Nasty business," said one of the soldiers. He spat to emphasize his point, but his gaze never left the body.

"Poor lad," said the second as he rubbed the hilt of his sword, which lay in its scabbard. "Bet he didn't even know they were comin' for him." He too seemed unable to look away from the mangled corpse.

The man in the white robe was younger than the other two, but he had a sternness about him that made him seem older. The soldiers stood behind him. "Unfortunate. But there will be many more casualties than this in the coming war," he said without turning his eyes from the mutilated flesh. "We must all play the part Edan has ordained for us, for a far greater outcome than our individual lives is at stake."

The soldiers waited for him to say something more as they all stared. The second soldier spoke up. "Shall we bury the body, m' lord?"

"No. The locals must not know we are here. Those are the orders."

"What about the pucas?" asked the first soldier.

"Leave them. We have enough now. The people in yonder village will have to deal with them. It's time for us to return to Torrlond."

The first soldier nodded. "I'll be glad enough to turn my back on this place. I've seen enough trees to last seven lifetimes."

"What about the local priest?" asked the second soldier.

"Bagsac?" The white-robed man smirked. "He has his orders too. He knows what to do." He snapped the spell by turning away from the dead boy. "We'll find the others and leave after sunset. We can't be seen with any of our new recruits. Remember: The supreme priest's orders are to move without attracting attention."

"Yes, m' lord," said both soldiers at once. They too turned away and followed the man in the white robe, leaving Oswy's body to the flies.

"DEAD!" SAID EDGIL. PAIN FLASHED WHEN HIS SWORD SMACKED Dayraven's back and sent him staggering forward. Laboring to breathe, Dayraven swallowed the pain and stabbed his sword into the earth. He grimaced and shook his head in disbelief at his father. *How?* thought the younger man. *Didn't even see it coming. How'd he do it? Again.*

Whenever they sparred, Edgil anticipated Dayraven's every move, somehow knowing when his son would make himself vulnerable. The old man always knew. And the sting on the young man's back bore out his father's word. Had it not been a wooden practice sword, and had his father not softened the blow, it might have severed Dayraven's spine. As it was, the sting would serve as a reminder.

Like everyone in the village of Kinsford, and indeed in the whole of the Mark, Dayraven respected Edgil. Yet his father's speed and intuition both astonished and frustrated him. Most young men his age were at least quicker than their fathers, and many were stronger, though not perhaps as cunning. But *his* father was Thegn Edgil, the hero of Kinsford. And though grey streaked his beard and his long, light brown hair, the warrior showed no sign of slowing. Under his white kirtle and tan breeches, his tall, slender body was muscled like a graceful predator. He wasn't even breathing hard.

Dayraven sat on the grass to catch his breath and sighed. The morning sun beat down. Sweat trickled along his neck and lower back under his kirtle. A satisfying ache permeated his muscles, especially in his right forearm from swinging his practice sword. For certain he would sleep well that night. As he tilted his head up, closed his eyes, and took in a deep breath, the living world around him — sun, grass, clear air — invaded his senses. But he wished he could beat the old man, if only once. Just down the slope, Imharr laughed.

"Lasted to the count of twelve that time, Day." Imharr brushed dark curls of his hair from his face. His brown eyes twinkled with amusement.

Dayraven smiled. He pulled up his practice sword and stood. "And how long do you suppose you'd last?" He stepped toward Imharr and, with one eyebrow cocked, whispered, "Longer than your meeting with Elfleda last night?"

The jest put a quick stop to Imharr's laughter. He reached for the leather bondsman's band around his upper arm and adjusted it, as he often did when he was in trouble. His previous evening's tryst with one of Kinsford's beauties was indeed short due to her father's untimely appearance at their appointed meeting place, her family's barn. Only Dayraven knew of Imharr's undignified retreat from his hiding place before the lovely Elfleda's arrival.

The bondsman grinned as he raised his practice sword and opened his mouth to retort, but a sharp command from Edgil cut him short. "Both of you now." With no more word, he raised his wooden sword and attacked.

A loud whack. Splinters spun off swords. Imharr was quick enough to parry the blow that flew down on them, but its force knocked him back several feet, leaving Dayraven to face Edgil. His father's firm instructions thundered in his mind: *Don't wait — attack first.*

He swung at his father, who flicked the blow aside with his sword and shoved his free elbow into his son's chest. When Dayraven fell backwards into Imharr, the bondsman dodged aside and deflected the thrust that blurred at him. Dayraven tripped and rolled. Wooden swords clacked as his father rained blows on Imharr. With every swing and crack, the bondsman parried and backed up a pace. *Get up. Go.* Dayraven sprang at his father from behind, but the cunning warrior maneuvered Imharr into the young man's path. *Here it comes — give it everything.*

When Edgil lunged, Dayraven swung hard to deflect the coming blow. His father darted back to let the young man's practice sword swerve into Imharr. Wood met the bone of Imharr's elbow. The bondsman grimaced and dropped his sword. Before Dayraven could look back at his father, he grunted as the flat of Edgil's sword slapped his ribs. *Oh, gods be good. Again . . .*

Thus vanquished, the two younger men panted and hung their heads. Since the sun's early rising they had suffered similar defeats at the older man's hands on the grassy slope outside Kinsford, and there was no finer way to spend a summer morning. Edgil stood over them, looking down with stern eyes.

"In battle, fight together with your companions in arms. Learn to fight together, or you'll not live long."

Dayraven nodded. "Yes, Father."

Edgil often gave such advice after thrashing them, and Dayraven heard his father's love beneath the unyielding words. The kingdom of the Mark had not warred for a long time, and there seemed little likelihood of him seeing a real battle. Yet threats existed in the world, so he understood his father's wisdom in preparing him.

Imharr rubbed his elbow while wincing, but his usual smile returned as he shook his head at Dayraven to tease him for his error. Edgil handed his practice sword to the bondsman and said, "Enough. The fields need tending. Take these home and meet me with food and drink. Dayraven, you have an errand to Urd. When you return, meet us in the fields. Don't be long."

"Yes, Father."

Dayraven and Imharr walked towards Kinsford while Edgil strode in the other direction toward one of their four hides of farmland outside the village. Without turning around, Edgil called out a final word. "Guthere says Ebba may ride with you, but mind you return soon."

Imharr nudged Dayraven with his elbow and grinned. Dayraven too smiled at the thought of a morning's ride with his betrothed on a beautiful summer day.

As the two young men walked down the grassy slope, Kinsford's wooden wall waited in the distance. Under the bright sun, the village's timber halls with their turf-covered roofs welcomed them. Behind that wall and under those roofs dwelled nearly everyone Dayraven held dear. Especially Ebba.

He glanced at Imharr. "Sorry about the elbow."

With his free hand Imharr punched Dayraven's shoulder, knocking him off balance. The bondsman chuckled. "Not to worry. Your father had us all tangled. Always two steps ahead of us, he is. He half meant for one of us to hit the other. Gave him a reason to lecture us: 'Learn to fight together, or you'll not live long.'"

Imharr's faultless imitation of Edgil's firm voice made Dayraven smile.

"Still, I could've done better."

"You're doing well enough, and you'll do better, Day. Not everyone has a father like yours. It's not always easy, trying to live up to him, but you'll be thankful for it in the end. He'll teach you much and more. You only need to be ready to take it all in here." Imharr tapped his head with his finger. "When the time's right, you'll stop thinking about it. Thinking just gets in the way. It'll be part of you. You'll see."

"I know. But sometimes it's like I see what's coming, and there's nothing I can do about it. He's fast, for certain. But there's something else. I know what he thinks I'll do, and I do it anyway . . . I do what he expects. I'm not sure I have words for it, but my mind isn't where it ought to be."

"Might be you were distracted. Your mind was already on that *ride* with Ebba." Imharr's playful wink made his meaning more clear than needed.

"I should've hit your head, not your elbow."

Imharr laughed, and Dayraven joined in a moment later. The younger man asked, "What about you?"

Imharr squinted with suspicion. "What about me?"

"You know. When are you going to ask one of those women you're always chasing to settle down with you?" He almost said aloud what they both knew: If Imharr wanted to wed and start his own farmstead outside Kinsford, Edgil would free him. The bondsman had enough silver tucked away for it.

Imharr grinned. "*They* chase me. There's a difference, you know. And it's more fun my way. Some are made for settling down. Others get a taste for a little adventure. Besides, a wife would keep me too busy."

"No doubt your nights at least would be busy."

Another punch struck Dayraven's shoulder, and at the same time Imharr's foot tripped him from behind, sending him rolling. He lay there on his back and laughed, taking in the sky's deep blue arching above and the smell of the grass. Sunlight dazzled his eyes.

"Quite the jester," said Imharr's voice above him. "We'll see how wide awake you are after your wedding night." He extended his hand, which Dayraven took with a firm grip, and pulled up the younger man. Both of them smiled.

"In the meantime, we'd best get moving. Some of us have work to do while you go out *riding*."

"How about 'Athelbertha'?"

Ebba giggled and then, with mock severity, frowned at him from her horse, which she rode sidesaddle. "That's even worse. Sounds like some old noblewoman."

Dayraven smiled at her, swaying a bit with the rhythm of his red mare, Rudumanu, plodding beneath him. "With a face like a prune from scowling too much?"

"Do you want your daughter to have a face like a prune?"

He pretended to look thoughtful, pursing his lips and scratching the light beard on his chin. "Hmmm. I suppose Athelbertha won't do, then. Our eldest daughter should have something prettier for a name." He grinned. "What about 'Burghild'?"

Ebba rolled her eyes and groaned. She flipped her long blonde braid over her shoulder, the way she often did when she had decided something. "Best leave the naming to me."

Dayraven smiled and nodded his head toward her. "As you say."

During the last couple miles of riding side by side, he had been teasing her by coming up with unfashionable names for their future children. The only sounds other than their banter were the clopping of their horses and, tied to Rudumanu's saddle, a sack jingling with jars of ointments and herbs, all the supplies Urd needed for the month. The curving green hills on the western outskirts of the Mark seemed to invite them to take their time as they rode.

When they neared a copse atop a grassy hillside, the two lovers looked at each other and smiled. He nodded toward the small cluster of trees, and with no word spoken, they rode towards its shade. After alighting from Rudumanu, he helped Ebba down from her horse. While the horses grazed nearby, Dayraven spread out his cloak beneath the trees, where he and Ebba sat next to one another.

The blue dress Ebba wore — her favorite, he knew — was a near match for the color of her eyes, which he gazed into. Her smile was playful. "How would it be if we didn't know each other? If we came from different parts of the world and never met?"

"Then," he said with a grin, "I'd search to the ends of Eormenlond until I found you, like the tale of Wilfar seeking Aelfscyn."

"Silly. You wouldn't even know to look for me."

"True love would guide me."

At this she laughed, and he with her, but then she frowned. "Isn't that a sad story?"

Dayraven shrugged. "Wilfar dies after he finds her, and Aelfscyn throws herself on a funeral pyre."

"Did she truly? Your head's full of sad old stories. Just don't expect me to throw myself on any fire for *you*."

He held his hand over his heart in mock agony. This drew a giggle from Ebba, and they smiled at each other. "You know," he said, "those stories may be sad, but they're more than that."

"Oh?" Ebba stuck her chin out and raised her eyebrows in challenge. "How do you mean?"

"Well . . ." Dayraven thought a moment, and he grew serious. "They tell us who we are, and where we come from."

"That sounds like something Urd told you."

"Well, perhaps she did, but it's still true."

"If it's true, give me an example."

Dayraven grinned as he realized Ebba's cleverness in tricking a story out of him. She loved hearing him tell the stories he learned from Urd and from the old woman's books. He knew she was proud of her future husband's learning. Other than Urd and the local priest of the Way, who was from Torrlond, Dayraven was the only one near Kinsford who could read.

In truth, one of his chief pleasures was telling Ebba stories, and not only for the admiration. The tales brought them closer, as if they were entering a world he summoned only for them. After they were wed, he planned to borrow one of Urd's books and teach Ebba and their children to read. "Very well," he said. "As it happens, not long ago I came across a tale in one of Urd's books that will serve."

Ebba sat up straighter, and her eyes lit up in anticipation, which made Dayraven smile even more. He continued, "It concerns the kingdoms of Adanon and Caergilion, in the south of Eormenlond."

"I know where they are, silly. Imharr was born in Adanon."

"Then you also know that Adanon and Caergilion have been foes for hundreds of years."

"Of course. Everyone in Eormenlond knows that."

"But do you know how the two kingdoms came to be foes?"

She smiled. "Tell me."

Her smile was so charming, so innocent and enticing at the same time, that Dayraven stopped just to gaze at her, until she scolded him, "Go on!"

"Alright," he laughed. "It all began with love."

"Love?" She raised one eyebrow in disbelief. "What sort of love brings such hate into the world?"

"Patience, my dear. You'll see."

"Very well, though I can see this will be another sad story. Tell on, and I shall listen."

Dayraven cleared his throat and leaned forward in an attempt to assume the air of a shaper or storyteller. "This is the tale of how Lothen, Duke of South Torrlond, wrested the land of Caergilion from the rulers of Adanon. Lothen settled there with his soldiers in the days of King Ednoth of Torrlond, long before the Mark existed, and the Southweald and Northweald were then one vast forest."

As he conjured up the right tone, Dayraven began to warm up to his story. "Generations of shapers have handed down songs of how Lothen won the kingdom of Caergilion to gain the love of Edgitha, daughter of King Ednoth. It's said Edgitha was so beautiful that every nobleman in Torrlond, even those already wed, admired her and desired to please her. Naturally, this led her to become somewhat haughty."

"Naturally," observed Ebba drily.

Dayraven ignored the interruption. "She refused all proposals brought to her father by suitors, until one day she proclaimed she would marry nothing less than a king. Since there were no unmarried kings at that time, it seemed Edgitha meant never to wed. However, one nobleman, Duke Lothen of South Torrlond, did not let that stop him. He was a young and headstrong but brave man who had recently come into his dukedom, and he had known Edgitha for many years since he was fostered at the king's court in Torrhelm. Lothen had long been smitten by Edgitha's beauty, and he determined to win her love. His lands bordered the Marar Mountains, and south of those mountains in those days lay one large kingdom: Adanon.

"Adanon was an old and powerful kingdom, but in recent years civil war and disease had weakened it. Its weakness suggested a daring plan to Lothen. He would conquer Adanon and become its king, and then he would return to Torrlond to ask for Edgitha's hand. After many preparations, he set out with his advisors and warriors over the Marar Mountains.

"For ten hard and bloody years they fought. Lothen and his troops could not conquer all of Adanon, but they succeeded in occupying the western and northern portions of the kingdom. After he gained enough victories to carve out a sizable kingdom, Lothen grew weary of war, and Adanon had bled so much that its leaders were eager to lay down their weapons. The two sides agreed to peace and drew the boundaries that exist to this day. Lothen named his kingdom Caergilion, and he returned to Torrlond to ask Edgitha to wed him. 'For your bride price I offer a kingdom,' he said to her, and she relented at last. He brought his queen with him to their new chief city, Iarfaen."

"All those people died so one man could wed a woman who thought too highly of herself?" Ebba's face reddened with indignation. "I don't call it love at all. It's pride that drove her, and it's stupid pride that drove *him*."

Dayraven smiled at her outburst, but he knew she was wise in her judgement. Perhaps pride and love were not as far apart as most folk thought. "I suppose you're right. But the tale's not finished yet."

"Oh." Her features calmed. "Let's have the ending then."

"Lothen's victory turned out bitter. Hearing Edgitha was the cause of the war, a surviving native nobleman stabbed her to death then slew himself with the same blade to avoid capture. Sorrowful at the loss, Lothen nonetheless declared he had seen enough bloodshed to last the rest of his life. He sought peace by marrying a noblewoman of the southern people. He urged his soldiers to follow his example and find wives among the people they conquered, for a great part of the men in those lands had perished.

"That's how the conquerors blended into the local people after a few generations, and their children spoke their mother's language, though they changed it with many words from the Northern Tongue. But the people of Adanon regarded those of Caergilion as half-breeds and their tongue, Western Ondunic, as barbaric. They blamed the rulers of Caergilion, descendants of Lothen, for dividing and weakening their once powerful kingdom. The people of Caergilion in turn despised those of Adanon, and for many hundreds of years those two kingdoms have sought to harm each other. Even today, soldiers and brigands of both sides raid across their borders, slaying the older folk and enslaving the younger."

When Dayraven nodded to signal the tale's end, Ebba sighed. "I knew it would be a sad one."

"But, you see, it tells us much."

"What? That people will slay and die for the most foolish things?"

"I suppose. And it tells us why Adanon and Caergilion will never have peace."

"Because of an old story?"

"Yes. The old tales take us to faraway times and places, but they're also where we come from. They tell us how we got here. Look at Imharr: he never would've come to the Mark if soldiers from Caergilion hadn't raided his family's farm in Adanon and enslaved him. Those soldiers never would've done that if the two kingdoms hadn't hated each other for so long. And they never would've hated each other if it hadn't been for Lothen's love for Edgitha. Or their pride, as it were."

Ebba smiled, and he guessed she was both pleased and amused at his skill in closing his argument. "That might be, but I'm glad to be from Kinsford right now."

Dayraven looked into Ebba's eyes. "So am I."

Leaning on him as they sat on his cloak, she took his hand and looked out over the land they called home. He followed her gaze east to the view opening out beneath them. In the summer months the undulating landscape was green and gentle. Below them, hawkweed, buttercups, daisies, and clover painted the hillside with flecks of red, yellow, white, and purple wavering and bobbing in the breeze. Among the wildflowers flitted buzzing insects. A morphing cloud-shadow at the hill's base slid over the landscape. Beyond, hills that Dayraven had known since childhood rose in waves behind one another until they blurred in the distance under the blue sky. To the north, the Folkwater River shimmered in the sun as it snaked between the hills, while the great forest, the Southweald, blanketed the lands to the south.

Mixed in with the meadow's grassy smell was the sweet scent of Ebba's body. The air was clean and bright and clear, and everything in the world seemed right where it should be. Knowing how fleeting the moment would be, Dayraven took a deep, slow breath and savored it as he tilted back his head. Far above, a large bird glided on the wind, a dark speck amidst the deep blue.

"Feels like I could fly today."

"Silly."

He gazed at Ebba again, focusing on her blue eyes and her face's delicate features. "Beautiful," he said as he traced his finger over the soft flesh of her cheek and down her neck.

Ebba looked down, but when he brought his face closer, she clasped his head in her hands and kissed him. Her lips were warm and pleasant, and her fingers ran through his hair, pulling it just enough to convey her desire. When she broke off the kiss, she looked up into his eyes and grinned before pulling him close for another. Dayraven placed his trembling hands on her back, moving them in gentle circles as he pressed her close. One of her breasts brushed his chest, sending a shiver rippling through his body. A quiet groan escaped her open mouth, which he covered with his lips. He lost himself in that kiss, and in the copse's shade the eager pleasure of youth swam over them.

Dayraven shifted one hand from Ebba's back toward her chest, but at the same moment, she released him from their kiss and clasped his hand. She sat straighter and wiped her mouth with the back of her free hand as she steadied her breathing. "We'd best get going to Urd's. Your father said come back soon to work the fields. And both our fathers know exactly how long this journey takes."

"Then we'll tell them Urd kept us with one of her stories. Likely she will anyway." He slid one hand to the curve of her waist.

Ebba pursed her soft, glistening lips in a frown. "All the more reason to get going. There'll be time later . . . *after* we're wed." Her frown turned into a teasing smile.

He could not help answering her smile with one of his own. After a long sigh, he stood up and offered his hand to her with a deep bow. "In that case, if my lady is ready, we will depart."

She took his hand, and he pulled her up into his arms for a final kiss, which she did not deny.

Before the kiss ended, something stirred the dry leaves on the ground nearby, startling the two lovers. A grey squirrel skittered from behind one oak tree halfway up the trunk of another, where it watched them. Ebba pointed at it. "We have company."

The creature fixed its dark, glassy eyes on Dayraven. He stepped forward a pace and knelt. Its face twitched, and its little mouth worked as if it were chewing on the meat of a nut. "This copse is its world," he said without turning back to Ebba. "Like Kinsford for us. It loves its home the same way we do."

He inched closer and spoke to the squirrel as if it could understand. "Don't be afraid, little one. Not everyone beyond your world means you harm." He held out his hand toward the creature, which sniffed the air.

Dayraven's awareness contracted around the squirrel. He heard its thoughts, if the wordless workings of the little creature's mind could be called such. Perhaps they were more raw emotions or instinct, but he perceived them nonetheless. He felt the squirrel's urge to flee from the strange monsters looming before it competing with the desire to defend its home and simple curiosity.

In the next moment, the creature's posture relaxed. *That's right, little friend,* he told it. *I won't harm you.*

Their thoughts met in the space narrowing between them as the squirrel climbed down from the tree trunk and approached Dayraven's outstretched hand. Such things often happened to him when his mind slipped in a certain way while he focused on something. Since he was young, he had a way with animals and an easy understanding of people. Sometimes he thought he saw himself from another's eyes, a kind of emotional understanding that leapt out. Thus, he thought little of it when the squirrel edged to within a few inches of his hand and cocked its head to the side as if posing a question.

But when he peered back with a smile at Ebba, her face was more surprised than amused. "Why do they always come so close to you . . . like they're tame?"

"Might be it thinks I have food. I don't know. I think it knows I won't hurt it. It's just something . . ."

The thudding of approaching hooves cut off Dayraven's explanation. The squirrel jerked and disappeared into the copse. He stood up and turned around. In the distance, Imharr rode his grey mare, Hraedflyht.

Ebba gazed across the meadow. "What's he doing here?"

Dayraven held her hand. "He's riding hard."

They did not need to wait long for Imharr, who headed toward their grazing horses. As he approached, Imharr reined in Hraedflyht, but he did not alight from the snorting mare. His face was enough to tell Dayraven something was wrong.

"Your pardon," said the bondsman as he nodded toward Ebba and then turned to Dayraven. "Far be it from me to interrupt young lovers, but you must come back to Kinsford."

"What happened?" asked Ebba. "Is everyone well?"

"All are well in Kinsford, as far as I know. I saw your father before I left. But something's happened." He looked again at Dayraven. "I can say little, but when Earl Stigand spoke to your father, he told me to fetch you back as soon as I found you. Best not wait."

Dayraven wondered what tidings the earl had given his father to cause such concern. A shadow in his mind belied the warmth of the clear day. Whatever was wrong, he was ready to stand by his father and Kinsford.

"Alright, then. The sooner we return, the sooner we'll learn what's happened." He hurried to ready the horses, and when he finished, they journeyed back to Kinsford speaking little.

2

WHERE MEMORIES DWELL

Scenes of Sequara's childhood flooded her mind along with an array of emotions – a poignant mixture of longing, affection, regret, and sorrow – when the farm came into view. Much like every other home in the region, the humble farmhouse was built from the tan limestone predominating in Asdralad's countryside, while the barn, which seemed in as much danger of toppling over as it always had, consisted of warped pieces of wood.

Pulling on the reins, Sequara stopped her mare for a moment to observe the scene and the emotions alike. She had spent countless hours playing and working among the olive trees surrounding her, and the scent of the nearby sea transported her to those days so that their illusion of safety and untroubled peace pervaded her once again. For a fleeting moment, she was that girl again, innocent of the deaths and duties that would take all this away from her forever.

And yet, somehow, those days remained somewhere within her, in the place where memories dwell – or at least some imagined impression of them did. Fragments of images, sounds, and smells: She knew better than to trust them, for in the act of caressing them over the years, she had changed them. Each one was part of the fiction of her life. But in the realm of origins she perceived the truth that such a life did not in fact exist, that it was a gentle breath indistinguishable from the endless air around it. Memories were all little lies strung together to confer the impression that a life had a story with its own meaning, that it existed apart from the energy whence it came and whither it would return. Unlike most people, Sequara could not long indulge in such comforts.

Behind her, Karad's horse whickered, snapping her mind back to the present world around her. Her bodyguard nudged his horse forward until he was next to her, squinting while gazing at the farmhouse. The veteran's leather armor creaked as he reached up to scratch his temple beneath his helm. "Not a bad spot to grow up in. Wouldn't mind a farm like that to settle on. Heera could grow her flowers there."

Sequara snorted. "In all the years you've been talking about retiring, your poor wife might have grown a sea of flowers." Feeling a familiar pang of guilt over it, she well knew the old soldier stayed on out of loyalty to her, as if no one else could protect her as well.

Karad's mouth quirked into a half smile, and he grunted. "Still. Not a bad spot."

"No. It wasn't bad." Sequara shook her head, and the slight smile she had not even realized was there disappeared. It was better to seal away the warm memories, for in attachment to them lay pain. Such pain would only cloud her judgement. She must never forget who she was now.

That was why it had been years since Sequara had returned to the farm, though it was less than half a day's ride north of Kiriath, and sometimes regret at what must seem like her indifference crept into her. As much as she tried to attain the state of enlightened detachment that seemed second nature to Queen Faldira, it was never indifference on her part. It simply would not do to give this particular corner of Asdralad more attention than any other, and her duties kept her far too busy anyway. Even now, she was unsure if she should have come, and she entertained the idea of turning her horse about and leaving. *What good can come of this?* she wondered for the thousandth time. She lifted the reins and then hesitated.

Children's giggles yanked her attention back to the farm. In the distance, one boy, the elder, chased his younger brother until they disappeared behind the farmhouse, unaware of her presence. She gazed at the home. Every sun-warmed stone of that dwelling was familiar to her, though in the few times she had returned during all her years away, it always seemed smaller than her childhood recollections made it. She knew it would be cooler inside the home, with its windows open to the sea breeze and the scents of woodsmoke, spices, and seafood permeating it.

She tugged on her silk tunic, which had begun to stick to her sweaty back, and took a deep breath.

"Shall I wait here for you, then?" Karad raised one of his eyebrows. No doubt he sensed her uncertainty. Having warded her since Queen Faldira declared Sequara her heir when she was but twelve, the man understood her well. Too well. Sequara doubted the queen had ever been so transparent to her bodyguards. But she could not resent Karad for being perceptive as well as loyal, and he always kept his concern for her to the smallest gestures.

She took a deep breath, once again taking in the dusty, salt-laden scent of her youth. "Yes. Thank you, Karad." The heels of her boots nudged her mare's sides, and it trotted toward the farmhouse.

The two boys came sprinting from behind the home, but they stopped and froze when they saw her. Their eyes wide, they stood for a moment with their mouths open before running back toward the house and disappearing inside the shadows within the open door. By this reaction Sequara understood they had recognized her, and a fresh pang of guilt raked her with sharp claws as she realized how little she knew them.

It was not her duty to know them. Surely they understood this.

When she rode within twenty paces of the door, Sequara pulled on the reins and alighted from her horse, her boots scraping on the hard, bare earth of the well worn yard. She arched her back and then bent over, rubbing her legs to ease muscles stiff from riding. It had been some time since she had ridden so far. Her dark blue tunic and matching loose trousers flapped when the sea breeze kicked up, blowing dust into her eyes. By the time she finished blinking it out and wiping her eyes, Elur had emerged from the doorway, no doubt warned by his sons of her presence.

For a time longer than was polite, he gazed at her with a blank expression. He was younger than she, only twenty-five, but years of labor in the sun had etched a few wrinkles around his eyes and darkened his skin to a rich brown. Though she was darker than most in Kiriath, Sequara was painfully aware of how, in his eyes, her bronze skin made her resemble the noble families he so scorned.

Elur glanced for a moment toward Karad in the distance before returning his gaze to her. Though he wore a frown, he inclined his head in a bow. "Majesty. What brings you to our 'umble farm?"

Sequara ignored the exaggerated rustic accent and the sarcastic bite in his words, knowing they came from hurt. She was careful to give away no emotion in her face, just as Queen Faldira had trained her. "I'm to leave Asdralad for a time." She left unsaid the fear lingering behind her words: that where she was going might be very dangerous, and there was a chance she might not return. Nonetheless, this revelation seemed to hang in the air between them during a long silence.

Elur's eyes widened for a moment, and then his face softened. "Oh. I see. I s'pose you can't tell me where you're heading." It was not a question.

"I cannot. I'm sorry."

"No need to be. When do you set out?"

"On the morrow."

"Then you'll stay the night? Shara'll have supper ready soon enough. Must be hungry."

She glanced at the ground for a moment before meeting his eyes. "I'm afraid I cannot. I leave at daybreak, and I must hasten back to Kiriath to make preparations. I came only to see you before my departure. To say . . ." She swallowed the words that almost slipped out as well as the tears that threatened to come.

Elur scratched his ear and looked down at the ground, giving her a moment to regain her composure.

She managed a half smile. "Besides, I don't think Shara truly wants me under her roof after what happened last time."

He winced and then chuckled, which widened her grin, and for the briefest moment they were children again with no cares or distance between them. Elur shook his head, and then his smile disappeared. "Mustn't blame Shara. She's afraid of you."

"I know. And the boys."

He frowned. "And the boys. Like every other villager on the island."

She gazed at him as the pain of his words seeped in. "And you, Elur?"

He squinted at her as if trying to make out something he could not quite see. "Sometimes." A small grin brightened his features. "Other times I remember the girl who used to put up with me, even when I was a pain in her arse. The one who used to take care of me." He shrugged. "Mostly, I reckon I just miss you."

I miss you too, little Brother. Sequara paused to master her voice. "In serving Asdralad, I serve you and your family."

"And everyone else." He nodded. "I know. The queen – may the Mother and Father bless her – made the right choice in you, and though sometimes I wish she hadn't made it, far be it from me to question her wisdom." Though Queen Faldira came from a noble family, Elur's hostility never extended to her. He drew himself up. "We're proud of you too, you know. Even Shara."

Sequara allowed a small smile and, mastering her emotions, resisted the urge to hug her brother. "Thank you. It helps me to know that. I will journey with a lighter heart."

They stood for an awkward moment, each leaving so much unsaid since it was easier, perhaps even better, that way. Finally, he scratched his ear again. "Sure you won't stay for supper at least?" The expectation of refusal lay beneath his words.

She smiled. "I have food and water in my saddle bag. I must leave to reach Kiriath before dark."

He did well to disguise his relief behind a nod. "Your horse?"

"We stopped at the inn in Ganbu. We'll stop again on the way back."

He nodded again. "Well. Stay safe, then, on this journey of yours. I reckon it must be something important for the queen to let you go."

"I think it might be." *Asdralad's survival might depend on it.* She did her best to hide all emotion from her face. "I'll try to come again after I return."

Elur grinned as if he did not quite believe her, but then he nodded. "We'll be here."

Sequara peered at him for a long moment, hoping it would not be the last time she saw him but committing his features to memory in case it was. "Take care, little Brother."

A brief widening of his eyes betrayed his surprise. She had not addressed him as her brother in many years, perhaps since the day she first left for Kiriath. His smile – so little changed from when he was a boy – almost broke her composure, and she took a deep breath before he said, "And you, Sister."

She placed her boot in a stirrup and heaved herself up while swinging her other leg over the mare's back. Once she was settled in the saddle, she looked down at Elur. "Give my greetings to Shara and the boys."

"Will do."

Sequara brought her horse about and commanded it to trot back through the olive grove. When she approached Karad, he turned his horse and fell in beside her without a word. Not once did she look back as she sought to quiet all the memories swirling from the place where they dwelled within her. She knew she would be caressing them during the long ride back to Kiriath.

AFTER ARRIVING AT THE VILLAGE OF GANBU, WHICH LAY HALFWAY between Elur's farm and Kiriath, Sequara and Karad walked their horses to the inn, where the innkeeper, bobbing his head several times in deference, stabled the steeds and had his son rub them down before feeding and watering them. The inn was not much bigger than the rest of the dwellings in the village and was made of the same tan limestone, though it boasted a well in its small, dusty courtyard. Within the shade and relative coolness of the inn's compact common room were three modest tables with benches. At two of the tables, locals drank watered down wine and ate mussels. Shadowed by Karad, Sequara headed toward the third with as little noise as possible.

The villagers went quiet, their eyes flicking between Sequara and Karad, whose black leather armor and white tunic gave him away as a palace guard. They all rose and gave her careful bows, to which she responded with a nod. "Thank you. Please continue with your meal." They waited to sit back down until she found a place on a bench at her table.

They stole occasional glances her way, but they resumed their interrupted conversations about the year's olive harvest and other local matters. By Karad's presence and her silks they might have assumed she was noble, but she suspected they knew who she was.

The sunlight streaming through the open doorway dimmed when someone new entered, a woman, and a man followed hard on her heels. By her simple, roughspun frock and thin but muscled body, the young woman appeared to be one of the many laborers or small farmers that made up the majority of the populace in Asdralad's countryside. Without the gift, Sequara imagined she would have looked much like her, and they were of an age. The woman's wide eyes and set jaw told of some distress before she reached Sequara's table and went down on her knees, gazing at the floor.

Karad's hand drifted toward the hilt of his sheathed sword, but Sequara directed a quick shake of the head to him. The veteran nodded and kept his hands at his sides, but he stood from the bench all the same to position himself closer to the distressed woman kneeling before Sequara.

The man behind her, likely her husband, bowed low and spoke first. "M'lady, so sorry to disturb. It's just she's that upset, seeing as how we lost t'other one a couple years back. So sorry." He swallowed his own distress and put his hand gently on the woman's shoulder. "Nila. Please, we shouldn't be disturbing the good lady."

Nila did not move. Still gazing at the floor, she seemed to address her husband. "She was one of us. She'll hear me out." She looked up at Sequara and held her eyes. Mastering the sobs that nearly broke from her throat, she spoke in a voice husky with emotion. "You are Lady Sequara."

Sequara nodded slowly. "I am."

A broken, desperate smile took over Nila's face, and, freeing itself from her lashes, a tear streaked down her cheek. The words spilled out of her too. "The Mother must have sent you. My child. My baby. Will you save her? Our village healer can do nothing to stop the fever. It took my Aran before. The same one, I know it. But this time the Mother sent *you*. Please, my lady. Will you help us?"

Using one of her breathing exercises to calm herself, Sequara mastered her emotions before she began reacting to the mother's distress, which reached deep within and shook her. She took Nila's face in her hands and bent toward her. "Of course. I will do what I can. Take me to your child."

Nila and her husband led Sequara out of the inn and through the village, with Karad following close behind in silence. A few other villagers, mostly children, gazed from their doorways in mute curiosity. When they arrived at a simple stone dwelling on the outskirts of Ganbu, the couple turned back to Sequara, Nila pleading with her eyes and her husband bowing low. "She's inside. Please," said the young mother, her voice breaking into a sob on the last word. Her husband opened the door and gestured for Sequara to enter.

Without a word spoken, Karad ducked in first. Suffering him to do his duty, Sequara followed into the one-room home, the couple coming in behind her. She blinked in the dim interior, which featured crude furniture and a small hearth that had bestowed the hut's smoky scent. In one corner, a small form lay on a sleeping pallet, a girl of about four years, thin and sunken-eyed. With light from the doorway spilling onto her face, the little girl moaned, her chapped lips twitching as she tried to roll her head to the side. Sweat plastered her curly hair to her forehead, but her body shivered as she kept her eyes clenched.

Sequara forgot everything else as she knelt next to the sleeping pallet. She reached toward the girl's forehead and brushed it with her fingers. It was clammy with fierce heat. She looked at the girl's mother. "You were right to seek me. The fever is high, but I will help her."

Nila nodded and put one hand on her husband's shoulder, and he leaned over to help steady his wife.

Sequara fixed her gaze on the little girl, placing one palm on her burning forehead. The girl remained still, but Sequara's eyes widened a fraction as she released herself into the realm of origins. Leaving behind her body, she joined her surroundings, aware of every emotion yet detached from all like an ethereal observer. She heard her voice chant the song of origin, "Druanil vardunay nanduinae . . ."

From the timeless realm of origins, she imparted some of her own energy to the little one's fevered body to fight the small organisms poisoning it. Dimly aware that time was passing for the mortals nearby, she remained in an eternal present, the repeated words of the chant echoing around and within her as more energy seeped from the vast source she tapped into the small body her flesh touched, spreading strength within it. As she shared her power with the girl, so too did the little one's mind open up to her, her thoughts and memories bleeding and swirling into her. Sequara knew the suffering and the joys the girl had experienced in her short life as if she had lived them, as if the little one's self had blended with her mind. All the while, the strength she gave the girl allowed her body to fight the invading organisms threatening it. The inexorable energy spread, the balance tipped, and the organisms that had been ravaging the small body dwindled until, after a last desperate stand, they succumbed.

Sequara returned to her body from the realm of origins, looking down at the girl, who opened her eyes and grinned. She was aware that the girl shared the peaceful sense of knowing her that always came when minds touched while healing. She grinned back.

Nila and her husband collapsed to their knees, the flood of their emotions bursting through in sobs, their bodies shuddering as they touched Sequara's boots in gratitude. Even Karad, watching over it all, brushed an eye with the back of his hand and cleared his throat.

Sequara allowed herself a brief but pure smile, feeling the rare satisfaction that came from having the gift when she healed. These were her people, and she had helped them. In that moment, the usual doubts as to her purpose quieted.

LATER THAT NIGHT, AFTER RETURNING TO THE PALACE, SEQUARA gazed out over Kiriath, and for a moment her thoughts strayed back to the little girl she had healed in Ganbu. She had left the village a bit tired but fulfilled. Healing was the one thing that always gave her happiness, but, in accordance with her training, she kept such emotions in check. She reminded herself that, in the days ahead, she would likely need to use the gift for altogether different purposes.

"Then all is ready?" Queen Faldira's words tugged Sequara back to the present. The elder woman's voice was as serene as ever, and yet Sequara could not help but feel the keen discernment within her, as if the queen perceived every thought in her mind, even with night's shadow cloaking her face.

She inclined her head in a slight bow. "Yes, my queen."

"Good." Asdralad's ruler gazed out from the height of the grounds just outside the palace doors, where the two women stood looking down at Kiriath's flickering lights and the bay beyond. Around those hearthfires and within Kiriath's homes and inns, folk gathered, ate, sang, played, jested, and made love, all blissfully unaware of the vast threat assembling far away on the mainland of Andumedan. As yet, the burden of that knowledge fell on the shoulders of only two: their queen and her chosen heir.

The elder woman's long hair swayed with the gentle breeze coming up from Halion Sound, and, under the moonlight, Sequara could just make out the silver strands that formed a stripe along the middle of her scalp. "Much depends on your secrecy. We have been left in the wake of the events unfolding, reacting too late. The deaths of those three Torrlonder priests in Caergilion have set everything in motion. Already it is impossible to prevent some of the coming bloodshed. Your success could make all the difference in averting more."

Sequara glanced back toward the palace doors, where two guards stood out of earshot. "I will do everything in my power."

"I know you will." Faldira turned toward her companion and looked down at the younger woman. "You may rely upon Karad. He will command the guards assigned to you. All of them are capable sailors and will have no trouble keeping up their disguise. As we discussed, it is vital that none of them know why you are there."

"Yes, my queen."

"Forgive me for laboring the point, but if even one of them fell into the supreme priest's hands, nothing in their minds would be hidden from him. Even Galdor's two agents know nothing except that they are to aid you in arriving at the meeting and report to him when it is finished. They have established themselves in Torrhelm and will await you there. In the meantime, they'll keep an eye on things to make sure all is safe."

"I understand."

Her dark eyes hidden in shadow, the queen gazed at Sequara, who perceived that her mentor was buying time with these reminders and had something important to say. Perhaps she was seeking the right words.

"You visited your brother today." It was not an accusation or a question, simply a statement without judgement and delivered in the queen's usual mild tone.

Nevertheless, the words took Sequara by surprise. She had requested leave to depart the palace for the day, but she had not told the queen where she was going. She took a moment to compose herself. "Yes, my queen."

"How was he?"

"Well. His boys are growing. Elsewise, little has changed."

"And what does he think of my making you heir to Asdralad's throne?"

Queen Faldira had never asked such a question. Sequara cleared her throat to give herself some time to answer. "He has great respect for your wisdom, my queen."

The queen laughed gently. "More respect than he ought to, most likely. But that is one decision I have never doubted. Not only because of the strength of the gift in you, but because of who you are, where you come from. We face great changes in the years ahead, I deem. The others would have been too wedded to tradition to deal with them." All the other candidates the queen had trained from childhood along with Sequara had come from the island's score or so of noble families, in whom the gift ran strong. Sequara was not the first commoner chosen to rule Asdralad, but it was still a rare occurrence.

The younger woman gazed at her feet. "I hope to prove worthy of your faith."

Queen Faldira drew closer and enfolded Sequara's hand in both of hers. They looked one another in the eyes. "I am sorry."

Sequara blinked and looked up at the queen's face in confusion. "For what, my queen?"

"For choosing you. For taking away your life. And now this. I wish I could go in your stead."

"Never. Asdralad needs you."

"As it will need you. But this trial is yours. It and the events that spring from it will shape your rule in days to come."

Sequara did not quite understand, but she nodded.

Queen Faldira drew one of her hands inside the cloak she wore over her dress. When it emerged, she held an object. She opened the younger woman's hand and placed something hard into it, gently closing her fingers around it.

Sequara glanced down. She found that she was grasping the hilt of a dagger, whose blade almost seemed to gleam as it caught the moonlight.

The queen's gaze was unwavering. "I do not know what risks or betrayals you might face, but you should expect them. As we discussed, you must avoid capture at any cost. Should our plans become known, Asdralad would face certain ruin."

Sequara's grip on the dagger's hilt tightened. She nodded. "I understand."

3
THE HUNT

"Life for life. Blood for blood. The beasts must pay for slaying Oslaf's son."

Thus said Edgil to Dayraven and Imharr after he told them of the shepherd boy's death at the farmstead south of Kinsford. Seldom had the Mark's folk heard of such a happening. The earl of Kinsford had asked Thegn Edgil to lead the hunt to avenge the boy and the sheep that the pucas tore to shreds, and Dayraven knew his father took the charge as a sacred duty. Outsiders had harmed their people. Edgil had taught him from boyhood there was no higher good than loyalty to the Mark, no higher duty than avenging their own.

After gathering the men of the hunting party and readying their weapons, they arrived at Oslaf's farmstead before evening. In the westering sun's waning light, they tracked the trail of blood to the Southweald, the great forest hemming in their lands to the south. They returned and stayed in Oslaf's barn through the night because it would have been fruitless, even perilous, to hunt pucas in the darkness, when the beasts would have the advantage of their night eyes.

Grief and hatred marked Oslaf's ravaged face when they arrived at his farm, and the stout farmer's voice trembled when he spoke of revenge for his only son. Freawina, Oslaf's wife, wept as she and her two daughters served bread, cheese, and mead to her guests with silent dignity. Dayraven watched them until his throat tightened and a knot twisted in his chest. He choked back his own tears at the mother's pain, which seemed to inhabit him. Gazing down at his food, he dared not speak.

He had known Oswy, a lad nearing manhood, only five or six years younger than he. Often they had played with the other boys at stick-fighting in the fields outside Kinsford during planting or harvest season, or had swum in the clear Folkwater running outside the village's North Gate. The boy's laughing smile appeared before him. His wit had been quick, and he had possessed a knack for making others laugh. He had been kind and good-natured, and he would have made a fine husband and father someday.

Life could be harsh and brief in the Mark, but the boy's end made no sense. A senseless event in a senseless world. Fate was mysterious and mighty, and even the gods submitted to it. At least folk thought the old gods did. Bagsac, priest of the Way from Torrlond, would say his god, Edan, determined the fates of everyone. But why would a god be so cruel as to end a boy's life in such a hideous way? No. That was no way to explain it. Perhaps there was no way. Dayraven's folk knew only one path to address it. *You'll be avenged, Oswy.* He tried to feel outrage at the lad's needless death, but only sorrow came, and he hid this sorrow lest his father and the others mistake it for weakness.

THEY SET OUT EARLY ON THE MORROW. IN THE MISTY GLOOM before dawn on the ninth day of Midsummer's Month, the hunting party departed in silence for the Southweald. Twenty men — some thegns, some freemen, and some bondsmen, but most tested warriors and woodsmen — rode their horses across the downs and gentle meadows whose deep green hid in the shadow before day.

Dayraven told himself he was proud to be among them, but his stomach gnawed on itself and seemed in no mood to keep the bread, cheese, and goat meat he had forced down it earlier. He swallowed the acidic taste. There was a death behind him, and death ahead. He made himself remember Oswy and the tears running down the cheeks of the boy's mother. Duty and loyalty to their people called them here, and with his father leading them, it would be death for the pucas. He would do his part too and seize this chance to show he was his father's son.

A warm breeze brushed the riders' faces as their horses cantered, and the familiar landscape rose and fell beneath them. Had their purpose been less grim, they could have passed for a hunting party intent on making the most of a pleasant day. This was a different sort of hunt. After passing the first outlying trees, they slowed to a trot. At the head of the party, just in front of Dayraven, Guthere spoke to Edgil. The mist half shrouded their forms, yet Guthere's voice grated in the silence: "Never in our time nor our fathers' time have the beasts been so rash. Raiding a farmstead miles from their lair."

"The pucas have grown bold or desperate, but they'll learn not to stray from their forest," said Edgil.

"Something's behind this. Nightgangers always skulk. Might be they kill one or two stray cattle by night. These took the boy in the light of morning. Unheard of."

"Something urges them. Don't know what, but they no longer feel safe."

"Perhaps Bagsac could tell us something."

"Perhaps. But this wood holds wonders even the priest with his wizardry would fear to meet."

"Then," said Oslaf, who rode to their left, "let's burn the whole cursed forest on the heads of all the rutting beasts in it."

Edgil looked ahead, but Guthere glanced at the farmer. "Careful what you say. We're nearing it."

In the growing light the forest's outline took shape. Massive and threatening, unending as the sea. The Southweald, out of which Dayraven's ancestors carved their settlements, was the single most dominant fact of life for the folk of the Mark. They lived from it and feared it. As the great forest loomed closer, Edgil ordered them to dismount and lead their horses on foot. The air was damp yet warm, and the tall, wet grass stuck to Dayraven's boots as he marched.

One of the horses neighed. They disliked the Southweald as much as the men did. Shushing under his breath, Dayraven stroked Rudumanu's nose. The mare looked out of her dark eyes at him and flickered her long lashes, assuring him she would follow. The horses reacted to the men's fear, but men and beasts followed the stone will of Edgil, who walked before them all. Dayraven tracked his father's silent movements.

As they halted before the trees, Imharr stood on Dayraven's right and cleared his throat. The bondsman smiled as he nodded at his readied bow. After glancing at his own empty hands, Dayraven hastened to untie his bow and quiver from Rudumanu's saddle. His fingers slipped while stringing the yew, but on his second attempt he succeeded. While putting the strap of his quiver over his head, he drew out an iron-tipped arrow and looked ahead. Instead of one towering shadow, oak, ash, elm, maple, beech, and fir greeted him with solemn stillness. He took a deep breath.

Tingeing the thick green foliage, the rays of the morning sun struck the leaves of the foremost trees through the thinning mist. Twisted and gnarled into coiling and writhing shapes, some of the ancient trees had endured many soft summers and biting winters even before Dayraven's remote ancestors laid axe to their sylvan brethren that once covered the downs. Deep and dark yawned the gaps between lichen-crusted trunks and boughs, and elderly clumps of tattered moss trailed from branches. Though the air felt still, as the men drew nigh the leaves hissed in a slight breeze as if in challenge to any foolish enough to enter beneath them.

The Southweald was a vast wave threatening to smother Dayraven. Though he had hunted deer and elk in it many times with Imharr and his father, who taught him that from this forest came life as well as death, it commanded more awe than love. A den of bears, wolves, pucas, trolls and creatures far more fell, it was also the giver of food and shelter, and a wise man respected it. Urd once said the folk of the Mark took their being from the Southweald, though Dayraven did not rightly understand what the old woman meant by that.

Light bathed the men in front of him and gleamed off the sword hilt lying in the baldric around his father's broad shoulder. The leathery skin on the long, muscular arm was taut as the older man grasped his spear. Dayraven's grip tightened on the smooth wood of his bow. Leather armor and boots creaked. Horses' hooves crushed grass and clopped against the hard earth. A distant thrush greeted the day with song.

They had come nigh the place where the trail of blood led yestereve. Edgil slowed the pace and scanned the forest's edge. He held up his fist, and they all froze while he stooped to the earth. With his body tensed, Edgil gazed at the ground. After standing, he listened for more than a moment while staring ahead at the trees. Dayraven tried to perceive what his father sensed. Even the thrush ceased its singing, but the breathing of the men around him was loud.

Then it appeared. Light glinted in one of its eyes. An instant later, under a fir's shadow, the rest of its hideous head took form. Sharp, jagged teeth protruding from a wide grin. The snub of a nose under large, yellow eyes glowing like a cat's. Large, pointed ears twitching in agitation. Dark green, hairless flesh blending with the trees. The creature leered at Dayraven, and hatred flashed from its eyes.

"Father . . ." Dayraven whispered, but the elder man silenced him with a raised palm.

"Wait for my word."

Guthere signaled the rest to ready their weapons.

One of the last to see the beasts was Oslaf. As soon as he understood what was happening, he brandished his spear at the forest and shrieked, "Nightgangers, I'll have your blood!" Before anyone could stop him, Oslaf was running at the forest with his spear in one hand and a long hunting knife in the other.

"Wait! It's a trap!" said Edgil.

But Oslaf, who was an enraged farmer avenging his son, not a disciplined warrior, rushed toward the trees. Several wiry bodies a little more than half a man's height leapt into the branches as they let out piercing cries like the high-pitched laughter of madmen. The horses whinnied and reared, and some men had trouble controlling them.

In the confusion, Dayraven dropped his arrow but caught it before it hit the grass. His sweaty fingers struggled to hold his bow, and for a moment all was chaos around him as he moved with dream-like slowness. Ahead were flashes of movement in the forest. With their three long fingers ending in dagger-like nails on each hand and foot, the pucas scattered into the trees as fast as a man might run or scampered into the dark forest on all fours. Others not far off answered the cries of the first. The farmer did not understand the pucas' cunning, but Dayraven realized the creatures would never allow the hunting party to see them so easily unless they wished it. They were waiting for them.

Edgil cursed, "Orm take the fool! They'll tear him to pieces if we don't hurry. Ready spears and arrows!"

His booming voice restored order, and Dayraven knew what he must do. *Now. For Oswy and the Mark.* He steeled himself and began to run by Imharr's side when his father spun around.

"Stay with the horses."

"But I . . ." was all Dayraven said before his father's fierce blue eyes silenced him.

He looked to Imharr for help, but the bondsman's quick nod told him to say no more. "It's alright, Day. We need you here."

Edgil barked, "Imharr, hurry!" He and the bondsman ran at a full sprint for the forest with sixteen others.

As the men rushed closer to the trees, Edgil's firm commands rose above all other shouts: "Eanmund, fall back! All of you, form a line! Guthere, take the left side. I'll take the right — when we enter, keep the men on both sides of you in sight at all times. Imharr, next to me!" From further in the forest came Oslaf's screams, whether in rage or in terror Dayraven could not tell, and the pucas' chilling cries.

In a moment the forest swallowed them. The shouting of men and shrieks of pucas continued a short while, and then the noises subsided. After they died out, only the nervous horses snorted nearby. Dayraven's heartbeat grew less wild, but he kept scanning the trees for movement. At first he held his bow ready, but after a brief space passed he knew he would not need it. The rush of excitement gave way to dull worry for the others as well as disappointment that he was not with them.

IN THE FULL LIGHT OF MORNING DAYRAVEN SOOTHED THE HORSES, whispering words of comfort in their ears and stroking their muscled necks. "Easy now. They'll all be back soon enough." *I hope*. They would.

His father was leading them, and Imharr was there too. They would bring them back.

The sun, which had burned away the shreds of mist and promised a hot day, began to warm Dayraven's body through his white kirtle and brown breeches. As he scratched Rudumanu's nose, she nuzzled his chest and blinked her dark eyes at him, which made him smile. The mare understood the danger had passed, and she snorted to assist in calming the other horses. Dayraven let out a long sigh. His gift with animals was half the reason his father kept him back. But only half the reason.

More than ten years before, as a lad of seven or eight years, he had managed to walk halfway to the Southweald before Imharr caught him and brought him home to Kinsford. His father punished him, but he forgot the punishment. He remembered, however, his father telling him that his mother would never have forgiven him had her son died young. Even then, as a boy, he understood he was all Edgil had left of his Eldelith.

Bringing to mind the sorrow of Freawina, young Oswy's mother at the farm, he tried to picture his own mother. His father, who never wed again in spite of the urgings of Guthere and others, seldom spoke of her. But Imharr, whom Edgil bought as a boy of six from slave merchants in the southern kingdom of Caergilion, sometimes described her for Dayraven.

He told Dayraven how kind she was to him when Edgil came back from the south to his new bride in the days when they began to make their home. She turned Imharr from a frightened boy into one of the family, teaching him the Northern Tongue and sharing the household work with him even when she grew big with child — the child who was supposed to fulfill the dream of a family and instead brought its end. Dayraven pictured his mother and, though he had never seen her, he imagined her as Imharr described her: a young and pretty woman with long light brown hair and gentle blue eyes. He whispered her name to himself: "Eldelith."

At that moment a raven's croak broke his daydream, and Dayraven looked up to seek his namesake in the trees. He searched in the direction whence it came, but the next time it called from another place. Scanning the leafy branches more closely, he sought in vain.

"Where are you?"

A third croak came from close by, and a big, black bird stared at him with beady eyes from the gnarled branch of a large oak. When it hopped like an old man from the shadows toward the branch's end, sunlight glistened on its jet body. Feathers thrust in sundry directions behind its large, horny beak, which bobbed up and down.

"Hello. Come to keep me company? Help me watch the horses if you like."

As if in answer, the raven croaked and flapped its wings three times. It leapt from the branch and swooped down towards him.

He flinched as the bird flitted over him, and when it passed, it turned from black to ghostly white before it disappeared. Thinking it must have been some trick of the morning light, he gazed up in the direction the bird had flown. Empty blue sky and a few wisps of far off clouds. After peering up for some time, he gave up and turned back to the forest. On the same branch of the oak perched the raven, staring at him like it had been waiting and was inviting him somewhere. An instant later it croaked again and gathered itself for flight. This time Dayraven knew it was no play of the light, but that the raven had turned transparent white. It vanished into the Southweald.

"Pretty trick," he muttered as he drifted toward the forest. This was no common raven. In the stories the folk of the Mark told, ravens played the role of tricksters and messengers, though their messages most often dealt with death. It was said they were wise enough to perceive the otherworld, and they could foretell someone's end. Dayraven loved such stories but had never believed them, not even as a child. The creature could pose no danger, but this strange bird was somehow meant for him, and it was trying to tell him something.

Since he had already tied the horses to some outlying trees, he looked back and explained to them, "I'll just have a look. Don't go anywhere."

Rudumanu neighed in remonstration.

"Don't worry, old girl. I'll be fine."

The rest of the horses stared back, and Dayraven thought about what his father would do if he found them unattended. *I'll be back long before them.* He took up his spear and bow. *Only a quick look.*

When he entered the damp coolness under the trees, the musty scent of untold years of decaying leaves on the forest floor greeted him. He waited for his eyes to adjust to the dimmer light while he scanned the trees for the raven. There was no sign of the earlier clash between the men and pucas save for trampled moss and broken ferns. He paused and listened to be sure none of the men were coming back, and then he thought of returning to the horses.

The ghost-raven croaked from a nearby ash to tell him where it was and flew deeper into the wood. He scratched his head and gazed at where he lost sight of it. Nothing but branches and leaves. It might be easy to dismiss it as a conjuring of his imagination and go back. But he *had* seen it.

He looked up at the forest's roof to take note of the sun's direction. A light wind swayed the uppermost branches. The sun broke through leaves in lances that shimmered in dew-laden spider webs before spotting the forest floor. He knew how deceiving the forest could be, but, thanks to his father, he was as good a woodsman as any among the folk of the Mark. After wiping sweat from his brow, he set off in the direction the raven had flown.

Soon enough it called, and he spotted it before it flew off again. The ghost-raven led him from tree to tree, entering deeper and deeper into the Southweald, and at times it changed hue again. Often it paused and stared as if making sure he followed. Each time he stopped, he thought of returning to the horses, but he could not shake the notion that the bird was telling him something. If ever he lost track of it, the raven croaked from its perch in a tree and took off again. It never stayed anywhere after he spotted it, thus keeping him guessing if it were some trick of his eyes that made the raven change colors, or if it were some portent. The sun rose higher as the raven led him on.

Stopping for a drink of water from his calfskin flask, he swallowed and took a long look in the direction of the horses. They were far out of hearing now. An involuntary shiver rippled through his body, and he took a deep breath. "Perhaps it's time to turn back."

The raven chortled behind him.

He swung around. Perching on the branch of an ash, the bird gazed at him with eyes that seemed to laugh.

"Are you telling me something? Leading me somewhere?"

The raven's only answer was to fade to white and flap further into the woods. He had little choice but to follow — the raven called him somehow, not least because of the name his mother had bestowed on him before she died giving birth. It was an unusual name in the Mark. According to Imharr, Eldelith had insisted on the name with her last breaths, speaking in a fey tone that Edgil could not deny. However it might have been, he began to wonder if the raven *was* a messenger. But what was the message?

"Urd would know," he said aloud, as if the dark trees crowding round him could understand. *If only I could show her the bird.* The raven croaked again from somewhere beyond his sight. He put away his flask and followed.

Soon after, as the raven clung to a branch, a vision of the others returning to the unattended horses seized him. He would need to explain himself to his father. That would never be easy, but it would be easier if he had the bird. *No one will believe unless I bring it*, he thought as he drew an arrow from his quiver. Setting his spear against a trunk, Dayraven readied his bow.

He drew out the process by checking his bowstring, wondering if the bird would fly off before he could loose. It remained in place for once. He thought of his father's displeasure and nocked the arrow. Sweat moistened his hand, so he wiped it on his kirtle. He was a sure shot, but, as the yew creaked while he aimed, he half hoped he would miss.

The raven stared from its perch. His hand trembled, and the feather fletching rubbed against his tense fingers. In his mind he saw the fingers release their grip on the shaft and heard the bowstring's twang. But he did not loose.

The creature went pale again and flew into the foliage. Dayraven sighed and smiled. Putting away his arrow and grasping his spear, he pursued the bird. He rounded a smooth, grey beech and picked up his pace while looking up for a sign of the raven. It called from behind a long, dense thicket blocking his way.

Until now, the trees had allowed patches of sunlight through, but this part of the forest was closer, mustier, and darker. Before Dayraven stood an imposing wall of rampaging brambles interweaving through twisted trunks and thick vines descending from above. The enveloping canopy cast a shadow that rendered it cave-like. This was where the raven had been leading him. *Best to be wary. Perhaps I should go back.*

He stepped forward and peered into the thicket. Through a few small chinks, he thought he could see a clearing on the other side. *Strange. Only one way to find out what it is.*

After resting his spear and bow against a tree and removing his quiver, he unsheathed the long hunting knife at his side and began to slash his way through. The thicket gave way as the blade's steel edge chopped and cracked slender branches and vines, and soon more light seeped through. It seemed there were no trees on the other side, but that made no sense in the midst of the Southweald. Since he had already come this far, he would find out what lay behind the barrier. As he sliced more brambles, the unnatural light grew brighter. The raven was silent and nowhere in sight, but now he was bent on his task. Something drew him on, and he needed to know what was behind the wall of brambles. At last he made a hole large enough to step through while crouching, like a small tunnel through the thicket. He blinked at the brightness before him and shuffled forward to discover what awaited him on the other side.

Dayraven emerged into a circular, grassy glade some fifty paces across. It was beyond strange that such a place should lie in the Southweald, for the trees all round the little lea were dense, and no one he knew would risk the peril of the forest to hew such a clearing. Without the trees' shade, he squinted in the warm sunlight. A sting on his cheek brought his hand to his face, where some branch or twig of the thicket had exacted slight revenge as he hacked his way through. Red oozed from a small scratch on the back of his hand as well. Tiny droplets of blood mingled with salty sweat on his tanned skin. He sheathed his hunting knife. When he looked up, he did not see the raven anywhere in the clearing. Instead, he saw the elf.

A stab of panic in his chest blossomed into numb shock. *Gods! What a fool for following! Then it's death the raven foretold.* With the sudden and chilling knowledge that he was about to die, he froze where he stood.

Though it took a woman's form, Dayraven knew this was an elf. He also knew he should turn around and run back through the thicket and outside the forest to the horses. But he could not, for he had looked in the elf's eyes, and his feet stood rooted to the earth.

Many stories among the folk of the Mark and the other kingdoms of Eormenlond spoke of the elves in the Southweald and other forests. Every child knew old tales of how, once or twice in every generation, some overbold individual wandered into the forest and disappeared only to be found days later in the elf-sleep. Always the victim's body lingered for a few days, but there was no waking from this sleep. Urd once called it the death of Angra, whereby the elf lured the spirit out of the body.

Other tales spoke of a few who were luckier, who saw an elf from a distance without looking into its eyes and fled home to tell of it. Sometimes the elf took the form of an animal or a bird, sometimes a person. But those few who survived had luck and their wits about them, for it was death to look into an elf's eyes. No wizard or sorcerer in all of Eormenlond, whether east or west, or even beyond the seas, knew the song of origin for the elves. Urd told tales of some few sorcerers, long ages ago, who wielded power over dragons, but no one knew whence the elves came or what they desired from those they took. All this raced through Dayraven's mind the moment he looked upon the elf-wife.

In the center of the lea she stood. She was the most beautiful woman, the most beautiful thing, he ever beheld. He understood desire from his secret meetings with Ebba, who waited for him in Kinsford. The elf-wife tore from him feelings of a different order. She had none of the earthy lure of flesh, but was something ethereal and distant and clear. The longing she awoke in him was like gazing at the bright stars on a cloudless night beneath the glow of Brynea, the river of fire in the night sky — only that was dim and pale compared to what now rippled through him. Part of him knew the deception behind the form standing before him. *This is sorcery. She's not what she appears.*

Such knowledge mattered naught, for he was a creature in a cruel and unbreakable snare. She blazed before him, and he could only stare, having lost any claim to mastery over his frozen body. His only movement was the involuntary and frantic thumping of his heart, which lurched and threatened to burst in his chest as his eyes locked onto her.

Of some fabric more fine than silk was her plain, white robe, which could not contain her radiance or was made of light itself. Her long golden hair cascaded behind her pale shoulders, while her lips were expressionless yet alluring. Most of all, her deep blue eyes would not release him. Cold they were, and without pity.

The part of Dayraven that understood the deception was a tiny voice growing more and more distant, and soon the throbbing in his body drowned it out. With her eyes the tall elf-wife commanded him to approach, eyes not so much cruel as indifferent. As his heart pounded harder, blood coursed through him in waves. His will could do nothing against the overwhelming need to come closer and touch her, to let her envelop him. The longing pierced deep down. Somehow this creature embodied all his desires wrapped up into one desire beyond his mortal life. It was a yearning he feared more than anything and that burned away all else. A necessity that meant death and annihilation. All else Dayraven had felt and done in his life faded like distant memories slipping away.

Though he knew it was useless, a small part of him insisted on fighting. Summoning all the will he had left, Dayraven lunged for the reality he once knew, clawing at anything he could hold. He tried to remember his home in Kinsford, the dwellings along the street, the faces he knew, but the elf's face submerged all. Struggling to speak, he found he could not, so he wrestled for control of his mind with the elf. He told his mind to close his eyes, but whether they would close or not, there was still only the beautiful, sublime face of the elf before him, nearer and nearer. Wrenching harder, he fought to at least utter a cry, but he heard nothing. He was losing himself, the only part left to him a helpless, incoherent, and desperate fear, and even that was fading.

But then something he did not expect happened. Something deep down in him, a voice that had always been with him, told him to let go.

So he did.

A moment came of stillness, an instant of bright clarity in which Dayraven perceived the life around him with a new crispness. His senses sharpened, and the world unveiled itself for the first time. There were the musty trees on the edges of the grassy lea with their translucent green foliage, the glaring summer sun warming his body, the pungency of his sweat, the iron tang of the red blood beading on his hand, the wind's whisper, and the song of the distant thrush.

He had been drowning and found himself on the surface. This, he knew, was how the world looked and felt, and everything he experienced before this moment was a dream. With this clarity he observed not only the world around him but himself, as if he were no longer contained in his body. And there in front of him wavered the elf-wife's form, now faint but surrounded by a bright light that was a breach in the fabric of the world, as if the world were a mask, and the elf a tear in it. In spite of the warmth of the summer day, a chill emanated from the tear. It was cold in that place. Perhaps his letting go surprised the elf. For a brief moment, Dayraven found himself able to speak between heavy, gasping breaths.

"What do you want from *me?*"

The elf stared at him, showing no emotion or concern at his absurdity. At the same time, Dayraven also heard the fleetingness of the *me* in his question, and its futility merged with the vibrations of his pulsing heart down in the empty center of his fragile bones. *Run* said his flesh. *Turn and run.* But then, as the wild hope of escape rushed back for a frantic moment, the clarity vanished, and there remained only the eyes in the elf's face and the throbbing desire to disappear in them.

With no more motion than a slight smile, the elf beckoned him to come, and he could no longer understand if the command came from the elf or from within him. The voice that pulled him back a moment before dwindled and succumbed. With every step closer the intensity of his desire grew until, with excruciating pressure, it began to shake him apart. Besides the elf-wife, there was only the consuming light.

Still he neared the elf, and, as his little life unraveled behind him, he realized he was Dayraven no longer. His home of Kinsford appeared, not as he had wished it to, but as something that never belonged to him. It was the point of a pin that the great forest of the Southweald dwarfed. Past the Southweald he had never walked, but his vision encompassed the hills of the Dweorghlithes rolling on the other side of the great forest and the Sundering Sea beyond, and then only the stars.

Shreds of fear dissipated along with his life. Only bliss remained. The bliss shattered him and sent him flying in pieces scattering over the world. Bright as a star, the elf opened her arms in an embrace to receive him, and the lives of Ebba, Imharr, Urd, his father and mother, and all the lives around him and before him were specks disappearing in the elf's brightness. Even then he understood that, as his father and the others hunted the pucas down to the youngest ones, it was all one vast energy raging against itself. Only the beauty and the terror kept them apart, kept the illusion of existence alive.

As the one who had been Dayraven perceived the end would be the same for all, peace and acceptance enveloped him. Now there remained only the victorious, unbearable embrace of annihilation. Locked to the elf's eyes, he met the embrace, accepting its inevitability. No clothes, no body, no sense of self. Garbled memories wrapped in flesh – all gone. Stretched over time and space. No distinction between him and the elf. Both one and the same with the light. Never existed. Always was light. Hiding from self. Life a game. Eternity's sublime, tragic jest. Light swallowing everything.

Darkness.

4
THE AWAKENING

Late in the afternoon, Edgil passed through the South Gate and returned to the muddy road running through Kinsford. He carried his son's body in his arms. The villagers gathered and murmured as they watched him falter now and then, gazing ahead with eyes widened as if he were fey and taking little heed of where he went. Cuts crisscrossed the thegn's arms, and drops of blood flecked his kirtle and leather jerkin. The body he held showed no sign of a wound. Edgil's face bore a blank expression, but in the eyes of stout Guthere, who led his friend's horse as well as his own, tears gathered and ran down his cheeks into his grey-blond beard. Behind them trudged all the men who had gone on the hunt save Oslaf and Imharr. They looked down at the brown earth in silence while leading their horses.

On both sides of the muddy road the halls of the thegns of Kinsford and their households clustered. Made of wood hewn from the Southweald and roofed with thatch or green turf in the manner of their ancestors, they were the dwellings of the warrior-farmers who were Earl Stigand's picked war troop. Smoke curled out of the louvers of a few homes, and smithying punctuated the laughter of playing children. But these noises ceased as word spread that the hunting party had returned.

As Edgil made his way with his burden, the hunters joined their families, who stood watching all wide-eyed. Soon the words "elf-sleep" passed the lips of many. With Guthere ten feet behind and a crowd closing in, Edgil bore his son's limp body down the road, which ended in the North Gate not long after it went by a building rising above the others in the village: Stanflet, the high-gabled hall of Stigand, Earl of Kinsford.

Of Kinsford's halls, only Stanflet's high roof boasted curved slate shingles overlapping in long rows. Proud and tall was the hall the earl's ancestors wrought long ago from towering trees in the place they settled. On the building's western side above three stone steps waited a large porch. Under the porch's roof and between its two carved columns of oak loomed doors more than twice the height of a tall man. The ancestors of Kinsford's folk long ago hewed those doors from ancient oaks of the Southweald and carved upon them images of their old gods: Bolthar wrestling the bull, Sithfar hidden in his cloak and holding his staff, Syn and Logan striving with ice and fire, Halmar riding the whale, Dyna with a sheaf of wheat, lovely Glora with her flower garland, and Regnor and Hruga seated over all.

When Edgil and Guthere neared Stanflet's entrance, a slender young woman in a blue frock shot out of the crowd behind. Ebba ran towards Edgil and wailed while clutching her braid. From her eyes tears streamed, and her cheeks were flushed. Before she reached Edgil, Guthere grabbed her by the arms and embraced her convulsing body, his broad face contorting as he stroked her head.

"Ebba, dear, you mustn't yet. I'm sorry, my child."

"Father," she sobbed, "tell me what happened! Let me go to him!"

"You will, my dear — first give the father time with his son."

An older woman, Sigitha, joined her husband and daughter, and they wept together as Edgil, alone with his grim burden, continued toward Earl Stigand's hall.

When Edgil stood in front of the great doors, they opened outward with a long creak. From the shadows within emerged Stigand in a plain brown kirtle, breeches, and boots. A large sword hung in its scabbard at his side. He towered a head above two of his household warriors, who were clad in byrnies and wore polished silver and bronze helms with bright nose guards and cheek guards. Between the guards stood the frowning earl as he looked upon his thegn with his burden. He stroked his long, grey-brown beard, and when he addressed Edgil, his gruff voice wavered.

"Hail, Edgil. What tale is there of the hunt?"

A long silence followed while Edgil stared as if he had heard nothing. But then his head snapped up.

"My lord, we avenged the boy, Oswy — we hunted the pucas to their lair, and the whole pack of beasts lies dead in the Southweald. But Oslaf is no more. I'm sorry. He was fey, and I couldn't keep him from his death. He slew many and now lies in a mound at his farm."

"Then he died well. I'll provide for his widow. But I see there's more to your tale. Come inside, my friend, and lay your son down on my table."

Edgil trudged up the steps, but before he crossed the threshold, a rasping voice broke in from behind. "What's this I hear of the elf-sleep? I must examine the body. Let me through." A hooded man in a white wool robe bustled through the onlookers, who parted before him. Other than his salient nose, his hood shadowed his features, but beneath the robe he appeared a thin man of middling height.

"Welcome, Bagsac," said Stigand with a scowl. "As a priest of the Way, your lore may be of use here. Guthere and Baldred, come as well. I want you to tell me what happened." The big man's face softened along with his tone. "Edgil, bring in your boy."

At that Edgil stepped inside. Stigand, Guthere, and Baldred followed, and the priest shuffled in behind. Once within the hall, they passed through two rows of columns made from great trunks of carved oak. These soared up to the ceiling, where interwove large rafters also made from the Southweald's trees. The late afternoon sun still shone through the louver above, while flickering torches in sconces lit the hall and scented it with their smoke.

The men proceeded until they reached the middle, where a long fire pit lay in the midst of the floor of grey stone that the years had polished smooth. Behind the oak columns and along both sides of the hall waited benches for times of feasting and counsel, and Stigand's high seat stood in the middle on the right side. Beyond the seats and adjoining the outer walls rested the raised wooden platforms whereon the greater part of the earl's household slept. On the walls above the sleeping platforms hung colorful tapestries telling the Mark's old stories with woven images.

Stigand ordered his guards to set up a table near the high seat. When it was ready, he nodded at Edgil and gestured toward the sturdy wooden table. With a blank intensity on his face, the thegn eased the slender body onto the table as if it were something fragile. Once it was at rest, he brushed a strand of his son's light brown hair from his face.

Dayraven's youthful face with its downy beard appeared asleep and peaceful. A scratch with droplets of dried blood stood out on his cheek. Slow and subtle was the rising and falling of his chest.

After Edgil stepped back, the priest Bagsac removed his hood, revealing patches of wiry grey hair protruding from the sides and back of his head around the bald crown. Out of deep-set sockets his beady eyes peeped, and their smallness gave his bony nose even more prominence. He licked his thin lips and began to approach the table. But Stigand held up his palm. "Let's hear the tale first, priest. Mayhap you'll learn something you need to know."

Bagsac's eyes squinted and his lips curled in what was perhaps a grin. "Of course. It may be of some use. Let us hear it."

Stigand nodded at his thegns Guthere and Baldred, and Guthere spoke, struggling to hold in tears that threatened to stream down his broad cheeks. "My lord, the tale's short, though the grief's great. When we returned from slaying the pucas, bearing Oslaf's body, we came back to the horses. Edgil had told Dayraven to mind them while we hunted, but he was gone. We found his fresh tracks in the forest and followed them till we came on his spear and bow leaning against a tree. Not far away we found his body. My lord," he stammered, "we couldn't wake him, though he seems unharmed. It's the elf-sleep. An elf took our Dayraven. I can say no more."

"Is there aught else?" asked the earl. "Any sign why Dayraven went into the wood alone?"

"My lord," said Baldred, "there was nothing. Only his tracks."

"It must be," interrupted Bagsac, "that the elf lured the boy." One of his eyes twitched as he turned on Edgil with a quivering smile. "With your permission, I must *examine* the body." There was a high-pitched strain in his voice, and he drew out certain words as if they had special meaning. "It is a matter of great *importance* that I see what magic these creatures have. There must be some traces of it in the body."

After hesitating, Edgil nodded in response, so the priest pulled back his white robe's sleeves and licked his lips again as he put his hands over Dayraven's chest. He closed his eyes and, after a pause, mumbled a low chant in a language the other men did not understand. The chant continued for many breaths. Guthere and Baldred gave each other solemn nods and raised their eyebrows, but Stigand stood watching the floor with arms crossed. Edgil stared at his son's body as if no one else were present. Once the priest finished chanting, he kept his eyes closed and his hands over Dayraven for another long moment of silence. He opened his eyes and removed his hands.

"Well?" asked Stigand with one eyebrow raised.

"I sense" — Bagsac paused with a scowl on his face — "that the boy's spirit is gone. We must hasten to burn the body and put it in a mound far from the village. The magic of elves is dangerous."

Edgil continued to look on his son.

No one spoke until the earl broke the silence with a sigh. "Well, my friend. You heard the priest. Let us honor Dayraven's body now that the spirit is gone."

The warrior stood for some time staring ahead. He said in a flat, hoarse voice, "How can I avenge his death?"

Stigand swallowed. "There's no shame in this, and I need you. Kinsford needs you. I'll pay the wergeld for your son, and none will hold you shamed."

Edgil appeared to ponder Stigand's offer. He looked down at the floor for a long while until he turned to the earl and nodded. "Kinsford gave me life. I remain with you, my lord."

When he finished speaking, horses neighed outside and, soon after, someone else entered the hall and walked toward them. It was Imharr. Mud spotted his boots, black breeches, and dark green kirtle, and his black, curly hair stuck to his sweaty face, where his usual smile was absent. He was not alone.

On his right arm leaned an old woman clad in a worn brown cloak. She wore her white hair bound behind her and walked with a short staff of gnarled wood. The torchlight twinkled in her bright, blue eyes, round which years had engraved many lines. Her expression revealed little of her thoughts as she hobbled down the hall between the oak columns rising high above her. In spite of her small stature and shabby appearance, she looked the men in the eyes as she tottered straight for them. As she approached, the clack of her staff on the stone floor echoed.

Bagsac's eye twitched again as his shrill voice broke out. "Why has the thrall brought her? You can do nothing here, old woman. The boy's spirit is gone. This matter does *not* concern you. You will only be able to mourn with the rest."

"Perhaps you're right." Her voice was clear though aged, and she smiled as she walked closer. "But the boy's my kin, and even you will not deny my right to see him."

Imharr looked toward Edgil and bowed his head. "My lord, I hope I've not done ill. I asked your leave to take Day's horse and fetch her. When you didn't answer, I did what I thought best."

"Whether ill done or not," said Stigand, "you acted out of love. That's pardon enough."

"But I warn you, old woman," said Bagsac, "don't try your witch-craft here. There are dangerous powers at work that you might unleash. I tell you all we must burn the body as soon as possible."

Edgil broke out of his stupor, looking ten years older and weary. "Urd. I've not forgotten Eldelith was your sister-daughter. For her sake, you have my leave to look upon her son. And Dayraven loved you. No one can deny that."

The men parted and let Urd through. Before she reached Dayraven's body, she turned to Edgil. "It's hard to see good men endure sorrow. But you are strong, Edgil." She took his large, calloused hand in her small, frail one and gazed up into his face.

He nodded and stared at the floor.

Urd came to Dayraven's body and looked at his face. She listened to his breathing and stroked the scratch on his cheek. Then she smiled and called out his name, "Dayraven. Dayraven, my child."

At this Bagsac snorted, but no one took heed.

The old woman listened to Dayraven's breathing, and then she looked up with her brow raised and a slight frown. She said to the somber men around her, "I deem this indeed an elf's work." Bagsac grinned as if at a simple child, but Urd's frown changed to a mischievous smile. "Yet his spirit remains."

The men's eyes narrowed as if they doubted their hearing, and the priest sputtered, "The woman's mad! Why listen to such nonsense? You once may have had some simple craft, witch, but you're plainly mad. I told you all the boy's gone. Why hesitate? There's need for haste."

Urd's voice rose as she looked to Edgil and Stigand. "Dayraven's still with us. I don't know how, but his spirit hides deep within him."

"But," said Stigand, "there's no tale of anyone ever waking from the elf-sleep."

"No one ever has," said Bagsac, "and no one ever will, unless by the power of Edan, who is greater than elves, or through His priests."

"My lord, we should do as the priest says," said Guthere to Stigand. The solid warrior's brow furrowed. "There's evil at work here. I felt it. It must've been the elf that stirred the pucas to attack us. When we destroyed its servants, it took another of us. It took our Dayraven. It's evil and will work more evil through what it touches."

"No, Guthere," said Urd, "it was not the elf that stirred the pucas. You should ask the priest and his masters in Torrhelm about that. He knows why the beasts are angry. Don't you, Bagsac? Tell them about the pucas and your war."

There was a silence, and all the men's eyes turned to the white-robed priest.

Stigand frowned. "What's she saying, priest?"

"She's mad. Mad, I tell you." The priest shook his head. "Don't listen to a word she says. In the holy name of Edan, we must burn the body before the evil spreads."

"Stay a moment. What's this she says of the pucas?" pursued the earl. "Do you know nothing of this?"

"They're not important. If the priests of the Way have a use for them, that's their business, and it need not concern you. The danger is with us now, in this hall."

"What are you saying, Bagsac? What do you know of the pucas?" said Stigand with more than a hint of anger rising in his voice. All the men looked to Bagsac. Edgil's brows lowered.

Bagsac's twitching eyes fixed on Edgil. "There are orders from the supreme priest himself. You've heard rumors of war in the south. Great preparations are underway. The consequences reach much further than this petty village. I warn you all: It would be best for anyone not to concern himself in the matter."

While the men talked, only Imharr noted Urd whispering over Dayraven's still body with her eyes closed. She clasped the young man's face, and she intoned his name again and again. Each time she said it, her face tensed a little more, as if she strained to hear something. Just as Bagsac finished his warning, she cried in a loud voice, "Dayraven, awake!"

The men all turned around at once. They stared slack-jawed and wide-eyed, for Urd stood over Dayraven, who opened his eyes and wobbled up into a sitting position.

"Edan save us!" screamed Bagsac as he jerked back several feet. Guthere and Baldred too stepped back, while Stigand and Edgil went tense and rigid. Only Imharr stood by as Dayraven blinked.

SOUND BROKE THROUGH DARKNESS. THE SOUND WAS OTHER THAN darkness, and it reminded him *he* was other than darkness. Again the sound came, and he recognized something about it. He strained to listen. *Dayraven.* In the darkness it was dim and muffled, but it was distinct enough to understand. *Dayraven.* That single word inundated him with uncountable feelings remote yet akin to him, and they seemed to blossom full grown out of nowhere.

He remembered. Yes, the voice was calling *him*. *Dayraven.* A little louder this time, and he thought even the voice sounded like someone he should know. At once he fled the darkness and raced toward his name, toward the life his name meant. *Dayraven, awake!*

And he did.

Instead of black, his world exploded into blood red and then, with open eyes, painful white until brightness resolved into sounds, shapes, and shades of color. At first the sounds and forms swam, but soon he recognized where he was as he forced his weary, enfeebled body to sit up, steadying himself with his hands against a wave of dizziness.

Dayraven found himself thrown back into a world familiar yet strange and removed from him. There stood Urd, Imharr, his father, Stigand, Guthere, and some others, including the priest Bagsac, all gawping at him. Though he knew he was in Stanflet, he felt odd, somehow outside himself. The whole inside of his head was numb, and his thoughts were thick and slow. Something like a loud, hollow whisper pulsed and rang in his ears. The feeling was so disorienting that when he tried to speak, no words came out, as if the link that connected his mouth to his mind were cut and hanging loose. Instead, the words seemed to echo all around him: *What happened . . . How'd I get here?*

The only response from the others was to back away from him, which confused him more. He struggled to return to his body so he could speak, but his will and his body remained severed. Everything in Stanflet took on a weird focus to Dayraven, and the tension in the hall pierced the flesh of his scalp like needles. He knew the faces gaping at him, but he could not remember entering the great hall.

Grasping for his last memories, he saw the horses on the outskirts of the Southweald as he waited for the others during the hunt for the pucas. Darkness followed. Something happened to him during the gap in his mind, and whatever it was brought him to Stanflet and to home, or to some foreign place masking as home. He tried to shake away the disorientation of looking at the scene before him as someone not in it. He was himself and at the same time a stranger to himself. Certainly these familiar faces regarded him with distrust. Worst of all, their raw fear somehow stabbed its way into his mind, where it churned and wrought such nausea that his stomach buckled and his mouth salivated. He retched when he tried to speak again. Dazed and bewildered, he shook his head and cringed. *Why can't I speak? What's happening?* His throat tightened, making it hard to take in air, and his heart reeled as it thumped.

"Slay it! She's awakened the elf! Slay it now!" cried Bagsac.

Guthere and Baldred drew their swords, but Imharr stood in front of Dayraven facing them and unsheathed his hunting knife. Edgil stood paralyzed, his gaze flicking between his son on one side and on the other side his fellow thegns, ready to cut the young man down. Urd held the hand of Dayraven, who grimaced and shook his head again to banish the nightmare he found himself in. He winced and shivered as the men's terror screamed in his mind, which was wide open to every emotion in the hall. *What's wrong with me? Can't think through the fear.*

"Who dares draw blade in Stanflet!" roared Earl Stigand, and everyone froze.

Guthere and Baldred's swords clanged on the floor, and Imharr dropped his hunting knife. All three knelt, and Guthere, stealing a glance at Dayraven, said to Stigand, "My lord, forgive me."

Unable to comprehend their actions, Dayraven watched them as if they were creatures he had never encountered before. But as the large earl asserted control, he started to return to his mind, where the nausea and the others' emotions diminished. He began to see as he was wont, and the throbbing whisper receded. *Thank the gods. I must try to think.*

"Rise, and put away your weapons." As the men obeyed, the earl's red face settled into a scowl. "Urd, what have you done here? Explain this."

The old woman gazed at Dayraven. "I only reminded Dayraven who he is. That was all he needed to awaken him. As for how he's here, I can't explain that. It's never happened before with the elf-sleep."

"You see!" said Bagsac, who was trembling behind an oak column. "She knows *nothing* of what this creature is. The magic of elves is potent, I tell you, and they are cunning. It has taken his body. I feel its power. It may seem to be the boy now, but if you let this malice dwell among us, it will take us all!"

Dayraven did not understand what Urd and the priest were saying. He comprehended only pieces of their conversation, as if half their words were in some strange tongue. They must have been speaking of someone he did not know, yet mention of elves reminded him of something terrible, something massive lurking just under the surface of his consciousness. *Elves? The elf-sleep? Where've I been?* Perhaps he would be able speak again soon.

"Edgil," said Stigand, "what do you say?"

The warrior blinked as he looked at Dayraven. "I don't know, my lord . . . I see my son here, and he's unchanged."

"Be wary," said the priest. "Don't be deceived, for these creatures know our desires and play upon them. It will seem to you it is your son, and then you'll be trapped. Its magic already works upon you. You should have burned the body in the forest when you found it."

Still not comprehending their speech, Dayraven at least knew where and who he was. Like tendrils of mist in the sun, the sensation that he was in the others' minds and the echoes of fear dissipated. He found his voice and reached out to Edgil. "Father, what's happening?" Resolving to stand, he was almost surprised when his legs obeyed his will and swung down from the table he sat upon. A surge of dizziness made the floor spin, but he was in command of his body at least.

When he wobbled to his full height by grasping the table with one hand, Baldred and Guthere and Stigand's guards all flinched back. Behind his column, Bagsac shook his fist as a spasm took over one of his eyes. "Stay where you are, foul creature!" He turned to Guthere and Baldred. "Don't let it move or speak, or it will enchant us all."

Stigand stepped forward. "If you're Dayraven, don't stir or speak. Stay where you are, and let us bind your hands and mouth."

Still unsure on his feet, Dayraven looked at his father, whose face only told of confusion, so he turned to Urd and Imharr at his side.

Urd nodded. "Do as he says. Your life depends on it now."

The urge to speak welled up, but Dayraven checked himself at Urd's calm warning. How could all this have come about? *What's wrong with them? What happened to me?*

But he only nodded to the earl, who ordered one of his guards, "Halga, fetch rope and a piece of cloth. Now."

The wide-eyed guard spat when he glanced at Dayraven before hurrying away, leaving Dayraven to wonder what he saw. *Why's he so afraid?*

"Don't be deceived by its compliance," said Bagsac. "It wants you to believe it's the boy so it can take you while you sleep."

"You fear so much, priest," said Urd. "No harm has come to anyone from Dayraven."

"Silence!" he said and came forward a step with his chest thrust out. "Your petty mind tricks have no effect on me, witch. I see now you're in league with it. You will betray us all."

The priest's hostility reminded Dayraven of the fear that grasped him moments before. *Have they all gone mad? Or have I?* He again stopped himself from speaking.

The guard Halga returned with rope and some black cloth, but he did not step close to Dayraven. The men looked at each other until Imharr said, "I'll do it. Give me the rope."

"See that he does it well," said Bagsac.

Stigand stepped closer and watched while Imharr tied Dayraven's hands behind him with the rope.

As the rope dug into his wrists and restricted his movement, Dayraven's breaths grew short and shallow, and he could not wipe his clammy palms on his kirtle as he wanted to. What if they all abandoned him? Were these the people he had known all his life, or was this some nightmare? *Steady.* Once more he fought the urge to implore. *Urd said not to speak. It will be alright.* The knots tightened around his wrists. A moment later, the black cloth appeared wound into a narrow strip in front of his face, and when Imharr's hands slipped it in his mouth he gagged. Coming only through his nose, his noisy breaths sped up and grew erratic.

Now he could not speak even if he willed to. The cloth dug into Dayraven's cheeks when Imharr pulled it taut and tied it off. The bondsman stepped forward to signal he was finished. Dayraven turned toward him. Imharr returned his gaze through glistening eyes, and he sniffed before looking down at the floor. Urd's face was unreadable, and his father's expression was almost desperate, but the others appeared grim or even hostile. *What are they going to do with me?*

Earl Stigand turned to the others and in his gruff voice said, "This is a matter for a folkmoot. Kinsford's thegns will decide Dayraven's fate at the Doomring. Baldred, sound the horn."

Another of Stigand's guards hurried behind the high seat and returned with a large white horn featuring three gilded bands with runes etched around them. Baldred took the ancient Horn of Kinsford from the guard, strode to the great doors of the hall, and winded the horn three times for all of Kinsford and beyond to hear. Three times the horn sang out high and clear, and Dayraven's father stood motionless. Ere the third blast's echo died, the tall warrior turned and walked with sagging shoulders toward Stanflet's doors.

Bound and gagged, Dayraven could say nothing as his father walked out of the hall. Edgil was a man of deep loyalty, but Dayraven understood some event had brought conflict between his father's two great loves: his people and his son. He wished he could tell his father he understood how torn he was, how it was impossible for him to act. A spear shaft nudged his back as two of Stigand's guards prodded him toward Stanflet's doors.

When Dayraven arrived outside the doors and stood under the porch's roof, he squinted at the brighter light outside, for the sun was just beginning its descent to the west. Kinsford's people were emerging from their homes and proceeding by Stanflet toward the North Gate. The nearest ones, faces he had known since childhood, looked at him in ways he never would have expected. Red-headed Eanmund, who had been on the hunt for the pucas, lowered his brows and glared before he spat and pushed his wife, two young sons, and daughter along. The widow Ethelburga, so affectionate to all of Kinsford's children, never turned her wide eyes from him as she passed, and she covered her open mouth with her fist. His friend Alwyn, plodding behind his father and mother, glanced once in his direction but then hunched his shoulders and kept his gaze away from Dayraven.

Kinsford being a small enough place, he knew them all as one knows family. Yet all viewed him with the same silent horror. *What have I done? Slain someone in a fit of madness? How is this happening? Am I walking in the world of dreams? I'm not asleep, and I'm not mad. I'm not mad.*

The gag prevented him from speaking. One of the guards, Halga, must have noticed his agitation, for he said from behind, "Wait. Let them all pass." This took some time, but after the last of Dayraven's people straggled by, the guards ordered him forward. As he descended the porch's steps and walked toward the North Gate, Urd and Imharr remained nearby. Urd met his glance with a gentle smile. There was some comfort in their presence, and the old woman and the bondsman at least seemed to know him. That was something to hold on to. The two guards walked a safe distance behind him while Urd and Imharr stayed close to his left. He looked behind once. Not a soul stirred on the muddy street that ran between the rows of timber halls. Thus abandoned, Kinsford appeared strange and alien.

As they left the North Gate and the village, the stream of people ahead of them wound its way by the Folkwater River for a few hundred feet then turned right onto a path leading up a flat-topped, barren hill overlooking Kinsford. Atop the hill was an ancient earthwork in the shape of a ring, the Doomring. The folk of Kinsford knew the ring had waited there long ages before their ancestors came and cut down the trees around the hill to make their settlement. Some held that the Dweorgs must have delved it for some purpose of their strange religion before any other peoples came to Eormenlond, and others that it was older than even the Dweorgs. However it came to be, the long centuries had worn it down to a grass-covered rim atop the hill. The earthwork remained the height of a bench and had gaps in it facing north, south, east, and west. Around it sat Kinsford's thegns in times of crisis.

By the time Dayraven and his escort came to the foot of the hill, nearly everyone in Kinsford, just under five hundred souls, had taken their places. He sighed beneath his gag as, more than a hundred feet above him, a few individuals struggled to the top. A fist gripped his heart when he began to climb the worn path snaking up the hill, and he tried to steady the short breaths coming from his nose. As a child he had feared and wondered at the hill and the faint, ancient voices murmuring from it. Always solemn, the Doomring grew the more so now that it became the place of his judgement. As he followed the path upward, he wondered why the only people he had known since his birth, his own folk, so feared him. He wondered how his father would look at him as he stood in the ring, if he would know him. *I'm still Dayraven, son of Edgil of the Mark. Nothing can change that. My father will know me. He and Urd will clear this madness.*

When Dayraven and those following him reached the summit, the people crowded out of his way to reveal the Doomring. He blinked at the thirty-nine bearded thegns sitting around the circle, each wearing a sword and bearing a round shield of linden wood painted according to his house. Their grave eyes turned to him. Also staring at him were the freemen, women, children, and bondsmen, who thronged behind the thegns. Earl Stigand occupied his usual place, while Edgil waited two seats to the earl's left. His father lowered his eyes and gazed like a wooden carving at the ground before him. Guthere sat nearby, and behind Guthere stood kind Sigitha wearing pity in her eyes, their young son Guthmund, and dearest Ebba.

Dayraven would have cried her name if he could have when he saw the tears streaming down Ebba's cheeks. She looked up at him, and their eyes met for a moment until Guthere realized what Dayraven was looking at, turned around, and commanded her, "Don't look in the eyes, I told you. It's unsafe for you more than any other, my child."

Ebba turned to the ground and sobbed.

Dayraven froze. *What's happened to them? I am Dayraven, son of Edgil.* A guard pushed him with his spear shaft through one of the four gaps in the ring toward its empty center.

As he stumbled to the middle of the ring, the sharp gazes of the people prodded him, all the people he ever knew. *What do they fear? It's only me.*

The bondsmen huddled to one side. Imharr stood out among them. He was the only one save one woman, old Kulva, with the dark hair and bronze skin of the far off south. The bondsman's eyes met Dayraven's, and he smiled and nodded. In truth, he had never seen Imharr looking so worried and desolate.

A shiver shook his spine and shoulders. Kinsford's gathered people surrounded him in every direction, speaking with wild eyes and eager voices to their neighbors of the wonder standing before them until they all understood the reason for the summons. The word "elf" came up more than once in their murmurings. For an eternity Stigand waited, and then he rose and sounded the Horn of Kinsford once.

When the horn's echo died, all were silent. The earl cleared his throat. "I, Stigand, son of Swithulf and Earl of Kinsford, call this folkmoot. Thegns of Kinsford, we are here to decide the doom of Dayraven, son of Thegn Edgil. An elf of the Southweald took him, but he stands here among us. Never in our time or the time of our ancestors has such a thing happened, for no tale tells that a man the elves took has awakened. I ask you all to think on the best path to follow. Who wishes to speak?"

As the earl spoke of the elf, Dayraven understood what was happening. Something enormous lurked under the surface of his awareness. He wanted to remember it, yet he feared to. *An elf. Yes. Something happened. I can't bring it up. There's a hole in my memory. In the Southweald, he said . . .*

Bagsac shot up from his seat across the wide ring from Stigand and removed his white hood. He strutted toward Dayraven a few paces and scowled at him, then turned around toward the people while sliding the pink tip of his tongue along his lips. "I, Bagsac, priest of the Way and faithful follower of Edan, speak through His authority on behalf of Kinsford's people. The Supreme Priest Bledla, who with his wisdom and power sits in the great city of Torrhelm, in his grace and mercy long ago sent me to you as a guide for such a time as this. I have called upon Edan, and He has warned me against this," and here he pointed at Dayraven and spat, "this elf-spirit, this demon sent to devour us! I tell you all now, and whoever says otherwise does not love this people, that this elf-spirit in the semblance of one who walked among us is come for the purpose of deceiving you and taking you while you sleep. You all saw the boy in his father's arms, and we all know it was an elf that devoured his spirit."

Bagsac shook his head as he paced around the circle and peered into the faces of the people with his beady eyes, one of which convulsed with a life of its own. The villagers leaned forward in anticipation of the priest's next words. "You heard the earl, and you all know that once an elf takes a spirit, it's gone forever. The boy's gone, I tell you. Gone. All that remains is the shell. What stands before you," he began lowly, but then raised his voice to a fevered pitch, "is a ghost-shadow, a hungry demon, an elf-dwola!"

Several people started back with widened eyes. "You may think," he continued at a lower pitch, "that he looks the same. You may feel no difference. But he is waiting, waiting until your guard is down, and then he will *strike*!" Many in the crowd flinched. "For your own sake, if you love one another, you will destroy this monster before it destroys you. Slay it now with your swords. Then burn the body and bury it far away in a mound, and let no one come to that cursed ground again. All this I say to you – those who follow the Way and those yet to embrace its salvation alike – in the name of Edan, for He has spoken to me," and he finished with hands folded in reverence.

The villagers all began talking at once. Dayraven shook his head, and he choked on the cloth in his mouth when he tried to voice his protest. *The old fool! Why does that mad priest hate me? I'm no elf-spirit. They must let me answer him. They must let me speak.*

Trying to remain calm, he mumbled beneath the gag, which left his mouth dry as it soaked up all his spit. No one heard him. The thegns spoke in low tones to their neighbors, and the crowd behind buzzed with excitement. They gazed at Dayraven with fear and even hatred in their eyes, and many voices grew angry. But the voices ebbed when Urd stood out from the crowd and, leaning on her staff, walked through the northern gap in the ring.

Bagsac, who had just sat down, popped up again. "She may not enter the ring, nor speak at this assembly."

"Often woman's counsel on this hill has helped Kinsford," said Stigand from his seat. "There's no law against a free woman speaking."

"But a mad woman, surely, has no right to give counsel," said Bagsac. "She may have been born here, but she gave up her part in this people when she disappeared for years and came back madder than ever. This witch, this heathen, is always leaving and coming back at the strangest times. Don't you wonder where she goes? Does she commune with the elves?" he asked as he wagged his finger. "What damns her most is *she* awakened the elf-dwola. Yes, she's in league with it. We'd best slay them both."

"Hold your tongue, priest."

Everyone fell silent, and all eyes turned to Edgil, who had spoken. He stood up and glared at Bagsac. "Urd's not on trial, and where she goes is her business. She's a daughter of a thegn of the Mark, and you'll hearken to her now."

Dayraven gazed at his father and knew he had made up his mind to save his son. Among the bondsmen, Imharr's smile returned. With a sigh beneath his gag, Dayraven raised his face to the sky and closed his eyes for a moment. *Thank the gods. Now they'll know. Urd will tell them. I am Dayraven, son of Edgil, and this nightmare will end.*

Bagsac glowered at Edgil and sat. Urd entered the circle and tottered with her staff toward Dayraven. She stopped then gazed around the whole circle at people's faces as if measuring their fear.

"Folk of Kinsford, you cannot know beyond a doubt whether this be Dayraven, or an elf-dwola come to devour you." Urd glanced at Dayraven, and he thought she winked as a smile played across her face. "But, search inside you," and here she looked at Edgil, "and seek the answer there." Turning to the crowd, she continued, "Yes. There's fear: fear of what has never happened before. Fear of what you do not know. Fear of becoming what you do not know." At this she regarded Dayraven, then looked around. "But is there not also something else? Doubt, perhaps? What if, for the first time ever, a man awoke from the elf-sleep, and this is our Dayraven standing here bound and gagged?"

The faces peered at Dayraven as if dreading his transformation into a monster at any moment. Urd went on. "Everything happens for a first time. Can you *know* this is not Dayraven? If it is," and she squinted as she gazed around the circle into the thegns' eyes, "then to slay him would be to murder one of our own. A blood-crime of the worst sort — impossible to avenge or repay."

The angry scowls on several men's countenances slid into doubtful frowns. Dayraven's neck and shoulders relaxed, and his whole body lightened. *Soon it will end.*

"Since you can never know for certain, there's only one way," Urd held up a finger, "to both save yourselves from danger and avoid the stain of murder."

She would win them over. If the gag had allowed him, Dayraven would have smiled. *It's coming. She'll show them who I am, and then they'll let me speak.* Many in the crowd leaned forward as the old woman paused. Dayraven awaited her next word.

"Exile."

His knees weakened and almost buckled when Urd said it. A cold numbness spread across his mind. *What? It can't be. Just tell them who I am.* Everything around him happened with unreal swiftness. He shook his head as the people of Kinsford debated with their neighbors. How could she have said it? Wasn't exile from the Mark, from his people and all he knew, worse than death?

These thoughts rushed through him as the people carried on discussions that blurred in his ears, though some shouts rose above the din.

"This is wise counsel!"

"Let it be done!"

Urd gazed at Stigand while the crowd's din rose. The earl nodded to the old woman. As he rose from his seat, Stigand turned toward Edgil. The tall warrior looked down, closed his eyes, and nodded in assent. All the while, Dayraven kept shaking his head in vain protest.

"Thegns of Kinsford!" the earl boomed, and all others fell silent. "You have heard the case, and are you now ready to render Dayraven's doom?"

"We are ready," the thirty-nine thegns said as they stood and unsheathed their swords, which reflected the setting sun's light.

The scene unfolded as if time had meandered for untold centuries only to reach this single point of Dayraven's fate. The world had come to this. He still shook his head in protest and pleaded with his eyes, but none paid heed.

"Who among you," asked Stigand, "would follow the counsel to banish Dayraven, son of Edgil, forever from the folk of the Mark and our land, never to return upon pain of death?"

A resounding clash of swords on the shields' iron bosses answered, and the men stood with the flats of their blades across their shields. Only Edgil held his sword at his side and stared ahead. Stigand looked at his friend, and, closing his eyes, Edgil clanged his sword on his shield.

It signaled the end of Dayraven's life. *No. Not this. Nothing to live for. No people. I am no one. Why? I've done nothing. Can't they see?* His body began to shake, and the world darkened around him.

"And are there any among you," continued the earl, "who would slay this man here and now as a danger to the folk of the Mark?"

There was a brief silence, which Bagsac broke as he stood. "You are unwise to let him go. You will see. You will regret not heeding me." He licked his lips as he donned his white hood. Turning from the Doom-ring, he broke through the crowd and walked down the hill.

Stigand ignored him. "Then I declare the doom of Dayraven, son of Thegn Edgil," and he looked with narrowed eyes at Dayraven. "You are hereby cut off from this people. I give you one day from this hour to leave, and if you should not depart or should ever return, then any man may slay you without guilt and without payment. Let no one of the Mark give this man shelter or aid. This folkmoot has ended."

Dayraven sank to his knees. *Exiled. I am no one.*

The people broke up and walked down the hill, few looking at him as they departed. Among them, one voice cried, "Father, let me go to him now! I must see him at least!"

Guthere held Ebba back. "No, child. Never again. It's best this way." He glanced back at Dayraven. Fear and mistrust dwelled in the eyes of the man who until that morning had been a second father to him. Sigitha, Ebba's mother, enfolded her sobbing daughter in an embrace, and they disappeared beneath the hill's crest. After they were gone, Dayraven's forehead sank to the earth and he groaned under his gag. *It can't be. It can't be. Ebba. Please.*

As the sun lowered on the horizon and the sky erupted in oranges and reds, one figure remained seated at the edge of the Doom-ring. Imharr approached Edgil and stood before him. The thegn rose and faced Imharr, and then he took out his hunting knife without a word. Gripping his bondsman's arm, Edgil cut the leather strap sewn around it in token of thralldom in a few swift strokes. He grasped Imharr by his shoulders.

"You're free." His voice was strained and rusty as if from disuse. He cleared his throat. "I am old and bound to Kinsford, to the Mark, sworn to Earl Stigand for life by a vow I cannot break. But you . . . You've been a brother to Dayraven. It would . . . help me to know you're with him. If you're willing."

Imharr glanced at his arm where the leather band had encircled it all those years. He nodded. "I would have asked for this anyway. I will stay with Dayraven."

Edgil still held him. "One last thing. I exiled him with my own hand, and I can't face him. Give him this for me, and he'll understand, and remember who he is." The thegn unbuckled the leather baldric around his shoulder and handed his scabbard and sword to Imharr. The westering sun's light glistened on the golden hilt, and the pommel's blood-colored gem quickened with an inner fire as the warrior handed over the weapon.

Edgil swung around and descended the hill. Imharr turned toward Dayraven and Urd, who huddled in the Doomring's center.

DAYRAVEN SAID NOTHING WHEN URD UNTIED THE CLOTH AROUND his mouth. He remained kneeling as the old woman began tugging at the rope binding his hands behind him. He stared ahead with a blank gaze. "Why? Why did you do it? Why did *he* exile me? Death would have been better."

She struggled with the bonds around his hands. "Oft must warm heart give cold rede. It was to save your life, and your father understood it was the only way. Don't speak of death now, child. The world is greater than the Mark. You'll live to look back on this day. Besides, there's something more I must tell you when you've calmed down. Hold still. Imharr, come help me with this!"

Imharr approached and cut the bonds from Dayraven's wrists with his hunting knife. When his hands were free, he remained sitting as the setting sun's last rays disappeared from the hill. In the gloaming, as the three sat in the Doomring's center atop the hill overlooking his former home, Dayraven gazed toward the darkness in the east.

5
UNDER THE STARS

At Urd's direction, Imharr left the Doomring to fetch horses, traveling clothes, supplies, weapons, and silver from Kinsford. She remained sitting on the hill with Dayraven in the cloaked silence as twilight surrendered to nightfall. The gentle wind's caress cooled him, promising the night would be as clear as the day was. Fires glowed below in the dwellings of Kinsford. Small islands of warmth and life in the midst of darkness. For a long while he stared at them and thought of all the people he knew in their homes, especially his father and Ebba. He would never again sit around the fire pit exchanging stories with his friends and elders nor hearken to the shaper bringing to life one of the old tales with harp and voice. This thought put him in mind of a song he once heard a wandering shaper sing of Beornmod the Exile:

Alas! The lone one longs for the land of his kin,
In his breast he buries the burden of his loss
As he fares among the foreign, far are his dear ones.
Though he sails over seas, his sorrow follows,
Cold is such company, his cares never fade . . .

The tiny fires of the stars leapt out high above, glimmering across vast expanses in answer to fires in the homes below. Having no will to speak, Dayraven lay down in the grass, which tickled his neck, and gazed up for silent minutes at the rising full moon and the sparks of the stars, so small and fragile and fleeting. *Most of it is darkness. One day the darkness will swallow them all.* Between points of light he traced images Urd had taught him to see: Bolthar and the bull, Sithfar and the wolf, Halmar and the whale, and Glora with her swan. Behind them all in an arch across the sky glowed Brynea, the River of Fire guarding the gods' realm. But all that was just old stories and fancy, and the shadowed world felt more godless than ever.

But then the stars reminded him of something. At once, instead of flickering points of light in the night sky, a pair of deep blue eyes loomed over him, and he gasped at the flash of memory. Time stood still, and the eyes grew larger and brighter until they became a white light. The white light, he recalled, was irresistible, and it spoke to him of the bliss of annihilation. His life began blurring with the light.

He closed his eyes and shook himself. When he opened his eyes again, the familiar world returned with the innocent stars twinkling above. He sat up with a jerk. His heart was pounding and his body shivering, and he remembered. The vision had lasted only a few heartbeats, but it changed much. There he sat in the Doomring, and Kinsford felt unbearably small to him at once. *Yes, I see it all now. It was an elf . . . and the raven. But what has it done to me?*

He struggled to suppress the disembodied quality that accompanied his recollection of the elf. Even the memory threatened to steal his identity and his humanity away. He could not shake away the feeling of being observed, an almost palpable tingle on his skin and a sough in his mind, but most fascinating and terrifying was the sensation that *he* was also the observer. *What's wrong with me?* Perhaps the people of Kinsford had been right to fear him.

Trembling in the darkness, he sat up and looked at Urd's outline. "Grandmother," he whispered, "it was there just now."

"What, child?"

"The elf. I remember now." He swallowed and paused, bracing himself to tell her. Speaking of what happened could be dangerous, could make it happen all over again. Urd waited in silence.

"I followed a raven into the Southweald. A ghost raven. At times it changed to pale white as I tracked it from tree to tree. It led me to a clearing, and I saw her. The elf. She called me, and I couldn't turn away. I couldn't even speak. She became a light surrounding me, and I joined the light, and then . . . I don't know. I heard your voice calling me, and I awoke in Stanflet."

"Is that everything?"

"Yes. I think so. But at first I couldn't see, or I saw too well, and everyone's fear was inside my mind. It was . . . hard to bear." He clutched his temples as if he could squeeze away the image of the elf and the disorienting sensation. Something was lodged in his mind, something more than just a memory.

"You knew their feelings, their thoughts, no?"

"Yes. That's how it seemed."

"Well, child, that makes quite a day. Ghost-birds and elves and now exile. You must have had enough by now, eh? Why a raven, I wonder?"

Somehow Urd's familiar voice banished the chill that had come over Dayraven with the memory of the elf. She was an anchor to the familiar world, and as he pulled himself closer, the disembodied sensation began to recede. Inhabiting his body once again, he took several deep breaths. He pondered her question, for he too wondered about the mysterious raven.

"I thought to ask you. Perhaps it was the elf luring me into the forest," he offered.

"Perhaps. Perhaps not. At any rate, you were meant to meet the elf."

"What do you mean? Who meant for me to meet it? And what is it? What are the elves, I mean? They're so terrible, yet so beautiful."

"Yes. Like life itself. No one knows the song of origin of the elves, for they're outside of time. Yet they're of this world, though they don't live in it as you and I do. They show themselves in the forests and waters, where life is strongest. Oh yes, long ere our people came to Eormenlond, long before the Andumae came, and even long before the Dweorgs, elves dwelled in Iltharwyn, the ancient forest that became the Southweald and Northweald after our ancestors came and clove it in half. The Andumae say looking upon an elf brings the death of Anghara, or as we here call her, Angra. The spirit returns whence it came without the body's death. The body's end is the death of Oruma, or Orm, as we call him. Few suffer the death of Angra, and for some reason your spirit traveled that path but came back."

In the moonlight Urd fixed her eyes on him. "That's something I must think about now: how and why you've come back."

After a while, horses clopped toward Dayraven and Urd through the darkness, and they stood up. In the moon's growing light, Imharr emerged leading Dayraven's horse, Rudumanu, and his own grey mare, Hraedflyht, up the hill. Each horse was laden for a journey.

Urd greeted Imharr, "Ah, there you are, son. You've always been such a good boy."

"Easy to be good when there's a beautiful woman waiting for you."

"Don't tease an old woman. Save it for one of your gullible village girls. Come on then, and help me onto your horse. My bones are weary, and we have a long walk tonight."

Imharr threw a bundled cloak to Dayraven and walked toward Urd. But before Imharr helped her up, Dayraven approached him. "Thank you." He grasped his friend's shoulder. "Thank you for everything. But you needn't come. Only I am an exile, and you have a life here, especially now that you're free. You could settle down and start a family. Half the young women in Kinsford would jump at the chance to wed you."

"Half? Must be at least three quarters," said Imharr with a smile. "But it really doesn't matter. I've a fancy to roam the world a bit before settling down, and I'm not sure one woman's enough for me anyway."

Urd snorted and rolled her eyes. "Shameless. Come help me on your horse, foolish young man."

A sigh escaped Dayraven. He had pictured himself wandering Eormenlond alone, but Imharr would journey with him to wherever he would go. It would be almost like taking Kinsford with him. The tightness in his chest lightened, but guilt tinged the relief. *I'm being selfish. He's doing this for my sake, taking on exile for me. I don't know how I can repay him.*

"Wait. Before we leave," said Imharr, "I have something for you. Your father asked me to give it to you."

Imharr drew back his cloak and unbuckled the baldric from his shoulder. He held out the scabbard and its sword. Dayraven gazed at the weapon with his mouth open until Imharr nodded at it and smiled. "Go on. It's yours."

Dayraven reached out with hesitant hands. He swallowed as he grasped the sword and held it before him. It felt lighter than he expected, perfectly balanced, and the hilt cooled his hand. When he drew the blade, it whispered a metallic ring as it slid from the scabbard.

In the moonlight they gazed on the Dweorg-wrought sword Edgil brought from Torrlond when he was a young man. The wavy-patterned blade reflected the moonlight and shimmered as if casting its own glow, and Dayraven traced the ancient runes of strength and protection forged on it. The red gem inlaid in the middle of the golden pommel appeared almost black.

"Sweothol," whispered Dayraven. "But how could he part with it?"

"He said it would remind you who you are."

"But I've always thought of it as part of him." Dayraven stared at the blade. "The king of Torrlond gave it to him."

"Yes, I recall that day well."

Dayraven nodded, his eyes still locked to the sword. "You've told me the story enough times that I sometimes fancy it my own memory. When he fought for Torrlond and saved King Ermenred's life after the war."

In the moonlight, Imharr's dark eyes kindled. "When the Caergilese attacked in the mountain pass, I saw your father slay Lord Diangal himself, and I was glad. Another Caergilese slaver gone from the world. Once it was over, King Ermenred drew Sweothol and handed it to your father after he refused a captaincy, saying he would rather return home to the Mark. Even then, though I was only a frightened boy and a newly bought slave, I was ready to follow him anywhere."

Dayraven still gazed at the sword. "I don't feel worthy of this. It was made for a leader."

"Yes," said Urd. She wore a sad smile. "Edgil was born a leader. But we'd best move on now. Put away the sword, Dayraven. And for the last time," she scolded Imharr, "get me on your horse before I die on this hill. We're going to my home to sleep for a few hours and prepare for what's next."

"Yes, m'lady." Imharr laughed as he bowed low, and Urd rolled her eyes.

Dayraven sheathed the sword and strapped the baldric round his shoulder. He thought his father's gift should somehow strengthen him and give him courage, but it was also much to live up to. *I will remember, Father.* Even if he could never return to Kinsford or the Mark, he would not forget where he came from, and no one could take that from him.

While Imharr helped Urd onto Hraedflyht, Dayraven put on his cloak and tried to swallow the tightness in his throat. He looked one last time behind him at the firelights in Kinsford. *Never again. I'll see it only in my memory.* He turned, and they descended the Doomring.

Urd rode as Dayraven and Imharr led the horses on foot. The moon glowed bright, but they journeyed at a slow pace over the folds of the downs. Traveling over the shadowed and silvered nightscape of gentle hills to the southeast of Kinsford, Dayraven found himself thinking of Imharr as a young boy watching Edgil fight Lord Diangal in the mountain pass. Now that this strange day had torn him from his home, he pondered how frightened Imharr must have been as a boy sold to a man from far away. How alone he must have felt after raiders from Caergilion slaughtered his family. Imharr seldom spoke of his former life, having told Dayraven the story of the attack on his family only once.

As he had observed to Ebba yesterday — had it been just yesterday that he sat with her in the shade of the copse overlooking the hillside? — men had long raided across the border between Caergilion and Adanon. Even if they did not know why, all over the kingdoms of Eormenlond, everyone knew Caergilion and Adanon had been foes for hundreds of years and would remain such until the world ended. Imharr's story was one of the countless tragedies in those centuries of hatred.

In one early morning raid in northern Adanon, soldiers from Caergilion slaughtered Imharr's father, mother, and elder brother and enslaved Imharr and his sister. Only once had Imharr told Dayraven how he saw the soldiers cut down his father and brother while his mother hid with her two younger children in their home. How he tried to kill the soldiers as they raped then slew his mother. How they laughed and mocked him as they held him and made him watch them rape his sister.

Imharr had told Dayraven these things some two years before, and, too shocked and clumsy to find the right words, he had just looked on as his friend's tears trickled down his cheeks. Reckoning the memory must be unbearable, he never asked him to speak about his family or his home.

But now, as they walked under the stars on the grassy hills, he wanted to understand. He was a little ashamed of not trying to before, realizing only his present trouble made him think of it. Perhaps, he reflected, knowledge that others endured sorrows enabled everyone to go on. Every story ever told, all the tales the shapers sang of people long turned to dust, confirmed this. He gazed at Imharr and asked, "What do you remember of your first home in Adanon?"

Imharr looked at Dayraven and then bowed his head. "Adanon is a far off place and a distant memory. Sometimes I dream of it. And sometimes I used to talk of the south with Kulva. Baldred's father Baldulf bought her when she was a young woman, so she remembers more than I do. But she was from further west in Adanon, near Harieth, many miles from where I was born, near the chief city of Palahon. Sometimes we spoke in our tongue, though her Ondunic is more like the western sort, and mine was pure eastern. Still, we understood one another, and that's how her memories became my memories. But the images of my family are my own. I can see my older sister. Might be she's alive somewhere. And I see my older brother and mother and father. I'll never forget them."

When Imharr finished speaking, an idea took root in Dayraven's mind. He thought about the idea for a moment, and then it all fell into place in a rush. *Yes. It all fits. Mayhap there's some hope after all.*

The story of his father's sword, won in battle against Caergilion.

The story of Imharr's family, who died at the hands of soldiers from Caergilion. And now, Dayraven remembered that, just a few weeks ago, merchants from Wolvendon, the Mark's chief city, had brought tidings to Kinsford that Torrlond's king, Earconwald II, son of Ermenred, was preparing a new war against Caergilion. They told of how, after a generation, troubles had again flared up over missionaries of the Way in the south.

The word was that a mob in Caergilion had murdered three priests sent to convert them, and that King Malruan of Caergilion refused to punish the murderers. King Earconwald and the supreme priest of the Way, the mighty wizard Bledla, were gathering their strength in Torrlond to retaliate. The news caused excitement in Kinsford, though few reckoned it would change anything in their corner of northwestern Eormenlond.

But now these tidings became momentous as Dayraven knew he was meant to be part of all this, that everything pointed in the same direction. Perhaps fate was pushing him. He would seize this chance and make everything right again. *This will make it worthwhile for Imharr to follow me into exile. I might even return to the Mark, and to Ebba, once I've proven I am Dayraven, son of Edgil, and no elf-dwola.*

As soon as it took full form in his mind, the idea burst out. "I have it," he said, breaking the night's stillness. "Would you like to avenge your family, Imharr?"

"What do you mean?"

"Torrlond's gathering for war, remember? This is our chance. Perhaps everything's happened to give us this chance. I'll go where Father went, and you'll avenge your family against Caergilion."

"What are you talking about?"

"Don't you see? We'll join Torrlond's ranks. We'll help King Earconwald defeat Caergilion. When it's over, we'll look for your sister." Seeking Imharr's sister occurred to him just as he was speaking, but it too made sense with everything else, and it would be a fitting way to repay his friend's loyalty. "What do you say?"

Imharr hesitated. They stopped walking, and Rudumanu and Hraedflyht waited for their masters. Under the moonlight, Dayraven sensed the idea catching hold in Imharr's heart. He was ready to go to Torrlond. But before he spoke, Urd uttered one word.

"No."

They both looked up at her dark, hooded outline atop Hraedflyht, for she had spoken with authority. She had brooded on top of the horse for such a while that Dayraven had almost forgotten her. But now something stirred her to speak with urgency.

"My child, something happened this day that never happened before: Your spirit survived a meeting with an elf. I don't know how, though I've always known you have the gift. Anyone with an understanding of the gift could have seen it even before today. You'd have made a fine wizard with proper training."

"The gift? But I'm not . . ."

"Think of how you've always perceived others' minds. Yes, Dayraven. You're not like your father, though you've always wanted to be. It's your mother you take after. I saw it in poor Eldelith too. Though my little sister, your true grandmother, had little trace of it, your mother could have been a great sorceress. But she married your father, so I said nothing. Then we lost her. I watched you grow up, and all the time I knew what was inside you. But I also saw you wanted to be like your father, a great warrior and a good man, and to have a family with that dear girl. So I let you be. A wizard's life is hard and lonely, my child, and you must want it. But this day's passing has changed everything."

He could not keep the confusion and disappointment from his voice. "I . . . I don't understand. A wizard? I've never . . . What must I do?"

"You must *not* go to Torrlond and fight for King Earconwald. Not all is what it seems, my child. Your life, your soul, would be in danger there. Your life is in danger here. Bagsac would not have given up so easily had he known the significance of you waking from the elf-sleep. He feels and fears the power in you, but he thinks it is because you are a creature of the elf."

"What power? What did the elf do to me?" Dayraven shivered as he realized he might not want to hear the answer. He guessed it had something to do with the disembodiment that hit him like a wave of nausea when he awoke in Stanflet and the now dim but persistent sensation that something lurked in his mind, like fingertips caressing the hairs on the back of his neck.

"You know. You feel it, don't you? Before today, you would've made a strong wizard, but now . . . My dear boy, I've never felt anything like it. One with the gift can sense the power in another, and I've been near some of the greatest to wield the gift in our age. You . . . It burns as bright as the sun in you now. I don't know how, but your meeting with the elf has changed you. There is vast power in you, and it's far too dangerous to leave alone."

"Dangerous? How?"

"When the world learns of you, many will seek to use you. *I* will seek to use you, my boy. Yes. You should know it, and I hope you'll trust me. And some will want to kill you. Bagsac will find out the truth soon enough, and when he does, he'll come for you — and not alone. That priest is a fool, but his master is not. When the Supreme Priest Bledla finds out about you, he'll want you either dead or in Torrlond to use you for his own ends. We must let him have neither."

Too many thoughts assaulted Dayraven at once. He began to wonder if the people of Kinsford were not right to exile him. Was he not something possessed and dangerous? There had to be a way to purge him of whatever the elf put inside him. There had to be a way to reclaim his life. *I don't want it. I don't want such power. I want my life.*

He shook his head and clutched his hair. "I don't understand, Grandmother. A moment ago everything made sense again. And now you tell me all this. Why would the supreme priest of the Way care about me? Where am I to go then? Do I stay with you?"

"No. You can't stay with me. Bagsac and his followers will come for you soon. The supreme priest will send him as soon as he learns of you. Bledla will not hesitate. He will know. He will wonder. And if he is what I believe him to be, he will consider you a threat."

"Why? I've done nothing to him."

"There's little time to explain and so much to tell you. It might only serve to confuse you, and I don't know how much you can take in at once."

"But why would the supreme priest of the Way want me dead?"

Urd sighed. "Very well. I suppose you should know this much. It concerns the Prophet Aldmund."

"The one who began the Way?"

"The same. In his writings, Aldmund spoke of a rebirth of his power. This rebirth was to happen in one who would help to usher in the Kingdom of Edan, a new prophet. Bledla believes *he* is the inheritor of Aldmund's power, that he is the second Prophet of Edan. But there are certain things about your survival today that might make him doubt. He will not like it. He will convince himself that you are a test, an obstacle he must overcome to fulfill the Kingdom of Edan. And he will do *anything* to fulfill the Kingdom of Edan."

"But I . . . I don't even know what this . . . this *thing* inside me is, let alone how to use it."

"Though you've no ability to use it yet, the power in you will frighten him. When he's frightened, he is most dangerous. If you're lucky, he'll send only Bagsac for you, but you must avoid all priests of the Way in case. They will sense you. Most will feel your presence only when they're near you, but there are a few, the most powerful ones, who may know you from afar. Your path will not be easy, and you must use great caution. You must stay here no longer than this night, and you must set out early on the morrow. You have a long journey before you."

Dayraven released a long sigh before nodding. "Alright. I'll heed your counsel. Where would you have me go?"

The old woman paused a moment. "To Galdor," she said at once. "He'll know what to do, and he's most fit to train you. Yes, you're too close to me, too dear. I've already wasted much time out of love for you. Galdor it must be. But you must travel hundreds of miles to reach him, and it's good you have Imharr with you. In spite of appearances, he has some sense about him."

"Thank you . . . I think." Imharr smiled and nodded.

"As usual, you speak in riddles, Grandmother. Who's Galdor? And where is he?" asked Dayraven.

"Far away in the kingdom of Ellond. You must journey east through the Mark and through the north of Torrlond, but stay far from the cities of Etinstone and Torrhelm. Better yet, turn north to Torrlond's town of Rimdale and find a ship bound for Ellond. You'll be less conspicuous there, and there will be fewer eyes to see you. The sooner you leave Torrlond behind, the better. When you reach Ellond, go to the chief city, Ellordor, and there ask for Galdor in the king's palace. All there know him, and I'll send him a message so he'll expect you. As for who he is, that you'll find out. Suffice it to know you'll be safe with him, for he's a wizard of the best sort, and the chief counselor to King Fullan of Ellond. As long as Galdor remains in Ellond, it will be safe for you, and safe from Torrlond."

"Safe from Torrlond? I don't understand." Dayraven looked in the hills' shadows, half expecting Bagsac and his followers to leap out. But only the horses munched fresh grass as their masters stopped to talk. "Ellond and Torrlond have always been allies. We're all kin. But you speak as if Torrlond were a threat to Ellond, and to us. How can that be, when King Earconwald is about to strike in the south against the enemy, Caergilion?"

"I told you not all is what it seems, my child. You'll learn this now that you're leaving Kinsford. King Earconwald and the Supreme Priest Bledla mask their true ambitions behind this war with Caergilion. They're preparing something far more terrible than revenge for their slain priests. And *you* are a threat to their plans. That is why they'll come for you. Bledla will never tolerate your existence unless he thinks he can control you. But our first move is to get you somewhere safe. Then you must learn to use this power that is in you."

"Learn to *use* it?"

"I've thought it over, and it's clear Galdor will know what to do with you. He is most fit to train you, and he will explain it all. There's no time now, my boy. You must trust me and go to Galdor."

"Wouldn't it be easier to rid me of this . . . power? Then I would be no threat to anyone, and I could return to Kinsford. Can't you get it out of me?" The whisper in his mind swelled, raking his thoughts with shadowy claws. A darkness loomed from it and threatened to swallow him. There had to be a way to escape. He did not want any part of elves or wizardry, and he did not wish to be an enemy of the supreme priest of the Way. Fighting for Torrlond to reclaim his home and his bride was far simpler.

Urd reached down from the horse and stroked Dayraven's cheek, and he knew her answer would end his hope. "I fear no mortal could remove the power that is in you. I cannot. Even if I could, I don't know that I would. It's part of you now, and you must find a way to reconcile yourself to this change."

His mouth hung open, but he could find no words. He shook his head.

"You have a purpose, Dayraven. You did not ask for it, but it has fallen to you. That is the way of it. You may have a role to play in the future of Eormenlond, and the lives of many will hang in the balance. But the first thing is to get you to safety. Then, you must see if you can learn to control what is in you."

Urd turned to Imharr. "My lad, will you see this boy safely to Ellond?"

"Yes, if you ask it."

"I do."

Imharr's reply came after a moment. "Alright."

"I'm sorry," said Urd. "Seeking your sister is a worthy quest, but the southwest will soon become a dangerous place, and it's the last place to send Dayraven just now, other than Torrlond itself. No," she said as she turned to Dayraven, "you must go to Galdor. Much more than you guess depends on it. He'll know what to do with what you have in you. It will take time, but if all goes well, you two might be able to search for Imharr's sister someday."

Too bewildered to argue, Dayraven said, "Alright, then. We'll go to Ellond and seek this Galdor. But why don't you come with us?"

"I think not. That would make it easier for Bagsac or someone worse to find you. This too is a matter I've given some thought. Better I stay behind and provide a diversion. Yes, I'll lead them away from you." She giggled like a child about to play a prank.

Dayraven opened his mouth to object, but Urd held up her hand. "Don't worry about me. I can take care of the likes of that foolish priest. There's more to this mad old witch than even you know, my dear boy. Besides, I have somewhere of my own to go. But we'll meet again, don't worry. For now, Galdor is best. Now, let's move on before my bones freeze. This horse is far less comfortable than my bed."

Before they resumed their path, Imharr took a spare cloak from his saddle pack and placed it over Urd's shoulders as she sat on the horse. They continued their journey under the stars.

THE GENTLE HILLS GAVE WAY TO MORE LEVEL GROUND, AND THEY walked at a faster pace. During the night they passed by dark outlines of a few hardy farmers' silent dwellings outside Kinsford, but the last two miles were only meadows. Once they saw by the moonlight a herd of elk grazing in a lea. Dayraven noticed Urd gazing at the dark forms of the animals, and he worried for the old woman. What would happen to her if Bagsac came for him? Should he insist that she come with them? *Not much good that would do. She's more stubborn than a boulder.*

He did not think she would change her mind, so he said nothing for the moment. A few of the elk turned their heads at the sound of horses and tensed to flee. But when the horses and people leading them plodded on at a distance, the elk returned to their grazing.

As Dayraven and Imharr continued on foot and Urd on horseback, their path took them south, closer to the Southweald, until no other living person lingered within miles. The end of their path brought them to something rising ahead in the darkness. A circle of tall oaks surrounded a large, grassy mound, and the wind rustled the leaves of the trees. After they entered the oak ring, a low, wooden door in the center of the mound grew visible, the first sign it was in fact Urd's turf-covered home.

Imharr helped Urd alight from the horse, and she put her hand on her hip as she tottered towards the door. The two young men led their steeds behind the mound, where another structure waited in the darkness. In a small shed behind the home lay a dozen sleeping goats, and there Dayraven and Imharr left Rudumanu and Hraedflyht to put them up for the night. After finishing this task, they went back to the door and ducked their heads to enter and join Urd inside.

The small dwelling glowed with the fire Urd had coaxed to life in the corner fire pit, and smoke curled out the small louver above. The single room was just large enough to hold a few pieces of crude, sooty furniture, a couple barrels for storing grain and water, a sleeping mat on a raised wooden platform, a few shelves on which rested pots and jars of dried foodstuffs and herbs, and the wooden chest in which Urd's spare clothes and six calfskin books lay.

Few in the Mark owned even a single book, and few enough could read. But all regarded such objects as treasures, and Dayraven knew Urd's books contained much lore, for she had taught him to read from three of them. The others, she told him, were written in High Andumaic, a language different from the Northern Tongue. What lore they held he did not know.

Though it was much smaller than his father's large, bare hall, Urd's cluttered home always seemed to welcome Dayraven. For the first time that day and night he relaxed, and some of the worry seeped out of him, leaving him to realize how weary his body was as the old woman prepared food. Suspended from a blackened beam over the fire pit was a chain ending in a hook. On this hook she hung by its handle a pot she filled with water. As the water boiled, she added some salted goat meat, dried vegetables, and herbs to the pot and told Dayraven to fetch bread from the room's single cupboard. When all was ready, she spooned the stew into three wooden bowls. The three of them sat on the straw-covered floor near the fire pit and ate the dry bread by dipping it in the stew. They said little as they ate, for they were tired and hungry. When they finished and washed their hands and faces in a basin of water, Urd looked hard at Dayraven and Imharr. "Now we sleep. You begin a long journey on the morrow."

While she went to her mat and grew motionless at once, Dayraven and Imharr wrapped themselves in their cloaks and lay on fresh straw on the floor. Dayraven lay awake some time thinking about the day's events and what the next day might bring. There had to be a way to reclaim his life. He wanted to see his father again, and Ebba . . . It was impossible that he could not wed her. He would see her again. He would find her somehow.

But for now, the only way forward seemed to be the path that Urd set before him. Perhaps this Galdor fellow could find a way to rid him of the elf's curse, or at least teach him enough that he would find a way himself. Urd was right about one thing: He was confused, not to mention frightened. A single day had transformed his world into something far less comfortable.

He found his jaw opening in an ear-popping yawn. Realizing how exhausted he was, he began to allow his mind and body to slacken, and the tension eased out of the muscles of his back and limbs. *I need to sleep.*

He sighed and let his mind slip into the state of half-awareness that precedes sleep. His last tired thought was of Urd's words about his future. *A wizard, she said. She said I must want to become one. If I don't, then what?*

As if in answer to his question, the air in the room shifted, and, beginning as a shaft of energy that quickened in his mind, a potent force invaded him, ripping his mind from his body with such unexpected and dizzying power that he gasped.

Dayraven's body lay on the floor of Urd's home, and nearby lay Imharr and Urd. Like a vapor caught in a breeze, he floated through the roof of the turf-covered mound and rose above it. His consciousness expanded so much that he became insubstantial as he mingled with the night air. The oaks outside in the darkness awaited him, and the wind hissing in their leaves was the voice of the land speaking to him in a slow and ancient language. As he drifted through the oaks and felt the centuries of quiet strength in their rough flesh and the quickening of life in their leafy veins, the voice of the land echoed in his mind and all around him. *Join me*, it whispered. The strange voice was familiar.

The elf! screamed his consciousness, and at once he slammed back into his body on the straw-covered floor of Urd's home.

His breaths came in rapid gasps, and his limbs shook as his normal vision and sense of his body returned. Dayraven clutched at his sweaty face and chest to make sure he was there. The shreds of his identity reclaimed their places within him as the disembodied state oozed away, leaving him with nausea and horror in its wake. The thing in his mind, the shard that the elf inserted there, diminished until it became a whisper. There it was lodged like a pebble in his shoe that prodded him but eluded his grasp.

The glowing coals in Urd's fire pit cast a ruddy light that revealed no presence other than Urd and Imharr in the home. Imharr's steady breathing told of his sleep, and Urd's form remained still.

Oh gods. It can't be. Curse you, he railed at the elf and the ominous presence it had inserted in his mind. *What have you done to me? I'm no elf-dwola, and I'm no wizard. Leave me alone!*

His breaths steadied. He did not wish to awaken Urd or Imharr. Somehow, it would be better not to tell them. Perhaps it would not happen again. *I will rid myself of this. I will take my life back. I am Dayraven of the Mark, son of Edgil, and I will wed Ebba.*

After some time, his breathing slowed, and at last his exhaustion got the better of him. But in his sleep a disturbing pair of deep blue eyes called him even as he fled them. And in his dream, since he could not escape, he turned around to face the eyes. It was then, with the faint sound of a raven's chortle echoing around him, he realized they were his own.

6
THE POWERS IN TORRHELM

Within Bagsac's stark and bare hall, its only resident sat at a small table mumbling a chant with eyes clenched and hands shivering over a glass ball, whence a blue light emanated. The ball, about the size of its owner's head, sat on a rumpled piece of white cloth, and as its brightness increased it revealed the strained features of the priest, who removed his white hood and gritted his teeth, his thin lips parted in a scowl. Sweat ran down his bald head into his face as he chanted. The light in the glass ball began to swirl, at first like thick liquid and then with gathering intensity, making confused shadows dance about the hall. With a trembling voice the priest said, "I, Bagsac, priest of the Way, call upon my lord, the Supreme Priest Bledla, who sits in majesty in Torrhelm. My lord, if it please you, hearken to my call."

A spasm took over one of Bagsac's eyes as he peered at the glass ball, the light of which turned from blue to burning white. The blurred form of his master's long white beard and hair, his sharp nose, and his deep-set, cold blue eyes animated the sphere. Though the glass ball distorted the face, which swam and morphed into grotesque forms, Bagsac quivered and bowed no less than he would have if those piercing eyes were gazing upon him in the flesh. That gaze could penetrate him even through the seeing crystal, exposing him and laying bare his every sin and every failing. Lagging a moment behind the movement of the supreme priest's lips, a deep, commanding voice emanated from the crystal.

"What is it, Bagsac? You are to use the seeing crystal only in the most important circumstances. I keep watch in many places, and there is urgent business at hand. Is it about the witch Urd?"

"My lord, it concerns Urd, and there is something more." Bagsac slapped his twitching eye and bared his teeth in a grin at the face in the glass ball.

"Go on."

"Ever since you bade me keep a closer watch on her, I found nothing of great interest, until today."

"Quickly, Bagsac — what is it?"

The priest licked his thin lips. "Remember, my lord, you also told me to study the elves and their magic, to see if we could understand more of their ways?"

"Yes, of course. What have you found?" The supreme priest's tone gave more than a hint of his rising impatience.

"Today," stuttered the priest, "an elf took a young man of Kinsford — the grand-nephew of Urd, in fact — in the Southweald. The boy's father brought him back, and I examined the body. It was the elf-sleep, for certain. But the old witch came, and she claimed she called the boy's spirit back. With my own eyes I saw the creature arise. It must have been an elf-dwola she awoke — perhaps she is one herself, my lord, or she is in league with the elves."

"Urd has no such power, and she is no elf-dwola." In the seeing crystal the supreme priest's eyes flickered. His voice slowed, and he asked the next question as much to himself as to Bagsac: "But, if it *was* the elf-sleep, how did she call the boy's spirit back?"

"My lord?" Bagsac hid the puzzled look on his face by wiping sweat from his brow with the sleeve of his white robe. "She claimed the boy's spirit was still in him somehow. I did not see what she did, but she called the boy's name."

"Are you saying the boy came back from the elf-sleep on his own, and that the witch claimed to *awaken* him?"

"Uh . . . yes, my lord. I think . . ." His eye resumed twitching.

"Now tell me, Bagsac: Did you feel the presence of the gift in the boy?"

"Oh, yes. So much power! I had felt the gift in the boy before, but he's a heathen, like most of the people out here, so I said nothing about it. But after the elf took him, it was like a blazing beacon." A frown clouded Bagsac's face. "But I thought he was an elf-dwola . . ."

Bledla's eyes narrowed. "And what is this boy's name, this grand-nephew of Urd the witch?"

Bagsac's voice quivered as if his master's gaze would flay him. "Dayraven, my lord. A most heathenish name. Son of Edgil."

"And does this Dayraven wield magic? Has Urd taught him anything?"

"Nothing, I think, my lord."

"You think?" One of Bledla's eyebrows arched up as he seemed to scowl, though it was possible the morphing of his face in the seeing crystal exaggerated the expression.

"I'm certain of it, my lord," squeaked the priest.

"Hmmm. And where is this young man now?"

Bagsac pulled at the collar of his robe like it was choking him. "Earl Stigand called a folkmoot. I urged the villagers to slay him, but Urd said they should exile him instead, and that is the course the fools took. The boy has gone with the witch now."

In the glass ball the wavering image of the supreme priest frowned. "Urd is clever, and she outwitted you this day. But I have learned more about this witch of late, and she will soon become a hindrance. We must brook no hindrance to Edan's will, for it would cause the unnecessary suffering and damnation of many. Take some loyal men with you and slay her." Bledla paused as if debating something before making up his mind. "And slay the boy too. If he has no lore as yet, he is no threat to us. But the witch must know his potential now, and she will want to train him against us. No doubt she has already corrupted him."

The priest grasped the hair on the sides of his head with both hands as if he were trying to pull out what was left of it. "But, my lord, what of the Mark's people? The boy is an exile, so I can remove him with impunity. But the witch? How can I slay her openly?"

"You are a priest of the Way, one of the Eternal of Edan. Reck not what those villagers might do. If any interfere with the coming of the Kingdom of the Eternal, then they cause great pain and suffering for themselves and those around them, and death is their rightful and most merciful end. There is no place for the coward in discharging Edan's will."

Bagsac cowered. "Yes, my lord."

"Now, I must attend to urgent business. You did well to tell me of this, and I rely on you to finish the matter. Report to me when it is accomplished. Blessed be the Eternal of Edan."

As his glass ball dimmed and the hall darkened, Bagsac sank on his bench and his head collapsed on the table before him. He let out a sigh and thought about which men he could rely on and how many he would need once he recovered his strength. It would take time to gather the right men, and he needed to rest after the strain of using the seeing crystal that linked him to the supreme priest. Soon the ball's glow went out, and the priest sat alone in darkness.

BLEDLA, THE SUPREME PRIEST OF THE WAY, SAT MOTIONLESS BEFORE the glass ball as it ceased glowing and left the shadow-filled chamber around him dimmer. Frowning and stroking his beard as he pondered Bagsac's report, he turned from his seeing crystal mounted on an iron base, which rested on a large, circular table before him. This was no time for such distractions – on the verge of fulfilling Edan's will. Still, he needed to think, for there were certain signs. *Waking from the elf-sleep? If that fool Bagsac is right, it could be taken to mean . . . But the boy's an unbeliever, like Urd. It cannot be. He would not be a fit vessel for the work of Edan.*

Bledla slid the crystal to one side, after which he reached with both hands for a large book that also lay on the table. The book's thick leather cover was red, and gilded clasps decorated its corners. With slow, deliberate movements, he lifted the tome and placed it before him. Closing his eyes and inhaling as he caressed the cover, he then opened it. He flipped a few of the vellum pages until he found the passage he sought.

The words were seared into his heart, and he could have recited them without the book, but he stroked the letters with his fingertips on the page and smiled at them, at the beauty of their expression and their truth. Ink on vellum. The bark of hawthorn branches processed with wine and iron salts to make the ink. The flesh of a calf, cleaned and bleached and stretched and scraped, to make the vellum. All to form words, which were nothing more than metaphors agreed upon to contain and convey truth. Such were the elements, mundane and intellectual, of the volume before him. Yet, brought together in this particular form to convey these particular truths, they became something far greater. They became sacred. Imbued with Edan's truth. Nothing was as familiar and dear to him as the book he now read from. In fact, Bledla had bound his soul to the words of the tome, words so established in his mind that he might have written them himself.

Indeed, the supreme priest was so linked to the words' true author, who lived hundreds of years ago, that at times it seemed he *had* written them. And with the power that Bledla wielded, who could argue that Aldmund, the Prophet of Edan, did not speak through his successor, the supreme priest of the Way?

After whispering a few sentences, he came to the most important passage. This he intoned in his deep voice: "'Thou shalt know Edan's life in the one that wieldeth the Way by the clear tokens of its glory. It will defy the eldest and greatest powers in Eormenlond. For only through Edan cometh power, and only Edan might ken the meaning of His gifts. When this Way thriveth through Eormenlond, thou shalt witness the Kingdom of the Eternal, and Edan will reign over us.' Blessed be the Eternal," he finished.

He closed his eyes again and let out a long breath. He had made the right decision. *The boy Dayraven is no follower of the Way. The demon-elves have sent an obstacle in my path. They know they will have no place in the Kingdom of the Eternal, and they fear their end. The end of all evil and suffering. Edan has allowed this to happen as a test.*

He gazed up at something beyond the dark ceiling. "I thank you, mighty and benevolent Edan, for sending me this test. Bagsac will kill the boy and the witch. I will not fail You. Your enemies will perish, and

Your kingdom will arrive in all its glory." And with that he dismissed the matter from his mind.

Bledla gathered his white woolen robe about him as he stood from his large chair and walked toward the arched window of his stone chamber with a hint of a smile on his face. Through the window's open shutters a breeze wafted from the darkness outside. Within the supreme priest's private chamber, little suggested his rank other than the large number of books and yellowed scrolls lining the scores of shelves. As one lone torch sputtered in a corner, its light failed to reach the corners of the high, vaulted ceiling. Filled with shadows above and below, the chamber almost whispered of the deep mysteries and old secrets it had witnessed. Bare and austere was the dark room, a testament to the self denial of the tall, thin man looking out its window.

From his view high in King Earconwald's royal palace, which bore the ancient name Sigseld, the supreme priest and chief advisor to the king surveyed the moonlit rows of stone spires and domes beneath him. Like a forest made for giants, the peaks of the buildings wound upward in defiance of laws that bound their inhabitants to earth. But higher than any other structure and perching over its nest on a wide mound at the city's center was the immense royal palace whence he looked out. Its turrets and spires above him seemed to threaten the thin clouds ghosting before the luminous moon.

All other parts of Torrhelm, chief city of Torrlond and greatest city of Eormenlond, lived under Sigseld's protective gaze. At this dark hour, most people slept in their houses of brick and stone, but far below clanked a troop of guards marching to their watch. Vast and teeming with innumerable points of firelight was the city spreading out beneath him. Yet even this city at the heart of the greatest and most blessed kingdom, this city with no rival in all of Eormenlond — even in the ancient kingdoms of the east — had its boundaries.

Bledla's smile broadened as he looked far, far out at the fire beacons on the guard towers interspersed along mighty Torrhelm's impenetrable stone wall. In his mind he saw beyond the wall to the great River Ea surging through the city on its way south. Past its meandering course he went, and he envisioned even further out the wide and fertile plains of South Torrlond, and beyond them, jagged peaks rising from the plains, the Marar Mountains. To the other side of the mountains his mind raced, to the kingdoms of the south, Caergilion and Adanon.

Bledla stroked his long white beard and beheld those kingdoms awaiting their destiny. *So soon. Everything I have labored for. So many years of painstaking preparation and planning. The efforts of a lifetime, and all through Edan's power and will. I am but Your humble servant. So beautiful. So perfect. Let it begin.* He trembled as he exclaimed, "Oh mighty Edan, soon it will all be Yours. We will usher in Your kingdom, the Kingdom of the Eternal, a haven for those who will dwell in peace, bliss, and adoration with You. Those who stand in our way will burn away as dross."

A knock at the door drew his attention. When the wizard turned from the window, he controlled his countenance to reflect the sobriety of his holy station. He walked to the other side of his room and unlatched the lock on the heavy wooden door. In the hallway, two soldiers in the white kirtles of the temple guards stood to the side. A third figure in a white robe towered over them. All three bowed to the supreme priest.

When he stood straight, the white-robed man more than equaled Bledla in height but was broad and stout as well. The torch he was carrying illuminated his blunt-featured face framed by flowing red hair, with grey streaking the middle of his long, red beard. In his fierce eyes flared a zeal Bledla approved of. When he rested a hand on the thick belt around his broad waist, the keys attached to it by a metal loop jingled.

"My lord, blessed be the Eternal," said the large man as he bowed his head to the supreme priest. His greeting echoed along the hallway.

"And the Kingdom of Edan." Bledla touched the man's inclined head. When he raised it, Bledla smiled. "How fare your guests, Heremod?"

"My lord, they are alive, as you commanded."

"Any further confessions?"

Heremod wore a solemn frown as he shook his head. "No, my lord. They are steeped in wickedness." The big man grinned, flashing his large, crooked teeth in the torchlight. "But I assure you their stubbornness has yielded them little comfort."

"Good. They may yet break."

Heremod wrinkled his broad nose, and his face grew troubled. "My lord, the others are all awaiting you there, including King Earconwald, who grows . . . ah, impatient."

The supreme priest's countenance did not flicker. "Then let us proceed."

"Yes, my lord."

Bledla turned to the two guards. "Stay here. I go to the dungeons."

"Yes, my lord. Blessed be the Eternal," answered the guards in unison before bowing again.

Bledla nodded his approval and proceeded next to Heremod along a torch-lit hallway. The hallway ended in an entrance to a spiral staircase of stone winding both up and down. The supreme priest and his companion stepped into it and descended.

Bledla took a deep breath before addressing Heremod. "Each of these stones we tread, each step, brings us closer to the fulfillment of our life's purpose."

Heremod nodded. "Yes, my lord."

As they continued downward, the supreme priest recalled another of his favorite passages from the Book of Aldmund, and he recited it. "'Each life is a journey, one guided by the holy hand of Edan toward its end.'"

"Aye. So spoke the Prophet."

Bledla allowed himself a momentary smile. "We are nearly there. Soon the reason for our lives will be revealed to all."

The big man grunted. "All lives go according to Edan's will." Their tall shadows shifted across the curved walls until they reached the bottom.

There they emerged from a door leading into a large hall lit by more torches along the walls. Two rows of large stone columns soared upward into the darkness, and the moonlight streaming in long, narrow windows far above suggested the hall's great height. Four guards in white-crested helms and white kirtles at the passageway's entrance bowed then stood at attention as Bledla walked by in his white robe like a tall wraith, his bulkier and even taller companion by his side. The clacking of their footsteps on the stone floor echoed throughout the dark, still hall.

Bledla stared ahead as he spoke. "There are those who, in their ignorance, will see us as cruel. They do not understand that, in doing Edan's will, we are doing the greatest possible kindness this world has ever known. 'Oft does cruelty to the flesh yield salvation of the spirit.' In the world to come, all who embrace Edan will be healed and whole. This wretched, fleeting world of polluted flesh will become a place of unending beauty and bliss. Thus, in firmness we show mercy. Through war in this realm, we bring peace in the eternal realm to come." His voice quivered with a hint of emotion. "This too is our sacrifice, and we make it with unshakeable resolve."

"It is the Way, my lord. Edan commands and sanctifies all we do." Heremod followed his solemn nod with a grin.

More torches lined both sides of the hall, revealing arched entranceways to other corridors with two silent temple guards of the Way posted at each. The guards stood like cold statues, breaking their poses only to make rigid bows as the two white-robed figures passed. They strode by two score of them before making their way to the last archway at the great hall's end. The two guards awaiting them there tugged on iron rings to open heavy, creaking doors, through which blackness yawned and waited.

A damp draft from the dark entrance ruffled the guards' white kirtles and swayed a strand of the supreme priest's white hair. The flame of Heremod's torch danced and sputtered in the draft. He and Bledla entered the darkness without a word. The door clanged shut behind them, and they descended.

Down the dark staircase led, once in a while reaching a short, level landing then changing direction in a zigzag pattern. The torch illuminated only a few feet at a time, and the narrow stairway seemed to lead to impossible depths below the castle. At first the passage's walls were smooth, but they grew rougher the further down the two reached. Thick and nigh impenetrable was the darkness in the passage, and silent was their going. The further they descended, the cooler and damper the air grew, until moisture oozed from the walls and dripped from the ceiling, plopping into small pools on the stairs.

At last it ended. At the stairway's bottom they came to a door of black iron, beneath which a dim light spilled onto the landing. Keys jingled as Heremod inserted one into the lock. The lock clicked, and, when the big man pushed, the thick door groaned open.

After Heremod closed and locked the door, they walked down a crude passageway. Torches set every twenty paces reflected in moisture coating the rough walls and in stagnant puddles on the uneven floor.

The two men passed several locked and barred doors of great size with thick iron bands on them. From behind these doors emanated low moaning, the tortured noise of afflicted humans or beasts. A moment later, the echo of their footsteps mingled with a cacophony of hideous laughter and terrified screaming from further down the hall. But when their passageway intersected with another and they turned right, the sounds grew fainter, and soon enough an eerie quiet returned.

The supreme priest broke the silence. "The cells grow full."

"Yes, my lord," answered the big man with a grin. "But only on the first level. There's still room below."

"Good. We must try to fill them within a few days. The time is coming. Even this place of torment takes on beauty as it serves Edan's purpose."

"Yes, my lord. We've arrived."

Two temple guards stood on either side of another large iron door. Light from the other side of the door spilled beneath it into the hallway. As the guards bowed, Heremod grasped the door's handle and pushed. A red glow emanated from within, and Bledla entered with Heremod behind him.

Bledla blinked at the light cast from the many torches mounted on the walls, and then he half smiled, knowing how the spectacle of the large chamber with smooth walls, floor, and ceiling of black, polished stone slid a sliver of fear into the minds of even the most wicked and hardened prisoners. Their first sight would be those sitting in judgement around the long stone table forming a large half circle nearly as wide as the room, with its ends reaching toward the door. Even the smoke of the torches could not mask the distinct sweet stench of decaying flesh lingering in the room.

Five of the seven stone seats behind the table bore occupants. Bledla inclined his head to the one in the central seat, the only person not wearing the white robe of the priests of the Way. Instead, his garments consisted of a red silk shirt patterned with gold leaves and a pair of black breeches tucked into black, shiny boots that he rested atop the table. He wore a fur-lined cloak, and a slim golden crown rested on his brow. The man's brown hair had grey patches at the sides, and grey peppered the trim, brown beard covering his strong jaw. A long and hawkish nose sat between keen grey eyes that conveyed he was used to being obeyed. He did not look pleased.

The four figures in white robes stood up, bowed to Bledla, and said, "Blessed be the Eternal."

The crowned man scowled and slouched in his seat with his legs crossed on the table, showing the soles of his boots. "You're late, Bledla." His voice was calm, even bored, but Bledla knew the anger beneath it.

"My apologies, your Majesty," answered the supreme priest, keeping his voice smooth with an effort. "A matter not irrelevant to our meeting detained me. I came as soon as I could." *Arrogant cur. Insolent fool. You insult me before my high priests with this pathetic display of defiance. For all your bluster, I know you fear me. You fear the power in me, especially in this place.*

The supreme priest locked eyes with King Earconwald. It was a subtle contest, but Bledla was determined to win. His high priests needed to know who possessed the real authority. *Your power is of the world, wretch, but mine comes from Edan. You are a trial to me, but Edan has commanded that Torrlond's power should serve Him, and so I tolerate you. For now.*

To Bledla's satisfaction, the king's gaze wavered first.

"Very well," Earconwald mumbled as he lowered his feet from the table. "I accept your apology. Let's get this over with. I hate this foul place."

As Heremod sat down, Bledla occupied the seat to the king's right and addressed his monarch. "Your Majesty, I assure you the work the High Priest Heremod does here, unpleasant as it may be, is necessary in bringing to fruition the Kingdom of the Eternal of Edan."

Earconwald smirked. "Yes, Bledla. I've heard it all before."

"Indeed. With your permission, Sire?"

"Yes." The king flicked his hand in a dismissive wave. "Get on with it."

"As you all will see in short order, we have a special reason for meeting in this place." Heremod smiled from ear to ear at Bledla's words. The supreme priest went on, "But first, let us review our plans and hear the reports from those who have just arrived." He turned to a bald man with a pointed black beard and a small, slender frame. "Morcar, how go the preparations in South Torrlond?"

The high priest smiled before inclining his head toward Bledla. "Well, my lord. When I set out, the dukes in the south had already begun issuing their orders for the mustering. Those priests powerful enough in the gift to assist in the campaign accompanied me here. We who dwell closest to the heathens in Caergilion, you will find, are the most zealous in our cause." Morcar looked around and smirked at the other high priests as if challenging them to disagree.

"Excellent." The supreme priest turned toward another man, this one blond with a trim beard gone silver on his chin. "Joruman. What of Etinstone?"

The High Priest Joruman nodded toward Bledla before answering. "Much the same, my lord. Etinstone is ready. As ready and *zealous* as anyone, I assure you." He glanced at Morcar with those last words and cocked one eyebrow to accompany his mocking grin.

Morcar answered with a frown, but, accustomed to the rivalry among the high priests, Bledla ignored the exchange. "Very good. And I know that Arna has the monastery here in Torrhelm well in hand, just as Colburga watches over the priestesses."

At these words, the oldest of the high priests, a grey-bearded, bald man sitting on the other side of the king, and the only woman in the room, large and blond haired, each bowed with the acknowledgement.

Bledla nodded to them each in turn before continuing. "We will be prepared for our retribution against Caergilion shortly. In three days," and here Bledla turned to King Earconwald, "your Majesty will hold the assembly with the dukes of your realm and almost half their captains. In a fortnight, the chosen companies, nearly half of

Torrlond's forces, will muster. Your companies from North Torrlond, Etinstone, and Torrhelm will converge at Hasumere, from there proceeding south to meet the companies of South Torrlond. All told, the army you will lead, when at full strength, will number almost ninety thousand, all under your personal command. And then . . ."

King Earconwald interrupted, "The journey to Hasumere better be worth it. It's out of the way."

Bledla frowned. "It is necessary, your Majesty. The prophecies are clear: 'In those days, even the beasts of the forests and the fens will serve their purpose in bringing about the Kingdom of the Eternal.'"

"I don't give a damn for your prophecies, Bledla. Is there a clear military advantage in diverting our forces to the fens?"

Bledla took a deep breath and forced a smile. "I can assure you, Sire, our task at Hasumere will be well worth it. It will spare thousands of your troops before the end."

Earconwald grunted, and the supreme priest resumed before his king could speak again, "We will use some of the forces we are gathering to defeat Caergilion, but the greatest weapon at our disposal, the most wonderful sign of Edan's power, we will keep in reserve. Caergilion is only the doorway into the rest of Eormenlond. Once we pass the Marar Mountains and smash it, Adanon will be at our mercy. After we finish in the south, we will move on to the rest of Eormenlond in the east. We will save our greatest surprise for any foolish enough to resist. The kingdoms of Eormenlond will submit to the Way so that the Kingdom of Edan and His Eternal may begin. As it is written in the Book of Aldmund, once all of Eormenlond lives under the Way, Edan will come and reign over the Eternal, and all others shall fall away."

"Blessed be the Eternal!" exclaimed the High Priestess Colburga, her fervor bursting out. As they caught Colburga's zeal, the high priests listened with eyes kindled and devout smiles illuminating their faces. They nodded with approval as their leader laid out the plans for the salvation of Eormenlond.

But Earconwald sat with one eyebrow cocked. "Yes, well, before anyone submits to your Way, they will submit to Torrlond, and to me."

Though he knew the petty man was goading him only to mask his fear and assert his authority, this was a challenge Bledla could not ignore. His steady gaze would have withered most men, but Earconwald had the advantage of his crown and his long familiarity with the wizard, so he only smirked as the stern supreme priest warned him, "The Kingdom of the Eternal will belong to the true believers, your Majesty. It is my sacred duty to tell you this. All others will return to dust or to the demons they worship and dwell in darkness. Your father knew this, and he died as one of a long line of pious kings, as one of the Eternal, to be resurrected by the power of Edan." *Unworthy wretch. Too late will you learn the truth.*

The High Priest Arna shifted in his seat to the king's left and opened his mouth to intervene. "Your Majesty . . ."

Earconwald cut him off by raising his palm in a quick motion.

With tension flaring between their leader and the king, the other high priests stared down in front of them. Unblinking, Bledla faced his earthly sovereign. *I must show them who the true master is. Yet we need this fool of a king for now. Edan give me patience.*

With a flushed and sneer-twisted face, Earconwald looked to his right and returned Bledla's gaze. "I'll take my chances, priest. I told you long ago not to utter such rubbish when we're in private. And do not forget it was my pious *father* who held Caergilion in his hands more than twenty years ago and marched out with a useless swiving treaty permitting a few white-robed priests to run around spewing their holy nonsense. That is no mastery!" He pounded the table. "Because of his piety, we must now conquer Caergilion again. In the meantime, as you've pointed out, our purposes coincide. Let's leave it at that, for now."

When the king finished speaking, he stared at Bledla with fury in his eyes as his nostrils flared, a warning sign the wizard recognized after so many years of observation and unheeded counsel. Earconwald would never dare to harm Bledla — even if the coward did not fear him, he needed the supreme priest's power for his worldly ambitions — but the wizard well knew there were ways the king could unleash his violence, and he had no time for such games.

"As you wish, Sire," returned Bledla as he softened his gaze into a smile. He swallowed his distaste and nodded his head in a slight bow, hoping it would be enough to appease the fool. *Let him think he has won for now. The last victory will be Edan's, and on the day of salvation I will watch him writhe.*

Earconwald's face relaxed into a vicious but satisfied grin. Once the supreme priest knew his superficial submission had placated the monarch and lessened the tension in the room, he spoke again. "But now we come to the reason for our presence in this place. With your Majesty's permission, the High Priest Heremod will conduct our prisoners here."

King Earconwald waved his hand at Heremod, who grinned and lumbered from the room with his keys jingling.

Bledla resumed speaking. "As you all know by now, our prisoners are spies in the employ of the traitor and heretic Galdor of Ellond, who sent them to convey a message and aid someone here in Torrhelm. What you do not know is Heremod and I learned more from the spies this afternoon concerning the conspiracy against us that Galdor leads. The conspiracy is broad and scattered far, though only in its infancy. Queen Faldira of Asdralad is one of its number, as may be King Tirgalan of Sundara. Also, there is the witch Urd, from the Mark. All are powerful in sorcery, though such unbelievers cannot hope to match us."

"And none of their kingdoms can vie with Torrlond's military power," remarked the High Priest Arna.

"Quite right," agreed Bledla. "Besides this, Galdor is in a precarious place, for we have strong support for the Way in Ellond. It will not be difficult to dislodge him and force King Fullan to bring Ellond to our side. As for the Mark, the witch Urd holds no sway there, and the people of our sister kingdom in the northwest will come to our heels when we call them, as they always have. King Ithamar of the Mark may not be devout enough, but he allows the priests of the Way freedom, and we have a number of followers there. Besides this, our ancient kinship is enough to guarantee the loyalty of the Mark."

The High Priest Joruman smiled. "So, at the moment, only the kingdoms of Asdralad and Sundara concern us, and they have little strength of arms."

Bledla nodded. "Correct. However, the members of Galdor's

conspiracy somehow know we are gathering powers never harnessed before for our assault on the unbelievers, though they may not yet know of our greatest weapon. Thus, we must strike before they bring other kingdoms to their cause or unite the south and east against us."

Earconwald waved a hand in dismissal. "There's nothing to worry about. A rapid assault on the south, and then we'll have one front to the east. By the time this little conspiracy becomes organized, we'll control more than half of Eormenlond. The old kingdoms of the Andumae in the east are crumbling. Their vigor is gone. Once all of western Eormenlond is ours, they'll never withstand us."

"No doubt you are correct, your Majesty," said Bledla. "But hitherto we have enjoyed the advantage of secrecy. All of Eormenlond believes our target is Caergilion. We sent the three martyrs there to stir the unbelievers against the Way, giving us a justifiable claim for our invasion. But, until now, we have kept hidden the knowledge that we will go beyond Caergilion to bring first Adanon and then the whole of Eormenlond under Torrlond's sway. If others discover this too soon, we risk Adanon and the other kingdoms of Eormenlond uniting behind Caergilion. We do not wish to allow them the time to prepare for war since we would lose the element of surprise. That would make our task more difficult and delay the spreading of the Way."

King Earconwald's smirk made plain his disdain. "Adanon will never aid Caergilion. They would rather see each other destroyed, even if uniting could save them. There's no difficulty there. Besides, there are far more ready soldiers in Torrlond than in the whole of their two kingdoms. But we'll strike soon, much sooner than they can guess, and our victory will be swift."

As the king finished speaking, the door clicked open, and Heremod returned smiling. Behind him filed in six guards in white kirtles, and among them two naked men with chains around their feet and hands limped in, half carried by the guards. The prisoners squinted and blinked, and their chains clinked as they tried to shield their eyes. The High Priestess Colburga's face wrinkled in disgust, while the other high priests and King Earconwald kept impassive expressions.

Bledla narrowed his eyes and craned his head forward like a large feline on the verge of springing for its prey. *Servants of the heretic Galdor.*

Traitor. Apostate. I have not caught you yet, but I will, and on that day I will rejoice with Edan in your downfall. In the meantime, these two will suffer for allowing you to seduce them away from Edan's truth.

The guards prodded the two men forward with their swords until the prisoners slouched in the center of the room in full view of their inquisitors sitting behind the stone table. Bruises, cuts, and filth covered both prisoners' bodies, and dried blood caked their mouths, wrists, hands, ankles, feet, and groins. Fresh trickles of red ran down their inner thighs and dripped from their anuses. The elder prisoner had disheveled brown-grey hair, while the younger, who shivered and shrank from Heremod, was blond.

The supreme priest locked his gaze onto the two prisoners. "We know the traitor Galdor sent you two spies to convey a message to someone here in Torrhelm. Tell us who this person is, and your deaths will be merciful and swift."

The younger of the two wretches glanced with wide eyes and jerky movements at all the faces in the room, but the elder stared at Bledla. "I told you . . ." He wheezed, and fresh blood oozed over his split lip. He continued with great difficulty, partly because he had no more teeth. "We don't know his name."

"I see. That is unfortunate." The supreme priest of the Way betrayed no emotion. He turned to Heremod, who stood behind the prisoners with the row of guards. "Heremod, remove the cover." *The will of Edan be done.*

"Yes, my lord." A gleam lit Heremod's eyes. He turned to the guards and ordered them, "You two. Hold the prisoners. You others, come help me."

Bledla watched with a stone face as four guards followed Heremod, who walked in front of the two prisoners and bent to the floor. Where he crouched was an outline in the otherwise smooth stone floor of a circle twelve feet in diameter. Because it was black iron, the circle blended in with the floor. But in three places there were iron handles welded onto the circle. Heremod took his keys and inserted one into holes next to each of the handles. Each turning of the key produced a loud click. At two of the handles he posted two guards each, while the large high priest took one of the handles himself. He counted, "one, two, *three*!" and all five men grunted as they lifted the iron cover a few inches, shuffled with it to the right, and let it down with a loud clang on the stone floor. They slid the cover to the right with a scraping noise to reveal a gaping hole in the ground some eleven feet in diameter.

How far down the black hole went was impossible to see, but warm, fetid air and an overwhelming, sickly reek of rotten flesh rushed into the room, prompting the High Priestess Colburga to cover her mouth and nose with the sleeve of her white robe. The two weary prisoners watched this proceeding as a guard behind each held them up by the arms, and the younger prisoner never stopped shaking.

"Move them closer." Bledla waved a hand at the guards, who shoved the two prisoners to the hole's edge.

He looked upon the two wretched heathens with a blade-like gaze. "As you declared, blessed Aldmund, 'Those who follow not the will of Edan shall in the end return to the dust whence they came.'"

Then he commanded Heremod, "Bring it up."

The red haired high priest grinned before he closed his eyes and chanted in an ancient tongue, "Ashdala midannon im inghuishway singallon. Valmala inghannon ar oruday ardallon."

As the large man repeated the phrases several times in his sandy voice, the other high priests looked with rapt expressions at the large hole in the floor, while King Earconwald watched with his lip curled in disgust. Other than Heremod's incantation, only quiet foreboding filled the chamber. Then the red-haired high priest ceased, opened his eyes, and revealed his jagged teeth in a broad smile.

After moments of silence, the room vibrated with a piercing shriek emanating from the hole. No human could have made such a shrill sound, for whatever produced it seemed to fill the entire hole. It told of some dread thing in the earth's bowels living to sate its unending hunger.

The younger prisoner, whose shaking increased in intensity, surprised the guard who held him by jumping back with unexpected force and pissing all over the floor. Slipping in the urine, the guard punched the young man in the back of the head and forced him back to the edge.

Bledla widened his eyes as he addressed the prisoners. "You have no doubt heard of gruddugs before, though I daresay you've never seen one. Amazing creatures. Eyeless, they live deep under the earth. Toothless, they devour their meals whole and digest them for weeks in their bellies. That is what they are: a mouth and a belly. Yet all of Edan's creatures have their purposes. Gruddugs live from the earth, but they grow much larger when one feeds them flesh. They are easy for one with the gift to control, but this one may soon outgrow its lair."

Turning to Heremod, the supreme priest said, "Dangle that one over the hole," and nodded toward the elder of the two prisoners. *He is the stronger of the two. The other's will may break.*

Without hesitating, Heremod punched the stomach of the man, who groaned and buckled over. He took rope from a guard and tied it around the chain holding the prisoner's hands. With one swift motion he picked up the man by his hair and threw him into the hole, but, as he held the rope, the man jerked to a stop, his arms stretched above him. While Heremod held him there, the man moaned, and the younger prisoner cried, "Brithmar! Don't leave me!"

"Pull him up a bit higher, Heremod, so his friend may see him," said Bledla.

Standing at the hole's edge, Heremod chuckled and hoisted up the rope as if he held a rag doll at its end, and the man in the hole cried out his agony. Two guards now held the younger prisoner, and one gripped his head to force him to look down the hole.

Just then the gruddug let out another shriek, this one even louder than the first. A sticky, oozing sound coming from the hole filled the room and grew louder. The prisoner hanging in the hole cried, "Orm take me swiftly!" while the room shook from the monster worming its way up. Then, with speed that made most of the onlookers flinch, an enormous mouth erupted a few feet out of the hole as it wrapped around the prisoner with a deafening sucking sound.

Showing itself for an instant, the gruddug resembled a colossal maggot dripping yellowish mucus from its white, translucent, fleshy hide. The outlines of its organs were visible through its skin, as was Brithmar's writhing form. Its reek stunned everyone, but somehow

Heremod held on to the rope for a moment to listen to the muffled screams of the man inside the creature. He released the rope with a laugh, and the gruddug disappeared into the hole with its meal.

The naked young prisoner stood wide-eyed and shaking with terrible convulsions. "Brithmar!"

"Do you wish to share his fate?" inquired Bledla.

Taking the young man's quivering for an answer, the supreme priest continued. "Then tell me, to whom were you to convey the message from Galdor?"

Turning his terrified eyes from the hole to Bledla, the prisoner shook his head along with the rest of his body.

"Your days are finished, heathen. It is too late for repentance, but I will give you a small measure of mercy if you cooperate now. There is only one last thing for you to tell me. If you confess the name of the person you were to meet here in Torrhelm, I will grant you a swift death. If not . . ." The supreme priest raised his eyebrows and glanced toward the hole.

The prisoner's eyes followed the wizard's, and his lower lip quivered as his mouth opened, but only a high-pitched, pleading whine came out.

"I grow weary of this useless interview," said Bledla in a tone all the more threatening for its casualness. "The wretch has lost his wits. There remains only one way to discover the truth. I will enter his mind and find it there."

The High Priest Arna sat up. "My lord." He continued in a whisper as he leaned closer, "There is a danger, as you know. What if he knows how to merge wills? He is Galdor's servant, after all, and he might have taken this precaution."

"Look at the wretch, Arna." The supreme priest smiled. "I know, oldest of friends, you speak out of love, but you need not worry. This unbeliever cannot even remember his own name. He will be no threat to me." *Edan give your servant the strength and wisdom to carry out your will.*

The smile transformed to a snarl as Bledla turned to the prisoner and growled, "Unbeliever. Vile heathen. Your mind will yield its secrets to me, whether you will or no." After he stood up from his seat and faced the young man, Bledla's eyes locked onto the quivering prisoner. Helpless, the wretch stared ahead at his inquisitor. The supreme priest chanted, "Druanil ecthonias di andyon dimniathon. Abu mihil inghanias mi rakhyon inlorathon."

As Bledla's resounding voice intoned the phrases again and again, the young man's eyes widened. His gaze darted around the room as if he sought a voice that he could not find, but then his eyes took on a dullness, and they settled on Bledla. The young prisoner began to shiver less.

When he stopped shivering altogether and stood still, he continued to stare at Bledla with a vacant face.

The supreme priest ceased chanting.

The others in the room said no word.

After a few silent moments, Bledla perceived in his own mind the ghostly images of an old man, an old woman, and a girl who resembled the young prisoner. The young man yearned toward them, but Bledla said, "No, boy, your family means nothing now. Show me the traitor, Galdor."

The image of a white-bearded old man appeared to the supreme priest, and Bledla suppressed the rage that arose at the thought of that heretic. He must remain focused.

"Yes. Good. Remember the day he told you and Brithmar of your errand here. Cleanse your mind of all else."

The ghost image of Galdor spoke to a ghost Brithmar, then nodded and smiled at Bledla.

"Yes, I see it now. Very good. Now, show me the one whom he told you to meet."

Blackness.

"You must have heard it. His name, show me his name."

The prisoner's mind remained dark.

Bledla probed deeper. "You cannot hide it from me. Denial will merely prolong your suffering."

The young man winced as if he had been pricked somewhere, and his mouth stretched in a rictus.

Still the supreme priest saw nothing. He tore further into the heathen's mind, which sought to flee from Bledla in rising terror. The supreme priest gripped it in a vise of steel.

"No, foolish boy, do not resist . . . You lie!"

The young man's head quivered again, and his face convulsed while his body remained stiff and erect.

"Lying heathen. Show me the one Galdor told you to meet." He had to be lying. Such defiance of Edan's will was intolerable. Bledla slashed and ripped for the truth.

The wretch's mouth gaped open while his head shook with more violence.

"Unbelieving dog. Show me!" Bledla's fingernails dug into the palms of his clenched hands, and he gritted his teeth. The prisoner's head slammed back and forth while his eyes rolled up in his head, and bloody drool seeped down his chin.

Agony and terror wracked the wretch's mind — Bledla well knew this since he experienced every emotion and measure of pain along with the man. But what was pain? A tool in the service of truth. And the supreme priest's righteous wrath was a towering inferno that seared the pain to ashes.

The prisoner's head grew bright red, and the veins on his temples and forehead protruded like bluish roots. Still the supreme priest shouted, "Show me, curse you!"

Arna winced. "My lord, he'll not take much more."

Bledla screamed even louder, "Show me!"

The young prisoner let out an inhuman scream as his head became purplish. His terror and anguish vied with the supreme priest's wrath, and all the emotions swirled together in Bledla's mind in a mighty and violent embrace. Such defiance of Edan's rightful commands warranted no mercy. The room blurred, and the heat of Bledla's body radiated from his flesh. Fueled by righteous rage, the supreme priest's will ascended ever higher to seize the wretch's mind and crush the truth from it. Bledla clenched his eyes and shrieked one last, long time, "Show meeeeee!!!"

With a gurgling sound, the young man's head splattered open like a squashed grape, and within, the prisoner's mind snapped and darkened. Wet droplets pattered on Bledla's face as bright red blood sprayed from the prisoner's nose, mouth, and eye sockets onto all the onlookers. The High Priestess Colburga gasped, and one of the blood-soaked guards who had been holding the prisoner vomited. The young man's stiff body swayed then fell to the floor onto what was left of his face with a wet splat.

No one in the room stirred or spoke.

The body lay unmoving as a red pool oozed and radiated from its head. Small chunks of pink and grey floated on the pool.

"Well, Bledla," sneered King Earconwald, who had spots of blood all over him, "it looks like you got it all out of him." He stood up from his seat and looked around the room. "This meeting has been most enlightening, but it is now over. I'll call for you tomorrow. Be sure you're not late."

Nearly staggered by the agonizing death he experienced along with the young prisoner, Bledla allowed himself a quick shake of the head. *Another sacrifice.* Considering it wiser and easier to allow Earconwald's anger to abate for a day, the supreme priest nodded acknowledgment toward his earthly sovereign. *It is well,* he thought with satisfaction. *He will fear me even more after this.* He kept his countenance expressionless to mask his irritation at the fool's impertinence.

As the king walked to the door, all others in the room stood up and bowed to him. After opening the door, King Earconwald turned around with a smirk. "You people are insane."

He left with the two guards outside as an escort, and the door banged shut.

Blood spattered all over his robe and running down his forehead to his sharp nose, Bledla gazed at the closed door. "So the heathens have always said of the Eternal, since the days of Aldmund. But the end times will reveal the truth. Then only will the unbelievers realize their woe while the Eternal triumph." *Then your day will come, vile king.*

He turned to Heremod, who still stood with the six guards. "Throw that corpse down the hole and cover up that stench."

Heremod ordered the guards, all trusted devotees of the Way, to execute the command. Once they tossed down the body, they slid back the iron cover, which fell into place with a loud and final clang.

The supreme priest declared, "Thus end all who oppose the Way of Edan, whether early or late."

His five high priests in their blood-speckled white robes beamed at their leader as he continued. "For, my beloved brethren in Edan, the long awaited time comes soon. I have foreseen it. We will live to see the accomplishment of the Kingdom of the Eternal. All the signs are in place. A mastery over the eldest of powers I will reveal, and through great strife shall we bring about Edan's will. The promised day of peace and bliss is nigh, and you will all stand next to me as we look on the glory of Edan."

"Blessed be the Eternal!" they cried in unison.

7
A DAWN ATTACK

Bearing a torch, Urd entered her goat shed in the dead of night. Inside, the ruddy light spilled onto the sleeping forms of the goats. On the other side of the shed, Rudumanu and Hraedflyht were still. The old woman crouched and stroked one of the sleepy kids. It responded in a trembling little voice.

She took up the bleating kid with one arm and bore it outside, its white coat crimsoned in the glow of torchlight, and as she walked toward the edge of her oak ring, she hummed a gentle lullaby, tender as when a mother puts her child to bed.

Just outside the oak ring, she crouched down and lay the sputtering torch in the grass where her goats had cropped it short. For more than a hundred heartbeats, she caressed the kid in her arms and listened to its soft bleating while she continued to hum within the circle of flickering light. Outside the torch's small sphere of illumination, darkness loomed.

Still crouching and cradling the goat, Urd slipped one hand up the opposite sleeve of her robe. When she withdrew the hand, the knife it held gleamed red in the torch's glow. She ceased humming to utter the words, "I thank thy spirit, little one." With a swift and strong motion she slit the kid's throat, and the wind whispered through the oak leaves. The little body gave a quick shudder. Dark blood – nearly black in the torchlight – poured from the white neck. Urd held the goat for a long time while its life spilled into the ground. The blood lessened to a trickle, then drops.

The old woman laid the kid's body on the grass. She reached up her sleeve again, and this time she produced a short length of rope, which she put aside. Releasing a long sigh, she set about dressing the meat before tying the carcass to an oak branch to drain.

DAYRAVEN AWOKE AND OPENED HIS EYES. A RUDDY GLOW FROM THE fire pit illuminated the room and cast long shadows across its walls. Staring up at the sooty ceiling beams of Urd's home, he reflected that his had not been a restful sleep. *Too many dreams*. However, even if his dreams had not been to his liking, at least he had remained where he was supposed to after he fell asleep. No more unpleasant partings from his body. The presence the elf put in his mind was still there, though it was faint — a shadow sensation, an elusive itch. But it was there, and it was foreign, for he had never felt it before his meeting with the elf. He also could imagine the faint echoes of the raven's call, as if it had been screaming outside Urd's home all night. There was no need to worry the others by telling them about it, or how, after they went to sleep, he had drifted outside and heard the elf calling. *Just the aftereffects of the elf-sleep. It may never happen again.*

A loud pop followed by a long sizzle drew his attention to the other side of the room. Urd stood in her brown cloak with her back to him, her long white hair braided behind her. He lay still and watched her near the fire pit, where a small black cauldron hung from the chain over a crackling fire. In the cauldron something boiled and steamed, and Urd bent with a hand on one hip to disperse the coals with an iron poker, lessening the fire. The shadow she cast across the room shrank. She was a small woman whose old body had grown fragile. After she stood, she turned to the side. The red glow revealed her calm features, the wrinkles on her face, and her bright eyes that were keen and beautiful. *She's borne many burdens, most we know nothing of. A lonely life. A witch's life. They say neither a witch nor a wizard has a people. I wonder if I've ever known her. I hope she'll be fine when we leave.*

The door of the little home opened, and Imharr ducked inside to tell Urd, "All packed and ready. We'll be able to leave as soon as we eat."

"Very good. The two of you can help me now." She spoke without turning around as she inspected the cauldron. "Did you sleep well, my child?"

Was there suspicion in her voice? Could she sense what had happened to him? "Well enough, though I think not for long. Is it dawn yet?" Dayraven stretched and stood, rubbing his eyes.

"Not quite," said Imharr. "Your aunt's an early riser. She had me up and packing some time ago. It seems she wants to be rid of us."

"Impudent young fellow," scolded Urd with a smile, but then her face grew serious. "There's need for haste, I fear. But first you must eat. You have a long journey ahead. Bring the cauldron outside." She took a heavy, long knife with a bone handle from her cupboard along with two iron scrapers and a large wooden bowl. Putting the knife and scrapers in the bowl, she took up a torch in her other hand and headed out the door.

After Dayraven splashed water on his face from a basin, he and Imharr used old strips of cloth to grasp the handles on the sides of the cauldron, which was full of steaming water, and carry it outside. It was still dark out, and Dayraven welcomed the light breeze fingering his kirtle as he glanced up at the glimmering stars. The position of the moon and stars told that it would not be long before dawn began bleeding into the sky.

"A clear morning," said Imharr. His voice seemed loud in the stillness. The water sloshed in the cauldron between them. "The day will be good to begin a journey."

"Yes." *A journey away from home.* Dayraven did not want to think about where it would take him, and a heaviness occupied his chest. This day would mean the end of everything familiar.

The two young men followed Urd's torch, bearing the cauldron just outside the ring of oaks. She motioned with her hand for them to come near her, where she stood over the dressed carcass of one of her goats lying on the grass. "Pour the water over it."

Dayraven and Imharr tipped the cauldron of scalding water over the carcass. Once they finished, she put the bowl with the knife and scrapers in Dayraven's hands. "Get to work, then." She handed the torch to Imharr and then shuffled back toward her home without another word.

The two of them first scraped the hairs off the body, and then they carved up the meat, placing the portions into the cauldron. Just as they were finishing, Urd returned with a bowl of hot oil smelling of herbs and salt. She turned to Imharr. "Be a good lad and build the fire back up, and put the gridiron over it."

The goat made a hearty breakfast. Urd finished before Dayraven and Imharr, and while they ate she sang part of an ancient song the shapers passed down about King Folcwalda of Ellond, who lived more than five hundred years before them:

Fierce was Folcwalda, the flinger of rings,
When he wended his way, he wielded his folk,
To the banks of the broad one, the blue Theodamar.
Over meadows they marched, from the mother of kingdoms,
From the homeland of heroes, the hallowed Ellorlond.
Unbarred he his breasthoard and brandished his spear,
The ranks he rallied, his rede he made known.
Their shields they shook, from sheaths sprang swords,
Bright were the battle-flames, the blades all keen,
When cried out their king, he kindled their wrath:
"Listen! Loaned is this life, not long are we here,
Ere death claims his due, in darkness enfolds us.
The rings come to rust, and rest takes the warriors.
The hawk flies not home, the horses are silent.
The ground will eft guard both the gold and the silver.
The sword of the soldier in sorrow abandoned
Lies shattered in shards, its sheath now empty.
Hushed is the harp, and the hall stands idle.
Friends are fleeting, family will perish.
Where have they wandered, the ones who came before?

Where linger the lost, the line of our folk?
In the mirk of the mound are a man's longest dreams,
E'en bold ones will bow, barrows will hold them.
But glory is granted ere the ground claims their bones
To the fearless who flee not from fate's mighty grip.
Ere death ends his days, man's deeds make his name.
Then go forth to win fame, folk of my heart!"

Dayraven knew the song, for Urd had taught it to him when he was young. It told how Folcwalda and his people broke out of Ellond over the Theodamar River and conquered the now vanished kingdom of Riodara, a name forgotten, but Urd told him it once was among the mightiest of the kingdoms of the Andumae. The land that had been Riodara became Torrlond, whence the folk of the Mark came. Folcwalda made himself King of Torrlond, and Ellond he gave to his eldest son, Fullan. Hence the kings of Torrlond and Ellond, descendants in unbroken lines from Folcwalda, were kin. Such glory placed Folcwalda among the greatest of heroes in all of Eormenlond's history. His was a story of bravery and new beginnings, and Dayraven wondered if the old woman sang it to strengthen him. He did not feel brave, and his own new beginning seemed more like an end.

Nevertheless, the song worked a certain magic on him. Its lulling chant awakened in his imagination the deeds of ancient days, and a vivid image of clashing armies swam before him. Blood ran, and thousands died. A kingdom ended. Another began. With her clear voice Urd sang the haunting song. As it brought to Dayraven's mind the endless generations of old, he wondered how many kingdoms of the world had come and gone like Riodara. He wondered if, five hundred years from his time, people would remember songs of the Mark. *We're all of us like them. It's all one story. But what will be my part in it now? A man without a home has no people to remember him. No kin to protect him.*

Urd broke off her song and added a stick of wood to the dying fire. While Dayraven and Imharr finished their food and washed up, the old woman looked long at Dayraven. When he returned her gaze, she said, "It's time."

The three walked out to the goat shed, where Rudumanu and Hraedflyht awaited their masters. Laden with leather packs of food and spare clothes as well as their masters' bows, the two mares stamped and neighed to signal they were ready.

Before getting on his horse, Dayraven turned to Urd. "This day is unwelcome. I'm loath to leave Father, Ebba, you, and all I know in Kinsford, and I don't know what will happen. But I want you to know you've given me strength."

"Dear child, the strength is in you. You have courage, and you'll find yourself. Go to Galdor. He'll be expecting you. We'll meet again." These last words the old woman paired with a nod.

"May fate grant it," he said.

He and Imharr climbed on their horses.

Seeming small and frail, Urd took a deep breath and looked up at them. "Ride northeast for the Folkwater. Once you meet it, cross the first ford over to the northern bank, then follow the river east to Wolvendon. Get more food and supplies there. Don't linger, and head east. When you leave behind the Mark and enter Torrlond, you'll find a wide road. Follow it east along the Withweald. The road runs east across North Torrlond, and further on another road crosses it going north. Take the road north to Rimdale. There you must buy passage on a ship bound for Ellond. Remember: Stay away from priests of the Way."

"Yes, Grandmother. We'll be careful."

Urd gazed at Dayraven and smiled. "'Careful' is not enough for a young man. Be *afraid*. May Sithfar, the god of travelers, watch over and shield you both." She looked up at Imharr. "You too will find yourself, my lad. Stay with him as long as you can."

Imharr grinned. "He won't get rid of me, my dear." He reached for Urd's hand and took it in his own. Bending from his horse, he kissed it.

"Goodbye, dear boy," said she.

Dayraven and Imharr rode at a trot behind the goat shed towards the edge of Urd's circle of oaks. They headed northeast as morning's red light bled over the hills. Dayraven turned around once before leaving the ring. Urd's small form in her brown cloak stood gazing after them near the goat shed. Along with the persistent whisper of the shard the elf had implanted in his mind, a pang of worry for the old woman spread through his chest.

"I hope she'll be alright."

Imharr followed his gaze. "Don't worry. If anyone knows how to fend for herself, it's our Urd."

URD FROWNED AS THE TWO RIDERS DISAPPEARED BEHIND HER OAKS, and she sighed when the first sun rays struck the back of her house. She sniffed and wiped at one of her eyes with a finger. No use being sentimental. There was little else she could have done. *The boy must be trained. So much power.* The old woman shivered. It had been many years since such fear had seized her. Had she sent him away because she feared him? Yes, and because she loved him. *No choice. I had to send him. But will he reach Galdor? I cannot see his path yet . . . For now, I must keep those priests away from him.*

She stood for some time with closed eyes, chanting beneath her breath. Her body swayed as if a breeze rocked it forward and backward until it went rigid, and her eyes popped open in a vacant stare. But it was not with her eyes that she perceived the world around her. The whisperings of the earth brushed against her spirit. Many subtle voices blended with one another, but among them was one that most concerned her. It spoke of heavy hooves biting into the grass and soil. Horses. At least ten. *Yes. They're coming. Time to prepare.*

She shook herself out of the trance, after which she exhaled as her shoulders drooped. Tottering toward the trees and walking around the circle of oaks in silence, she peered up at their branches. *First, Galdor must know the boy is coming.* When she stopped at the oak ring's western end, near the entranceway, she hummed a slow tune. The rising sun gilded the tops of the trees. Branches swayed and leaves bobbed in a gentle breeze. Her humming grew in volume until Urd sang to the oaks, "Tulimmin ingdhali vinyoro ar dwinnin. Im niamin ushtali bahoro an gwannin."

As soon as she finished the second phrase, a small spotted eagle glided down from one of the oaks and settled on the ground before her. The bird's dun feathers darkened to deep brown on the wings and tail, and white flecks lined its wings. Its sharp beak curved downward at the end, and its dark eyes seemed eager for flight. She stepped nearer. "I have need of your swift wings."

The eagle stared up at her with comprehension in its eyes and hopped closer. She bent down with hands resting on her stiff knees and smiled as her gaze met the bird's. Mere inches from it, she stroked its feathers while locking eyes with it. The old woman had sung many spells to it, and they were each long used to the other's company. Its hunter's mind was swift to link with hers.

Images from Urd's thoughts seeped into the bird, memories of Dayraven and Imharr. These impressions, along with the sense of Urd's feelings about the young men, imprinted themselves in the bird, waiting for one with the gift to unlock them. When she finished, she stood up and urged it. "Go to Galdor. You know the way. Fly with speed, wind-rider."

Up rose the eagle with a few flaps of its wings. In a circle it flew around Urd's home before it cried out once and soared toward the rising sun, which dazzled the old woman's eyes, and then it was gone. *You've never failed me. Do not fail me now.*

Urd turned around and walked back to her turf covered home. Passing the house, she stopped at the goat shed, outside of which the goats grazed and stuttered. As she addressed them, she smiled like a mother at her newborn child. "I must go for some time. Stay within the oaks, little ones, and you'll be fine. No wolves will enter the ring. If I don't return ere summer's end, find a warm place for the winter. I should try Eorp's farmstead if I were you, just a few miles to the west across some nice meadows." In silence the goats all stared at her, and then they gave her a chorus of bleats before returning to their grazing.

The old woman turned around and made her way into her home, where she packed a few things in a small leather bag and took up her walking staff. She emerged from her home with these things and sat down cross-legged in front of the door as if waiting for someone. *Now, I must arrange a proper welcome.*

Closing her eyes, she chanted in a whisper, but her voice took on more volume as she continued. "Ahuronai in dumalin ar gwalinor miladon. Indagathai mi turolin in regabor segradon. Tulimmin heshtali hingworo ar druno. Im niamin ringdhali saryoro ni vanyo." Many times

Urd repeated the phrases, and for a long while nothing notable happened.

But then, at first in an unremarkable trickle, birds began to alight in her oaks. The trickle became a steady stream until a flood of birds flew towards her home and landed in her trees with no more noise than the fluttering of their wings. The flood grew to a multitude, and it seemed hardly feasible for even the thick branches of such great trees to shelter so many birds. Swallows, mourning doves, woodpeckers, blackbirds, crows, sparrows, robins, starlings, and many more: they all flocked to Urd's oaks and disappeared behind their leaves. Urd chanted for several moments after the last birds arrived, and then she ceased. With her eyes still shut, she nodded with a satisfied smile on her face.

More time passed, and the old woman yet held her eyes closed. For a long while she sat motionless, almost deathlike in the still air. Then a small change came over her face, her eyebrows rising and her brow furrowing. Opening her eyes, she stared ahead at the western edge of her oak ring and grinned.

Just outside the oak ring's entranceway, a hooded man in a white robe sat astride a white horse. Behind him rode up a dozen men of the Mark, all known adherents of the Way. The horsemen, who bore spears and shields, hesitated outside, but the man in the white robe pointed and directed them to spread out and surround the oak ring. The men urged their horses to their stations, and some disappeared from Urd's view as they rode for the ring's eastern side behind her home.

She looked on their proceedings without stirring. After the horsemen took their positions, Urd cried out to the man in the white robe, who remained on his horse outside the ring.

"Greetings, Bagsac. You needn't linger so long. I'm right here, as you can see." *Poor fool. Come to do your master's bidding. He'll need to send more than this gaggle of geese.*

"Witch!" screamed Bagsac, priest of the Way. "Don't think I'm not aware you've woven countless spells within the circle of these trees. I know your power is greatest in there, but that will not save you now."

"We'll see."

After a few moments of inaction, Bagsac yelled across to her,

"Come out with the boy Dayraven and meet me, and I may spare your life."

"Come in and meet me, and I may not spare yours." Her smile lit her face, and her voice echoed among the oaks, as if the wind rustling in the leaves carried the words or the trees whispered the threat along with their mistress. Several of the men flinched and urged their steeds back a few paces, never taking their gazes from the oaks, and the horses whinnied at the ghostly echo in the trees.

BEHIND URD'S HOUSE AT THE OAK RING'S EASTERN END, FOUR horsemen rode within, as Bagsac had instructed them. When Urd's voice crept from the trees, they halted their horses and looked at one another. Nothing else happened, so one of them, a burly thegn with a blond beard and fierce eyes, motioned forward with his hand.

They moved in near silence toward the house by the goat shed, where the goats grazed nearby. Since the goats ignored them, they rode closer to the back of Urd's home. As they neared it, the thegn drew a sword, and the other three readied their spears. In front of the mound and out of their vision, the priest Bagsac and the witch shouted at one another. The swordsman motioned for one of the spearmen to follow him around the right side of the turf covered house, and he pointed at the other side to direct the other two around that way. They rode closer and glanced at each other. The thegn raised his hand in the air, where it hovered until he grimaced and brought it down in a swift motion, the signal to strike.

WHILE BAGSAC'S MEN POSITIONED THEMSELVES FOR THE ATTACK, from the edge of Urd's oak ring in front of her home, the priest shouted, "Foolish and stubborn woman! You should have submitted to the Way when I gave you the chance. Edan is merciful but mighty, and only His Eternal will gain victory. The supreme priest himself ordered me to give you one last chance to repent. Come out with Dayraven, and promise to cease worshiping your demons. I will bless you both into the path of salvation."

Urd laughed. "I don't need your salvation, Bagsac. Since only the Eternal will live forever, I would find myself in rather poor company. Imagine the lot of you running around in your white robes singing praises — even Edan would tire of you!" She rocked where she sat as she chortled.

Bagsac scowled at her. "Blasphemer! I have given you your last chance!"

Urd stopped laughing. She stood with the aid of her staff and leveled her gaze at Bagsac. "I know why you've come, priest. Waste no more time with your games."

No longer did she smile as she shut her eyes and chanted in a loud, clear voice, "Hrondin ar dwinnor ghannash in valir! Blunnin im ghodor utanash ar vardir!" After Urd cried out her spell, she raised one arm with her palm facing outward.

Horses neighed and screamed. The four men who had crept to the rear of the old witch's home galloped behind her on their steeds, two from the right and two from the left. With their beasts' hooves churning up clods of dirt and grass, they raced forward at full speed.

The horses and the men clinging to them did not close on the old woman. They streaked past her, rushing for the western side of the oak ring. The three spearmen fumbled and dropped their weapons. None of the four riders controlled the animals they bounced on, and they struggled to clutch onto the beasts.

As the horses shot toward the western edge of the oak ring, the priest awaiting them there held his hands aloft and wove his counter spell: "Hrondin ar dwinnor ghannash in valir! Innin im gwalor runash in bundir!"

The four steeds sped up.

He repeated the spell, but the horses sprinted towards him with their riders flailing. "Curse her! I can't break her spell while they're in the ring." Then he realized his peril. Eyes widening, he turned his horse around and galloped in the other direction.

Three horses with their riders chased the priest. When Urd waved her hand, the fourth mount, upon which the thegn with the sword clung for life, galloped not out the western entrance to the ring, but veered at the last moment under an oak. The change in direction was so sudden that the man had no time to duck and avoid the large, gnarled branch snaking out of the tree.

With a thud the man's head met the branch, snapping him back as the branch quivered and several leaves fluttered to the ground. The horse stopped running and, after a moment of indecisive wavering, the man's limp body slouched to the right and fell onto the grass. His steed galloped back toward the house, where Urd waited.

The remaining eight men surrounding the oak ring looked on. For a moment they stayed where Bagsac posted them, but after some fidgeting, first one then the rest of the adherents of the Way rode in the direction the priest had fled when the three horses chased him.

In the distance, Bagsac with his hood and hair waving behind him urged on his white steed while the three horses and their discomfited riders followed. But then, after more than a furlong, the priest turned his horse around. Facing his closing pursuers, he once more chanted his counter spell, "Hrondin ar dwinnor ghannash in valir! Innin im gwalor runash in bundir!"

This time, far outside the circle of oaks, his spell worked, and the three men regained control of their snorting and panting horses a few feet from Bagsac. Once the three stopped, they leapt off and cursed at the beasts. The other eight men rode up.

"Idiots!" screeched the priest as they halted. One of his eyes twitched with rapid blinks. "Why aren't you where I told you to be?"

One man answered, "Forgive us, my lord, but when you fled . . ."

"Fled? I did not flee!" Bagsac's face reddened as his wiry hair danced about the bald crown of his head. "A priest of the Way *never* flees. I was merely dealing with the witch's spell. Where's Heardred?" He looked over his followers.

"His horse ran under one of the trees, and he, well . . . fell off."

The priest's eyes went wide. "Then he's in the witch's hands, and she has his steed. She'll escape. Back! Ride back, I tell you!" He turned on the three men whose horses had been enchanted and waved his arms. "Haste, fools! Make haste!"

The three looked at their horses before leaping back on them, and then the eleven men galloped back to the oak ring behind Bagsac.

When they reached the entranceway and halted, the horsemen

remained behind Bagsac. Urd had not escaped but still waited beside her turf covered home atop Heardred's dark steed as she faced them.

"What's the matter?" she said. "Can't deal with an old woman, priest?"

"What have you done to Heardred, witch?"

"Less than he would have done to me, I think you'll find. When he wakes, if he's still himself, be sure to thank him for the fine horse." Urd laughed at the priest and his followers hovering behind him.

Bagsac made a fist, licked his lips, and spun toward his men. "If we rush at her, she won't have time to cast a spell, or she'll hurry, and I'll be able to counteract it even in the ring."

The men blinked and stared at him without word or movement, but the priest went on. "On my word, ride straight for her and cast your spears at the first chance. She won't be able to control all your horses, and I'll ride behind you to protect you. If she flees, ride her down and slay her — she can't cast a spell while fleeing. Be careful of the boy and his thrall. They may be hiding somewhere. Be quick!"

They looked at each other and then at the ground.

"Do as I say!" hissed the priest. When no response came, he licked his lips and slid one hand down his face, after which he bared his teeth in a trembling smile. "If you wish to dwell with the Eternal through the salvation of Edan, you must obey His will and slay His enemies. Edan will shield you."

Several men stirred and readied themselves at this final word, and the others followed suit. Urd remained unmoving on her horse as the men arrayed themselves in a line for the attack.

"Now!" screamed Bagsac. "For Edan!"

When they galloped forward, the men shouted their battle cry: "the Eternal!" Bagsac rode behind and urged them on. "For Edan! Bring her down! Bring her down!"

In response, Urd sang, "Tulimmin hushtali ar dwinnon im dargas. Orwinnin vardali im urnon ni bedlas."

Before the men rode within casting range, the swarm of birds Urd had called to her oaks leapt out of them and, with a piercing chorus of squawks and chirps, shot toward the men on horseback. The multitudes darkened the sky at once and overshadowed the men, who looked up and quailed at the attacking cloud. All around the men the birds flew, and then, swifter than eyes could follow, hundreds dove straight for each, including the white robed priest.

The men stopped their horses and sought a way out, but none could see for all the birds flying at their faces and herding them back into the ring. The birds pecked and scratched the hapless men, who shrieked as they tried to protect their faces with arms and shields. A chaos of feathers and screeches enveloped them.

Though the birds did not attack the horses, the spooked beasts stamped and neighed and reared. Two men fell from their steeds, and two others drove theirs into each other then tumbled off. The horses whinnied and galloped out of the oak ring without their masters.

Amidst the shrill noise of birds and the screams of men, Bagsac's tortured voice broke out, "Tulimmin . . . ardanui . . . im diamul . . . Aaahh! Get out of the ring! Get out of the oak ring!"

But none knew in what direction to flee, so they thrashed and flapped, riding or running about as if mad while blood ran from their cuts and scratches.

Urd laughed at the men flailing about in the swarm of birds. The white-robed priest and two of the men still mounted were gaining their way back to the oak ring's western entrance. Her lips formed a grim smile, and then she sang out, "Ahuronai singhallon im diadin ar vonwy. Holdunai rindallon in taravin ar vishwy." She repeated the phrases several times, and after the last time she nodded. Turning her steed to the ring's eastern side, she urged it to trot ahead.

As she passed by the shed, Urd stopped the mount for a moment near the goats. "I'd get inside your shed if I were you. They'll soon be getting a nasty surprise. Goodbye, my dears."

With a chuckle, she glanced one last time at Bagsac and his men yelling and running about within the tempest of birds. She clucked at her horse and dug in her heels, riding east and leaving the scene of chaos behind.

STILL ASTRIDE THEIR HORSES, BAGSAC AND HIS TWO MEN MADE IT out of the oak ring, where the birds abandoned them and flew back toward the remaining men screaming and wallowing within. Blood ran out of cuts on the priest's forehead, nose, and cheeks. Feathers poked out of his robe and wiry hair. He tore off his hood, and one of his eyes juddered along with half his face. "Curse the witch! I'll have vengeance on the heathen. Tulimmin ardanui im diamul . . ."

But before he finished his counter spell, a deep rumbling invaded the air and the ground quaked. The rumbling rose at once to a furious pounding like a thousand giant drums. The priest ceased his spell as the three men looked at each other. Then they turned around.

Screams burst from the throats of all three, and the priest's white steed neighed and reared. Bagsac lost his grip and fell off his mount, which galloped into the oak ring, and the other two men rode back within, the only direction left to them.

"Wait!" wailed the priest. He sprang from the ground as if whip-wielding demons urged him. "Edan save us!" He sprinted into the oak ring with his white robe and wiry hair waving and feathers trailing him.

Behind him thundered a herd of two hundred elk with wrath and fire in their dark eyes.

A large branch presented itself as the priest ran into the circle. With remarkable agility and speed, Bagsac jumped and grasped the branch while his legs dangled beneath him. That did not save him, however, since one of the larger elk crashed into his tailbone with its antlered head. But that at least gave him the momentum to swing his legs up onto the branch. After securing his perch, the priest once again became the favorite target of thousands of frenzied birds.

"Aaaaahh! Edan curse that witch! I'll rip out her eyes! Argh! Bloody birds! Ah! Edan save us!" The priest spluttered fragments of chants as he struggled to bring up the words of the counter spell he needed.

At that point all of Bagsac's men had lost their weapons and their horses in the confusion. Those still standing found refuge, like the priest, from the herd of stampeding elk by running for the nearest oak. This was no help against the swarm of birds still harassing them, and the men clung to their branches as they whimpered and cried out at their small but numerous attackers, which prevented any from leaving the oak ring.

The herd of elk, an unstoppable force of muscle and antler, raged like a river straight through the compound and out the eastern side of the oak ring, bringing the remaining horses along with it. Urd's goats, biding their time in their shed, watched the elk part around them then disappear, leaving a dust cloud in their wake. On its way out the eastern end of the oak circle, the herd trampled over any tracks Dayraven and Imharr or Urd had left.

The dust settled. But thousands of birds still twittered and whistled as they dove to attack. The goats returned to their grazing while the men in the trees swatted at the birds and Bagsac collected enough wits to attempt to counteract Urd's spell.

"Tulimmin ardanui im diamul ni dwinwy! Orwinnin vardali ni burlo on dagdas!" The priest's pinched voice wavered, but after he uttered it a number of times, the spell began to have the desired effect.

At first in ones and twos and then in large groups, the swarm of birds left off attacking the men. They flew away from the oak ring in sundry directions, diminishing to specks and then disappearing.

All was quiet.

Eight bloodied and battered figures with feathers sticking to their wounds and in their beards and hair descended with little grace from the oaks. Bagsac groaned the loudest and fell off his oak branch. When he picked himself up, a grimace stretched his face, and he bent over and held his hand to his backside. He began hobbling toward the nearest farmstead. "Not my fault," he mumbled to himself as he began rehearsing protestations. His eyes took turns at twitching.

8
SECRET KNOWLEDGE

The High Priest Joruman passed from a columned, sun-lit cloister through a door leading into the scriptorium of Torrhelm's monastery. His eyes adjusted to the dimness inside. Motes of dust floated in swaths of sunlight streaming through high, arched windows, and candles at each of the hundred desks arranged in rows provided more light. On a stool before every one of the desks sat a white-robed priest or a yellow-robed apprentice. Awareness of the gift in each of them tugged at his mind, though of course not one was nearly as powerful as he. High above the priests and apprentices toiling over illustrated and sometimes gilded copies of the Book of Aldmund and other religious tomes, faint echoes of quills scratching on vellum played among the ribs of the smoke-stained, vaulted ceiling — the only sound in the tomb-like scriptorium.

Impressive, thought Joruman. Nothing on this scale existed in his monastery in Etinstone. He glanced at the *Life of Hildeflaed* the nearest apprentice was replicating. *But a waste of resources.* Had he been in charge, the priests and apprentices would not be mindlessly churning out copies of the lives of saints and martyrs, filled with nursery tales, spurious "miracles," and spiritual triumphs over heathens revealing the supposed might and truth of Edan. Instead, they would be contributing toward the proliferation of books with real lore, books that delved into the true mysteries of life, books of knowledge that revealed the way things worked in the world.

The patter of his sandals on the stone floor reverberated as he walked through the room. None of the priests or apprentices writing at the desks glanced up to notice him, but the grave priest who was serving as monitor bowed toward Joruman when the high priest walked by. He acknowledged the man with a curt nod and proceeded toward the door at the other end of the room, which opened into his destination.

Even after reacquainting himself with the place for many days, Joruman smiled at the vast chamber he entered. The vaulted ceiling was higher in the library than in the scriptorium. Three levels of arched windows invited stripes of sunlight to brighten sections of the shelves, which lined the walls and stood in orderly rows occupying the entire room, as immense as it was. A man could spend the rest of his life gleaning knowledge from the books and scrolls packed into those shelves. They climbed so high above ground level that one needed a ladder to reach the upper volumes. The monastery's library deserved its fame as the greatest repository of lore in Eormenlond. And though a majority of the books and scrolls filling its thousands of shelves was the same sort of pious rubbish being replicated in the scriptorium, it also contained a mine of real knowledge waiting for the right mind to delve into it.

Joruman drywashed his hands in anticipation of what treasures he might uncover today. That morning a summons had come from the High Priest Arna, but he still had some time for a little research. He was getting closer to what he was seeking. Valmitru's *Treatise on the Body and Soul* had alluded to another text by an ancient Andumaic sorceress called Ishdhara, or Isdara, or some other variant of the name depending on the source.

Whatever her true name was, Ishdhara claimed to have found evidence that the gift was separate from the sorcerer or sorceress wielding it. In other words, the gift was not intrinsic to the individual in whom it dwelled. Most promising was Ishdhara's hypothesis that it must be possible to isolate the gift. If it was possible to isolate it, then it must also be possible to separate it. He could feel it: He was on the verge of confirming years of speculation.

He was not certain it would be possible to find Ishdhara's text. To begin with, he did not even know the title. Furthermore, it was not like he could simply ask for it. Valmitru's *Treatise* had been hard enough to track down. A hundred years ago, zealots had burned every translation of it into the Northern Tongue because of the heresies it contained. The copy Joruman discovered was, of course, in High Andumaic, and it was buried in the middle of a dry tome containing early histories and lineages of the kings and queens of Sundara. Thus, lacking the cleverness to find it, the devout idiots who destroyed knowledge in favor of brute superstition overlooked it. It might be the only copy remaining outside of the Andumaic kingdoms, so he had already brought it to his temporary quarters and was pondering how he might steal it or at least keep it somewhere safe. To find Ishdhara's text, it might be necessary to travel to Sildharan or Asdralad, but Bledla and Earconwald's imminent war would make that impossible. However, once the war was over and Torrlond was supreme in Eormenlond, the lore of every kingdom would be at his fingertips.

The high priest made his way between the rows of shelves, nodding to acknowledge the bows of the few priests he encountered. Except for sporadic whispers, the library was as silent as the scriptorium. Joruman ignored them all as he breathed in the comforting scent of musty books and the outside world receded. He had nearly reached the section where he found Valmitru's *Treatise* when something caught his eye.

With her back turned to him, a woman stood at the end of a row of shelves immersed in the book she held. Long and curly red hair cascaded down the priestess's white robe nearly to her backside, whose shapeliness even the robe could not entirely conceal. The high priest stroked his beard and toyed with the ring on the little finger of his right hand. Perhaps a quick detour would not hurt.

Unlike the Supreme Priest Bledla, Joruman did not despise pleasure, and he never saw the sense in the strict adherence to celibacy among the priesthood. Pious notions of purity based on denial of human nature held no appeal to him, though he was wise enough to tread carefully. He entered the row of shelves and pretended to search for a text. As he neared the priestess, he slipped out a few volumes and thumbed through them before replacing them. Most of the books in that section were of the mystical and spiritual sort, such as Eosa's *Union with Edan* or Lady Ethelbertha's *Meditations*. A waste of good vellum. When he was near enough to the priestess, he glanced over her shoulder at what she was reading with such intense interest that she did not seem to notice him:

"*In the mildest caress of the wind is it present for the one who walks that narrow path. Such elevation does it bestow that the true spiritual followers will perceive it in their limbs, in their thoughts, and, yea verily, in their souls . . .*"

That was all he needed: Alwyn's *Mysteries of Edan's Presence*. He was quite sure of it, though he had not seen the volume since he was an apprentice, and even then he had been inclined to mock it.

So that way blows the wind.

Just when he turned back to affect engagement with the volumes on the shelves, the priestess glanced at him.

"The High Priest Joruman?" Though she whispered, the awe in her voice was apparent. By now she would also sense the immense power of the gift in him, which dwarfed the tiny amount of it in her.

Removing his finger from the spine of a book, he turned toward the voice and raised his eyebrows as if noticing the priestess for the first time. Gazing up at him was a face lovely enough to match the hair and backside. Fervor emanated from her hazel eyes.

"Hello, my child," he said in a quiet voice. "My apologies for intruding on your space. Far be it from me to divert a scholar from her pursuits, but I was searching for a copy of a text that has long been dear to my heart. I thought it might be somewhere near here."

She blinked, and her mouth hung open. "What text is it, my lord?"

He graced her with a smooth, well-lubricated smile. "*Mysteries of Edan's Presence*. It's by a great spiritualist named Alwyn, who died some eighty years ago. Have you heard of it?"

LYING NAKED BENEATH THE SHEETS ON HIS BED, JORUMAN SIGHED AS he watched the young priestess pull her white robe over her head to cover the milky curves of her body once again. She gave him a shy smile as she adjusted her glorious curly red hair, which had become a bit tousled during their rather vigorous activity.

He knew the type well. Daughter of an earl. Aspiring to spiritual enlightenment. Locked away and bored. Ripe for the picking. With just enough of the gift to gain her entry as an apprentice and squeak by as a priestess, the girl would have wasted her real assets in holy contemplation had it not been for the allure of his position and power. The only hard part had been slipping her into his temporary quarters in the monastery unnoticed.

Yes, Torrhelm was full of fine pleasures and delicacies. Etinstone, the seat of his high priesthood and a large enough city, was provincial in comparison. The true power — with access to all the knowledge he needed — was in Torrhelm. But soon the time would come. After years of wandering in the wilderness, he could taste the change in the wind, and he would make sure it blew in a direction favorable to him and his goals. Earconwald had confirmed their agreement soon after he arrived in Torrhelm. All he needed to do was remain useful to the king and play his role in the coming war, and it would be a matter of time. As he fantasized once more about the imminent day when a rise in his fortunes would allow him to remain in Torrlond's chief city for good, he allowed himself a satisfied grin.

"Are you *sure* you have no time to teach me some more today, my lord?" Perhaps mistaking his grin as directed at her, the young lady gave him a decidedly less shy smile. She was not as naïve as she had pretended when he began seducing her. Of course, the wine had helped to loosen her up, but he knew what gave him access to those perfect breasts and pried open those delectable thighs: power. There was nothing more seductive.

He fished in his head for her name. Was it Gida, or did she say Enid? *No matter*. "No, my dear. As tempting as it is, I think not. I must attend to important matters of the kingdom. However, you may stop by later, perhaps tonight. I believe it would be profitable to continue your tutorial. You show great promise. There are deeper mysteries into which I will induct you. Scriptures few eyes have read. Paths to Edan few feet have trod." He favored her with a crooked grin.

Her smile widened, brightening her beautiful face, and she inclined her head in a slight bow. "As you say, my lord."

"Needless to say, you must use the utmost discretion. Few are privileged to know what I will reveal to you. Understood?"

Her eyes took on an innocent look again, and she nodded. "Oh, yes, my lord. I won't tell anyone. Just like you told me."

"Of course you won't, my dear. Now." He pointed toward the door. "I must prepare for my duties. Don't forget to leave without attracting any notice."

"Yes, my lord." She bent to retrieve her sandals, giving him one last tempting view of the shape of her backside beneath her robe. After she slipped them on, she looked at him again and blinked her eyes.

He pointed again at the door across the room. "Tonight, my dear."

She smiled and nodded, and without another word, she walked across the chamber to the door. After unbolting it and peeking into the hallway, she glanced one last time at him, slipped out, and closed the door without a noise behind her.

With her final glance, a stab of guilt prodded him, and he worried for a moment about the young woman. Unlike him, she had little power to protect herself. She could be stripped of her position and cast out, perhaps even imprisoned or worse. In many ways, if they were caught, the price would be much higher for her simply because she was a woman. He did not wish such a lovely creature any ill. *It's the Way that's to blame. Full of hypocrisy, fear, and rot.* But he would work to change all that someday. In the meantime, he had instructed her carefully. Flicking aside the guilt, he promised himself he would be sure to protect the young woman — and any other of his dalliances — when he came into power.

Joruman smirked and then stretched as he yawned. He pulled the sheet off and picked up his own white robe from the floor. After donning the garment, he looked around at his temporary quarters in Torrhelm's monastery. With a large bed, shelves of books, a well-stocked wine rack, comfortable furniture, and private bathing facilities, his apartments were adequate to his tastes. Of course, when he made the permanent move to Torrhelm, he would reside in something far more grand, and he would need plenty of room for his private experiments.

His mind jerked back to the present. It would be unwise to be late for the meeting with Arna. His fellow high priest had requested that he pay him a visit, and he did not know why. He doubted it was to share a glass of wine and chat. Arna was nearly as ascetic as the Supreme Priest Bledla, though only half as mad. And though Joruman's power in the gift was roughly equal to Arna's, the older high priest was far closer to Bledla and therefore enjoyed more authority. In the unofficial hierarchy among the five high priests, Arna was the highest. It would be unwise just yet to cross Bledla's old friend. It was important to keep up the right appearances, and no one was better at that than Joruman.

Still, he reflected as he washed up with a clean basin of water and dried his face and hands on a fresh towel, it would be useful to know what Arna wanted before setting foot in the bear's den. He hated not knowing things. It was impossible that the old man should have gotten wind about the agreement with Earconwald, but he might have heard something to Joruman's disadvantage. He supposed he would find out shortly. He hung up his towel, left his apartments, and walked through the long, dim hallways of the monastery toward the High Priest Arna's chambers.

"ENTER," SAID THE GRAVELLY VOICE FROM WITHIN FOLLOWING Joruman's knock on the thick oak door.

He twisted the brass knob and pushed the door, which groaned on its hinges, to reveal Arna's large but sparsely furnished front chamber. Occupying the center of the room was a wide desk, on which piles of disordered manuscripts lay. At the back of the room was the small alcove in which the high priest slept on a plain sleeping mat. Shelves full of books and scrolls lined the walls, and more piles of manuscripts occupied large sections of the floor near the shelves.

Though it was a chaotic mess, the volume of knowledge there gave Joruman a pang of jealousy. Many of the scrolls and books were the dull records and accounts pertaining to the monastery's upkeep, but he knew Arna was a keen scholar like himself, and he would have given much for a few hours to browse through the man's private collection.

He might have asked for the favor, but the old high priest sat at his desk with an expression that was not quite severe enough to call a frown, yet neither was it exactly welcoming. He was not Bledla, but Arna could be intimidating as well. And, on second thought, the old man might have been a touch more powerful than Joruman was in the gift. But no doubt his age and experience contributed to the disparity.

"Joruman. Please be seated." Arna gestured toward the plain chair positioned before his desk.

He complied and stroked his beard as he looked the older man in the eyes and smiled. "To what do I owe the pleasure of your request for my company?"

Lines appeared on the splotchy forehead under Arna's bald head, and the web of wrinkles around his eyes deepened when they narrowed. The high priest sighed. "You know I've long taken an interest in your contributions to the Way."

"Of course. You were the one who put my name forward for the position of high priest when old Byrnhelm passed on to Edan. I'm not likely to forget that."

Arna gave a half smile. "Yes. Even when you began your training here in this monastery, a boy fresh from your village, you were . . . different. In addition to the power of the gift in you, you were eager, and you had a keen scholarly mind."

"Coming from you, that's a real compliment."

"You were such a serious lad. If I remember it aright, you had just lost your mother before you came to us."

Joruman glanced down at his mother's ring on the pinky finger of his right hand. "That's right."

"How old were you? Thirteen?"

"Twelve."

"Ah. A difficult age at which to lose one's mother. Of course, at no age is it easy."

"Yes."

The two men stared at one another, Arna seeming to wait for Joruman to say more. The older man broke off his gaze to look down at his desk. "I recall a particular conversation we had back then. You asked me if it was possible to commune with the souls of the dead, or to bring them back to life."

"And you told me that death was the great mystery. That it was in Edan's hands. That we all must succumb to it, and to Edan's will, and hope to see our loved ones in the Kingdom of the Eternal."

"So you remember. I did say those things. And I didn't think you were inclined to believe me."

"I was grieving, and I was a foolish boy."

"But a driven one. You may not have uncovered a way to defy mortality, but you learned a great deal. You outstripped every other boy your age as a scholar. In fact, you put to shame all the boys older than you as well."

"Grief was a weapon in those days, and I had much to learn. But I'm sure you didn't ask me here to flatter me."

The old man's nod was solemn. "Quite right. I'll get straight to the point. I've heard rumors of a disturbing nature."

Joruman summoned a casual smile. "I take it these rumors concern me?"

"They do."

"And I suppose you are not at liberty to reveal to me the person or persons who so helpfully passed on these rumors to you?"

"I fear I am not."

"Naturally. And if no accuser is willing to stand forth and swear truth to such rumors, then they are nothing more than conjecture at best, slander at worst."

Arna grunted to acknowledge Joruman's point, though he did not know if the old man was agreeing with him.

Joruman waited for more. "And . . . What do they say?"

Arna cleared his throat and looked down at his desk again before returning his gaze to Joruman. Something was disturbing the old man, but there was no way he could have heard even a whisper of Joruman's hopes. Was there? Only Earconwald had even a clue, and the king would gain nothing from telling anyone. No, he and the king had too much to gain from each other for betrayal to mar their plans.

"Joruman. I don't need to tell you that when we become priests, we swear a vow. A vow of dedication. We devote ourselves to Edan and to the Way, and to nothing else, for there is no greater purpose in this life for those blessed with the gift. This vow includes obedience to the faith and to the laws handed down through Edan's divine voice, which speaks through the priesthood, and most especially through the supreme priest. Needless to say, such laws apply with greater strictness to those few elevated to the office to which you and I have been called to serve."

Joruman blinked. "Yes." *I knew all that before I was an apprentice. Every village boy and girl knows much the same. Get to the point, old man.*

"The reason I have called you here is to give you a chance to address the rumors about you. That is to say, before I find myself compelled to trouble the Supreme Priest Bledla with the matter, I wanted to offer you the opportunity to explain or refute them."

"I'm most grateful." *Get to the bloody point, fool.*

Arna folded his hands in front of him. "The rumors I have heard state that, in direct contradiction to the laws of the Way for a priest or priestess, you keep in Etinstone a . . ." He cleared his throat. ". . . a certain woman who is your mistress."

When the words emerged from the grave high priest, Joruman could not help himself. A bark of laughter escaped him, and he laughed more at the astonishment on Arna's face. *Is that all? Aldmund's balls, I thought he might have known . . .*

"This is a serious matter, I assure you."

Joruman waved his hands. "You misunderstand me." He collected himself and forced his smile down. "I appreciate the gravity of the situation. It's just that, if you knew how absurd such a notion is . . ."

"The individuals who passed on the rumors to me did not think they were absurd."

"Well, I may tell you they are." *For one thing, I never allow a woman to linger long enough to deserve the title 'mistress'. But perhaps I should begin to take better care.*

"Are you certain?"

"Of course. By my faith in Edan, I swear to you that I keep no mistress. There. Is that enough?"

"Well . . . I don't know."

"Look, Arna. It's the nature of the powerful — men like you and me — that rumors gather round them. Others become jealous of them and may try to weaken them or even bring them down by spreading lies. Sometimes honest and good men, having heard such slander, become the unintentional instruments of a miscarriage of justice. If I were clever and had an enemy, I would whisper false secrets in such a way that they would travel to the ears of an honest man, and then I would watch as the honest man attempts to impose justice on my enemy. All the while, there is minimal risk to me."

"I suppose that's possible." The old high priest scratched his beard.

"In fact, there are rumors about everyone who enjoys a measure of power. Just look at the whisperings I've heard recently: The illegitimate child Duke Guthfrid's daughter bore was in fact his own. Lady Osburga did not lose her jewels to a thief as reported but sold them to claw her way out of gambling debts. Our fellow High Priest Morcar keeps only young and slender boys as his closest servants and often orders them to spend the night in his chamber. And the High Priest Heremod does unspeakable things to the poor wretches he tortures down in his dungeon. Well, I suppose the last is hardly a rumor." *Let him chew on all that.*

"The Supreme Priest Bledla believes Heremod's work is important."

But you don't, do you? We both know Heremod is a sadistic monster. And Bledla's fucking insane. "Of course he does. But you see my point? Why, I would imagine there are slanderous rumors even about you, my friend. Some youthful indiscretion, perhaps? Some secret plot?" He was careful to assume an incredulous tone, as if suggesting any rumor about the High Priest Arna would be inherently ridiculous.

Yet Arna's face looked uncomfortable. Was it also turning a little red? There was something there Joruman would have to find out about, but now was the time to untighten the screws a little. "And if I ever heard such a thing about you, do you know what I would do? Knowing your piety and unquestionable service to Edan, I would dismiss it for what it was: a vile *rumor*."

Arna collected himself and crossed his arms before him. "So you deny it?"

"Of course. It is false. What more can I say?"

The old man paused a long time and pulled at his grey beard. "In that case, I'll let the matter rest. That is, unless the rumors persist, in which event, it may be necessary to look into them further."

I hear your warning, old man. "Rumors are stubborn things that take on a life of their own. Even the Prophet Aldmund was not immune to them, I'm sure you recall. There are stories that he kept a secret wife and had three sons by her."

Arna's eyebrows arched up. "Apocryphal stories. None of them appear in the approved canon."

"Yes, of course. But you are a scholar, are you not? You and I both know some of those apocrypha are older than the stories the Way has sanctified as divinely inspired. It was not even one hundred fifty years ago that our predecessors agreed upon the canon at the Third Council of Torrhelm, and most of what they canonized dated from only twenty or so years before it."

"The dates are in dispute. There is a measure of linguistic evidence to suggest . . ."

"Oh, come. We both know you don't believe that. To be sure, the authors made clumsy attempts to make the scriptures seem older, inserting half understood archaisms and such. But even a half-hearted linguistic analysis reveals the truth. Some of the *apocrypha*, on the other hand, are much older, even belonging to thirty years after Aldmund's death."

"What's your point?"

"Only that rumors can be persistent and dangerous, my friend." *Though often enough there are truths embedded in them, and I will find out those most dangerous to you if I must.*

The High Priest Arna's eyes widened, and Joruman guessed the old man took the hint. The two gazed at each other for a long while: a test of sorts. He smiled, and Arna looked down at his desk yet again and sighed as if he would much rather be reading the manuscripts upon it than having this conversation.

"Very well," said the old man. "I'll keep that in mind."

"Thank you. Is that all?"

"Yes. Blessed be the Eternal." Arna foraged for a manuscript on his desk and took up a quill, which he dipped in a bottle of ink.

"And the Kingdom of Edan." Joruman rose and moved for the door. Before he reached it, however, he turned around. "Arna?"

The old man looked up from his manuscript. "Yes?"

"When I have the leisure, might I have the honor of looking through your private collection sometime?"

In response to the puzzled frown on Arna's face, Joruman clarified with a gesture towards the shelves. "Your books and scrolls, I mean."

"Oh. Of course."

"Thank you." Joruman turned and grinned on his way out.

ARNA STOPPED PRETENDING TO READ THE MANUSCRIPT AND SAGGED in his chair after Joruman exited and shut the door. He took a deep breath and sighed, and he sat there for a long while.

"I'm not made for politics or games of power," he said to the air. He shook his head. "I should have been a hermit, not a high priest."

What was it Joruman had said? *"Some youthful indiscretion, perhaps? Some secret plot?"*

Was it merely a lucky guess? A tactic of desperation? Joruman was a shrewd man who probably hid numerous indiscretions and secret plots of his own. But what if he knew something?

Surely he could know nothing of what happened so long ago. Even now, Arna could not keep back the dizzying and terrifying memories of that time. Only Bledla and one other had an inkling of what had happened. No one else could have knowledge of Arna's secret buried beneath the accumulation of years. The others from those days were all long gone now, and only the three of them had ever known anyway. Bledla would never tell anyone. He would never even speak about it. As far as the supreme priest was concerned, all was forgiven and forgotten.

For Arna, it was a wound that had healed on the surface long ago, but deep beneath it twinged. The grief and passion had stilled, but in their place remained the dull ache of loss, as if a piece of him were missing. It was not supposed to be that way. He was not supposed to have such wild regrets. He had renounced all his desire. Whether or not it was unnatural, as Bledla had insisted, he no longer knew. But he had renounced it. Why, then, had it never left him? *Edan forgive me.*

As for the other who of course knew, he had sworn himself to secrecy when they parted. Whatever else he had done in all the years, however wrong he might have been, he would never break that promise. Arna would never believe it.

No. Joruman knew nothing. He was an ambitious, talented, powerful, and dangerous man, but he knew nothing of that.

Still, the cunning high priest likely had some idea about Arna's doubts. Did he know just how deep and wrenching they were at times? Exploiting their mutual scholarly interests, he had been clever to bring up the apocrypha. They *were* much older than the books in the approved canon. They might contain truths long forgotten, inconveniences piety had covered up. Based on his research, Arna even wondered if parts of the Book of Aldmund were inauthentic, the inventions of later well-meaning and pious perpetrators of fraud. But he had never dared to voice such thoughts to anyone.

Sometimes it seemed Arna had nothing left but doubts. The sad irony was how his youthful devotion had urged him to dig deeper into the truth. The deeper he reached, the more nebulous the truth became. Back then he had thought his studies were bringing him closer to Edan, but everything he discovered made it harder to believe what he was supposed to. Blind faith would have been far easier. But it was too late for that. Everything was crumbling beneath him, and he did not know what to stand on. As another scholar who had searched too deeply into things to preserve a simple faith, Joruman might guess how much he doubted. But Arna was sure the man knew nothing of what happened all those years ago.

But what of the other matter? The business of the present? "*Some youthful indiscretion, perhaps? Some secret plot?*" Joruman's words echoed in his mind like an accusation.

In some ways, it was not another matter at all. It had everything to do with the past. Arna was sure he never would have dared if not for what happened all those years ago. It left *something* in him, and, though it ran counter to everything he was taught to believe, at times he believed it was the best part of him. Sometimes it seemed so right, and he ached and mourned for what he had renounced. Sometimes he believed he had never been happier in his life than he was in those too brief years. He was an old man now, but his memories of those heady days were vivid, while the events of the recent past were dull and grey. Had he been wrong then? Had he betrayed the best part of himself? Was it the real reason he had decided to act now? Or, as he told himself every day, was it a matter of his conviction? His conscience?

Does it matter? Whatever the cause, he had finally acted. Spreading the Way to all of Eormenlond to bring about salvation and the Kingdom of the Eternal had always been a dream he shared with Bledla, ever since their young days in the monastery. But he had imagined it so differently – as acts of charity that would win converts over many years, showing the light of Edan to those most in need. Bledla had long spoken of it that way too, and he could not remember when the change had happened in his old friend, when war became the path to Eormenlond's salvation. And Earconwald, the most corrupt king in Torrlond's history, was happy to use Bledla's crusade as a mask for his worldly ambitions. Arna shook his head and sighed.

He thought for a long time. At length, he decided Joruman could not know anything of his current intentions either. If he did, Arna doubted he would still be alive. If Bledla heard the slightest whisper about what he had done, what he was about to do, death might be a mercy. He would become one of Heremod's hapless, blood-soaked victims. Like the two wretched men murdered in the dungeon deep beneath Sigseld. Horrible deaths. Bledla had exploded the poor boy's brains. Edan help him. So much power. So much rage. The event haunted Arna's dreams. Those deaths were on his hands as much as Bledla's.

He shook his head to banish the bloody image. There was no turning back now. Whether he was wrong or right, he would see it through.

At any rate, he decided he would not worry about Joruman. The cunning man was only posturing. Wiggling and threatening his way out of trouble. Whatever schemes he was hatching, it would not be Arna's role to deal with him. In truth, he had no desire to follow up on the rumors about Joruman. They were mostlike true, or something close to the truth. But the priests who informed him had their motives, and Arna more than half suspected they were in the High Priest Morcar's camp. Let the younger generation take their turn at grabbing for power and stabbing each other in the back. What did Joruman's infractions matter to him?

Arna was tired of the game. He had never played it with any heart. It was Bledla who had promoted him to high priest, an office the most ambitious coveted. Always he had been in Bledla's shadow, and the supreme priest had pulled him along. Until recently, he had returned the supreme priest's trust with faithful devotion, often protecting and defending his superior and even denying himself in the process. But he had never wanted the power, and he was sick with the role he felt forced to play. Now he was withdrawing. He knew he would have little effect on the great events of the near future. There was only one final, big part for him. And then? *Rest. It will be over for me one way or another. No more doubts. No more fears.*

Only one question ate at him now: Which betrayal was worse? The one of long ago, or the present one? Perhaps he would never know. *Edan forgive me.*

As soon as he entered the hallway, Joruman's grin disappeared. A rival, most likely Morcar and possibly Heremod, was trying to discredit him with Arna and thereby with Bledla. It was a futile stab that he could afford to meet with light retaliation for the moment. Nothing traceable to him. He would have one of his agent priests in Torrhelm, perhaps Nothgar or Widhelm, take care of the matter. He had nothing to worry about from the High Priest Arna, but something about his conversation with him teased a corner of his mind. It was the half-buried memory of that time from his boyhood. Why had the old man brought it up?

So raw from the loss of his mother, he had looked up to Arna as his mentor, the sort of man he wanted to become: wise, learned, and powerful. But on the day that Arna told him he should accept death because dear ones who passed on were in Edan's hands, the old man had disappointed him. It was a lie that failed to bring back the one who mattered most, the one who had given him life and purpose.

He sighed as he realized it had been a long time since he thought of her. She was the only person who ever truly loved him, and she it was who taught him to use his mind. He could still remember her beautiful blond hair. But her face was gone. As a boy, he had tried in vain to recall it. Every time he thought of her, there was the hair and even the sound of her pretty voice, but the face was only a blank smudge. It had enraged him that he could not bring to mind her face. All he had of her now was the gold ring with a small garnet he always wore on his right hand. Death was a cruel thief indeed.

While the wasting disease killed his mother over those long months, he had tried so hard to make her live. She became weaker and thinner every week until her flaccid flesh hung from her protruding bones. Near the end, she slipped the ring from her finger, little more than bones held together by ligaments, and put it in his hand. He believed that if he loved her enough, she would not pass away. But she had, of course, died. She left him, just as the father he never knew left him when he was a baby.

For years he tried to find a way to bring her back, or at least to speak with her. Death yielded no secrets. At length, he faced the truth. He did it without flinching, and he resolved never to fool himself, to delve and seek the truth through the exercise of his mind and the power of the gift no matter how painful it was. It was in those years that the most important revelation of his life had come to him. The truth might be painful, but it was also the only lasting power. Knowledge did not earn one any friends or any comfort, but it was the only thing that was real. Those who pursued it without mercy lived an authentic existence. The first step as a boy had been to dismiss the Kingdom of the Eternal and the popular notion of Edan for what they were: lies for cowards and fools.

He had known by some instinct that such doctrines were both an admission of defeat and a delusion. Putting death in Edan's hands was like closing one's eyes in the darkness and pretending it was not there. Joruman was no such fool. He did not need religion as a false comfort to cloak the stark truth from him. The Kingdom of the Eternal was a childish fabrication, a ridiculous fantasy that weak-minded people told themselves they trusted in because they could not face the permanence of death. To be sure, the Way was a convenient means to control the populace. Those in power pandered to the delusion that after their corpses had rotted, the people's miserable lives might continue if only they would believe hard enough in Edan. Armed with such faith, they would go to war and kill and die. Pathetic.

But Joruman had a far greater vision. Once he was in a position to do so, he would dispense with the lies. He would reform the Way into what it could be: a beacon of learning, an army in pursuit of truth. And the gift, which offered the greatest capacity to see the reality underlying the illusions human beings were so apt to fool themselves with, would be its weapon. That was the only real hope for the best of humanity — those with sufficient amounts of both the gift and intellectual courage — to emerge in their rightful places and guide civilization into what it should be. It would be painful, and he would have to outwit fierce opposition to achieve it. The spilling of blood would be inevitable. But he would set in motion nothing less than the transformation of religion into a vehicle of truth.

Truth was *not* arrived at through mystical prophecies or the misunderstood ravings of a madman recorded by his zealous followers hundreds of years ago in a book to which one must surrender one's mind. It was only the mind that could conceive truth through meticulous study and the courage to face the darkness. Only through that long and noble process could there be any hope of reaching the furthest frontier of all, of achieving the greatest conquest. Probably not within Joruman's lifetime, but one day, humanity would conquer not just disease but death itself. On that dream he had never given up, for he realized now how much it had spurred him and ennobled him even as a child.

As a boy, Joruman had faced the darkness and become a man. Of course, he had not succeeded in defeating death then as his mother slipped away from him inch by tormenting inch, but he was proud that he had tried. In those days of wild grief, he had wanted his mother back so much.

He shook his head and let go of the memories. He had learned a great deal since those early days. He had grown and become so much more than Arna, the man he once looked up to, because he was willing to find the truth in all things. No hiding. No cringing. Now he was on the verge of even greater achievements, and nothing would stop him.

Fidgeting with his ring, he walked toward his apartments and looked forward to the company of Gida, or whatever her name was, later that evening.

9
THE WAY BACK

"We'd best get moving. If you keep your mouth hanging open any longer, a fly's bound to wander in." Astride Hraedflyht on a slight rise offering their first clear view of Wolvendon nestled against the vast Folkmere, Imharr was smiling at Dayraven. The younger man could only shake his head.

"So big," was all he said as he sat atop Rudumanu and gawked.

Beyond his vision the Folkmere extended, though he strained to see the far shore in the hazy distance. As it reflected the sky and rippled in the breeze, the lake's blue-grey surface shone like a giant sheet of glass across the landscape. For some time Dayraven and Imharr had halted to take in the sight. Dayraven had never seen anything so large. If the Folkmere was only a lake, how vast was the Great Sea surrounding Eormenlond?

At length, near the end of the third day after setting out from Urd's home, they rode into Wolvendon. Most of the journey had passed with Dayraven mourning the end of his life and, between long silences, Imharr attempting to comfort him with his humor and stories, to which Dayraven tried his best to respond. He missed his home, his father, and, most of all, Ebba. Thus, Wolvendon presented a welcome, though fleeting, distraction from his brooding.

The simple wooden homes of the villages on the outskirts of the the Mark's chief city gave way to larger structures, and greater crowds of people pressed all around. The smells of burning wood and roasting fish mingled together in the air. Folk everywhere went about their business, and though Dayraven had never seen so many people gathered in one place, the city remained on a scale that did not overawe him. It felt strangely familiar to him, like a much larger version of Kinsford. He almost wished he had come to stay in Wolvendon, perhaps under happier circumstances, having heard many tales of the city and knowing he would have come to love it.

Urd had told him how, in the depths of history, their people came from Torrlond and carved their way over many years through the great forest they encountered until they reached the Folkmere. On the shore of the lake they built their city of Wolvendon until it grew and throve, becoming the Mark's heart. Even now the streets fanned out from the wharves and quays lining the Folkmere, the lifeblood of the city. Though folk said Wolvendon was more like a town next to Torrlond's vast cities of Etinstone and Torrhelm, it seemed large enough to Dayraven.

On the muddy streets passed a great stream of people, horses, and wagons, with the occasional chicken or dog getting underfoot, and in places crowds thronged around merchants and mongers selling their wares from large carts. Occasional shouts punctuated the constant hum of conversations, and at times a barking dog or crying child would add to the din. The greater part of the buildings were wrought of timber, for it was in abundance in the Mark and was its chief source of livelihood along with the fish in the lake. The dwellings were not much different from the simple homes in Kinsford, yet they were somewhat larger and roofed with slate.

A few of the newer and grander buildings were made of stone, and conspicuous among them was the Temple of the Way. As they rode by on the opposite side of the street, Dayraven and Imharr kept their distance from its columned façade. Three white-robed priests climbed to the top of the entranceway's huge stone steps and hovered outside its tall doors. Looming over the priests were two giant figures in the form of bronze reliefs on the doors. The reliefs portrayed an ancient king on one door and a severe old man in a robe on the other. The latter, Dayraven supposed, must have been the Prophet Aldmund.

Remembering Urd's words about the priests' ability to sense the presence of the gift, he pulled up the hood of his cloak and urged Rudumanu to pick up her pace a bit. Something – a feeling akin to being watched, which he recognized from being near Urd and occasionally the priest Bagsac – emanated from those distant figures, and he wondered if he was perceiving the gift in them. If Urd was right that he always had the gift, he must have sensed it in her and in Bagsac for years without even knowing what it was. He hoped those priests were too far to feel the power the elf put in him, but there was no reason to take chances. He looked back one last time at the imposing building. The three priests were gone.

Further down the street, they encountered a different sort of building, one that chased Dayraven's worries out of his mind for a moment. In stark contrast to the temple was the ancient hall of the kings of the Mark, Widuru, which resembled Stanflet as an elder brother does a younger.

The high-gabled hall's roof soared above the city's other structures, and ornate carved patterns — knots and swirls dancing in and out of each other — decorated its timber façade. Thick oak columns with more intricate carvings supported the roof of the porch, beneath which weathered stone steps led to the entrance. On the massive doors were hewn splendid portrayals of the gods, and Dayraven realized the images on Stanflet's doors were but a poor imitation of the masterpiece before him.

Above all the other gods, Regnor and Hruga gazed down with benevolence from their thrones. Bolthar's muscles strained as he grappled with the maddened bull. From Syn's gaping mouth a freezing vapor curled toward Logan, whereas he shot raging flames from his hands toward her. Dyna's arms opened in blessing over a field of wheat. From the rough sea emerged Halmar atop a giant whale, while Glora glided above him on a graceful swan. Aloof from the others, Sithfar stood shadowed in his cloak and seemed to point his staff at the viewer, as if in warning that soon he would accompany him or her on life's final journey.

Dayraven's eyes lingered on the carvings, tracing the skill with which their creators brought life leaping out of the wood. *Such power and beauty. Those craftsmen were great masters.* In the presence of those doors he could almost suppose the gods were real. When he was a little boy, he had pretended to believe the stories of the gods were true, hearing Bolthar's heavy steps in the thunder and seeing Glora's hair in the rainbow. He could not remember when he first admitted they were not real in the way that people and cows and trees were, but Urd had taught him there was a different sort of truth in the gods. They may never have walked the earth, but they were the strange messengers of a people's dreams, the visitations of their joy and desire and fear and sorrow. All that was real enough, and perhaps there was no better way to deal with such things than through the gods. Such thoughts he had always kept between him and Urd, for he had no wish to disturb the beliefs of others in the old gods, those who thought them living beings and sacrificed to them out of awe. Anyway, they were easier to understand than the Way's Edan, who seemed so much more remote in his perfection and mastery.

I'll stick with the old gods, thought Dayraven as he gazed on the wondrous carvings. He wished it had been possible to enter the ancient hall through those enormous oak doors and have a glimpse of its court, for in Kinsford everyone spoke of young King Ithamar and Queen Aethelwaru as generous and wise leaders. With a sigh, he allowed Imharr to lead him away from Widuru.

But even passing through the city whetted his imagination. It was his first view of a world larger than his home. And the Folkmere seemed to him endless, a place wrapped in the mists of history and large enough to spawn great legends and stories to tell over a fire.

Dayraven and Imharr could have passed many days in Wolvendon had they not remembered the urgency in Urd's warnings about Bagsac and other priests of the Way. "We'll stay one night," said Imharr. "First thing is to find an inn. We can buy some food there since ours is running low."

"And a hot meal?"

"Of course. Accompanied by some of Wolvendon's finest ale."

. . .

THE COMPANIONS SETTLED ON A LIKELY INN WHOSE CHIEF recommendation was its distance from the Temple of the Way, and it seemed clean and friendly enough as well. Once they decided on the place, they tied Rudumanu and Hraedflyht to a post outside. Though it did not appear large enough to boast many rooms, the sign hanging over the wooden door — a somewhat crude carving of a stout woman wielding a fish — pronounced it an inn.

When the two young men entered the one-story building, they saw it extended back much further than they had guessed from the outside. A generous common room with tables and benches greeted them, and thick wooden beams supported the rafters holding up the roof. From the louver above a pale light descended, and torches in sconces added to the hall's warmth. At the further end of the hall was a doorway leading to a passage, down which Dayraven supposed there must be rooms for the guests. On the right side of the hall, smoke and the smell of grilling meat emanated from an open doorway.

Dayraven took a deep whiff. "I like it already."

A pretty young woman with curly blond hair emerged from the doorway whence the aroma came and walked toward them.

"I like it too," said Imharr with his eyes wandering over the green frock hugging the curves of the young woman's figure and lingering where its loosely laced top revealed a glimpse of cleavage.

Dayraven elbowed his friend, who raised his gaze to the young woman's eyes, and a smile lit up Imharr's handsome face. "Greetings. We're wanting a room for the night."

The young woman turned toward them and met Imharr with a sly, disarming smile of her own. But she did not respond. Instead, a gruff voice broke in from behind: "Then you'll be wanting to settle with me."

Dayraven and Imharr jerked around. A large, broad-shouldered man with little hair left on top of his head and a thick grey-blond beard stared down at them. He was middle-aged and pot-bellied, but the rolled-up sleeves of his kirtle revealed big, muscular forearms, and his look said he would put up with no nonsense. He must have followed behind them in the door. "Acha, you may help your mother with tonight's meal. I'll handle these young fellows."

His scowl said he thought himself more than capable of handling Dayraven and Imharr. The young lady obeyed her father, but not without raising her eyebrows in playful regret at Imharr.

"For one night you say? You have silver?" The innkeeper's bushy eyebrows lowered over his eyes as if to warn that the wrong answer would see them turned out on the street. At the same time, his frown suggested he knew exactly what Imharr had been thinking about his daughter.

"Uh, yes . . . Yes, sir," stammered Imharr. He reached for the bondsman's armband that was no longer on his arm and settled for tugging at his sleeve.

Dayraven smiled at his friend.

"And you'll be wanting a meal." It was a statement, not a question.

"Uh, yes sir. Please."

"Smells tasty in here," suggested Dayraven.

The innkeeper's broad face broke out in a huge smile. "My wife's cooking. Best venison in Wolvendon." His big, thick hand slapped Dayraven's shoulder like a slab of meat, and the large man guffawed as if he had made a jest. Dayraven and Imharr glanced at each other and mustered a nervous laugh.

The man stopped chuckling, but his smile remained to suggest they were all friends now. "Very well. I'm Wulfgar. I have a room for you, and I'll have my stable boy tend to the horses you left outside. First, I'll show you your room, and if you like it, we'll settle up. Afterwards, you may come for the evening meal, though it's a bit early as yet. If you're in the mood for company, others will turn up later. It's never quiet here at supper. The fare in the Fisherman's Wife will not disappoint you."

It did not. Not long after they left their few belongings in their small but comfortable room, the two friends sat groaning with full bellies and empty trenchers at a table in the stuffy common hall. Imharr sighed with pleasure. He was nursing his third cup of ale, and once in a while he stole a glance at the innkeeper's daughter as she served the other guests. Wulfgar had been right about another thing: Though it was still early, the room was already filling up with plenty of folk. Some were travelers like Dayraven and Imharr, and most of these kept to their own tables. From their talk and laughter, others seemed to be locals who frequented the Fisherman's Wife.

The food — grilled venison with beans and garlic fried in butter and fresh bread — had been excellent, but sitting down had given Dayraven too much time to think about home. He ached for Ebba, feeling her absence with an oppressive tightness in his chest. He would have been happy even to hear one of his father's stern lectures. His insides twisted, but he tried to put on a brave face so as not to worry Imharr. Perhaps it would distract him to see a bit more of Wolvendon. He stretched and yawned.

"My head's muddled after all that food. I think I'll go have a look outside. See the city a bit. You coming?"

Imharr was looking across the room at Acha's ample backside as she bent over to put trenchers down on a table. "What? Oh, yes. Fine. I'll . . . stay here."

Dayraven grinned. "I'm not the only one with a muddled head."

"Well, someone has to get more food for the journey. We're running low."

"I'm sure Acha would be happy to help you with that."

His friend returned the smile. "I'm counting on it."

"Just stay out of trouble."

A serious frown replaced Imharr's grin. "I should be telling you the same. Keep away from the Temple of the Way."

"Not to worry. I won't go within a stone's throw of the place. You're the one who'll be dealing with Wulfgar. I think the old fellow has eyes in the back of his head. But good luck all the same."

"Many thanks. Don't be gone too long." Imharr grinned again. "And don't wait up for me."

As Imharr's gaze returned to the young lady, Dayraven rose and walked by a few tables before reaching the door of the inn. When he opened it, the fresh air met him. A cool breeze knifed through summer's heat, and the sky had darkened with the onset of evening. Dayraven took a deep breath and stepped outside.

The street was far less crowded than before since the merchants and hawkers had disappeared along with their customers. A handful of folk still walked about, but not enough to intrude on Dayraven's thoughts as he took in the scene. His full stomach, the pleasant evening, and his imaginings about his forebears once belonging to this place combined to lighten his thoughts. He took in the sights of the buildings and streets, allowing his feet to wander where they would. Past many admirable structures he walked, and he nodded with approval at the sense of order in the city. In spite of its size, Wolvendon was a tidy place, and there was a certain uniformity to the homes. Though some were larger than others, no portion of the city seemed too grand or squalid. The stout buildings testified to the equality of the place. This city's dwellers took pride in every stretch of it.

In the midst of his musings, Dayraven realized his feet were taking him to one structure that differed in scale from the rest. He desired once again to see Widuru, ancient hall of the kings of the Mark. One last glimpse before they set out on the morrow. Besides, he might not ever have another chance to see it. Though it was just down the street from the Temple of the Way, he would not linger long, and he need not go too near the temple. After that, he would return to the inn to make sure Imharr was not getting into too much trouble.

From the alley where he walked he followed his instincts back towards Wolvendon's main street. When he emerged on it, he recognized where he was and headed toward Widuru. Even the central thoroughfare was deserted as darkness took hold over the city. But Widuru was easy to find as it loomed over the structures nearest it, and torches set in sconces outside the great oak doors illuminated their carvings of the gods and a portion of the great hall's engraved façade. The red glow from the torches painted the images and cast wavering shadows that disappeared in the outer darkness. The powerful portrayals of the gods stirred with life.

How long had the proud hall stood there? How many kings had it housed, and how many generations had it seen come and go? Remaining motionless in the darkness across from Widuru, Dayraven gazed at it in silence. His eyes traced the lines of the intricate carvings, and he longed to open the wide doors and enter the hall that bore witness to so many years of the coming and passing of his people.

A door did open. Not one of the large oak doors, but a smaller door off to the right that he had not noticed since the carvings concealed it. A white-robed man emerged into the torchlight outside the door. Dayraven became aware of a familiar tingling in the back of his mind – a subtle suspicion of watching eyes – just before his body tensed. He held his breath, hoping the shadows would be enough to hide him from the priest of the Way. His pulse throbbed so hard in his ears that he imagined for a fleeting moment it would reveal him.

The priest paused. He gazed into the darkness where Dayraven stood. Since the torches burned behind the man, his hood concealed his face in shadow. "Edan's salvation. Who are you?"

Dayraven bolted in the other direction. *Fool. Now you've done it.*

"Stop!" shouted the priest behind him.

Dayraven did not stop. Heart pounding in his chest, he did not even look back. His legs propelled him through the darkness, and only a small part of him was mindful that he might crash into something unseen. Between the shadowy forms of buildings he rushed, and the wind hushed by his ears. He hardly knew where he was going, but he knew he must flee. Of course the priest had sensed him. But perhaps he could outrun him.

Turning around, he saw and heard no sign of pursuit, but he did not stop running. If he had luck with him, mayhap the priest was no longer close enough to feel the power in him. He turned down a side street then ducked into an alley, hoping any pursuer would be less likely to spot him there. But as he hurried down the passage, his mind conjured images of dark figures trapping him in the narrow space. He tried to quiet his gasping breaths. Something could be hiding in the shadows ahead, and he would not know until he was upon it. He slowed his pace and peered down the alley. Nothing stirred. *Stay calm. Panic breeds mistakes.* Looking behind him again, he spotted no movement, so he hurried forward until he emerged on another street. As his wits returned, a simple plan formed in his mind. *Get back to the inn. We need to leave this night. Find Imharr and leave.*

Dayraven arrived at the Fisherman's Wife panting and sweating. It was dark and quiet outside, but from within came the bustle of the patrons. Before reaching for the door, he paused to catch his breath and scan the street. No one had followed him. He must have lost the priest. Still, it was too risky to stay the night. He did not know where they would go, but he and Imharr had to pack their horses and leave. The innkeeper would not care as long as he had his silver.

The first person he saw upon entering the common hall was Wulfgar himself. The big man was wiping a table with a rag. He looked up at Dayraven with a frown and narrowed eyes.

"Evening," said Dayraven. He swallowed and tried to steady his breathing.

Wulfgar's face relaxed. The innkeeper smiled and nodded before going back to his work. Guests remained seated at tables in the common hall, most of them in one noisy group that was throwing dice and drinking ale. Dayraven walked past them to the hall leading to his room.

When he opened the door, he did not find Imharr there. "Damn." He ran his fingers through his sweaty hair and exhaled through clenched teeth. Then he remembered. *Acha, the innkeeper's daughter.* Knowing Imharr, there was one logical place to look.

He threw their few belongings in their leather bags, fumbled on the baldric with his father's sword, and donned his cloak. When he left the room with the bags slung over his shoulder, he headed not toward the common hall but in the opposite direction. At the far end of the corridor giving access to all the rooms, he came to a door leading out the back of the inn. Before opening it, he took a torch from a sconce in the hallway.

The darkness outside was silent. After taking care to close the door behind him without a noise, Dayraven walked some fifty feet to reach the stables behind the inn. The smell of horses and fresh hay met him when he opened the stable's small side door. When he closed it, he heard a bump and a muffled curse. He raised his torch to illuminate the stables. "Imharr. Time to go."

Dayraven did not wait for his friend to come out. With blankets over their backs and fresh hay and water set before them, Rudumanu and Hraedflyht waited next to each other among the dozen horses stabled there. Their saddles hung on wooden pegs next to the stables.

Setting the torch in a sconce, Dayraven set about saddling his horse first. His hands trembled as he pulled the straps into the buckles. He was still at this task when Imharr's face poked around the corner of the stall. A piece of straw stuck out of his curly hair.

"What's going on?"

"We have company. In a white robe."

"Damn. I was starting to like this place." Imharr nodded. "Let me help." He fetched Hraedflyht's saddle from its peg and threw it on his horse.

Another figure emerged into the torchlight. Acha appeared as pretty as ever, but her frock was a bit ruffled, and it too had several pieces of straw clinging to it. Her cheeks seemed flushed as well.

Imharr smiled at the innkeeper's daughter. "Acha here was just helping me with the extra provisions we bought. I thought it would be easier to put them in the saddle packs now so we could leave at first light."

It would've been even easier if you'd brought a torch, thought Dayraven, but he only said to her, "Thank you for your help. If the food's even half as good as tonight's meal, we'll be well fed. I'm sorry for . . . our hasty leavetaking."

Her smile was a bit weak, and her wide eyes blinked as she neared Imharr. "What's happening? Must you leave so soon? When night's fallen?"

"Alas, my dear, I fear we must." Imharr stroked her cheek with the back of his hand.

"Is there some sort of trouble? Father'd not be happy if you brought trouble to the inn."

Imharr tightened the straps of Hraedflyht's saddle. "That's why we must go. We'll take the trouble with us and leave you good folk in peace. Though, of course, we leave with heavy hearts."

Acha's pouting lips suggested she might like a bit of the trouble if it meant more of Imharr's company. She sighed, "Very well. But mind you leave quietly." She went up on her tiptoes to give Imharr a last kiss, followed by a sly smile. "And come see me if you return."

"I'll be sure to."

Dayraven raised his eyebrows at his friend and nodded toward the large main doors at the other end of the stable. "I'll open the doors if you lead the horses out." He didn't wait for an answer. Though he had outrun the priest, he still felt a sense of urgency. Something crept into the edge of his awareness, like someone was watching him from behind. As ever, the shard the elf had inserted in him whispered in his mind.

When he reached the stable doors, he lifted the wooden beam barring them shut and set it aside. He pulled on them, and they creaked as they swung inward to reveal the darkness behind them.

A shadowed form leapt out of the darkness and crashed into him, shoving him against the open door. Bright streaks flashed when his head slammed into wood.

"Got 'im!"

The owner of the gruff voice was a large, helmed man whom Dayraven had never seen before. His strong arms pinned Dayraven's neck to the door with a spear shaft, and he was wearing a chainmail byrny under his kirtle. A sword hung in its scabbard at his hip.

The man's warm breath stank of ale. With his thick arms bearing down on him, Dayraven was helpless to move. Though he pushed against it, the spear shaft on his neck constricted his breathing, and his throat made gasping sounds as he struggled to take in air. Behind the man stood two more dressed and armed like him. With them was the white-robed priest of the Way. Dayraven seethed through his clenched teeth and strained harder to thrust the wooden shaft away, but it did not budge.

"Hold him. Cover his mouth so he may not utter a spell," ordered the priest.

One of the other armed men moved forward, but before he reached Dayraven, something blurred from the left to smash into the face of the man who held him. The big man's head snapped back. He went limp and collapsed, and Imharr stood over him with his fists clenched.

With a hoarse gasp, air rushed into Dayraven's throat, which he rubbed as he leaned back on the stable door to keep from falling over.

Imharr snatched the fallen man's spear to parry a blow from one of the other armed men. Wood cracked. Imharr used the momentum to swing the end of the spear shaft he held into the man's face. Bone crunched, and the man went down screaming. The third man and Imharr rushed at each other. Their spears clashed once, twice, thrice in a quick series of thrusts.

"Stop!" commanded the priest. "In the name of Edan!" He stepped forward with one arm raised toward the fighting men.

The man who swung at Imharr did not see the priest, and when he took back his spear for another thrust, he struck the priest's face with the butt end of the shaft. The shrieking priest clutched his face and went down. When the spearman looked behind him, Imharr whacked him on the head with his spear shaft. His helm rang with the blow, and he toppled over.

"Get on your horse!" yelled Imharr as he threw down the spear.

Rudumanu snorted just inside the stable. Dayraven tripped over something as he ran to her, but he kept his footing. He leapt on his horse, and Imharr was astride Hraedflyht beside him. Before them, the three armed men and the priest were struggling to rise.

"Ride!" Imharr surged forward on his steed. The priest and one of his followers dived out of his path. Dayraven gripped his rein and dug his heels into Rudumanu, who bolted after Hraedflyht.

They urged their horses past the inn and emerged into the dark street, where they could gallop away.

"Let's go, old girl," said Dayraven to his mare. She seemed eager to comply as the horses' clopping hooves dug into the street. The wind rushed by his ears. *We've made it*, he thought as the priest's indistinct shouting receded.

Out of the night air, an almost physical sensation brushed up against Dayraven's awareness, as if a sudden gust had pushed him from behind. The feeling nagged at him. Something was not right. This was confirmed when Rudumanu slowed down and then stopped altogether in spite of Dayraven's heels digging at her sides. Had it not been for the danger behind them, he would have felt a fool flapping his legs atop a motionless horse in the middle of the street.

Imharr sat atop Hraedflyht in the same bewildered position. “What’s going on?”

Dayraven pounded his heels in, but Rudumanu did not budge. “I don’t know. They just stopped.”

Then he understood the odd sensation he had felt. “The priest.”

The horses turned around and began trotting back toward the inn. Dayraven pulled on the rein, but Rudumanu ignored every attempt to stop her. *Gods, the horses have no choice.*

Up ahead, four shadowed figures stood in the road. Three held spears. Other people began to wander out of their doorways with torches in hand, no doubt to find out what all the noise was about. The ruddy light of the torches outlined the white-robed man and his three followers and cast their long shadows toward Dayraven and Imharr. The priest of the Way strode forward, crying out his spell in a clear, ringing voice: “Hrondin ar dwinnor singhal di landir! Blunnin im ghodor mordwin ar fardhir!” His three followers raised their spears as they grew closer.

The next thought that occurred to Dayraven was to leap off Rudumanu and run. But he realized they would never get far afoot. The priest and his followers could call others to their aid, and their capture would be a matter of time. But what else could he do? *Must gain control of the horses. Stop the priest. But how?*

He swallowed and spun his head in every direction to seek a way out. “Shit.” The urge to flee was drowning out his other thoughts, which would not link together to form a coherent plan. *Leap off and flee.* But that was no good, and one look at Imharr confirmed this.

“Unsheathe your sword.” Imharr glared ahead at their assailants. “I’ll take out the priest. You ride away at the first chance. Damn me for an idiot for dropping that spear.” He gripped his hunting knife in one hand, and the naked blade gleamed in the growing torchlight. His other hand was on his saddle, ready to push off and hurl him into their attackers.

Too desperate. They would not escape a second time, and they mostlike would die trying. But there seemed no other choice. Dayraven knew his friend would die for him. He must not allow Imharr to fall alone. *Never flee without him. We’ll go together.* His hand shook as he forced it toward Sweothol beneath his cloak. Could he kill a man?

The horses trotted closer to their pursuers. Instead of grasping the sword's hilt, his hand stopped over his galloping heart as if trying to hold it in place. "Shit. Shitshitshit. Stay calm." He shut his eyes and drew in deep breaths. His father's words about the dread before combat came to him. *Every man feels it. Do not seek to crush it, but let it flow out and fuel you. Keep control of your mind, but let the fear loose at the same time.*

"Shit."

His eyes still shut, Dayraven tried to let the fear loose, but it stayed lodged where it was. But something else did happen. Instead of finding the focus he needed to wield his blade, he seemed to have summoned the sleeping force within his mind. Its whisper morphing into a roar, the thing the elf put there awakened, and a pair of vast eyes flashed before him.

The shadow presence swelled and pierced his fractured thoughts like a shard of glass. It erupted to blur the boundaries of his being. The force swept him outside of himself, and in his place the disembodied elf-state arose. His body shuddered, and he tore away from it. *No! Not now!*

But it was too late. Those last shreds of his thoughts and fears dissipated into the night. Just as had happened in Urd's home, he expanded into the world around him. Even as his own emotions spun away and left him detached, myriad lives seeped into the edges of his consciousness. The dark city sprang to life with thousands — even millions — of points of energy as he witnessed the scene transpiring below him. His body rode on Rudumanu next to Imharr and Hraedflyht, and the emotions of the dozens of surprised onlookers screamed within him. Imharr's fierce determination to protect his young friend was hard like a blade. The raw anger of the armed men burned like a wound. Most of all, the words of the priest echoed in his mind: "Hrondin ar dwinnor singhal di landir! Blunnin im ghodor mordwin ar fardhir!"

As the words stirred in his consciousness, a strange peace enveloped him. Even as all the emotions assailed him, he became an unmoved presence, a powerful and impartial observer taking in everything. He understood Imharr's protective rage. He encompassed the frightened folk of Wolvendon staring in wonder from their homes. And he even took in the men and the priest who hunted him in the belief that he was a dangerous threat they must contain. All struggled to conquer their fear. All shared the desperate desire to live. His awareness touched them all, and for every one he offered a tender compassion, a gentle desire to allay their fear and anger. It was this desire that produced a sudden revelation.

He did not know whence — mayhap it came from the foreign presence that he could no longer distinguish from himself — but in this state of mind a strange new perception sprang to life in Dayraven.

The priest. His body no longer contained him. Like Dayraven, the energy that normally dwelled in his body spread outward. This perception did not belong to Dayraven's ordinary senses, nor did it belong to time and space, but nonetheless the feeling was as strong as if he saw or felt the man's energy as a visible or tangible thing. When the priest uttered the song of origin, his expanded mind reached and flowed into the energy inhabiting the horses. A part of him became the horses. At the same time, a part of him remained in touch with his individual will, and that will, having connected with the beasts' minds, now overpowered and wielded them. Confused and frightened, Rudumanu and Hraedflyht could not resist — for they could not perceive it — the will making their bodies move.

But it all unfolded with clarity to Dayraven's mind: He and the priest dwelled in a realm different from that of the senses, a realm more vivid than anything he ever experienced before. The elf-state was timeless and real, whereas his ordinary life was a fleeting and vague dream. And in this realm, the boundaries ruling the ordinary world — the world of dreams, the world of forms — dissipated like mist. Life — all of it — was one energy. Those who could perceive this energy could also wield it in others, as long as they remained in touch with their will. A voice from the world — or was it the elf? — whispered a thought to him: To make the fear go away, he must break the bond between the priest and the horses.

With this thought, energy rushed from Dayraven: not from his body, but from the disembodied entity hovering above and around it. It seemed to pulse in every direction, but it concentrated on the frightened horses. He would free the horses from their fear. As the sun in the heat of the clear day shines far brighter than a lone star in the cold night, the energy pulsing from Dayraven dwarfed the priest's. His energy met the priest's within the captive animals — this was the force holding them against their will — and calmly snapped it like a twig.

The priest of the Way screamed and collapsed onto his knees. His hands jerked to his ears, and his face hit the street when he crumpled forward. The three armed men pivoted to their leader, as did the many onlookers. For an instant, Dayraven too felt the man's searing pain. So terrible and fearful. As the pain reminded him that he was a separate entity from this suffering man, Dayraven recoiled from it like hot metal burning him.

He crashed back into his body, and his normal sense of the world returned, which left him almost blind in its torch-illuminated dimness. *Of course, it's night now.* In that other state he had not needed vision. To fend off the wave of dizziness rocking him, he closed his eyes and gritted his teeth. He wavered on top of Rudumanu but held fast, and when he regained control, he looked toward Imharr.

His friend's eyes were wide, and his mouth hung open as he stared at Dayraven. Then Imharr seemed to notice he could command his horse again. After sheathing his knife and taking up the rein, he nodded and said, "Let's go."

With a flick of their reins, they turned their horses about and galloped down the street. Shadows in the night flew by in a blur, the only sounds their horses' hooves thudding on the street and the wind rushing by Dayraven's ears. The next moments went by in a haze, but when he took notice of his surroundings, there were fewer of the dark outlines of buildings around them.

As they rode through the darkness out of the city and headed north, he allowed Imharr to lead the way. The elf's power had torn him from his body again. Was the indifference of the elf-state still in control, or was he simply numb with shock? He could not recall how to direct his horse. Fortunately, Rudumanu followed Hraedflyht. All he needed to do was stay on his mare. Adrift in his thoughts, he could not decide which emotion should be strongest: relief at their escape, awe at the power dwelling in him, or dread of what the elf's presence had done to him. He could grasp none of them yet. Would he be able to return to his former life? With his stomach sinking, for the first time since the elf took him in the Southweald, he feared there might be no way back.

10
WOVEN OF WORDS

Something was wrong. Sequara was supposed to meet Brithmar and Immin at the Silver Boar, an inn and tavern in East Torrhelm. They were not there, but the innkeeper, a toothless, sweaty fellow wearing a greasy apron over his worn kirtle, told her two men matching their description had been there not more than five or six days before. Where they were now he did not know or care since they had paid in advance for their room.

"None o' my business if folk pay for rooms they don't sleep in." He pushed his lank hair away from his eyes and ogled her, staring at her chest before looking her in the face again. "What brings a foreign girl such as you askin' after such men, anyhow?"

"Silk from Asdralad. I sell it. They want to buy it."

One of the least squalid establishments in East Torrhelm and not too far from the docks, the Silver Boar was a common meeting place for foreign merchants and their agents in Torrlond's chief city. There were also fewer priests of the Way around than in the much more prosperous West Torrhelm. Sequara had given the innkeeper extra silver for his trouble — and to keep his mouth shut — but she did not doubt his silence would end if anyone with more silver came asking about someone looking for the two men.

All this had her feeling more than nervous. She was in enough danger as it was, and now Galdor's two men were missing. They were supposed to be her eyes and ears in this city, so their unexplained absence left her feeling blind and deaf. The younger one, Immin, she did not know at all. But she had once met Brithmar a few years before when he accompanied the wizard on a visit to Asdralad. He seemed a decent, quiet, and capable man, and Queen Faldira told her Brithmar was one of Galdor's most dependable servants. So where was he?

As dawn's dim light began to prod at the darkness outside, she lay on the straw mattress of a sleeping pallet in her private room in the Silver Boar. Though it did not quite befit a wealthy silk merchant from Asdralad, the innkeeper had made sure to charge her as if it did. But the room had the added benefit of a window should she need to exit in a hurry, and for that she was willing to pay. Not that it would be easy to get far in this city filled with soldiers and priests of the Way.

Sequara at first thought that if Galdor's two men did not show up by morning, she would make her way back to Torrhelm's docks, where her men awaited her in a merchant ship loaded with some of Asdralad's finest and most colorful silks, and sail back to her beloved island. But that would mean defeat, and she hated that idea more than she feared to stay. *No*, she thought, *I must have what I came for. Too much depends on it.*

Before morning arrived, she resolved to stay in Torrhelm and go ahead as planned without Galdor's men. Rising with the sun, she sat on the straw mattress and gazed at the dagger Queen Faldira had given her. Before concealing it under her frock, she repeated in her mind the queen's instructions about avoiding capture until the calm indifference she had trained so hard to master suffused her.

Instead of her wine-red gown from Asdralad, she wore the dull garb of a local serving woman. There was no point in attracting attention, but she hated to trade her finely woven clothes for the rough brown frock and dun apron. She bound her long, raven-dark hair under a kerchief, and for the final detail she slipped a leather band around her arm, the mark of a slave in these barbaric lands.

Slaves in Torrhelm came from all over Eormenlond. Most were natives of Torrlond who fell into debt, but many were captives from the south and east, usually victims of raids by tribes of the Wildlands or the Thjoths. She spoke the Northern Tongue with an accent, but no one would question a slave's foreign accent, and this way she was far less conspicuous than a colorful silk merchant. The only danger was that one of those damned white-robed priests might sense the gift in her.

Shutting the door to her room, she walked without a sound down a dark corridor by a few closed doors and the entrance to the kitchen, where the innkeeper was yelling at someone unfortunate enough to be his servant about burning porridge. She slipped out of the Silver Boar without the innkeeper or anyone else seeing her, on her way stealing a basket from a table to complete the disguise of a serving woman on an errand for her mistress.

When she emerged from the tavern's door, dawn revealed East Torrhelm's filthy streets. A thin mist from the River Ea obscured the grey, sooty buildings of wood and stone crowding together, a few leaning drunkenly on others. The taverns lining the street were all quiet, but metallic pounding from a large armory and the frantic bellowing of animals from a shambles and tannery nearby filled the morning air.

In contrast to West Torrhelm, where all was solid and stately, this part of Torrlond's chief city seemed impermanent, the detritus of many lands washed up into one place to do the dirty work of a mighty kingdom. The scents of dung, acrid smoke, dead animals, and human sweat assaulted Sequara all at once, and dozens of workers shuffled along the muddy street, many heading for their errands or work in West Torrhelm. Borrowing the place's gloom, the ragged people inhabiting it seemed taciturn and withdrawn, as if they understood their dirt and grime and stench should not infringe much on West Torrhelm, or anywhere else for that matter.

Sequara was grateful for the mist as she plunged into the river of people, horses, chickens and stray dogs along with the occasional pig or cow being led to slaughter. Most of those around her were too tired or hung over to hurry much, but when a column of twenty soldiers clanked by, the workers jostled to get out of the way, and one skeletal man who reeked of piss and ale nearly knocked Sequara into the mud.

Like the rest, she avoided staring at the soldiers in their byrnies and grey kirtles, and she held her breath until they passed. *No priest among them, thank Oruma and Anghara.* She headed for the nearest bridge leading to West Torrhelm.

West Torrhelm presented a much cleaner face, but Sequara was no more comfortable among its huge structures vying to block out the sun. *This place is cold and full of shadows even in the summer months.* The cobbled streets were wide, and the stately and grand stone homes and businesses of the wealthy frowned down at her as she passed by. Their inhabitants, who dressed in the finest garments and decorated their fingers and necks with conspicuous jewelry, strolled among these buildings with an ease that spoke of their right to be there. Those dressed like Sequara kept their heads down and went about their business.

The street she followed ended in a spacious, cobbled square lined on its four sides with more of the proud, columned buildings. The sky opened up as a great crowd murmured and hustled in front of her.

In the midst of the open square, a huge bronze statue of an ancient, bearded king holding a sword aloft gazed down from high atop a stone pedestal. Indifferent to the statue's solemn dignity, a few pigeons perched on its shoulders and crown, staining them with white rivulets of their shit. Though she had never seen it before, Sequara knew the statue depicted Folcwalda, founder of Torrlond. People here regarded him as the greatest of heroes from long ago, but to those from Asdralad and the rest of the Andumae, he was a murderous invader. Beneath his watchful gaze, hundreds of mongers shouted out the great value and cheap prices of their wares in competition for thousands of customers milling about. Vegetables and fruits, fabric and clothes, ironware and leather goods, farm animals and slaves from all over Eormenlond: All were for sale in a great, bustling chaos.

Though many slaves had light skin and blond, brown, and red hair, nearly half of those at auction were the darker-skinned natives of Asdralad's kindred kingdoms in the south and east. Chained together and clothed with rags that ill concealed their bodies, some might have even come from Asdralad, though raiders seldom sailed out to the island kingdom. Even worse, many for sale were children.

Sequara spat to ward away evil as, not more than thirty feet away, a fat man with a whip scowled and pushed a dark-haired Andumaic girl up onto a wooden platform to be sold. Slaying the man would have been a simple thing for her, and she imagined several appropriate spells or simply plunging her dagger into his folds of flesh. But what good would it accomplish?

She fought the urge to rescue the girl, to buy her and take her away, for she was disguised as a slave herself, and a slave could not buy a slave. *I must do nothing to endanger what I'm here for, or I'll risk countless other lives.* Though she knew the eastern and southern kingdoms had used slaves for generations, she also knew it was the white-skinned barbarians who long ago brought the practice to Andumedan, which they transformed into their Eormenlond. *Some of them may have learned to build cities from us, but they're all still savages*, she thought, forgetting in her anger that a couple of her dearest friends came from the northern kingdoms.

At least Sequara could feel the sun's warmth in this square. More than that, she knew she must be getting close to the appointed meeting place, for this abomination had to be Great Cheaping, Torrhelm's largest market.

Following her instructions, she made her way towards the northwestern corner of Great Cheaping. As she passed by them, some mongers looked her over as if expecting her to steal something, but most ignored her. A slave wasn't worth bothering over.

At length, she faced the square's northern boundary and counted the alleys running between storied buildings, most of which belonged to wealthy wine merchants, cloth merchants, goldsmiths, and silversmiths. The third from the left was a narrow path squeezed between a textile shop and a goldsmith's shop. Trying not to appear in a hurry, she entered the pinched alley and left Great Cheaping's din behind her.

The little alley zigzagged, narrowed, and widened according to the dictates of the buildings overshadowing it. The cobbles were wet where someone had emptied a slop pail from a window high above, but otherwise the place was pleasant and clean enough. It was also confined. A perfect place to spring a trap, reminding her of the dagger's hilt pressing into her stomach where she had tied it under her frock.

After she passed the fifth building on the left down the alley, she found what she was looking for: a white sign depicting a needle and scissors over a door bearing a knocker in the shape of a horse's head. She opened the door to the tailor's shop to reveal another closed door to her left as well as a dark staircase leading up.

After checking up and down the alley for anyone following her, Sequara ducked into the door and closed it behind her. When her eyes adjusted to the stairway's dimness, she climbed the wooden stairs, which creaked under her feet. At the top of the stairs, dust motes settled in pale light spilling from an open doorway to her right. A door further away to her left and one across from her were closed.

The presence of the gift was strong. Someone powerful was nearby. The idea that this meeting was a trap seemed more plausible than ever. She headed for the open doorway.

Though she walked without noise, a voice from inside the room greeted her before she entered. "Hello. Have you come for an order, or would you be making one?" The voice grated with age, and when Sequara came to the doorway, its owner turned out to be a white-bearded man with deep lines etched in his face. He was not the one with the gift.

He sat behind a long wooden table covered with disordered piles of clothing and fabric. Behind him was a window, whence the light streamed in. But on every other available surface of the walls were mounted wooden poles, from which hung large spools of fabric, some unfurled to the floor. The little shop was a chaos of cloth that threatened to smother the old man, who smiled cheerfully but was looking a bit to Sequara's left. After a moment, she realized he was blind.

"Hello? Is it Mistress Ethelburga? Your gown's nearly ready, my lady. Otha's out on an errand, but I'm sure I could find it to show you."

Sequara nearly forgot what the message told her to say, but she collected herself. "No, I am not Ethelburga, sir. I come from afar seeking that which is woven of words."

The old man's smile changed to a puzzled frown as he looked with a blank gaze to Sequara's right, and she worried she had spoken the words to the wrong person. But then he startled her, exclaiming, "Ah! Yes, I see. Of course." His smile returned, and he squinted as he pointed towards the door and whispered, "You'll find what you seek behind the door at the end of the hall."

"Thank you." She ducked out of the room. She touched the dagger beneath her frock while walking back into the dark hallway towards the furthest door. The sense of the gift grew stronger again. Someone with great power was waiting behind the door. Whoever it was would have perceived her presence by now.

When she reached the door, her hand hesitated before grasping the wooden latch. She pushed the door inward. It creaked open and revealed a long, dark room. The light from behind her fell on numerous shadowy shapes. Except for a narrow passage in the middle, rolls of cloth filled the entire room. A storage room, and by the smell of it, a thick layer of dust had settled on all the old cloth.

"Close the door," hissed a man's voice, making her start. She squinted to peer through the darkness. One of the shadowed rolls of cloth at the room's far end stepped toward her and took the shape of a robed man. Sequara could see no details in the darkness, but she did not need vision to tell her that this was the one with great power. From across the room she sensed the gift within him in great measure. Here was a man who knew the songs of origin with depth few in Eormenlond could match. She was not sure *she* could match him, but she readied her mind as she closed the door.

"You are a priest of the Way." She was pleased at how steady she kept her voice.

"Do not try to learn my identity. If you knew, it would put more at risk than you realize. But you are Queen Faldira's chosen one, are you not?" The man took another pace forward, but she could still see nothing of his hooded features.

Sequara fought the urge to back out the door and run. *I must have what I came for. I will not fail.* Yet she was unsure how much to tell this man. His message said he would help them by offering a secret that could save them all, but this could equally be a trap. Queen Faldira had warned her to expect anything. "Let's trade our secrets with more fairness than that. If I don't know who you are, how can I tell you who I am?"

"We're not here to trade."

"Then why? Why would you give us this thing?"

The man in the shadows laughed, but there was no joy in his laughter, and his voice sounded aged. "There's some irony, you know, in this. Long ago, the Prophet Aldmund obtained this particular song of origin from Asdralad. He visited your island after his exile. Of that I'm certain, though many here would deny it. And now, after the passage of centuries, I'm giving it back to you. My reward will come later if somehow my actions bear the fruit I'm hoping for. But you are wise not to trust. Galdor's two men fell into the wrong hands. They're dead."

She thought of Brithmar and his quiet manner. "How?"

"That doesn't matter. What matters is the Supreme Priest Bledla and King Earconwald know everything they knew, including the fact that someone was coming from Asdralad. They're expecting you."

Her mind raced to her ship. "My men? Are they safe?"

"Yes, for now. I sent someone to warn them. Three should be hiding in a tavern by the docks until you arrive. The rest are waiting for you downriver with your ship. You must not go back to the Silver Boar. The innkeeper is no doubt enjoying a handsome reward for revealing your presence. I delayed the arrival of the priests and soldiers who came to arrest you, but they're waiting for your return. You did well to change your appearance. At the moment, every priest and soldier in Torrhelm is on the lookout for a beautiful and well dressed silk merchant from Asdralad."

Sequara smirked at the description of her. *No ordinary priest,* she thought. *Not with access to that kind of knowledge.* "I won't ask how you delayed my pursuers, but you have my gratitude."

The priest sighed, and he sounded weary. "In the end, it will all mean nothing if no one can use the song of origin."

Now we come to the matter. "Can you not use it?"

"Only one I know among the living can wield it: the Supreme Priest Bledla. And he will use it. That's why one of you must master it. It's the only way to stop the coming destruction. And if none of you can, find someone, or you will all perish. The coming war will mostlike be a slaughter, and the only way to prevent it depends on someone else mastering this spell. That would prove Bledla is not . . . the second Prophet. There must be balance. Many lives depend on it."

"But why can you not . . ."

The shadowed figure cut her off. "We're wasting time we do not have." He spoke with urgency now, almost desperation. "Learn the song from me and return to your queen. Pass it on to her and to Galdor, though I fear neither will be able to wield it. You, I sense, also have great power, but in this matter great is not enough. We must hope, slim though the chance is. Listen now."

Sequara realized that opening her mind to this man would make her vulnerable to him. If he should betray her, she would have little defense. But if she did not let him teach her the song, she could not bring it back to Asdralad. *Too much at stake. I've come this far.*

"Alright." She calmed her mind. "I'm ready."

The dark room was void of distractions, but Sequara had to cleanse herself of all thoughts. For a mind as well trained as hers, this was not difficult once she made the decision to learn the song of origin from the priest. Thus, when he chanted in his gravelly but steady voice in the eldest of tongues, her thoughts and memories wrapped around the words and made them part of her:

Urkhalion an dwinathon ni partholan varlas,
Valdarion ar hiraethon im rhegolan wirdas.
Gholgoniae sheerdalu di vorway maghona,
Dardhuniae sintalu ar donway bildhona.

Back to the beginning their minds went, to creation time, where those with the gift traveled to behold the nature of things and with such understanding could influence them in the world of forms. While he sang, a song of origin like no other she knew unfolded. She perceived in its dangerous vastness a cold cunning and angry heat, and at the heart of the words was wisdom both ancient and sharp. A keen intelligence differing from humankind's dwelled in the words. It was foreign but somehow akin. But most of all, the immense strength in the song threatened to overwhelm her with the certain knowledge that a person was but a small and fleeting creature in comparison to what it spoke of.

When he ceased chanting, the mundane world returned to Sequara's awareness in the form of the dim room with its molding fabrics.

"Very good," said the priest. "You grasped it swiftly. Queen Faldira has trained you well. At another time, I might have learned much on your island. We might have gained much from each other's wisdom and lore. But such was not meant to be. Pass on the song. I pray you're able to use it, or find someone who can soon. The time is coming. It begins in a few short weeks. Caergilion first, then Adanon, then the whole of Eormenlond. None will long remain safe if you fail."

Sequara looked at the man in the shadows, and more than ever she imagined a great weight of age and grief upon him. "I'll do what I can. I hope you'll see the reward you seek."

"Perhaps I will. Perhaps. But go now. Back to the docks. Pass the place where your ship lay, and keep walking. Don't stop for anything. There'll be soldiers posted there, and priests. Just keep out of their way, and keep a distance from the priests, though not one there can match you on his own. Walk southward along the river. Your three men will see you and join you when it's safe. I've provided them with a rowboat, and with that they'll take you downriver where your ship is hidden. Sail swiftly home, for time's running short. May Edan shield you."

"And may your eyes behold Oruma and Anghara's blessings."

The priest said nothing for a moment as they stared at one another in the dim room, but then she thought his head nodded. "Thank you." His voice was raw.

She opened the door and walked into the hallway. She did not look into the tailor's shop but descended the stairs, taking care to keep quiet. When she reached the door at the bottom, she paused a moment before opening it. She took a breath, pressed the latch, and pulled the door. The outdoor brightness at first dazzled her eyes, but when she spotted no one along the little alley, she breathed in the air.

Now I must reach my ship so we can go home, she thought. *I bring a most precious cargo.* She readied herself as she headed back toward the vulgar bustle of Great Cheaping.

TORRHELM'S DOCKS STANK OF REFUSE, ROT, AND FILTHY WATER. IN the brown river floated garbage, pieces of wood, and the occasional animal carcass. The sweaty sailors and dockworkers did not smell much better, and Sequara was on the verge of laying low the next man who pinched or groped her. However, most of the time it was impossible to tell who the guilty party was in the press of humanity moving and shouting along the docks. And in any case she could not draw attention to herself. There were scores of soldiers milling around, and they were watching for something or someone. *Do nothing to endanger the mission. I must return to Asdralad with the song of origin.* It did not help that, beyond the warehouses lying closest to the docks, every other building in the nearby streets was a tavern — and those that were not were brothels.

People conversed and shouted mostly in the Northern Tongue, but mixed in were the strange, trilling sounds of Ondunic and various common dialects of Andumaic that Sequara's ears half comprehended, accustomed as they were to High Andumaic. A group of tall, light-haired barbarians spoke in sharp, harsh syllables that identified them as Thjoths from Grimrik. A couple of them eyed her like predators as she walked by. Those were dangerous men, pirates and raiders without a conscience among them like as not. But none of this — the stench, the noise, or the boorishness of the men wherever they came from — bothered her as much as one thing: the presence of those damned white-robed priests.

So far, by waiting in alleys or crossing the street, she had been able to avoid the priests. She was far more powerful than any of the six she had spotted, which meant they could not feel the gift in her unless they got close. But one chance meeting, and one of them might discover her. If this happened, he would certainly call on the others, and that could be a problem, especially with all the soldiers nearby. She must remain wary without appearing to care overmuch about them. *Call no attention to yourself. Keep your head down and stay aware.* But where were her men? She had expected to encounter them long before now. *He said three of them should be waiting for me. I've already passed where the ship was docked.*

She stepped around a pile of crates that workers were unloading from a ship and paused to look around. Nothing but sailors, workers, soldiers, and a few whores out for an early start. A sigh escaped her, and she hoped the priests and soldiers had not somehow found her followers. Even with the warning her informant had sent them, they were vulnerable here. Many would remember the merchant ship from Asdralad carrying silk, and none would hesitate to inform the priests and soldiers of her men's whereabouts for a small price. In this place life was a cheap thing. There was nothing to do but keep moving.

"My lady. We've been waiting for you."

Sequara nearly jumped and twisted around, but, recognizing Karad's voice, she composed herself and answered back in High Andumaic. "Quiet and inconspicuous. To the rowboat now."

"Yes, my lady."

Two men fell in with her. Dressed as a common sailor, Karad walked beside her. Her bodyguard had been upset at the idea of letting Sequara enter the city alone, but the instructions from their source had been clear that she must come unaccompanied. She glanced behind her to see who the other man was. *Unan. Good.* Unan was strong and quiet. Like Karad, he was solid and dependable. But where was the third?

"I was told three of you remained."

Karad nodded. "We sent Aravh ahead to look after the boat."

"Then let us hope we find him there. Lead on."

They pushed through the throng until it thinned out along a less busy portion of the docks. Soon it became possible for the three of them to walk abreast. All the time Sequara was watchful for priests, but there was no sign of one, and even the soldiers seemed to have disappeared.

"Just down here. Around the bend," said Karad.

They walked a little further, and Sequara had to remind herself not to appear in a hurry. Just as Karad said, there was the third man, young Aravh, standing by a narrow dock. Tethered to the dock was a small, bobbing rowboat. *At last, we can leave this wretched place. Home is coming.*

But it seemed to her that Aravh's youthful face sickened when he caught sight of her, and he threw his bound hands up as he cried in Andumaic, "My lady! No! There's a trap!" Two arrows sprouted from his chest, and he went down groaning.

Karad jumped in front of the sorceress, and the veteran grunted as two more arrows thudded into his right shoulder and left thigh.

"Karad!" Sequara's training kicked in to force her emotions down. She needed calm.

A dozen grey-kirtled soldiers appeared from behind a nearby tavern. Four carried bows, and the rest drew their swords as they approached. Leading them was a white-robed priest of the Way, who grinned as if he had caught a helpless animal in a snare.

Sequara threw down her basket as she gazed at her assailants and gritted her teeth. *I must not fail.* Her mind slipped into the realm of origins, and as she thrust her arms forward, the air around her shifted and leapt alive with a current of energy. The priest must have sensed her power awakening, for his grin disappeared and his eyes widened. He was right to fear. She was strong enough to call forth *almakhti*, or what the barbarians named wizard's fire. He began his counter spell, but she ignored him since she knew the gift was far stronger in her. *Too late, priest.*

"Alakathon indomiel ar galathon anrhuniae! Vortalion marduniel im paradon khalghoniae!" As soon as Sequara shouted the song of origin, a jagged blue bolt of concentrated energy crackled from her extended fingertips and streaked toward the priest and soldiers, casting their forms into eerie light and inky shadows. It forked and exploded. A violent blue-white flash split the air and writhed in snaking currents around the screaming soldiers and priest, whose spell the energy shattered, and their bodies flew backward.

A moment later, fourteen corpses lay still and smoking on the street. Aravh had risen behind them, and he died in agony along with the Torrlonders. The anguish of all fourteen echoed in her mind, and she nearly staggered with it.

No. No time to grieve now. Every priest in Torrhelm will have sensed that spell. "Help Karad into the boat," she ordered Unan. "I'll untie it."

She ignored the many sailors and dockworkers streaming out of the taverns for a look at the source of the lightning that seemed to have struck from nowhere. As she fumbled at the knot and cursed it, she heard Karad grunting in pain then falling into the boat with Unan's help. A murmur of dozens of voices rose behind her by the time she finished untying the rope and jumped in the boat, which rocked as she sat down in the stern. Karad lay in the bottom looking up at her, his agony written on his face. Unan sat above him facing her, and his hands grasped the oars. "Row," she commanded, and Unan obeyed.

"The ship's downstream," said Unan as the wooden oars groaned against the oarlocks and splashed in the water. "The current will take us there in no time."

Sequara started to answer, but the words caught in her throat, and tears threatened to gather in her eyes. *I killed him. Aravh. He was trying to save me, and I killed him.* She managed to nod to Unan.

"My lady," said Karad between gritted teeth as he winced and gazed up at her. "You had no choice. He would have died anyway." Blood was pooling and soaking into the boat beneath him.

No. I could have saved him, she thought. And worst of all was that she knew his final thoughts. His agony and dismay still reverberated in her mind. In fact, though it was Aravh's emotions that most haunted her, the horror of all the men she slew echoed like ghosts in her mind. But she said nothing of this. They were all in Oruma's hands now, and they would remain so until Anghara gathered their energy for the next birth. Her work was here in the present, in the world of forms. Karad was in pain and needed help, but he was still concerned for her. *A perceptive man. The closest thing I've had to a father.* She shook her head to dispel the emotions welling up in her. *I must stay calm to help him.*

As Unan's oars splashed and groaned, splashed and groaned, she reached into her frock and pulled out her dagger. Leaning forward, she got on her knees and straddled Karad's legs, keeping careful not to lose her balance. She pointed the tip of her blade towards the arrow embedded in the man's thigh. "This will hurt."

He looked her in the eyes and nodded.

"After I dig out each arrow, I will heal you, but there will be much pain."

"I'm ready, my lady." He grasped a piece of rope, stuffed it in his mouth, and, with the cords of his jaw muscles lining his cheeks, bit down hard.

And I'm ready to return home, she thought as she looked behind. There was still no sign of pursuit, though a large crowd had gathered on the dock where the bodies lay.

Turning her attention to the wound in Karad's thigh, she sliced open his breeches around the arrow shaft. The arrowhead had bitten straight through the flesh and buried itself deep inside the meat of his leg. Only the wooden shaft protruded from the bloody gash. From the shape of the wound she was certain the head was barbed. *Anghara have mercy.*

This was truly going to hurt. She must be strong. She *would* be strong for the sake of these men who died and bled for her and for the welfare of Asdralad. Karad's wounds were serious, and soon he would bleed to death without her intervention. Keeping her face expressionless, she positioned the tip of her blade next to the shaft and pressed. Karad groaned, clutched the side of the boat, and bit down harder as beads of sweat ran down his forehead. The sharp dagger sliced into the skin and muscle of the man's trembling thigh, and he growled as more blood oozed out. *I'm more than ready to return home.*

11
AT THE CROSSROADS

Imharr pointed toward the lake, a vast mass whose scale was hidden in the mirk of night. "We need to cross to the other side. It narrows as we head north. Might be there's a ferry or a ford, but we won't find it now. We'll look for something at first light." They kept their horses to a walk. Neither of them said a word about stopping.

As the two friends rode near the shoreline, the stars reflected on the surface of the Folkmere, creating a twin image of Brynea's glow gazing back at the heavens. Gentle waves lapped the shore. The only other sound was the clopping of their horses. Riding by the lake on such a clear night might have been peaceful save that the glimmering lights put Dayraven in mind of the elf and its haunting eyes. *What has it done to me?*

The thing in his mind was sleeping again, a hiss of breath sliding along the edges of his consciousness. He tried to make sense of the moment when the mysterious shard of the elf's presence awakened and pierced his being. Its energy was so vast that it broke the priest's power over Rudumanu and Hraedflyht as if flicking away a moth. He could still hear the priest's anguish and shock when the man's hold over the beasts snapped. *I hope I didn't kill him.*

He decided he had not. Somehow, he convinced himself, he would have known. At any rate, Urd had been right. There was a vast amount of power in him. There were moments when what he might do with it intrigued him, but his fear of it was greater. *It's not* my *power. It's not me at all. It's more likely to control me than I am to control it. What if it takes over?*

Imharr had been silent a while, but now that they had slowed down enough to talk, the inevitable question Dayraven had been dreading came: "What happened back there?"

He hesitated and sighed. "I don't know."

"Did you . . . do something?" The darkness hid Imharr's face, but Dayraven could hear the concern in his friend's voice. Was there fear too?

"I was reaching for the sword when . . . The priest fell over. Not sure why. Everything happened so fast. It was all blurry." This was at least half true, but he was still lying to his friend. Why not tell Imharr everything? *Because he would fear me. Then I would lose everyone.*

"Mayhap the priest lost control of his power. That can happen to them, I've heard." Imharr did not sound convinced, but Dayraven decided to go along with him for now.

"I've heard the same. Might be. Leastwise, I'm not sure the priest meant to harm me."

"Why would you say that? If he didn't mean harm, he picked a strange way of introducing himself."

Because I heard his thoughts in my mind, along with yours and the thoughts of every person there. "He could've had his men kill me at the stables. Stuck me with a spear instead of holding me. He wanted to ask questions."

"Because he sensed the power in you? Like Urd said?"

Dayraven winced. "Yes. I was standing outside Widuru, and he came out. He must have felt it in me. The gift. Urd said it's always been there. Mayhap that's what he sensed. Mayhap it was whatever the elf put there. I think it . . . frightened him. Either way, I ran like a fool. I think he just wanted to ask questions."

"Looking for a new white-robe?"

"Might be."

"Good thing you ran. You'd make a terrible priest. They don't let them near any women, you know."

"Then *you'd* make the unhappiest priest ever."

"Now that's the truth. Anyway, let's try to stick to Urd's advice from now on and stay away from white-robes."

"Aye." Dayraven slouched forward as some of the tension eased out of his body. Now that they were out of danger, their hasty exit from Wolvendon seemed almost comical. "Sorry about Acha."

"Not to worry. She's a beauty, but I had to leave somehow. Running off like madmen made it easier. No time to give excuses."

"She probably thinks you're some sort of outlaw."

"In that case, she'll never get over me."

Dayraven grinned at his friend and thanked the gods for him.

DAWN'S ARRIVAL REVEALED THE FOLKMERE HAD NARROWED ENOUGH for them to make out the opposite shore. The sun had not been up long when they came upon a village of simple wooden huts with thatched roofs, and the first thing to greet them from the village was a ferry tied up at a dilapidated but serviceable dock. An old man emerged from the hut nearest the ferry. He smiled and squinted at them as they approached. "Looking for passage, friends?"

The ferryman proved a friendly old fellow who did not mind taking them as his only passengers so early in the morning, charging the standard fare. From his almost incessant talking as the water gurgled beneath them, he seemed eager for the company.

"Hwitwater tumbles down from the Hemeldowns and runs through the Northweald, where she slows till she widens into the Folkmere, right here. Hwitwater's a rough, foamy sort. Not like t'other one. The Withweald runs soft. Her waters're clear, even blue in hue. But the two mingle in the Folkmere, which runs out as the Folkwater. Now, Folkwater winds all the way to Birch Bay and joins the Great Sea with no end. I been all over these rivers — been a riverman since I was a lad." He favored them with a toothless grin.

They did not tell him they came from Kinsford, by which the Folkwater ran on its way to the Great Sea.

"Course," said the old fellow without missing a beat, "you're headed east. Elsewise, why cross over, eh? Headed for Torrlond?"

Dayraven and Imharr glanced at each other. Dayraven scratched his ear and swallowed. "Uh . . ."

The riverman nodded as if Dayraven had answered him. "After we cross, stick hard by the northern shore till it narrows into the Withweald. East 'gainst the river runs the path, and after three days o' riding, the path widens into a broad road. A real sight it is, too. That there road is where Torrlond begins, and it runs clear across the northern plains till it reaches the kingdom of Ellond, though *I* ain't never been that far. Great big mountains out there that touch the clouds, they say." He chuckled as if he did not quite believe it.

As the old fellow talked on and the breeze ruffled his clothes and hair, Dayraven imagined the great east-west road snaking across Torrlond's broad northern plains until it came in view of the Osham Mountains, whose white, jagged peaks soared far above the earth and, if legend held true, harbored dragons. But the road Urd told them to take branched away north much sooner, leading to the town of Rimdale.

He knew the wide east-west road was only the beginning of the mighty works folk awed at in Torrlond. Greatest among these were the marvels in Etinstone and, most especially, Torrhelm. Urd had forbidden him to go near those cities, and he would have heeded her advice even if his encounter with the priest in Wolvendon had not reinforced her warning. It was a shame, though, as he had long dreamed of seeing Torrlond someday. He was still reeling from everything that had happened to him, but among the many unwelcome changes was this new mistrust of Torrlond, the kingdom of his ancestors that still claimed kinship with the Mark. He shook his head. *Nothing is the same any longer.* Along with the constant whisper in his mind, he recalled the ghost-raven's chortle, and it seemed to mock him and all his shattered dreams.

But not seeing the great cities of Torrlond was the least of his problems. The ache in his heart over being torn from home, from Ebba and his father and everything he knew, was like a physical weight. The only purpose left to him was to go to Ellond, where Urd told him to find the wizard Galdor. Perhaps this man could teach him to control the monstrosity that the elf put inside his mind. There was even a sliver of hope – one he hardly dared to acknowledge – that Galdor might be able to rid him of his curse.

"YOU KNOW, YOU CAN TELL ME WHAT REALLY HAPPENED BACK IN Wolvendon." Imharr lay on the ground, his hands behind his head as he gazed upward and sucked on a long blade of grass protruding from his mouth.

Sitting next to his friend, Dayraven tensed. They were resting just off the road. The green landscape to the east where the wide road beckoned spread out beyond them in placid risings and hills, and like the clean blue sky above, there seemed no end to it. Down the middle and paralleling the road, the clear and calm Withweald split the plains as it meandered from the distant horizon, and on the banks of the river grew pockets of brush and willows. At the moment, no other wayfarers interrupted their view of the infinite land.

Imharr spat out the blade of grass. He sat up, and his brow lowered. "You don't need to be afraid. It's me."

Dayraven sighed. "I know."

"The white-robe and his three companions weren't just paying us a friendly visit. Whatever it was you did, you were defending yourself."

The younger man shook his head. "I don't know what I did. But yes, I think I did something. Used the power inside me to break the priest's control over Rudumanu and Hraedflyht. I think I hurt him. I felt his pain."

"You had a right."

"Perhaps. But I'm afraid."

"Afraid of what?" Imharr's voice grew quieter.

"Of what's inside me." The elf-shard brushed his mind like a finger caressing the tiny hairs on the flesh of his back. Dayraven flinched. "I want my life back. I wish things could go back to the way they were. I wish I could go *home*."

Imharr put his hand on Dayraven's shoulder. "I'm sorry, Day, but your life is . . . changed."

The younger man sighed again. "I know." He looked Imharr in the eyes and, with gratitude and a little guilt, thought of the suffering and wrenching losses his friend had lived through. *He's already given so much to me. I don't think I'll ever be able to repay him.* But there was one thing at least he could offer. "When this is over . . . when I'm better, we'll seek your sister."

Imharr's eyes widened for a moment, and Dayraven could see the pain in the broken smile his friend used to cover his first reaction. "Right now, we have to get you to this Galdor fellow. Then, we'll take it from there, see what happens."

Dayraven nodded. "Thank you. I don't know if I could do this alone."

Imharr grinned, this time with his usual mischief, which banished Dayraven's fears for a moment. "Well, I've heard the women in Ellond are lovely." He winked at Dayraven. "This gives me a chance to find out, doesn't it?"

Dayraven rolled his eyes, but he could not help smiling back at his friend.

THE CHILDREN PLAYING IN THE FIELDS BENEATH THE VILLAGE NAMED it Dunham. Lying on both sides of the road at a place where it wound to the top of a small hill, it consisted of wooden homes with thatched roofs that were not so different from those common in the Mark. It was large enough to boast one small inn with a tavern attached to it that the children named The Burrow. With its thatched roof and timber-framed stucco walls, the inn presented two thick-glassed windows on each side of a sturdy oak door. A tidy arrangement of flowers accented each of the windows.

Dayraven looked at Imharr as they stood outside the The Burrow. Their last hot meal had been back in Wolvendon. Imharr nodded, and without a word between them, they made their decision. When the two friends tied their horses outside and opened the door, a stuffy and cozy interior invited them in.

A buzz of talk and laughter and the smoky smell of grilling meat met the friends inside the tavern. Many of the village's men had gathered there for a bite and some gossip over a mug of ale. As soon as Imharr asked for a table, the burly innkeeper smiled. "We've a spot for you. You've come a ways?"

"Yes," said Imharr.

"You've the speech of Markmen."

"That's right," said Dayraven.

"Markmen always welcome at my inn," said the innkeeper with a nod.

Once they were seated at a corner table and sipping from their first mugs of ale, Dayraven glanced at six soldiers that had also stopped at the tavern. In the last two days on the road, the friends had passed by a dozen such soldiers. On the left shoulders of their grey kirtles they wore the king of Torrlond's ensign: a white-capped silver mountain with a gold crown over it on a blue background. The soldiers wore the kirtles over their linked byrnies, though one had a corselet of overlapping steel plates and a costly shield with a brass ensign of Torrlond set in the middle. This same man had two red stripes over the ensign on his sleeve and a red crest on his helm, by which Dayraven guessed he held a higher rank. All the soldiers had removed their steel helms of a conical shape with long nose guards, but they wore their swords at their sides. Their round linden shields painted with the king's ensign rested against a wall near their table. They joked and laughed as they sat together and ate their food. One slapped another on the back, and their laughter broke out twice as loud.

The ale and the warmth of the tavern lulled Dayraven. But when his meal came — hot pork sausages and fresh-baked bread to dip in the grease — he set to eagerly. While Dayraven and Imharr ate with little talk and plenty of satisfied grunts, the soldiers and the locals carried on their loud conversations. When he was finished, Dayraven sat back on his bench, leaning on the wall behind him and sighing as he reached for his second mug of ale. He happened to look up when someone new entered the tavern: a man in a hooded white robe.

Dayraven's hand froze before reaching his ale. He jerked up in his seat as the locals greeted the priest with cheers and friendly pats on the back. At once, all of Urd's warnings rushed back to him. Had

Bagsac or someone worse caught up with them? The door was the only way out of the tavern. *I've been too careless.*

The presence of the elf susurrated in his mind. Surely the priest could feel it. The white-robed man glanced in Dayraven and Imharr's direction and then spoke to the innkeeper. Answering with a smile, the innkeeper pointed toward them. The priest nodded and wove through the crowd towards their table.

By now Imharr had noticed the man too, and his hand reached under the table for the knife at his side. Sweothol was a heavy weight in the baldric on Dayraven's shoulder. He and Imharr would never have a chance if the priest called the soldiers to his aid. *It can't end like this. Stay calm.* He braced himself.

The priest approached with a friendly smile. "You are visitors?"

The two friends looked at one another and then stared back at the priest. Both of their mouths hung open.

"Yes," said Imharr. "Travellers. From the Mark."

"May I?" The priest removed his hood and gestured at an empty place on the bench opposite Dayraven.

"Uh . . . yes. Please join us." Imharr's hand moved away from his knife.

Tall and slim with a balding head and a dark beard, this priest of the Way betrayed no immediate interest in elf-dwolas. As he sat, he introduced himself. "I'm Osfrid, priest of the Way for several villages in these parts." The innkeeper plunked a mug of ale in front of Osfrid and nodded in deference to him before attending to others.

Osfrid raised his mug toward Dayraven and Imharr and smiled. "To guests." He took a long draft of his ale.

The two friends glanced at each other while he drank. Dayraven cleared his throat. "So, are you from Dunham?"

The priest nodded as he wiped his lips with the back of his hand. "My folk have been here as far back as we can reckon. Dunham's stood on this hill for hundreds of years."

Imharr raised his eyebrows as if he found this revelation fascinating. "Has it now?"

"Indeed. You might be interested to know it was a stopping point for the folk who went on to settle the Mark from Torrlond. It's said some of the villagers went with them." Osfrid smiled. "Might be we're kin."

Such lore sparked Dayraven's imagination, but he was unable to forget one uncomfortable fact. Awareness of the presence of the gift in the man tingled in his mind. He recognized it as something he had always felt in Urd's company, though it was far more muted in Osfrid. Always he had thought of this feeling as part of Urd's personality, as part of the mystery of the woman. But this priest exuded that same presence. Bagsac had it too, he realized. And the priest he had encountered in Wolvendon. He remembered sensing it when he was inside the stables of the Fisherman's Wife and the priest was waiting outside. He had not known what it was, but now he understood. It was a power he perceived, something almost alive and separate from the person, the same way he might sense the presence of someone creeping up behind him. *And if I feel it in him, he must sense it in me. Why does he say nothing of it?*

Finding courage from some unknown place, he decided it was time to stop running. "As a priest, you have . . . what folk call the gift."

Imharr tensed and sat up straighter.

Osfrid nodded and smiled at Dayraven. "Yes. But I think you don't need me to tell you that."

"Then you . . . sense it in me as well."

The priest laughed. "The same way a man senses the sun when it's daytime. As soon as I walked in, I felt it all around you. I don't know how you can contain it all. Never have I felt the presence of the gift with so much strength. I confess, that's the real reason I came here to join you."

"Then you want to make me become a priest?"

Osfrid stared at Dayraven before answering. "No. I don't want to *make* you do anything. One must want to be a priest of the Way. It's not just a matter of having the gift. It's a calling."

"A calling?"

"One must hear Edan calling to devote his or her life to Him." The priest took another drink before gesturing toward Dayraven with his mug. "There are those with the gift who are not priests or priestesses of the Way. Some who follow the old gods become wizards or witches, and there are those who are powerful in sorcery in the east and in the south — there such sorcerers and sorceresses worship their two gods. And then there are some who never learn to use the gift. They live their lives as normal folk, never realizing or caring about the power dwelling in them. There always were such folk, and there always will be."

"Then . . . they needn't become priests or priestesses?"

Osfrid's smile was gentle, his eyes patient and perhaps a little sad, but strong with a resolution Dayraven did not understand. "Learning to use the gift is one thing. Devotion to Edan is another matter. Neither is an easy path, and one must be prepared to give up much to use the gift. To become a priest, one must give up even more. But we believe they are worthy sacrifices. The Eternal will be the inheritors of Edan's kingdom, and it's a priest's duty to bring that kingdom to fruition by bearing witness to it. A priest must have the gift, but he must also feel the calling. I hope you may hear it one day, but if you don't . . ." He shrugged and took another draft of his ale. "Edan's purpose is mysterious, but I have learned to trust it."

"How do I know Edan is calling?"

"You'll know. When the time is right, you'll know. The important thing is to be patient and listen. You have the gift in greater measure than in any I have ever met, but as for how Edan is speaking to you . . . Well, that's a matter for you to decide, and no one else."

Dayraven repeated the priest's words in his mind. He shut his mouth after realizing it was hanging open. *Then, perhaps after Galdor shows me how to use the power in me, I will decide what to do with my life.* For some reason he could not understand, the priest's words gave him a glimmer of hope.

Osfrid tipped his mug up and drained it before setting it on the table. "I must excuse myself. There's an ailing widow nearby I promised to meet. A good woman. It's been a pleasure sharing a table with you both." He rose from his seat. "Oh, and if your way lies east of the crossroads, be careful: The brigands who lurk along the road there have become such a pestilence that they've sent soldiers up from Etinstone to deal with them."

"We'll keep watch for them," said Imharr.

"Good. Even if we never meet again, I'll remember you. May Edan guide you and grant you peace."

Not knowing the proper response, Dayraven nodded and said, "Thank you."

When the priest was gone, Imharr leaned toward Dayraven. "Why didn't they send us a fellow like that instead of old Bagsac?"

"Don't know, but they're not all so bad, are they? It's plain the people here like him." *He's a good man. A wise man.* Dayraven tried to nurse the glimmer of hope he felt. Perhaps there would be a life he could claim after Galdor helped him.

WHEN THEY LEFT THE VILLAGE, DAYRAVEN'S MIND WAS STILL ON what he would do once Galdor helped him, so he hardly noticed the sky had darkened while they were in the tavern. The air grew cooler and moister as an unruly breeze kicked up and lashed the friends' hair and cloaks. Soon iron-grey clouds clamped down on them, and they unleashed their heavy rain. Imharr pointed his thumb back as he sat atop Hraedflyht. He shouted over the fat, pelting drops, "What about turning back to seek shelter in Dunham?"

Dayraven shouted back, "Let's press on! There might be some shelter ahead!" In truth, the hope that his conversation with the priest had kindled was growing in his mind, and, feeling the first hint of happiness since his encounter with the elf, he did not mind the rain too much. He even dared to entertain thoughts of somehow reuniting with Ebba after Galdor trained him. First, he would help Imharr find his sister, and then he could find a way back to Ebba. They might not be able to live in the Mark, but he was sure she would follow him wherever he might go. Perhaps this Galdor would have a place for him. The folk of Ellond too were kin of the Markmen. Mother of Kingdoms they called it, for those who spoke the Northern Tongue all sprang from it. He could make a life there.

The strengthening storm agreed more and more with his mood, and the rain did not dampen his imagination. Thunder rumbled in the sky. The horses whinnied at streaks of lightning flashing and forking over the wide landscape. Like slow waves of a vast sea the meadows rolled. Never had Dayraven beheld so much open land, and it seemed to hold out some unspoken promise to him. Here was where the gods dwelled and strove. A grim beauty pervaded it. When the lightning flashed, for an instant it illuminated the plains and infused them with a vibrancy that extended to him.

But there was nowhere to take shelter, so they rode in the downpour as Rudumanu and Hraedflyht plodded along the now muddy road, on which puddles collected and rivulets sprang to life. In the rain they met few fellow travelers, but one informed them the closest shelter in their direction was an inn just a mile south of the crossroads on the north-south road, which still lay some miles distant.

"Our way turns north at the crossroads, not south!" shouted Imharr over the downpour to his friend. "But if this storm doesn't stop before long, might be we'll have to go a bit out of our way to seek shelter."

Let it rain, thought Dayraven. *It doesn't matter.* He dreamed of his meeting with Galdor, and he resolved to work hard to master the power within him.

The two friends kept riding through the storm. The rain did not cease, but after a while it lessened. A few breaks appeared in the dark clouds as they rolled overhead.

"Might be we'll skip that inn after all," said Imharr, but not without some regret in his voice.

With the rain diminishing to a drizzle, they could see further into the distance. Ahead of them appeared the thin brown line of the north-south road, which crossed the one they traveled on. They halted a moment as they stood on a slight rising in the land giving them a clear view. The undulations of the landscape hid the crossroads, but it had to be not far ahead. Imharr pointed north. "That way lies our path."

Dayraven's gaze followed the curving brown ribbon of the north-south road in the distance. The land beckoned to him, promising faith that he had a future not entirely beyond his control. It inspired a sudden desire to run loose and celebrate the birth of hope in his mind. He smiled at Imharr. "Let's race to the crossroads."

"What?"

"Let's race. Last one to the crossroads has to tend the horses and make supper this evening."

"Supper?"

"Best hurry." With a quick thrust of his heels, Dayraven urged Rudumanu forward, and the red mare responded.

"Have you lost your senses? Orm take you!" cursed Imharr as he brought Hraedflyht to a gallop behind his friend.

The road turned and dipped into a depression, and Dayraven lost sight of the north-south road. As if in answer to Rudumanu and Hraedflyht's galloping, the rain poured hard again. Rudumanu's hooves thudded and splashed, and the rain stung Dayraven's face. He looked back once. Imharr rode behind him, his face tight with concentration. Hraedflyht's muscles strained and quivered and her hooves sent mud flying with each thundering step. Dayraven laughed aloud.

Imharr was gaining on him, but he reckoned the crossroads would soon appear. His friend was a better horseman than he, so it was only a matter of time before the older man overtook him. He glanced behind once more: Imharr's jaw was clenched and his eyes determined as he leaned forward. His cloak flew behind him as his steed pounded the muddy road. Dayraven turned a bend. Just past a large outcrop of rock to the right was the crossroads. He was going to win.

He opened his mouth to laugh in triumph, but the laugh died in his throat at a sight materializing ahead of him. In the middle of the crossroads, two riders appeared through the thick rain barreling toward him. They leaned forward in their saddles, but, seeing him in their path, they yelled and yanked on their reins, almost falling off as they commanded their stocky mounts to a sudden halt. The horses neighed as their hooves slipped and dug into the road. To avoid a collision, Dayraven reined in Rudumanu, who staggered in the mud in an effort to obey. When the mare gained her footing, some thirty paces separated Dayraven from the two strangers.

The two riders leapt off their steeds and landed on their heavy boots to face eastward, whence they had ridden. Their backs were now turned to Dayraven, but there was something strange about their appearance. They were the height of mere boys but broader than most men and had long, thick beards. Both tore large axes from their belts, and the bigger one also drew a large, broad dagger. The two men must have been Dweorgs, of which he had only heard tales. Imharr shouted behind him, "Whoa!" Snorting in protest, Hraedflyht slid to a noisy stop just before colliding with Rudumanu.

Arrows whizzed from the east at the pair of Dweorgs. All disappeared in the mud save one that pinged from the smaller Dweorg's chest. He must have worn a good byrny under his kirtle. Emerging from the rain like an apparition, a dozen riders shot into view with a terrible din of hooves and shouts and yelps. They wore dark cloaks and hoods. The brigands the priest Osfrid warned them about back in Dunham.

Slinging their bows over their heads, the brigands drew swords as they bore down on their prey. Hooves pounded the earth. Mud flew and spattered. A tide of muscle and steel surged toward the Dweorgs.

The larger Dweorg yelled something in a strange language and hurled his broad dagger at the foremost brigand, who threatened to ride him down. The dagger flew straight toward the brigand's head, which snapped back. With the hilt protruding from his forehead, his arms flung outward as if preparing for an embrace. His sword dropped from his hand just before his limp body reeled backward and splashed in the mud. The horse kept running toward the two Dweorgs, who leapt out of its path.

The other brigands charged forward, one cutting at the smaller of the pair with his short sword. But the Dweorg pivoted to the side and swung his broad axe in one motion. Something fell, and the screaming horseman held up a bleeding stump where his sword arm had been. The remaining brigands rode by without getting close enough to slash at their intended victims. Focused on their prey, none of them seemed to notice Dayraven and Imharr as they brought their horses to a halt and turned them around for another attack.

Dayraven gazed mesmerized and unmoving. Three choices presented themselves: run away, stand by and watch, or do something. The first two he dismissed as cowardly, so he steeled himself and shouted the first thing he could think of: "Stop, in the king's name!"

Dweorgs and brigands alike turned toward Dayraven and Imharr.

At once, staying out of the fight seemed more wise than cowardly. But Dayraven had little time to think over his error.

Something buzzed in the air near his head. An arrow sprouted from the chest of one of the brigands and from another's throat. The first grunted, and the second hacked up blood as his hands clutched his neck. Before the brigand collapsed from his horse, a hand grabbed Dayraven by his cloak with sudden force and pulled him off Rudumanu. Dirty water and mud splashed all around him, and the ground hit him so hard that it knocked the wind out of him and jolted his elbows. The water soaked his front and chilled him.

He lay between the two horses next to Imharr, who must have pulled him down. Ahead, two more brigands cried out with arrows embedded in them, one in the arm and one in his thigh.

Shouts erupted behind him. Amidst the clinking of mail and pounding of boots, more than a dozen men clad in grey kirtles ran by the two friends, stomping so near as to splash mud on them. These spear-wielding soldiers must have been hiding behind the outcrop of rock. They cast their weapons of ash and steel. Most of the spears hurtled and thudded into the brigands' horses, which screamed and bucked. One black clad man fell off his mount with a shaft through his torso.

The remaining brigands leapt off their wounded steeds, which neighed and galloped away in madness. The rushing soldiers drew swords. Men on both sides yelled, and steel clashed. Now outnumbered, the brigands formed a ring and fought with desperate courage. One shrieked as a sword pierced his thigh. A blade chopped into his neck and silenced him. Another parried a thrust but then lost a third of his skull to a swooping blow. Blood and brains spewed out onto the mud before the body followed.

One brigand dodged a thrust and arced his sword toward a soldier's neck. Trailing the blade, a sticky rope of blood spattered from the gash, and the soldier's body went limp. Another brigand parried a blow with his sword and plunged a dagger in his other hand into his attacker's eye so that it disappeared up to the hilt. The soldier stood transfixed and stared with his remaining eye, as if trying to understand what just happened. When the brigand withdrew the blade with a red spurt in its wake, the soldier tottered backwards.

But it was only a matter of time before the superior numbers won out. Sixteen soldiers and the two Dweorgs surrounded the last two brigands, who paced like caged beasts. The two screamed defiance and rushed at the enclosing circle. Merciless blades hacked them to pieces.

Fourteen bodies lay in the mud, and red puddles collected around them. The rain continued to patter down, making momentary craters in the puddles. The only other sound was the groaning of three wounded and prostrate brigands. A soldier approached each of the writhing men. One tried to drag himself away, rasping, "No. No! Mercy! Please!" Three blades rose and fell, rose and fell, rose and fell, each time chopping with a quick, sticky sound into meat and bone. Groaning and pleading ceased. All was still under the hushing rain.

Dayraven lay next to Imharr blinking at the scene. His heart squirmed in his chest, and he was still trying to make sense of what happened when one of the soldiers turned toward Imharr and him and pointed.

"You fucking idiots!"

Unlike the other soldiers, who wore plain helms and byrnies under their grey kirtles, this man wore the crested helm and steel corselet that proclaimed his higher rank. "Fools! What are you doing here?"

Imharr raised himself and stood, and Dayraven followed suit. They were dripping and muddy.

"We're travelers," said Imharr, "making our way north at the crossroads."

The full of extent of his folly grew apparent to Dayraven. The fifteen remaining soldiers and two Dweorgs approached behind their commander. They did not look pleased.

"You fucking fools fucked up our trap!" shouted the man in the crested helm, who strode so close that Dayraven could see the rage in his bright blue eyes. Droplets of blood slid down his corselet as the rain smeared them. "We nearly had those scum right under us, where we could've picked them off with no worries. That was the fucking plan. But you came galloping in the middle to just about ruin everything. As it is, I lost two fucking men!" He turned toward his soldiers. "Are they dead?"

"Yes, m'lord. Leofgar and Tuda."

"Leofgar and Tuda!" the leader repeated at Dayraven's face, as if he and Imharr should recognize the names. "What do you say to that?"

"I'm sorry . . . for the loss of your men," stammered Dayraven.

"Sorry? *Sorry*? Oh, you will be. What did I hear you say? 'Stop, in the king's name?' Is that what you said?"

"I . . . I was trying to help. I saw the two Dweorgs being attacked, and I . . . thought I should do something."

Standing among the soldiers, the two Dweorgs crossed their arms in front of their chests and stared at Dayraven like all the rest.

"They were the fucking bait, stupid!" The commander pointed at the Dweorgs. "They were supposed to lead the brigands under the outcrop. Only *you* got in the way," he yelled as he jabbed his finger at Dayraven's chest, "and now I have two dead soldiers!"

"I'm sorry."

The soldier ignored Dayraven's apology. "'Stop, in the king's name?' Do you know what the penalty is for impersonating the king's soldiers?" His chin thrust out, and his wide eyes threatened violence.

"Pretty sure it's death or mutilation, lieutenant." The soldier who had spoken spat. "Might be both, though not in that order."

Dayraven gawked at the man. "I . . . no. I didn't mean . . ."

"A treasonous offense, boy." The lieutenant nodded. "Know what that means?"

"I . . ."

"Punishable by death."

"Let's string the fuckers up here, lieutenant," said another of the soldiers.

Imharr held up his palms. "Hold on, now. We just happened to be in the wrong place at the wrong time. He was trying to help. You can't hang us for that."

The soldiers moved toward the two friends, some of them grinning. Battle lust still animated their eyes, and it seemed they had found a convenient place to vent it.

Dayraven backed up a pace. His hand fumbled toward Sweothol, which lay in its baldric under his cloak. At the same time, the shard of the elf's presence in his mind stirred with a sharp breath. *Shit. Not now.*

"Ahem."

It was one of the Dweorgs who cleared his throat, the smaller of the two. Everyone turned to the short, thick-bearded man, who stepped forward and held his palms in the air. He flashed a teeth-baring grin, and Dayraven's mind snapped back to the present as the Dweorg bowed to the leader and sniffed. "If I may, lieutenant? We are one of the realm's mercenary companies, are we not?"

The commander rolled his eyes with undisguised annoyance. "Yes. Obviously."

The Dweorg showed his teeth again in a smile. "Exactly. Now, if I recall it aright, having just researched the matter before joining our esteemed company, I believe the laws state there's *another* punishment for those who impersonate the king's soldiers."

The lieutenant's eyes narrowed. "Yeah? Might be. Make your point, Dweorg. It's pissing out here."

"In the stead of death, the guilty party may choose to serve in one of the realm's mercenary companies."

Now the commander glowered at the Dweorg. "So."

"And *our* mercenary company has two men to replace: Leofgar and Tuda, may they rest in peace."

The leader frowned, and he put a finger to his bearded chin. "Hmmm."

The Dweorg gave a satisfied nod. "Right. Seems to me you have two new recruits before you. Is it not fitting they should take the places of the men whose deaths they may have unwillfully contributed to?"

"Might be." The commander pursed his lips and shook his head. "But look at them. They have no byrnies, no helms, and no weapons. Can't make soldiers out of unarmed men. Especially stupid ones."

The Dweorg held up one palm and smiled. "That's a matter we Dweorgs can address once we return to Etinstone. Weaponsmithying was our trade, after all. We'll see to it they have the proper gear."

The lieutenant raised one eyebrow and thought a moment longer, and then he nodded at the Dweorg. "If that may be, then you have the right of it, Dweorg. Saves me finding replacements, at least." He turned toward Dayraven and Imharr. "Well? What will it be? Death by hanging, or joining the Mercenary Company of Etinstone?"

"Hard to say which would be worse," jested one of the soldiers, and the others laughed.

Dayraven turned to Imharr, who shrugged at his friend. He looked at the smaller of the Dweorgs, who smiled at him.

Imharr sighed and glared at the lieutenant. "A drowning man takes hold of whatever comes in his grasp. Seems we have little choice."

The commander smirked at him. "So it seems. Now, since this is a mercenary company, you needn't swear fidelity to the Way. However, this is one of the sanctioned mercenary companies of Torrlond, so you must avow fealty to King Earconwald. Right? Your names?"

Imharr and Dayraven glanced at each other, and the former sighed before answering. "Imharr."

A lump formed in Dayraven's throat. *How are we going to get to Galdor?* His heart pounding, he could think of no way out of the mess they had landed in. "Dayraven."

The lieutenant frowned and squinted at him. "'Dayraven?' Bit odd. What sort of name is that?"

"The one my mother gave me."

The man held up a palm and grinned. "No need to get touchy, boy. Right. Imharr and Dayraven, in joining the Mercenary Company of Etinstone, do you swear by whatever god or gods you follow to be faithful to Torrlond's king and serve him in whatever cause he sees fit to employ you, and to obey his officers, who represent his person, unto death or until such time as he or his representative releases you from his service?" The bored monotone in which the lieutenant recited the oath suggested he had said it many times before.

Dayraven and Imharr looked again at one another.

The man waved his hand and rolled his eyes. "Say 'I do so swear.'"

"I do so swear," they repeated together.

"Congratulations on joining the company. I'm Thegn Ludecan, lieutenant and second in command. You can start by burying the two men you got killed as well as the scum lying over there." He jerked his thumb toward the dead bandits.

Lieutenant Ludecan turned to the two Dweorgs. "Since you're so keen on their company, you Dweorgs can help them." The officer swept the remaining soldiers with his gaze. "The rest of you, go collect your horses. Adda and Eafa, our two new friends have need of spades. Bring yours to them. Eorp, collect all the weapons of the dead. Don't need those falling into the wrong hands, do we?"

As most of the soldiers began walking back toward the outcrop, the lieutenant grabbed Dayraven by the cloak. "And listen well, now, because I'll tell you only once." He glowered at his two newest recruits as he lowered his voice to a growl. "If you even *think* about deserting, I will hang you and, law or not, mutilate you first. And don't test me on it." He raised his voice again. "The boys would love a little sport. Wouldn't you, boys?"

Two men walking away looked over their shoulders. "Aye, m'lord."

"That we would." Each sounded more bored than eager for sport, but Dayraven did not feel like testing the matter just then.

The lieutenant released Dayraven and looked up at the clouds, whose swollen darkness promised plenty more of the rain that was pelting them. "Make it quick so we can all get out of this piss." He glanced at the dead bandits. "We've finished our job here, and we need to head back to Etinstone to report for the mustering. We rejoin the rest of the company in four days." He gave Dayraven's shoulder a slap and favored him with a fierce grin. "War's brewing, lads." The officer followed his men toward the outcrop.

Dayraven and Imharr turned around, their only remaining company for the moment the two stout Dweorgs. These two stood with their arms crossed, watching their fellow soldiers disappear in the rain. They were well more than a head shorter than the average man of the Mark or Torrlond, the taller being at least two inches under five feet. But Dayraven had no doubt about the strength in their broad bodies after witnessing the smaller one's axe stroke. On their heads they wore solid helms with cheek guards and ornamentation in the form of bronze dragons breathing fire as interweaving knots. Dark lines and dots like some form of writing marked the length of their pale, hairy forearms, which resembled squat tree branches.

"Damn," said Imharr. "What just happened?"

The larger Dweorg patted the axe in his belt and stepped forward. His long brown beard waved and dripped raindrops when he rumbled at Dayraven and Imharr, "Fine mess you got yourselves in. Don't think of scampering away, either. Lieutenant's a man of his word, seems to me, and his men would kill you as quick as they'd scratch a flea." He stomped over to the corpse with his broad dagger in its face, put his boot on the chest, and plucked the blade out. After spitting on the body, he wiped the blade in the wet grass to the side of the road.

Dayraven stared at the stout fellow. "Sorry. I truly thought you needed some help."

"You?" scoffed the Dweorg. "Giving us help? Ha! When has your sort ever given us help? And now you offer it when it's not wanted."

The smaller Dweorg waved his hand. "Hlokk. Enough." Turning to Dayraven and Imharr, he said, "Forgive my brother, friends. He's hot-tempered even at the best of times, and the anger of battle has a way of lingering. But we're grateful for your help."

"No," said Dayraven. "It's you who helped us. Thank you."

The smaller Dweorg, who seemed the elder of the two, nodded and said, "Since we've already helped each other, and it seems we'll be in one another's company for some time, perhaps we should introduce ourselves." He had a greying beard retaining some of its original reddish brown color. A web of wrinkles surrounded the large brown eyes above his broad nose, and in them Dayraven perceived warmth, kindness, and sorrow. "I'm Gnorn," he said with a deep bow, "and this is my brother, Hlokk. We're pleased to make your acquaintance." Hlokk jammed his dagger in its sheath at his side, gave a wry grin, and bowed as well.

"As are we." Not sure how to respond in the manner of Dweorgs, Dayraven bowed in return. When he looked at Imharr and gestured with his hand, his friend followed suit.

The one called Gnorn smiled. "Though it matters naught to us, I guess by your speech you're not from here."

"Are you from here?"

"As you may have observed from our comrades' behavior, the Torrlonders do not count us among them, though we have long lived in their kingdom. In fact, we recently joined King Earconwald's forces, in which there are few of our kind, perhaps none other than we two."

"Well, you have the right of it. We are strangers here. I'm Dayraven, and this is my friend, Imharr. We come from the Mark, near the Southweald. To the south of that forest lie the Dweorghlithes, where folk say there are more of your kind."

Hlokk spat.

Gnorn frowned. "Those who dwell in the Dweorghlithes are indeed our kind, yet you should know not all Dweorgs love one another."

Imharr half shouted to be heard over the rain, "And though I am myself quite curious about Dweorg-lore, perhaps you could enlighten us on the matter somewhere drier after we've finished our task. Besides, I believe the good lieutenant wanted us to hurry along."

Dayraven glanced back toward the outcrop, whence some of the soldiers were already leading their horses toward them.

"Aye," said Gnorn. "Let's begin with Leofgar and Tuda."

USING BORROWED TOOLS, DAYRAVEN AND IMHARR DUG SHALLOW graves while the two Dweorgs dug with spades from the packs on their horses. A few soldiers pitched in to speed things along since none of them wanted to sit in the rain. The others stood nearby jesting or even dicing. Some had already rifled the corpses for anything of value, including their two former comrades.

Burying the dead was the custom of the Way, which prevailed in Torrlond. Some had begun to follow this example in the Mark as well, but in Kinsford most continued to burn their dead on a pyre. Dayraven had witnessed several funerals in his home village, where the mesmerizing, greedy flames devoured the body as friends and kin keened and mourned. It was a poignant way to say goodbye, a freeing of grief. It was strange for him to dispose of bodies by digging a hole and throwing them into it. But he and the others went about their grim task, scooping out the muddy earth with their tools.

"Well, this lot won't be bothering any more travelers," growled Hlokk.

"But they acquitted themselves well enough in the end, didn't they," remarked his brother.

"Aye. To the death, they did."

The brothers nodded at each other.

The Dweorgs seemed to communicate more than their words meant in their exchange. Dayraven wondered what it was, but he kept at his digging.

When they had the holes deep enough, the grave diggers lugged the limp bodies by the arms and legs and dropped them in. Some of the dicing soldiers had glanced over when Leofgar and Tuda were laid to rest, but there was little other reaction as most continued with their laughing, gambling, and cursing. No one said a word, and there was no ceremony. Dayraven and the rest used their spades to fill the holes back in with the wet soil. Steel grated on rocks and grit. Rain fell and dripped from the toilers.

As bodies disappeared beneath mud, Dayraven wished he knew some fitting words for the occasion. Someone in the world would grieve for them. A mother, a father, a brother or sister, a child. For someone, their deaths would bring home how fleeting the world was. Moments before, their flesh had contained their lives. The elf-shard brushed against his awareness and whispered in his mind, seeming to say that death was cold and lonely.

When they packed the last of the soil in place, they wiped their muddy hands on the grass. The other soldiers were already readying their horses for the ride south to the inn.

When Dayraven handed his borrowed spade back to the soldier called Eafa, the grizzled veteran gave him a gentle smile. "Best not take it to heart, lad. A soldier's got to get used to it."

Dayraven nodded and tried to return the smile.

"At least we can get dry now," said Imharr.

BEFORE LONG, AS DARK DAY GAVE WAY TO DARKER EVENING, THEY came to the inn. Large, crooked beams of wood formed the building's supporting framework, between which lay white stucco walls. Unlike The Burrow in Dunham, this was a large, sprawling structure standing on its own. It was in fact a series of connected buildings with an inner courtyard, and the rain slid off its slate roof in rivulets and drops. Other than the row of stables not far away, there were no other structures in sight. Dayraven wondered that a place like this should exist only for wayfarers, and he supposed it was big enough to shelter nearly a whole village. It seemed out of place without any other dwellings nearby, but from the inn's thick glass windows the welcoming glow of firelight shone.

Hlokk rubbed his hands together and sighed. Dayraven too looked forward to the food and warmth within. Along with the rest of their company, they rode through the courtyard toward the front door, outside of which four soldiers with spears sheltered under a porch roof. Over the porch hung a sign depicting two long bones crossing each other, and the script below read, "The Crossroads Inn."

After they alighted from their horses and untied their travel packs to bring inside, stablehands took their horses. Dayraven and Imharr stayed close to the two Dweorgs as they walked through puddles up to the spearmen, who stood above them at the top of three stone steps nodding to the other wet soldiers passing within. Their familiar greetings told Dayraven that the four were part of the same company as their companions, and indeed they wore the same ensigns on the left sleeves of their grey kirtles, declaring them King Earconwald's soldiers.

"Greetings," said Gnorn as he set foot on the first step. One of the soldiers presented the tip of his spear to him. Hlokk tensed and growled under his breath. Standing in the rain, Dayraven and Imharr waited next to the Dweorgs.

"Dweorg scum," said the soldier holding out his spear, "Go sleep in the stables. The inn's for soldiers."

"Then," replied Gnorn, still smiling, "we have no quarrel. As you well know, we are king's men."

The soldier smirked. "No stinkin' Dweorg's a king's man. Always grubbin' after other folks' things."

Hlokk's hands fidgeted before one rested on his axe. His large nose twitched and bushy eyebrows lowered as the rain dripped from his beard.

"Let them pass, Wonred. They're all with us."

Lieutenant Ludecan came from behind them, and the one called Wonred lifted his spear. The lieutenant smiled at the Dweorgs as well as his two newest recruits. "We rise early on the morrow and head back to Etinstone. On the march back, see to it you keep clear of the rest of the men since they don't wish to ride with you. Once we arrive in Etinstone, you have a day of leave for the Day of Edan. Do as you like until the mustering. Just be sure you arrive on time." He looked at Dayraven and Imharr. "*You* will report to me before the mustering to present yourselves with the proper weapons and gear. Your Dweorg friends will make sure you're equipped. Any failure on your part, and I'll make good on my earlier threat. Understood?"

"Yes, my lord," said Gnorn.

"Good. Now go inside and find out your quarters from the innkeeper. The four of you can stay together. Then get some food." Lieutenant Ludecan stepped ahead of them and disappeared inside the inn. The four of them followed, with Wonred scowling at them as they passed by.

The absence of constant rain was a relief as soon as they entered the light and warmth of the inn, which buzzed with eager conversations and loud laughter. Whitewashed walls and plenty of candles and torches in sconces gave the place a merry air. Red-faced serving women bustled about, and one of them fetched the innkeeper for the four friends as they waited by the entranceway, dripping enough that puddles collected under them. A stairway in front of them led up to a second story, and Dayraven guessed the Crossroads Inn must have dozens, if not scores, of rooms. Through an open doorway to their left was a glimpse of the generous common room. Already there were plenty of guests and soldiers dining there, and the smell of roasted meat brought all his senses alive.

As he stood waiting, Dayraven realized how tired he was, his muscles sore and his hands blistered from the digging, and his stomach growling at the scent of food. The first thing would be to get dry, warm, and fed. Then, he and Imharr would have to figure what they were going to do next and if there might be some means of escape from the mercenary company. Somehow, instead of finding Galdor, they were headed toward exactly where Urd told them not to go.

. . .

After changing into spare clothes from their packs and leaving their wet ones to dry in their room, Dayraven, Imharr, Gnorn, and Hlokk emerged in the common room. The din of conversations quieted. Many guests and soldiers stopped talking and stared at Dayraven's two new companions. Some scowled and muttered half heard curses about Dweorgs, but after some time they ignored them and went back to their talk. The four of them found a small table of their own in a corner of the smoky room, where a large fireplace crackled and a couple dozen soldiers ate, talked, and gambled among other guests. Near their table was a window. The rain hushed and pattered on the thick glass. Warm and dry, Dayraven listened and sagged into his chair.

Gnorn bought them drinks and their meal — mutton with cabbage and bread — and additional rounds of ale followed. While they ate, two musicians among the soldiers wove a pensive tune with fiddle and pipe, quieting the conversations a bit. The four listened and said little, but after the food was gone and they each sipped their third mug of ale, they spoke more. Feeling safe in their corner, Dayraven asked Gnorn, "Why fight for Torrlond when its folk treat you the way they do?"

Gnorn half smiled. "You mean because we're Dweorgs? Truth is, we don't fight for Torrlond. We fight for our own reasons. But before judging us, ask yourself why any man fights. Everyone has his own reasons, in the end."

"What sort of reasons?"

"A mob in Caergilion slew three missionaries of the Way, they say. Is that really why Torrlond makes war on its neighbor? To be sure, many soldiers believe in the Way, and in their hearts they hope to find salvation fighting for it. Yet more do not truly believe but find a convenient reason to conquer someone weaker and take what they can from them. Some fight because they have little choice and must feed their families somehow. Still others fight for glory" — the Dweorg looked Dayraven in the eye — "a chance at great deeds so their names will last a few years longer." Gnorn paused a moment to shake his head. "My brother Hlokk and I fight for a way out."

"What do you mean?"

"It goes back many winters before you were born, long before we or our fathers' fathers were born." Gnorn's eyes glistened with the ancient sorrow he referred to.

"Well, you promised to teach us some Dweorg-lore, and we're ready. Right, Imharr?"

"Day's always keen for that sort of stuff." Imharr was sitting back and smiling at the contents of his mug.

Gnorn frowned for a moment at Dayraven as if weighing his character. "Alright. Ever heard of the Dweorgs of the Fyrnhowes?"

Dayraven and Imharr both shook their heads, so Gnorn said, "You know the kingdom of Grimrik, of course?"

Grimrik, as Dayraven knew from a map in one of Urd's books, lay some hundred leagues as the crow flies north and east of where they were now. The peoples of Eormenlond feared and respected the Thjoths, the tall and fierce folk of Grimrik. Only their love of fighting, stories told, surpassed their lust for seafaring. The Thjoths spoke a language different from the Northern Tongue, yet somehow like it, making the words harsh and outlandish. Urd once told Dayraven the Thjoths came hundreds of years before from the Wildlands far off in the east and were kin of the tribes of savage Ilarchae living there. He said to Gnorn, "Yes, we've heard of it. Many say its people, the Thjoths, are hard and warlike."

Hlokk grunted and frowned.

"Such folk speak soothly," said Gnorn as he bowed his head. "Reavers and scourges of the coasts. Murderers and slavers. Thieves and usurpers. The Thjoths haven't always held the land they call Grimrik. Before them, for more centuries than your people or even the Andumae can remember, we Dweorgs of the Fyrnhowes dwelled there."

"What happened?" asked Imharr.

"Nearly two hundred winters ago, the Thjoths broke out of the Wildlands in the east. They raided the coasts of Ellond and Torrlond, and then a leader of theirs called Dragvendil lusted for a new kingdom for himself. At first he turned towards Ellond, but he found King Froda too strong when they met in battle at sea."

Gnorn stopped and swallowed. "The next year, he attacked us Dweorgs in our ancient strongholds in the Fyrnhowes. Our people resisted stoutly, but we were few, and we had the misfortune to kill one of Dragvendil's young sons. Dragvendil swore to destroy us or die in the attempt. We Dweorgs are hardy folk, but the Thjoths have an inhuman ferocity, a lust for death. Over twenty grim years, they reduced our people to desperate starvation and a daily struggle for life. At length, in the year 1530 by your reckoning, our people fled. Dragvendil founded his chief city hard by a waterfall where he slaughtered thousands of us — men, women, and children — and he named that city Valfoss. His new kingdom he called Grimrik, and his descendants rule it to this day."

So Dayraven was speaking with fellow exiles. He rubbed his jaw and asked, "How did your people come to dwell in Torrlond?"

Gnorn sighed and shook his head. "The few Dweorgs of the Fyrnhowes who survived sought shelter in Torrlond. King Ethelwulf, knowing the reputation of our craftsmen and our herblore, saw an opportunity. He invited our people to stay in Torrlond's cities to earn their living, and though many died on that sorrowful journey, the survivors straggled into Etinstone. There we gained a livelihood as goldsmiths, silversmiths, and weaponsmiths. Hlokk and I are weaponsmiths, as our family has been for generations."

"But," asked Dayraven, "why didn't your people seek shelter among the Dweorgs in the North Downs, the Hemeldowns, or the Dweorghlithes?"

"As I told you before," replied Gnorn, "the Dweorg kingdoms harbor little love for one another. Our quarrels and hatreds are older than the coming of your people or the coming of the Andumae to Eormenlond, and it would take me years to tell you of them. Suffice it to say the other Dweorgs would have naught to do with our people. None would ever help us. Thus we've lived through almost two centuries in a land that never truly welcomed us. The Torrlonders use our skills, but they don't love us, and how can we prosper where we're despised? In Etinstone, we survivors have dwindled over the years to a pathetic few. And that's why Hlokk and I decided to join Torrlond's army."

Dayraven shook his head. "I don't understand."

The thick wrinkles framing Gnorn's mournful eyes deepened as he smiled gently. "We wish to end things with dignity."

In response to Dayraven's stare, Gnorn continued. "There aren't enough women-folk among us, and none are eligible for Hlokk or me according to our customs. We can have no children, and we've nothing to live for. Rather than linger feebly with our ignoble lives in Etinstone, we wish to die with honor, in battle. Among our people, it's the noblest way to part from this world. Then we can join our ancestors, since there aren't enough of the living." Hlokk looked down at the floor as his brother finished speaking.

Dayraven gazed at Gnorn for a long moment. "It's a sad tale."

"Yes. Though few enough know it these days. We survivors pass it on, but once we're gone, only the silent land will remember. Not far north of here are hundreds of small mounds on the plains. Those are the barrows of the Dweorgs who died in Torrlond on the way to Etinstone when our folk first left our land. So many perished along the way. We Dweorgs live close to the land, and we understand this place you call Eormenlond better than you, for we've dwelled here longest. Our people could not bear to leave the place they called home for thousands of years. Now none of us has returned to that land for almost two centuries."

"I'm sorry," said Dayraven.

"Good of you to listen. You have a kindness in you that's uncommon among your folk. Not meaning to offend, of course. Mayhap it's uncommon among any folk, but . . . Well, might be it's the ale talking now. At least someone will know our fate when we're gone."

Dayraven indeed felt a strange connection with the two Dweorgs. They were his fellow exiles and, for the moment, companions in arms. "Fate is what brought us together, it seems."

"You needn't remain, you know." Gnorn looked around the room. As he lowered his voice, the others leaned forward. "Lieutenant Ludecan will have the exits to the inn guarded, as well as the stables. It would be unwise to attempt to leave now, and on the ride south there will likely be little chance. But once we're in Etinstone, we can find a way to get you out safely. Before anyone knows you're gone, you could be miles from the city on your way to wherever you were going."

"But Lieutenant Ludecan . . ."

"For all his talk of hanging, neither Ludecan nor anyone else will have time to hunt you. War is coming."

"But he'll know. He'll suspect your involvement, and you'll be punished. Might be he'll hang you in our stead. There would be no honor in abandoning friends like that. Right, Imharr?"

Imharr pursed his lips and scratched his head. "Well . . ." He shrugged. "We only just met." At Dayraven's outraged expression, Imharr held up his palms. "Alright. You're right. We can't have it look like Gnorn and Hlokk are involved. But we've got to get you where Urd said, don't we?"

Dayraven nodded. "There'll be a chance. Somewhere between Etinstone and where we're going. Might be even sooner. We'll know it when it comes." *I just hope we won't meet any priests before then.* He took a deep breath. "We'll find a way."

Imharr gazed at Dayraven for a while. His face was grave, and Dayraven knew he weighed the possibilities in his mind. At length, he sighed. "Aye. For now, we stay with the company." He looked at Gnorn. "If you don't mind, we'll tag along with you two for a spell. But the first chance we get without getting you into trouble, we'll be gone."

Gnorn smiled. "Then it's settled. Tomorrow, we journey to Etinstone. But I suggest we get some sleep now since we've been told we leave early."

12
THE CALL TO WAR

The ruler of the mighty kingdom of Torrlond stood on a stone balcony high in Sigseld, his royal palace, surveying his chief city. A strong gust tossed his hair back as he peered at the vast sprawl under the nearly cloudless sky. Smoke from thousands of fires fed the haze always hovering over the city.

This city, *his* city, the largest and grandest in all of Eormenlond, held about one hundred thousand souls, or one in sixty of Torrlond's people. Nothing like the conglomeration of life beneath him had ever existed in Eormenlond before, and no other kingdom could boast anything like it. It was fitting. No king like him had ever existed in Eormenlond before, for he would unite all the kingdoms under his rule.

King Earconwald II fingered the jewel encrusted hilt of his sword in its gold-inlaid scabbard. He wore his bejeweled golden crown as well as a rich robe of red, gold, and black over a shining steel corselet with a gilded engraving of the royal ensign on its breast. Always his best on formal occasions, he smiled as he gazed from Sigseld down upon the spires and domes glistening in the sun.

Far below, his ant-like subjects swarmed on busy streets turning and crisscrossing one another like parts of a vast maze. Merchants and laborers, soldiers and thralls, nobles and whores — all their activities and aspirations served one purpose: to make him richer and more powerful. His palace was the center of it all, and was not his royal person, the direct descendant of Folcwalda and living embodiment of his lineage, the reason for Sigseld's existence? In his sacred body dwelled the royal house of Torrlond, the heart of the kingdom, on which all else depended and around which all else revolved. His noble ancestors had performed great deeds. Why should he not enjoy the fruits of them?

Not just that: He would better them. It was his right to rule, his prerogative to conquer. Sages and loremasters wrote histories of the great and powerful, and he would ensure that his name would live forever in their annals. The monuments to his greatness would endure, and the shapers would sing of him as the ruler who had the courage and the vision to unite all of Eormenlond.

Earconwald laughed aloud as his eyes followed the streets out to the thick walls and towers encompassing the city. Nothing in all of Eormenlond could breach those walls, and no one would ever dare try. He reveled in the proud commercial buildings around Great Cheaping with their pretentious columns and large windows. He grinned with approval at both the towering homes of the wealthiest denizens in the western half of the city and the squalid, disease-ridden slums huddling together east of the River Ea, where more masses from Torrlond's countryside and abroad crowded each year to swell the greatest of cities.

But then his eyes turned back to the city's center and chanced upon the Temple of the Way's large dome and the adjacent monastery's sharp spires, the only buildings that dared to rival the size and splendor of Sigseld. The king's wolfish grin soured into a snarl.

Earconwald turned from the balcony and strode through the open door of an arched entranceway into a large room of smooth stone. On the room's opposite wall was another door, though this one was closed and barred. A rug with decorative patterns covered the chamber's stone floor, and on the walls hung bright-colored tapestries depicting long dead kings and queens, their eyes gazing down in pious solemnity. A large fireplace took up most of one wall, and light streamed in from windows with open shutters on the outer wall. Splendid oak chairs and a large oak table occupied another side of the room, and on the table sat an empty gold goblet, two empty plates, and a clear and elegant glass bottle one quarter full of red wine. An enormous bed in the center dominated the chamber. Intricate carvings covered the bed's frame and posts beneath a canopy of red and golden hued fabric.

Heaped on the bed were dark brown bear furs, atop of which lay a woman in a crimson dress holding a gold goblet. Beneath a gold circlet on her head, the woman's blonde hair flowed down past her shoulders. Jeweled rings weighed down her hands, while gold bracelets encircled her wrists and a belt of golden fabric enclosed her slender waist. The woman was not old — more than a decade younger than Earconwald — but she was no longer young either. Though still beautiful and desirable, there was something worn and tired about her as she languished on the bed with a cushion propping her up. When Earconwald entered the room, she took a furtive but deep draft from her goblet.

"My dear Moda," said Earconwald with a smirk, "you'll consume all the wine my vineyards in South Torrlond produce."

Queen Moda tried to laugh casually, but tension broke through her silky voice. "Then you'll simply take more from Caergilion when you conquer it, my lord. The wine of the southern kingdoms is superior anyway."

Walking towards the bed, Earconwald smiled at her as if at a naughty child. "Don't try to please me now, my dear. I told you to keep yourself presentable for today's ceremony with my dukes and captains. And what have you done? Snuck more behind my back? It would seem I can't leave you for a moment." He spoke with slow deliberation, each word a nail he was driving in.

As he neared, she sat up in the bed and cast her eyes down at the floor. Her voice quivered, though he knew how easily she could produce such an effect. "I'm sorry, my lord. Only a little more. I'm sure I'll be fine."

Earconwald closed in on her. Why did she burden him with her weakness and stupidity? He lashed out and struck away the goblet, which clanged on the floor. It stung his hand, but he was not about to show her that. Moda winced and shrank from him, which made him grin. He leaned down and hissed in her ear, "*I'll* say whether or not you're fine."

She clenched her eyes shut as he raised his hand to strike, but he hesitated and then smirked down at her. "Not now, I think. It wouldn't do to have your cheek too flushed. Would it, my dear?"

Moda trembled and nodded, which curled his lip in a look of both disgust and pleasure.

"Look beautiful for my dukes and the captains of my army — like a queen they'd go off to die for. Play your part and say as little as possible. Since you've failed to provide me with an heir, you can at least serve some purpose. When the ceremony is finished, drink yourself to oblivion for all I care."

A knock sounded at the closed door. Earconwald scowled at his queen a moment longer before breaking off his gaze. As he strode to the door, the king cocked up his chin and conjured a smile of regal benevolence.

He unbarred the door with a clack and opened it to reveal five soldiers standing at attention on the other side. The one in front was a grey-bearded man wearing a corselet of scale mail and a red crested helm as well as a crimson mantle over his shoulders. Over his ensign were three red stripes, and from his neck hung a brass and golden horn by a golden chain. As the four guards stood rigid, the older man bowed low and said, "Your Majesty, your dukes and captains and the priests are assembled in the hall. We wait to escort you at your pleasure."

King Earconwald smiled as at an old friend and put his hand on the soldier's shoulder. "Thank you, Earl Nothelm. Queen Moda and I were just preparing to come. By my word, it's good to see you this day. How's Sibwaru?"

"She's well. Thank you, Sire." Nothelm bowed his head. Captain of the king's household guard, the old earl was a man who performed his duties with great competence and never asked questions. *A good soldier*, thought the king. *Loyal and stubborn as a hound. A useful man. Just the sort who'll conquer Eormenlond for me.*

"Good. I'm glad of it." Earconwald turned to Moda, who approached from behind, and held out his arm. "Come, my dear." After the Queen dutifully took her lord's arm, he faced Captain Nothelm. "Lead us down, my friend."

BOASTING MARTIAL SCULPTURES IN BRONZE RELIEF AND GOLDEN bands, the ornate doors to the Great Golden Hall awaited the king. As Earconwald and his queen approached, the two guards at each of the splendid doors bowed and opened them. A loud din of men conversing emerged. But when Captain Nothelm stepped forward and winded the horn hanging around his neck three times, all fell silent.

King Earconwald paused and held his head high. Then, with Queen Moda at his side, he strutted inside.

Throbbing martial rhythms flooded the hall from drummers stationed inside the doors. The king kept time with slow, deliberate steps. From the hall's eastern side, light streamed in through tall windows of clear glass held within a delicate stone framework, while those to the west were less bright in the late morning. Two long rows of thick, black marble columns projected back to the hall's far end, where waited a large throne of black marble atop seven wide stairs. Behind the throne, a wall of gold cast its aura throughout, gilding the faces of spectators gaping at it. Light also poured in intricate windows above the Golden Wall. Even the floor consisted of variegated squares of black and white marble, each outlined in gold. Soldiers bearing polished weapons and helms and wearing the king's ensign on their grey kirtles stood like sculptures before each of the black columns, which soared up to the vaulted ceiling high above. Those who arched their heads back to cast their eyes upward saw the ceiling also was gilded.

Nearly nine hundred captains of Earconwald's vast and invincible army crowded the hall. Many of the captains were earls, though an almost equal number were thegns who had proven themselves worthy of command through some bold deed, competence in the field, or long-standing service. Not close enough to real power to lust for much more of it, they were nevertheless wealthy enough to be invested in Torrlond's military success. Their titles and land guaranteed their fervor for their kingdom and king, and their lack of imagination made them trustworthy. Faithful and doughty, they were the backbone of Torrlond's army.

As king and queen walked down the empty central aisle, the captains all bowed low, their faces expressing the eagerness of the rolling drums. On the hall's left side near the front stood the five high priests of the Way and a dozen of their attendant priests, all wearing their white robes. At the front of the right side waited the elegant and mostly grey-haired dukes of Torrlond, the fifteen highest ranking nobles after the king. Earconwald knew them all well. Ambitious men. Dangerous if not properly controlled. *Best to be wary when they're all around.*

However, he had tucked away enough knowledge about their weaknesses and desires to play them off against each other. His spies in all their households kept him well informed, and he allowed their informants to remain in his, sometimes feeding them false information for the purpose of manipulating the dukes. It was an often deadly game over which he enjoyed firm control. None of them were cunning enough to rival him.

Queen Moda mustered a dignified air while King Earconwald beamed a benevolent smile to his loyal captains, the leaders of his force with no rival in all of Eormenlond. In front of an oak chair to the throne's left stood the Supreme Priest Bledla in his plain white robe, stern and austere. *And here before me is the most dangerous one of all,* thought the king. *Someday that blade will try to cut me, but I'll be ready.*

As king and queen neared the throne, the supreme priest and chief advisor bowed and greeted his sovereign with a smile. The king acknowledged Bledla with a slight nod and ascended the seven steps leading to the throne while his queen took her position before an oak chair to its right.

The drums ceased. Earconwald paused a moment with his back to everyone in the hall. It was best to let their adulation grow in intensity by lingering a bit longer. Knowing all eyes were on him, he relished the dramatic tension, and then he turned around to face his subjects. *Now. Let them adore me.*

A wave of ecstasy burst loose as ear-splitting cheers broke out and reverberated throughout the Great Golden Hall of Sigseld. His lips curling upward, the king gazed over the assembled.

They ceased cheering only when Earconwald motioned downward with his palms to still them. "My faithful subjects! My people!"

More loud cheers.

Earconwald grinned until they died down. "Today is a great day for Torrlond!"

Still more shouts erupted and rolled on until he resumed.

"Esteemed priests of the Way, my noble dukes, and my captains, who command the greatest force in Eormenlond!" A loud chorus of yells followed, and it was some time before Earconwald went on.

"You represent nearly half of Torrlond's mighty army, you chosen ones. You've come from North Torrlond." Three dukes bowed and somewhat less than two hundred captains, each wearing the king's ensign with three red stripes over it on their shoulders, broke out in cheers. "From Torrhelm and its surrounding regions," and five dukes bowed while a third of the captains, by far the largest contingent, roared. "From South Torrlond." This time three dukes stooped while their captains cheered. "And from Etinstone and its environs," and at these words, four dukes bowed in acknowledgment as over two hundred captains yelled in support of their king.

But one captain among those of Etinstone — conspicuous by his great height and large, muscular build as well as his light blond hair and beard — only grinned as if he found the whole spectacle amusing. The king remembered that man. *The savage from Grimrik. Strange fellow.*

Earconwald proceeded. "In just ten days, on the heels of midsummer, the Day of Edan, your chosen companies will muster. Then, while your brethren stay behind to defend our great land, we go forth to defend our honor!" A loud hurray from the assembly.

As the voices calmed, Earconwald assumed a frown of grim determination. "For we go, my brothers, to avenge an act of perfidy, an act both shameful and cowardly, an act worthy of only vile animals. In kindness and concern for our fellow men in Eormenlond, we sent priests of the Way, men of purity and the Eternal of Edan, to enlighten those who live in darkness. We are light in the darkness, and Edan calls us to spread His salvation. But often when a man extends a hand to a beast, it bites the helping hand. Thus, the land to our south, a land of darkness, has done. The kingdom of Caergilion, ever a land of violence, is guilty of the blood of three priests of the Way who dedicated their lives to Edan, men of purity and devotion, and Edan's chosen. What's more, our other priests risking their lives in the southern kingdoms are in danger, and the demon worshipers of Caergilion may even intend to crawl across our border and commit such cowardly acts against our people in South Torrlond. We must never allow this. For the three blessed martyrs, Edan must have vengeance!"

Many in the assembly could not contain themselves. Their contorted faces grew red as they shook their fists and shouted. Pleased with himself, Earconwald paused to let his audience rage. *So easy. A stroke of genius, telling them Caergilion might invade. They'll hate them even more, and I will ascend on their zeal. Now, let them think they're virtuous for hating.*

The audience quieted, waiting for the next word. Earconwald continued in a calmer voice, exuding magnanimity and determination. "But it's not only revenge that compels us to visit Edan's wrath upon our neighbors. Edan is mighty, but He is merciful. The supreme priest" — the king looked down at Bledla, who smiled — "has impressed upon us our obligation, as those Edan has chosen, to spread His salvation to all of Eormenlond. This we do not for our own sakes, but for the welfare of those who don't know their own highest good. Caergilion has shown that sending messengers is not enough. There's only one way to tame a beast: Show it who the master is!"

Confident shouts and claps met these words.

"Yes, for our neighbors' good we come to show them the truth, the only truth there is, the only way to salvation. At first, they'll hate us, no doubt. But, when they learn of Edan's mercy, they'll see us as their deliverers. They'll know we made open the path to salvation, the only way to the Kingdom of Edan, the giver of life. That's why your hearts must be the harder, your arms the stronger, your resolve the firmer. You strike for Torrlond, you strike for Edan, and you strike even for the welfare of those whom you will defeat. And the sign of our righteousness will go with us, for you will see Edan manifested through his servants, the priests of the Way, led by the supreme priest, who has no equal in his mastery of the magic arts."

Bledla smiled coolly while many among the captains gazed at him with wide eyes and undisguised awe.

Earconwald continued, "You'll see wonders not witnessed in all the ages of men, sure signs that Edan is with us. Through the vessel of His priests, Edan will show He goes with us in the struggle. And our victory will be the sign of His power. You may thus go with Edan's strength in you, confident He guides your hand and your sword. We fight not just for this world or the kingdoms of men, but for the Kingdom of the Eternal. We cannot fail, and our enemies will join us in the ranks of the Eternal or perish, as all unbelievers must. Yes! Those who refuse Edan's call will perish, but some will see the path of salvation. The scales will fall off their eyes, and they'll bathe in the light that only the Eternal can know. Blessed be the Eternal!"

Nearly one thousand deafening voices shouted back, "Blessed be the Eternal!"

From the top of the seven steps, Earconwald surveyed his captains and dukes and the priests of the Way as they roared and held their fists aloft. Their faces were flushed with zeal, and their angry eyes burned to take revenge, or spread the Way, or do whatever their king told them. The energy was so intense that Earconwald's heartbeat sped as he grew intoxicated with the fervor his words evoked. He checked himself. *Truth and salvation — what drivel. Yes, the Way is useful. Bledla's power helps to win their loyalty. But I mustn't rely on the old fool too much. Fortunately, he needs me more than I need him.*

Few faces in the crowd remained calm. One, however, was the tall, blond captain from Etinstone who had not cheered before. He looked on his comrades' excitement with a frown that expressed detached curiosity, perhaps indifference. Earconwald's gaze rested on him a moment. *You, my barbarian friend, may be the only sane person here other than me.* He laughed inwardly and continued.

"When we march to Caergilion and to victory, remember the three martyrs who gave their lives for the Way. Remember your wives and children, whom you make safe from our enemies by striking ere they strike us. Remember Torrlond, the kingdom that gave birth to you, greatest kingdom in all of Eormenlond. And remember Edan, to whom we consecrate ourselves as we go forward to spread His salvation."

More wild cheers resounded throughout the hall. When they calmed, King Earconwald smiled from ear to ear. "Today, let us remain here in Torrhelm together as brothers."

Addressing the captains, he held out his hands to them in a gesture of welcome. "You will feast here in Sigseld, my royal palace, while I meet with the dukes of our realm and the supreme priest accompanied by his high priests. After you dine, each duke will hold gatherings with his captains. Report to your liege lords, and they will convey your orders. Depart tomorrow for your posts all over Torrlond and muster your soldiers for the appointed day. The time comes soon to defeat our foe. You are the strength of our realm, the hope of the Eternal. Edan grant victory and go with you all."

Shouts rang out and drums throbbed once again as King Earconwald stepped down from his throne and began to walk back down the central aisle through the charged hall. Next to him came Queen Moda, and behind them strode the tall supreme priest, whose five high priests trailed him. Last in the procession came the fifteen stately dukes.

As their leaders passed, the captains on both sides of the hall cheered and bowed low. All was polished pomp and glory, except one moment when Queen Moda stumbled in her haste to keep up with King Earconwald's longer strides. *Idiot. Drunken slattern,* thought the king as he glanced at her. She caught his look, and her eyes widened with sudden apprehension. He kept a perfect smile on his face as he imagined what he would do to her. *She's conspired to ruin my moment. But I'll repay her this evening.*

When they exited the hall and the captains' shouts receded behind them, King Earconwald proceeded along the spacious corridor. Captain Nothelm and two of his guards preceded him. The Supreme Priest Bledla walked beside his king, and Queen Moda drifted behind as they conversed. Following her, the five high priests talked among themselves, while the fifteen dukes discussed their lord's speech in flowery terms just loud enough for those walking before them to hear. Two more of Nothelm's guards brought up the rear.

Earconwald smiled at the dukes' effusive efforts to compliment him. Though he knew how shallow they were, the king expected such blandishments. He pretended to ignore them as he listened to his chief advisor.

Bledla spoke in a soft, deep voice to his sovereign. "A successful speech, Sire. You stirred them in the right direction, and they will pass their fervor on to their soldiers. Yet I could not help but notice a few lacked in zeal. Who was the large fellow, the light haired one among the captains of Etinstone?"

Earconwald cocked an eyebrow. "Ah, you saw him? That was Orvandil, Captain of the Mercenary Company of Etinstone. Some time ago he appeared and volunteered for our army. He'd been wandering around for years after getting into some sort of trouble in Grimrik. He's the one who rescued Duke Edbert's daughter from the Ilarchae raiders a couple years ago. They say he slew more than a dozen of them by himself — one savage killing others. Did it for the reward, of course, but Edbert insisted I make a captain out of him. He's proved able enough. Among the Thjoths he was some sort of nobleman. I imagine he holds to whatever barbaric superstitions his ancestors brought from the Wildlands."

"I see," said the supreme priest. "His lack of zeal is more understandable then. Such a one is no doubt fit to lead a mercenary company. Yet, I wonder, is it wise to suffer such unbelievers to fight amongst us, side by side with the ranks of the Eternal?"

Earconwald smirked. *Stupid old man. Such a soldier is as useful a tool as you are.* "The mercenary companies have always been of service. Their men join out of desperation, and desperate men often make bold fighters. As for Orvandil, you'll not find a better captain in our army, nor a fiercer warrior. He's the sort who'll kill for little or nothing, and he's not likely to care for the show I put on back there. But that doesn't mean he's not useful. In fact, I find him more sensible for it."

"Surely, your Majesty, you're not blind to the devotion your words evoked in your soldiers?" Bledla's voice quieted even more. "Does that hold no importance to you?"

As they passed by several guards, the king smiled. Earconwald was pleased with himself, but he spoke with deliberate ennui. "Yes, they seem quite excited about the whole thing. Nothing rouses the people more than an enemy. You'll find they do anything we ask when there's someone to fear and hate."

"No doubt you're correct, Sire. Yet what we just witnessed in the hall was a thing sublime, I hope you'll allow. Fervor for the truth has no rival in beauty. In fact, your words were so stirring I almost thought you believed them yourself." The tall supreme priest laced his smile with too obvious irony.

Earconwald forced a laugh. "Truth. For all your power, old man, only your fear makes you believe in such a thing as truth. Believing's your job, Bledla. I don't choose to fool myself. As for what we saw in there, I grant there's something sublime about so much hate -- a great leader can do much if he focuses it. All that's required is to keep the people angry and afraid, and that's where your Way is useful." Earconwald looked at the supreme priest to challenge him to reply.

Only a hint of Bledla's anger escaped in a slight widening of his eyes, and his voice lowered even more. "The Way is the path of Edan, the only salvation, and anyone who thinks to use it for his own ends will discover, whether early or late, he is Edan's pawn."

Earconwald stared at his chief advisor. "On this matter, as you're well aware, old teacher, we disagree. My father lived in fear of your religion, cringing within the petty limits it imposed and clawing at any wretched hope for salvation. I don't fear to take what I desire, and no god, whether your Edan or any other, will stop me." The king spoke softly, but he made the threat beneath his pleasant demeanor unmistakable.

Bledla swallowed and stared ahead. "Yes, your Majesty. We have an understanding. If my words failed to please, I spoke with your welfare in mind."

"I'll determine my welfare. That's the end of the matter."

Just then, Nothelm stopped ahead of them and held up his hand. He was staring at one of a pair of guards standing in the hall about a dozen paces ahead of them. "A moment, please, your Majesty," said the captain.

Earconwald nodded at Nothelm, who turned and barked out to the guard, "You there!"

The two guards straightened and looked ahead.

"What's your name?"

One guard turned his puzzled eyes to his comrade, who continued to stand motionless. The still one's helm hid his features, but he seemed composed and focused.

Nothelm approached him. "Your name, man! I don't know you, and I better find out soon how you . . ."

The man drew his sword and sliced it into his companion's unprotected neck in one quick motion. The second guard's eyes widened as a spray of blood erupted from his throat. From his open mouth came a hacking sound. His hand clutched at the wound, and his life spilled out between his fingers. Before he withered to the floor, his killer had turned and sprinted toward the king's party.

Queen Moda screamed. The dukes gasped. Captain Nothelm unsheathed his blade and shouted, "Protect the king!"

Two men jumped in front of Earconwald with naked blades. He jerked back and thrust his hands before his face until he realized the men were Nothelm's guards defending him. He fumbled at the jeweled hilt of the sword at his side, but his hand trembled too much to grasp it.

Steel clanged once, twice, thrice as the intruder met Nothelm with a swift series of slashes. The man danced in a deadly blur. The old earl parried with skill, but this man was quick as a viper, and the fourth thrust found the flesh of Nothelm's thigh.

The captain of the king's guard grunted and held his sword askew when he raised it to parry the next blow. Six of his rushing guards arrived. A din of clashing armor and swords broke the air as they crashed into the man and overwhelmed him, pinning him to the floor. Their blades rose and fell, chopping through mail and helm into flesh in a frenzy of strokes.

"Stop!" yelled Nothelm through gritted teeth. His wounded leg buckled, but he kept his footing. "Don't kill him!"

The crimsoned swords ceased arcing a moment later.

Nothelm limped over and pushed one of his men out of the way.

He shouted at the still body on the floor, "Who are you? Who paid you to attack the king?"

No answer came.

"Damn your bones!"

The six guards who had tackled the would be assassin stood in silence. One of them held his hand to his bleeding side where the swordsman's blade had hacked through his byrny.

Nothelm knelt down and removed the ruined helm to reveal the man's bloody face and red hair. The corpse's light brown eyes stared up blankly. "I don't know this man."

"No doubt a hired assassin," said Bledla, who looked on with his somber face.

"Yes," agreed Nothelm as he turned back to the supreme priest. "But who hired him?"

"I fear he's taken that secret with him," said Bledla.

King Earconwald's hands were still shaking. He wiped his brow, which was clammy with sweat. *Secrets. Who hired him, indeed? Surely not Bledla. On the eve of our conquest, he knows he still needs me. Moda?* He glanced at the queen, whose hand was raised to her mouth. The wide eyes in her pale face still gazed at the corpse as if it might rise up again. *One of my dukes, perhaps? Which would profit most from my death? My pious cousin and heir, Ethelred? How convenient for him if I should die.* The group of dukes murmured and stared with looks of shock and outrage at the carnage. Duke Ethelred exclaimed the loudest, "Who would dare?"

Captain Nothelm approached King Earconwald and went down on his knees. "Your majesty, I'm sorry I failed you. He should never have gotten as far as he did. I submit myself to your mercy and beg your forgiveness." The old captain's wounded leg shook, and he cast his gaze to the floor.

Earconwald only half heard the words as he wracked his mind for the answer: *Who sent the assassin? The wizard Galdor, perhaps. King Malruan of Caergilion? But I can't be certain he was even meant for me.* He stared open-mouthed at the corpse of the attacker until he realized everyone was waiting for him to answer Nothelm. He must compose himself. *I'm not afraid. I am the king.* His heart was still pounding, but he forced a smile and extended his hand to rest on Nothelm's shoulder. Grasping something helped him to still its trembling.

"Rise, Captain Nothelm. There's nothing to forgive. Your faithfulness and diligence have prevented a worse disaster. I only sorrow at your wound and the loss of your soldier." He kept his voice steady and strong. *I must be magnanimous. Show no fear. But which of my enemies or my servants would gain most by my death?*

The old earl rose to his feet with a grimace. "Like as not, your Majesty, there'll be one more dead somewhere: the man who should have been standing where the assassin was. We'll need to conduct a search."

"Of course, captain. But first, I command you to tend to your wound and your soldier's wound. One of Bledla's priests must heal you." *It would have taken someone with easy access to Sigseld to place the assassin here.*

The supreme priest nodded. "The High Priestess Colburga is most skilled at healing."

The large woman stepped away from the other high priests. With her lips pursed in a frown, she looked nearly as severe as Bledla. "It would be best to stop the bleeding soon."

"Thank you," said Nothelm. He faced Earconwald and bowed. "I'll leave lieutenant Hondwin in charge of conducting you and the dukes, your Majesty." One of the soldiers stepped forward and bowed.

"Very well," said the king. "You may go now."

Nothelm hobbled off in the company of his wounded soldier and the High Priestess Colburga.

Earconwald turned to the party of priests and dukes and showed them a broad smile. He held out his hands as if welcoming them. "Well, with the entertainment done, we may begin our feast."

Nervous chuckles grew into hearty, though forced, laughter from the dukes.

"We give thanks to Edan," said Duke Ethelred, "for your safety, your Majesty."

"Aye."

"Well said."

A chorus of affirmative grunts came from the other dukes.

"Thank you, my loyal subjects." *Which of you bastards dared to hire him?*

Earconwald turned toward his queen and smiled. "No doubt, my dear, you wish to retire after the day's excitement." *Would you have dared?*

Moda's wide eyes blinked up at him. "My lord, I'm glad beyond words you're unharmed." Her voice shook.

How he loathed that stupid look on her face. Remembering how she stumbled in the great hall on their way out and feeling his still unvented displeasure over it, he gave the queen a quick smile. "You may return to your chamber."

Moda looked down at the floor. "Thank you, my lord."

"Expect me in the evening." *Our meeting will not be a pleasant one . . . for you, at least.* As the queen ascended the stairs along with two guards, the supreme priest and his four high priests as well as the fifteen dukes bowed to her.

Earconwald turned toward them. "This way, comrades. We meet in my private chambers. By Edan, it's good to see you all." *Which of you?* "Come, Heahmund. Guthfrid, it's been so long, but you look no older. What's your secret — could it be that young wife of yours?" *Who would gain most by it?* The dukes all chuckled, including Guthfrid. They followed their king, and as they passed by the many guards down the hallway, their laughter echoed. *That's right. Laugh. I know what lurks behind your smiles. But I am the king, and I don't fear you.*

13
THE OLD WORKS OF GIANTS

"I hear Dweorg women are as hairy-arsed as the men. Must be like fucking a goat!" Up ahead, Wonred led the laughter that broke out among the mercenary company after his jest. Hooves clopping and mail clinking, they rode ahead of Dayraven, Imharr, Gnorn, and Hlokk, who stayed in the dusty rear as they followed the road to Etinstone.

"Seems he knows all about goat fucking," said Imharr loud enough for the entire company to hear.

Wonred turned around to glare, but the rest of the soldiers laughed and guffawed even louder than before.

"Steady on, lads!" came the lieutenant's voice from the front of the column. "I've a bottle of wine from South Torrlond waiting for me back at the quarters, and the fool who delays that meeting will be emptying latrines for the rest of his miserable days."

In the distance, the great buildings of Etinstone rose into view like an alien growth sprawling all over the plain. Dayraven tried to remember to keep his mouth closed in an attempt not to appear as awestruck and naïve as he felt. Riding behind the rest of the Mercenary Company in accordance with Lieutenant Ludecan's orders, the four companions had spent the journey conversing together and, most of the time, did their best to ignore the rest of the company. As Gnorn had predicted, there had been no opportunity for Dayraven and Imharr to desert the company along the way, with Lieutenant Ludecan or his most trusted men keeping an eye on the pair.

Amidst his anxiety about how he would reach Galdor, Dayraven had at least enjoyed the company of the two Dweorgs. A few of the other soldiers, like old Eafa and a little fellow called Sebbi, had made some attempts at conversation with him and Imharr. Part of Dayraven was even glad he would get a glimpse of one of Torrlond's great cities, though the worry about how he would avoid all the priests in Etinstone gnawed at him. Still, he could not take his eyes off the view unfolding before him. Never had he seen anything like a vast city, never dreamed of anything like it. Gazing ahead at the clusters of towers, spires, and domes soaring upward from the flat, green plain, he mused aloud, "How can folk pile up so much stone? How could any city be larger?"

Gnorn grunted. "Torrhelm is thrice the size. Even Etinstone seems small when you've been to Torrlond's chief city. Grand and cursed, a place like no other is Torrhelm. Yet Etinstone's the elder of the two."

"What do you know of its history?" asked Dayraven.

Gnorn, a loremaster among his people, smiled as his squat horse plodded along. He began with a line now familiar to Dayraven and Imharr: "Dweorgs' memories are long, for we watched the coming of the Andumae and your people. The land we ride in now was not always known as Torrlond. 'Land of Towers' the conquerors named it, such was their awe of the remnants of the kingdom they laid low."

Knowing the ritual, Dayraven smiled and responded, "From a book I learned it was once an Andumaic kingdom called Riodara. But our ancestors came from Ellond and conquered it in the time of King Folcwalda and his son Fullan."

"You have more lore than most of your people," said Gnorn, "but that's only part of the story. Let me tell you the rest." Riding behind their two companions, Imharr and Hlokk both rolled their eyes. Much of the past two days' riding had passed with Gnorn reciting old stories to Dayraven, or Dayraven telling tales of the Mark to the Dweorg.

Imharr groaned. "Another old tale. You two could keep on till your beards grow to the ground and you forget there's a world to live in now."

Hlokk laughed. "Your friend might turn into a Dweorg. No other people is fonder of useless old stories, and no other Dweorg more than my brother."

Ignoring Imharr and Hlokk, Gnorn warmed up to his audience of one. "Almost a thousand years ago, before your people's coming to Eormenlond, the Andumae began their great War of the Four Kingdoms, which lasted over a hundred years. It was in truth between their two mightiest kingdoms, Sildharan and Riodara, but the strife enveloped the others. The war raged on until, in the year 992 by your reckoning, the Red Death came."

"The Red Death? A plague?"

"Aye. No one knew whence it came, but the plague spread everywhere. It afflicted the Dweorgs as well. Our old hill fortresses could not keep out the fever that burned its victims and the terrible boils that covered their bodies with seeping wounds the size of your fist. Half of all people died. The sorcery of the Andumae did not avail them, and our herblore failed us. Villages disappeared forever. Dragons returned to wreak destruction and avenge old quarrels. Between war and plague, much lore disappeared. The kingdoms of the Andumae dwindled. Many believed civilization would succumb, and only wild beasts would roam the land."

"No wonder. Imagine half the people dead. Your kin. Your friends. They must have thought the world would end."

"Yes. But it did not. By the year 1039, the plague ended, but not the war. Then another death came in the form of men. In 1039 the Andumae discovered what they called in their tongue the Ilarchae, the fiery-haired ones."

"The same Ilarchae who live in the Wildlands to the east?"

"Yes," answered Gnorn. His sad eyes narrowed. "But listen, and you'll see. By the time the Andumae found them, the Ilarchae had been massing in northeastern Eormenlond for perhaps a century. Though they at times sent ships to fetch timber from the Ironwood, the Andumae never settled the rough lands beyond the Amlar Mountains. In the Ironwood dwell elves and wolves and ancient beasts, and in the eastern Amlar Mountains the trolls and dragons remain in greatest numbers. At their eastern end lies Slith, greatest of fens, wherein dwell foul aglaks."

"Doesn't sound very hospitable." Mention of elves made Dayraven wince. The presence in his mind murmured and skimmed along the corners of his awareness. He swallowed and waited for Gnorn to continue.

"Nor is it. It would take a hardy folk to settle it, but no one can say the Ilarchae are not stubborn. According to their own stories, they first landed on Enga Isle. From cold regions to the north they came and crossed many small islands over hundreds of years to reach Eormenlond. Tall and light haired, they had not so much craftsmanship as we Dweorgs, nor powerful magic like the Andumae. But they had strength and reckless courage, and that led them over the Great Sea to Eormenlond. Since none among the Ilarchae knew true writing, no one knows for certain why they came."

"That's still true," said Dayraven. "They say the Ilarchae know nothing of books."

Gnorn looked at Dayraven for a moment, and then he smiled. "The Ilarchae in the *Wildlands* know nothing of books, it's true."

Dayraven wondered what the Dweorg meant by that. There was something sad, perhaps a suggestion of irony, in his smile. But he said nothing as Gnorn continued the tale.

"As fate had it, a party of Riodarae foresters sent to the Ironwood to collect timber for ships came upon some of the Ilarchae, who attacked them. Young King Adoager, seeking an advantage to tip the balance in the ongoing war against Sildharan, decided to befriend the fierce newcomers, who were many tribes that fought one another and joined in temporary confederations for war. With promises of land as spoil, the Riodarae lured a large number of the barbarians into their war. This was Adoager's fateful mistake.

"Seeing the stature and boldness of the Ilarchae, Adoager put them at the forefront of his armies. As well as opening up another front against Sildharan to the northeast, Adoager welcomed many Ilarchae into Riodara. Thus, the Ilarchae fought against Sildharan from the northeast and west. For twenty-eight years they aided Adoager, until, in 1067, under their chieftain Hingwar, the Ilarchae took the city of Thulhan — one of the three great cities of Sildharan and long before a city of the Riodarae. This was a prize Adoager had long awaited, but his desire blinded him to the coming danger. Seeing the splendor of the Andumae and remembering promises of land, Hingwar demanded Thulhan come under his rule. This Adoager denied, and his quarrel with Hingwar that followed was the beginning of Riodara's end."

"But Riodara was destroyed by the Ellonders under King Folcwalda," said Dayraven. He knew this since he had read about it in Urd's books, and a few of the remaining shapers still sang tales like the one Urd had sung on the morning he and Imharr left her home, songs that told of Folcwalda of Ellond crossing the Theodamar River and defeating the Riodarae. It was they who settled Torrlond, and some of their descendants had carved out the Mark.

"Aye, that's true enough. And that's as far back as most of your loremasters will go. But the Dweorgs remember. Ever wondered where the Ellonders came from?"

Like most folk in the Mark, Dayraven assumed Ellond had always been there. Mother of kingdoms, they called it. History began with Ellond, and there was no king more ancient than Folcwalda. Before his time, there were only the gods and heroes, the ancestors of the kings. "Well, I thought . . ."

Gnorn smiled again. "Listen, and I'll tell you. Turning on their one time allies, the Ilarchae became foes of the Riodarae. Queen Dara of Sildharan made peace with the Ilarchae. In return, Hingwar yielded the city of Thulhan back to Sildharan. Thanks to King Adoager, the Ilarchae already dwelled in great numbers in Riodara, which they called in their tongue Ellorlond. In later days that name shortened to Ellond, for the Ilarchae slew Adoager and drove the Riodarae over the Theodamar River, and Hingwar claimed the kingdom of Ellond in 1069. Thus ended the War of the Four Kingdoms, which broke the power of the Andumae over these lands. The three kingdoms of the Andumae to the east began a time of peace and rebuilding. For Riodara there would be little of that."

Dayraven took in the truth like someone opening his eyes for the first time. "But that means . . . You're saying . . ."

"Yes." Gnorn nodded with a sad frown on his face. "Now hear it out to the end. Stung by defeat but not ruined, the Riodarae rallied and held the Ilarchae to the Theodamar. There the border remained for some eighty years of skirmishes as the Ilarchae built their city of Ellordor across the river from Minulhan, chief city of the Riodarae. The Ellonders strengthened their numbers with kinfolk, more Ilarchae, from the Wildlands. In the year 1152, they broke loose.

"In that year the Ellonders under King Folcwalda shattered the once beautiful city of Minulhan. Nineteen years later, the second greatest Riodarae city, Derahan, shared that fate. Of Minulhan only ghostly ruins linger. The destruction of Derahan was less complete, and the Ilarchae took it, renaming it Etinstone, or 'Giants' Stone', since they reasoned only giants could pile stone so high. The surviving Riodarae retreated south, where the victorious Ilarchae pushed them over the Marar Mountains to join their distant kin. Yet some stayed to die in their land, becoming slaves of the Ilarchae.

"As you know, Folcwalda founded Torrhelm on the River Ea and gave the kingdom of Ellond to his son Fullan. Torrlond grew in strength over the years, though the ships of the Ilarchae from the Wildlands ceased coming. The tribes of Ilarchae remaining in the east became sundered from their kin who crossed over. Their dealings with the Andumae so changed the Ellonders and Torrlonders that they forgot their kinship with the Ilarchae."

When Gnorn ceased, the clip-clop of their horses and the chirping of birds sounded louder than usual. In the near silence, Dayraven took in one important thing: The Dweorg's tale altered his view of the world and who he believed he was. In the bright sun he gazed ahead at Etinstone and wondered what it was like when it was Derahan and the Riodarae dwelled there. He also pondered the Ilarchae, his apparent ancestors, who destroyed that civilization to replace it with another. Folk in the Mark had little good to say of the barbarians dwelling in the Wildlands.

"If you speak the truth," he said to Gnorn, "then the folk of Ellond, Torrlond, and the Mark are all, like the Thjoths of Grimrik, kin of the Ilarchae. We come from them."

"Yes. To a Dweorg, you're all one and the same. Of course, a few of you have learned some manners," he said with a broad smile.

Dayraven laughed. The soldiers from the mercenary company riding ahead of them would never guess at the truth of their origins. "Many in the Mark and I'd wager here in Torrlond would quarrel over such lore. Yet my heart tells me you speak the truth."

"I advise you not to repeat the tale to the Torrlonders. They'd take it amiss to be called the relatives of savages." Gnorn winked and chuckled.

THE CITY'S OUTER WALL WAS A STONE BARRIER MORE THAN THRICE THE height of a tall man. With his hand on his brow to shield his eyes from the sun, Dayraven beheld the solid structure with its crenellated top. The wooden wall around Kinsford was a mere fence in comparison. Dismounting from their horses, Gnorn and Hlokk led Dayraven and Imharr toward the city's northern gate. Two helmed guards with the king's ensign on their grey kirtles stood on both sides of the gate with long spears in their hands and swords at their sides. Other guards peered down from atop the wall, looking bored as people streamed in both directions beneath them. Lieutenant Ludecan waited before the gate holding his horse's rein. All the other soldiers of the mercenary company had disappeared within.

"Alright, you four. The Day of Edan is tomorrow, so spend it as you like." The officer pointed at Dayraven and Imharr. "But I expect you two to present yourselves to me in our compound with your proper weapons and gear before evening's end. Understood?"

"We'll find their gear right away, my lord," said Gnorn.

"Good. Remember: before evening's end." Ludecan looked Gnorn in the eyes and gave a grim smile. "The first place I'll look for any of you that goes missing is among *your* kin." The threat of what would happen if they failed to show up was clear in the officer's tone, and at that moment Dayraven knew he would be marching out of Etinstone with the mercenary company. He would not repay Gnorn and Hlokk by risking harm to their folk. A chance to leave would come later, when he and Imharr could desert without implicating the Dweorgs.

"Yes, my lord." Gnorn nodded his head in a slight bow.

"Until then." Lieutenant Ludecan turned his back on them, and the crowd swallowed him along with his horse.

Gnorn motioned with his head for Dayraven and Imharr to follow. The way into Etinstone teemed with traffic going and coming: merchants carrying their wares, tradesmen clanking with their tools, farmers carting produce to market, travelers seeking shelter, soldiers being idle, thralls running errands, citizens milling about, horses waiting in the competition for space, dogs weaving their way underfoot, children playing and crying, and beggars of every age looking for a sympathetic face in the massive huddle crowding together.

It was a rough, chaotic sea of human and animal flesh. Passersby jostled Dayraven without an apology or a hello. He might have objected to some of the elbows, but he was busy staring at the volume of life and the scale of the tall buildings — some of stone, some of brick, some of wood — that hemmed them in and overshadowed them. Just one busy street would have swallowed all of Kinsford. At the same time, the press of the multitudes was stifling.

Even as they crushed together, people seemed oblivious to one another, all going about their own business. Merchants hawked their wares. Shouts like a fight broke out somewhere. Animals neighed and brayed. And the hum of voices drowned out even a neighbor's words. Worst was the stench of the place. From a row of butcher shops emanated the odor of decaying flesh. Filth festered in the open drainage ways at the sides of the cobbled streets. It was nigh impossible to avoid the horse and dog droppings. And the bodies all around stank of sweat and ale. There was no plan to it, no sense of what held it all together. Yet the city dwellers with their blank faces knew how to negotiate the chaos they lived in.

"Such a place would soon drive me mad, though I'm glad for a sight of it," shouted Dayraven to Imharr.

Gnorn, who led his horse ahead of them, turned around and laughed. "Splendor and squalor, lad! Splendor and squalor!"

They left the press when they proceeded down a narrow side street. Dayraven sighed. He and Imharr could now walk together as they led Rudumanu and Hraedflyht, and Gnorn and Hlokk led their own stocky horses before them. Taverns lined the street, and shadowed alleys ran between them.

When they walked by one such alley, Dayraven noticed at its entrance a young, pretty woman clad in a loose green frock with a low neckline. Her tussled brown hair curled in tendrils past her white neck, and she wore many gaudy bracelets. She leered at Dayraven. Finding it difficult to look away, he smiled. To his surprise, she pursed her lips in a kiss. His cheeks flushed as he turned away and kept walking.

Imharr glanced back and chuckled. "People here seem very friendly."

Gnorn turned around. "For the right amount of silver. But you'd best be careful. Some pleasures cost more than your wealth." The Dweorg winked.

Dayraven did not like to admit it, but the woman put him in mind of Ebba. He wanted to believe his love for her was about more than flesh. He cared for Ebba and wanted her happiness, but he also longed to kiss her again, to hold her until nothing else mattered. Wondering how she fared back in Kinsford, he hung his head and looked down at the cobbled street.

He had left so many dreams behind. *They're dead. And who am I without them?* A mass of apprehensions and yearnings that changed with his surroundings, he and all his emotions would someday fade into the world's pulse. What was one small mote of awareness like him?

Such thoughts stemmed from his encounter with the elf with its promise of oblivion. The steady hiss in his mind sharpened, and the elf-shard quickened as its shadow darkened his vision and its greed grew palpable. He could see those eyes again, and the temptation to slip into them grew until he felt that condition of strange perception, the elf-state. He slammed a door in his mind to those thoughts.

It worked. To his surprise, the ordinary world returned with the vivid sights, smells, and sounds of Etinstone. He could smother the elf-state. Even without training, it was possible to control the thing. Right there in the street, a big smile crossed his face. For the moment the foreign presence slept again, a bare hiss. Someday, with Galdor's help, he would learn to wield it, and the sliver of the elf lodged in his mind would no longer torment him. Once again he thought of finding Imharr's sister and then risking a return to the Mark and to Kinsford to ask Ebba to wed him, just as his father returned to his Eldelith. *I'll reclaim something of my life.*

Emerging from the side street, they entered the flow of another busy thoroughfare, which crowded out Dayraven's daydream of Ebba as he fought to stay behind Hlokk. But the street soon widened into a square, allowing him to lead his horse beside Imharr again. On the outskirts of the cobbled square, mongers ranged their various carts of produce. At the center stood a large monument supporting a life-sized bronze sculpture of a king atop a horse. The crowned and bearded king held his sword aloft, eyes set in determination as he looked back and called upon his followers. His helm and armor bespoke an earlier age to Dayraven's imagination, while his steed reared on its hind legs, its mane flowing onto its muscled neck. A throng of men and women gathered around the monument, listening to a man shout from steps leading up from its base.

Gnorn stopped a moment, and the four listened from the outskirts of the crowd. The young man shouting appeared not much older than Dayraven, and he wore the white robe of the priests of the Way. Behind his brown beard, the man's face was red, and his contagious anger flowed along with his message out to the crowd.

Dayraven sensed the presence of the gift in the man. It was akin to knowing that someone just outside the periphery of his vision was staring at him, but the sensation emanated from the priest. Now attuned to it, he knew this priest was much less powerful than Urd, for the feeling was far weaker than it was with her. The priest spoke with such a rush of zeal and fury that spittle flew from his mouth as his words tumbled out. Hoping the priest did not sense him but fascinated by the display at the same time, Dayraven crossed his arms before him and stood at a distance as the man delivered his diatribe.

"Yes, my brethren. It's the only path before us now. Before the serpent strikes again, you must *cut* off its head!" He slashed with one hand and with the other grasped an imaginary serpent that he held aloft. "In our day it comes to a fight between good and evil, and good will prevail. War is the only honorable path, and by sacrificing your sons, your labor, and your lives, you lay the path to your salvation. Yes! Edan will take your sacrifice unto Himself, and He'll open the way to salvation when you dwell in the Kingdom of the Eternal. The serpents of Caergilion will never stand, for Edan is with us. We'll stamp out the impure unbelievers, and they'll be dust beneath our feet. Yes, the impure will wallow in their vice. The impure will fall away when we defeat them. The impure will inherit darkness and death, while the followers of Edan will forever live in His light!"

While the priest thundered his frenzied message, men and women shouted, "Blessed be the Eternal!" The charged atmosphere was both exciting and frightening, and the small crowd seemed ready to run off and conquer Caergilion itself. Dayraven had heard enough. Though the man took no notice of him from that distance, he did not want to risk coming under the notice of this priest. He nodded to Gnorn to signal they should move on.

Once out of earshot of the shouting at the monument, Imharr said, "He doesn't seem to like the impure. I wonder what the good priest would think of our lady in the green dress back in the alley?"

Hlokk snorted. "He's no doubt her most loyal patron. Ha!"

As interested in the monument as the speech, Dayraven asked Gnorn, "What king is the statue back there?"

"That, my lad, is the first King Earconwald, who reigned nigh three hundred years ago. In his day your kingdom of the Mark gained its freedom in the year 1412 by your reckoning. 'Twas also the time of Aldmund, the wizard and prophet who first proclaimed the Way. Aldmund played a key role in convincing King Earconwald to grant your ancestors their . . ."

"Pray, dear brother," said Hlokk, "it seems our friends must stay with the mercenary company for the time being, which means we must equip them. If you begin another of your tales now, we'll never make it in time for our meeting with the good lieutenant this evening. In fact, we'll miss the entire war while you two discuss the deeds of men whose bones have long lain in the earth."

"Hmmm," said Gnorn. "We'll continue our discussion when less appreciative ears are absent, lad. But my brother's right. We'd better find you two the required gear. You have a fine sword, of old Dweorg make." He nodded with knowing approval at Sweothol poking out of Dayraven's cloak. "But Imharr lacks one as yet, and you both need byrnies and helms. Though you stand before two of the finest weapon-smiths ever to inhabit this city, unfortunately, Hlokk and I sold or gave away everything except what we now wear. But we have a couple friends in the trade who might give you a deal. You have some silver with you?"

Dayraven and Imharr looked at one another. They were running low on silver.

Gnorn raised one eyebrow and scratched his broad nose. "Well, you do have these horses to trade, and that'll get you somewhere, I suppose."

Dayraven stared at Rudumanu. He stroked her cheek, and she answered with a flicker of her eyes. He was not sure he could leave her with a stranger in this city.

Gnorn looked at him and nodded. "Don't worry, lad. She'll be safer here, and I'll not let you trade her to the wrong sort. Besides, you'll have to leave her somewhere if you're departing the city with us. We in the mercenary company are foot soldiers in war time. We'll be marching and leaving the cavalry to our betters." He patted his horse's nose and broke out in a broad smile. "Anyway, Dweorgs wouldn't be much use in combat on the stubby little fellows we ride. Ha!"

Gnorn and Hlokk led Dayraven and Imharr down a few small streets to the quiet quarter of Etinstone where the Dweorgs clustered. After the bustle, it was almost too quiet. No children played. Far fewer people milled about, and most who shared the street with them were bearded Dweorg men, all stout and under five feet tall. The Dweorgs who met Gnorn and Hlokk nodded or took off their hats by way of greeting. A few curious gazes lingered on Dayraven and Imharr.

More peaceful than the rest of the city, the Dweorg quarter was also cleaner. The small, square dwellings of grey stone were indistinct from one another, but their inhabitants cultivated an abundance of colorful flowers, herbs, and vines on the windowsills and exteriors of their homes. The greenery gave the place a welcoming feel, softening the harshness that grated on Dayraven's nerves elsewhere in the city. Among the modest but tidy rows of stone houses nestled more than two score soot covered shops of goldsmiths, silversmiths, and weaponsmiths. Over the entrances hung large signs advertising their trades, and from their louvers thin smoke curled out while hammers tapped on metal within.

Beneath a sign depicting a hammer and tongs, the four travelers entered the open doorway of one noisy shop. Stiflingly hot inside, the shop brimmed with piles of weapons and arms in various stages of completion — swords, axes, daggers, spearheads, shields, byrnies, and the like. Metal filings and twisted pieces of iron covered the floors and shelves, and the heavy scent of charcoal drifted in the room despite the open door and the louver above the raised stone forge. A pile of charcoal occupied one whole corner of the shop. On the other side, hot coals glowed in the duck's nest of the four-foot long forge, near which rested a bellows made of leather and wood and a barrel of dirty water.

To the left of the barrel stood a Dweorg the height of Gnorn and about the same age with dark brown hair and a greying beard. Sweat dripped from his nose as he clanged away with a fat hammer at a piece of red-hot flattened iron he held with tongs over his anvil. Though he faced the door, he did not appear to notice the newcomers.

"Greetings, Bur!" shouted Gnorn.

The Dweorg ceased banging, dipping the heated metal in the barrel of water with a hiss and a puff of steam. The tongs and now dark piece of iron he put aside on a shelf behind him. He wiped his sooty brow with a cloth that he tucked back into a pocket of his thick leather apron. Putting one broad hand on his hip, he scowled at the four companions. The other hand still gripped the hammer as if he meant to use it to chase away intruders. His large brown eyes locked onto Gnorn and Hlokk. "Still intent on your madness, then?"

Gnorn winked at Dayraven and Imharr. "Bur runs what used to be the second best weaponsmithy in all of Torrlond. Now it's the best." Turning to Bur, he continued, "These are friends who have joined us in the mercenary company. May I present Imharr and Dayraven, and I might add the latter promises to become a fine loremaster with the right sort of training."

Bur frowned at Gnorn and did not bother to look at Dayraven and Imharr as he tugged on his thick beard. "He promises to become dead along with you two oafs if he's joined the mercenary company."

"Glad we caught you in a good mood," said Gnorn, baring his teeth in a smile.

Dayraven wondered what Bur was like in a bad mood.

The weaponsmith continued to scowl. "So you came here to impress me with your new friends?"

"Not quite. You see, we met Imharr and Dayraven under some interesting circumstances. Brigands were chasing us on the road when our two friends here came to help us."

"Should've left you to the brigands."

"Ha!" Gnorn laughed. "I knew you'd see my point."

"No, I don't."

"Ah, well. As I mentioned before, our two friends wish to join us in the mercenary company. Imharr, however, has need of a good blade, and so I of course thought of you."

"Of course. Looks like they both need a byrny, a helm, and a shield as well."

"I see your powers of observation are as strong as ever."

"And since you thought of *me*, your friends mostlike don't have enough silver to pay for said sword, byrnies, helms, and shields."

"Exactly right again."

Bur crossed his arms and glared at Gnorn, saying nothing. Dayraven had a feeling the negotiations were not going well.

Gnorn spoke again. "However, they do have two fine mares to trade, and Hlokk and I will also throw in our own steeds to sweeten the bargain."

The Dweorg's sudden generous gesture surprised Dayraven, but Bur seemed unimpressed.

"Bargain? More like robbery. Horseflesh for *my* work? I should toss you out on your ears. Better yet, knock some sense into your head." Bur hit the open palm of his thick hand with the hammer.

Hlokk and Gnorn both laughed and slapped their knees. Dayraven and Imharr looked at each other, and Dayraven wondered if he ought to laugh too. "We do have a little silver," he offered.

Bur ignored him. The weaponsmith threw his hammer down on a shelf and turned his broad back to the four friends. Metal clanged as he rummaged through some rods and scraps of things on his shelf, muttering the whole time. "*Horses* for a Dweorg-wrought blade. Most-like starved old nags to boot. So you want to rob me *and* saddle me with your beasts. Your own business if you want to go off and get yourselves killed. Why drag me into it, eh? Hard enough as it is."

Gnorn smiled and winked again at Dayraven and Imharr.

Bur was vigorously polishing something with a rag. When he turned around again, in his hands he held a sword. "Here's something I knocked off a few days ago. The fine fellow who ordered it had the cheek to offer half of what we agreed, so I told him to get out before I stuffed it up his arse and cut him a bigger hole."

"Ha!" Hlokk bellowed in laughter. Gnorn chuckled.

Bur continued to scowl. "Not my best work since the fool wanted it done fast. Nothing fancy, mind you, but might be it'll do for what you're wanting."

Dayraven stared at the blade the Dweorg held out. He remembered to breathe. He glanced at Imharr, whose eyes were wide. The keen edges of the Dweorg-wrought sword gleamed, and the steel seemed to quicken with life as the wavy patterns forged into it caught the light in the smithy.

It was worth a fortune.

Gnorn grunted. "Hmmm. It'll do."

Bur held it toward Imharr. "Well, try it out. See how it feels."

Imharr reached for the simple but sturdy hilt. His hand grasped it, and as he held up the sword, the red glow of the forge danced on its surface.

"Give it swing," said Hlokk.

Imharr stepped back and sliced the air thrice. His eyes never left the blade.

"How's the balance?" asked Gnorn.

"It's perfect."

Gnorn nodded. "One more thing: needs a name."

Imharr kept gazing at the sword, and his jaw clenched as his face hardened. "Wreaker."

"A good name," said Hlokk.

DAYRAVEN SAID A DIFFICULT GOODBYE TO RUDUMANU AFTER HE helped Bur lead the horses to his stable behind the shop. He patted her nose and held his cheek to hers. "Farewell, old girl. You've been faithful many years. I'll miss you."

The red mare neighed once.

For the first time, Bur looked at Dayraven. "Don't worry, lad. I'll take care of her for Gnorn's sake. He's the best of us. Should you outlive him and Hlokk, don't burn their bodies after the old manner of your folk or bury them lying down as the Torrlonders do, but bury them sitting up in a mound, and be sure they face north."

Dayraven nodded, feeling a slight pang of guilt that, if things went as he planned, he would not be around to attend to his new friends if they should die in battle.

"And while they live," continued the weaponsmith, "be true to them. Heed my counsel, lad: Stay by them. You'll not find more loyal friends than Dweorgs, and none more so than those two brothers."

Dayraven tried to swallow the sense of betrayal arising in him. "I'll do my best." He nodded, in part to conceal the ill taste of the lie in his mouth.

Bur frowned and nodded in return, and then the two left the stable.

Dayraven and Imharr put on their new byrnies over their kirtles. Smelling of oil, iron, and leather, the linked mail was a heavy but welcome weight on Dayraven's shoulders, and the supple lining inside it made it comfortable but warm. He wondered how much it would slow his movement. It would take some getting used to, along with the helm pressing into his forehead and obstructing his vision with its nose guard. They put on their cloaks, strapped on their new linden shields with iron bosses, and left Bur's shop. The four companions hastened towards Etinstone's center in the early evening.

"If we hurry," said Gnorn, "after we report to Lieutenant Ludecan at the company's compound, we'll make it back to a friend's home in time for a good meal before bed."

Without the horses, they walked faster through the city, though they had to carry their own packs. Dayraven sighed as he thought about Rudumanu, but then he gazed down at himself. For the first time ever, he wore a byrny and helm and carried a shield, all of Dweorg-make. With Sweothol to complete his gear, he reckoned he looked the part of a warrior. He glanced at Imharr, who appeared a hero of old, and his friend turned his way at the same time. Imharr grinned at him, and, in spite of all his worries, he could not help returning it.

WITH THE LINKS OF THEIR BYRNIES CLINKING, DAYRAVEN AND Imharr paced behind Gnorn and Hlokk when they entered the courtyard housing the mercenary company. A broken gate leaned on the wall of the compound since it was attached only by one rusted and bent hinge. Large tufts of grass poked through the cracked cobblestones, many of which had disintegrated into gravel. Under a dead tree with various names and crudities carved in it, a dozen soldiers wearing the king's ensign on their worn, grey kirtles sat in a group throwing dice. Shouts of triumph or frustration came each time the dice rattled and rolled on the stones. A few other soldiers milled about the courtyard, at the far end of which was a large, rectangular building with a yellowed, stucco exterior. The stucco was so old and decayed that the stones beneath it showed in many places. Many tiles had fallen off the slate roof, while vulgar markings and semi-literate messages covered the crumbling walls.

"Welcome to the home of the esteemed Mercenary Company of Etinstone," said Gnorn. "It could do with a little tidying."

As the four companions passed the tree, the disheveled soldiers glared at them. "Fuckin' Dweorgs," muttered someone. Someone else spat, then a cup rattled with dice, and the soldiers turned their attention back to their gambling.

When they neared the building, the door burst open and slammed against the exterior wall. A large soldier emerged from it and stomped toward them, glowering ahead and taking no notice of them. The friends parted to give him room to walk between them. As he passed, he veered toward Dayraven and elbowed him, knocking him back a couple paces.

"Watch where you're goin', boy." The man wore a patch over one eye and had only a few grey teeth dangling in his mouth beneath his enflamed nose. He stank of ale and stale piss, and behind his matted beard he snarled as he glared at Dayraven with his one eye.

Dayraven's face flushed hot, and some wrathful instinct he had no time to stifle made him thrust his chest forward as he looked up into the man's face. Part of him wanted to ignore the insult, but it was too late. He forced a quick smile. "I have no quarrel with you. But it was you who fell into me." The words tumbled out before he had time to think about them. Had they been the right ones?

The man reached at his side and, after missing the hilt twice, unsheathed his large sword. "Sayin' I'm drunk? I'll gut you, boy."

Dayraven wondered if he had made a mistake, but now it was look like a coward or stand his ground. Excited shouts came from the gamblers under the tree, and they rushed over. More witnesses. He could not shame himself now.

"Fight!"

"Wigstan's at it again!"

"Come on!"

"Five silver pieces on Wigstan! Any takers?"

A crowd of some twenty men surrounded the four friends and the big soldier, many of them shouting to encourage the latter. "Come on, Wigstan! Take him out!" Dayraven recognized a few of them from the Crossroads Inn and the march to Etinstone.

"Let's go, Dayraven," said Gnorn. "Plenty of fighting to come."

"Fight me, boy!" screamed Wigstan as his spittle flew on Dayraven. "'Less you wanna hide behind your Dweorg-nanny."

"Pay him no mind, Day," said Imharr.

"Who's this pretty boy?" Wigstan pointed his sword at Imharr. "Your wetnurse?"

Dayraven gritted his teeth and lowered his eyebrows. He wondered what his father would have done in his place. In spite of his status as a warrior, Edgil was always restrained and slow to anger. Taking a deep breath, he took his hand off his sword hilt, not even realizing he had put it there in the first place. But he did not want to appear afraid, so he said, "I'll not fight a drunk."

"Coward!" The flat of Wigstan's sword smacked Dayraven's chest.

His hand moved ahead of his thoughts. Sweothol was out and pointed at the big man. He was surprised he was not shaking.

"Day," said Imharr.

Without looking back at his friend, Dayraven said, "I'll handle him." There was ice in his voice, and he focused the way his father had taught him.

"Nice sword, boy. I'll take it after I kill you."

"Come take it if you can. Drunk."

Wigstan roared and clove the air with his sword. But the big man was clumsy and befuddled with drink, and Dayraven dodged aside as his attacker lurched by.

The crowd cheered and widened the circle to give the fighters room. Dayraven tried to ignore his thumping heart as he readied himself for the next assault. His body was stiff and tense, and the byrny slowed him. What if the sword's hilt slipped in his sweaty hand? His father's voice echoed in his mind: *Observe your opponent. Look for his weaknesses and use them.* That would not be hard in this case. This man was drunk and ungainly. If he could conquer his fear, he would win.

Wigstan charged and slashed, but this time the big man was so unbalanced that Dayraven hardly even needed to move to avoid him. His first opportunity came, and he seized it by kicking at the drunkard's foot as he reeled past.

Wigstan's arms flailed as he crashed to the ground with a grunt. His sword clanged on the stones several feet away, and Dayraven hurried to his sprawled form in a rush of excitement. When the big man raised himself on his hands and knees and looked up, Dayraven held Sweothol's tip an inch from his one good eye. It was over. It had to be over.

"Do you yield?"

Wigstan growled and roared.

"Yield, or you'll be needing another eye patch." Those were clever words. He had not even thought about them before they came out, but he supposed they were good for a time like this.

The big man spat. "I yield."

The crowd laughed and murmured their approval, and Dayraven grinned. Trying not to shake, he looked for Imharr and smiled when he saw his friend.

Imharr returned the smile and nodded, but then his eyes widened and mouth gaped open. "Look out, Day!"

Dayraven spun around. A blur of movement. The world flashed white and then red, and the rough stone of the courtyard slammed into his body. Sweothol rang on the ground.

When he shook his head and focused, his nose throbbed. Wetness trickled onto his upper lip. He looked around.

Wigstan was reaching for Sweothol. But another blade and two axes appeared in front of the big man, whose hand froze.

"Back off, or I'll shove this steel down your vile throat," said Imharr.

Wigstan gazed at Imharr and at Gnorn and Hlokk, who handled their axes. He rose to his full height, spat, and stalked toward his sword, wavering as he went. After he bent down and picked up his big weapon, he looked back at Imharr and pointed the blade at him. "Watch your back, wetnurse." He staggered toward the gate and left the courtyard.

Those who had gathered to watch the fight exchanged coins and returned to their affairs, some still laughing and joking. The gamblers reassembled under the tree and began throwing dice again as if nothing had happened.

Imharr sheathed Wreaker and picked up Sweothol. Dayraven rose as his friend approached, and though his nose ached and bled, he smiled. "Some of our comrades seem the rough sort, don't they?"

"Well done, Dayraven," said Gnorn.

Imharr held Sweothol toward Dayraven. "Here."

Dayraven grasped his sword and sheathed it in his baldric, and then he noticed his friend was still looking at him.

Imharr smiled. "Your father would be proud. But next time don't turn your back."

"I won't forget that lesson anytime soon. At least not until my nose stops bleeding."

Gnorn held out a handkerchief. "Stick this on your face. Now that you look a little prettier, we'd better show you two to Lieutenant Ludecan. This way."

They entered the dilapidated building and ascended a flight of creaky stairs. At the top, they came to a closed door with two armed guards posted by it. One asked their business.

Gnorn answered, "Our companions are reporting to the lieutenant."

The guard knocked on the door, and from within came the gruff voice of Ludecan, who did not hide his annoyance. "Enter." The guard opened the door.

Inside the chamber, pieces of the walls and ceiling lay on the floor. Amidst the rubble sat Ludecan, who had removed his crested helm to reveal curly hair the same color as his beard: brown with plenty of grey. He still wore his scaled corselet for soldiers of higher rank. On the crude table before him sat an opened bottle of wine, his helm, a candle, a bottle of ink, and several pieces of parchment, which he now looked up from. He gazed at the four companions with his bright blue eyes.

"Ah, you're here." He glanced at Dayraven, who still held the handkerchief to his face. "What happened to your nose?"

"A fellow named Wigstan punched it after I beat him in a swordfight, my lord. He yielded, and I looked away."

"That was fucking stupid."

"I know."

"I'm quite familiar with Wigstan's charms. He was here just before you, in fact. Didn't leave in the best of moods since I didn't give him what he wanted. You'd best look out for him if he remembers you when he's sober. He's much more dangerous then."

"Thank you, my lord."

"Now, show me your blades."

Dayraven and Imharr unsheathed their weapons and presented them hilt forward.

"Impressive. Dweorg-wrought, of course. Put them away." They obeyed, and he continued, "Some items of business. I've enrolled your names on this parchment, but I'm obliged to ask you some questions."

He turned to Imharr. "You look like a southerner. How do I know you're not a spy from Caergilion?"

"My lord," said Imharr, "I was born in Adanon, which is a fair enough reason to not mind joining you against Caergilion."

"Why'd you leave Adanon?"

"The Caergilese killed my family and enslaved me when I was six. Most of my life I lived in the Mark."

Dayraven nodded at how convincing it all sounded. Of course, Imharr had not needed to lie about any of it.

"Yes," replied Ludecan, "and you picked up their wretched accent as well. That's good enough for me." He now turned to Dayraven. "You've both sworn the oath already. Now, I must ask you man to man: Do you intend to remain loyal to this company and obey your superiors in it?"

"Yes, my lord," answered the two. Lying even to Ludecan did not feel right to Dayraven, but he forced out the words.

"Good. Dweorg, Markman, southerner: I don't give a shit what you are, as long as you're loyal and fight well."

The lieutenant bent down under the table and from a pile picked up two pieces of woven cloth, which he flung at Dayraven and Imharr. Dayraven caught and looked at his. It was a woven image of the ensign of the king: snow-capped silver mountain with a gold crown overhead on a blue background.

"You'll need those," said Ludecan. "Get yourselves grey kirtles to go over your byrnies and sew your ensigns onto the left sleeve at the shoulder. Your first pay comes a fortnight after we leave the city. We muster in two days, at which point you report to the courtyard outside by mid-day. Until then, you're on leave. If you fail to show, as I've said, either you or someone dear to you will pay." He glanced at Gnorn. "In the meantime, you can stay here in our quarters if you wish."

"We have other accommodations in the city, my lord," said Gnorn.

"Then I'd stay there if I were you. Goodbye." Ludecan looked down at his parchments and started to write something with his quill.

The four companions turned to leave, but the lieutenant caught their attention with a last word. "When we muster, you'll meet the captain." He grinned as he looked at Gnorn and Hlokk. "You fellows ought to enjoy that."

Since he looked down at his parchments once again and resumed writing, the four companions took that as their dismissal and departed. After they left the building, Imharr asked Hlokk, "What do you suppose he meant by his last remark about the captain?"

Hlokk shrugged. "Don't know. Never met him. We heard he was called to Torrhelm when we joined less than a week ago. The next day, we rode for the crossroads to deal with the brigands. I imagine we'll find out in two days."

As the four companions left the mercenary company's compound, Dayraven still held the handkerchief to his bleeding nose. Beneath it, though, he was smiling. The throbbing pain in his nose meant little. The fight against the drunk Wigstan was nothing to boast of, but he had not shamed himself. Other than foolishly turning away from his opponent too soon like a green boy, he had done well.

But what pleased him most was that he had not felt the coming of the elf-state the whole time. The shard embedded in his mind had not pierced him or even stirred. He had remained himself, not ripped from his body and detached in the midst of crisis like some ethereal observer. There was no sign of slipping away at all, even with the swirling emotions. He had not sensed anyone else's thoughts or feelings.

The uncomfortable sensation that a piece of the elf lurked in his mind was still there, of course. Its hush formed a constant backdrop to his thoughts. But he had willed it to remain asleep, and it had obeyed. He could control it. He could contain it. This meant everything: With help from Galdor, he could be the man he wanted to be.

The trick would be for him and Imharr to find the right moment to escape after they left Etinstone. Though guilt prodded him at the idea of abandoning Gnorn and Hlokk, and though his brief altercation with Wigstan had him feeling almost like he could make it as a soldier, he knew he needed to get to the wizard Galdor. Everything depended on that. He pondered how it might happen all the way to the Dweorg quarter, where Gnorn and Hlokk led them to stay until the Mercenary Company would muster in two days.

14
THE ETERNAL WORSHIP

The Day of Edan. Summer solstice. The day before Torrlond's army sets out to make ready the coming of the Kingdom of the Eternal. Salvation. Everlasting peace. Bledla took a deep breath. *I am ready.*

Within the mighty Temple of the Way, the Supreme Priest Bledla waited for the moment when Edan would stir him to begin the annual ritual. He gazed down at the circular slab of black marble he stood upon, taking in the large bronze runes embedded in it, which stated: 'Here lies Aldmund, Prophet of Edan, until the coming of the Kingdom of the Eternal.'

Bledla lifted his eyes. In front of him, a sturdy oak stand held a large dark red book with gilded corners, his personal copy of The Book of Aldmund. On both sides of him a four-foot wide iron brazier rested on three legs. Hot coals glowed in the braziers, supplying additional light to what streamed through the small windows lining the dome's base. At the peak of the dome's ribbed structure, some four hundred feet above where Bledla stood, a glass-covered, round window set in a framework of stone let a column of sunlight shine down upon him.

He felt the presence of the five high priests ranged in a row behind him on the large, circular tomb. The rest of the priests and noblemen gathered below on the checkered marble floor, including King Earconwald and the five dukes whose seats lay nearest Torrhelm, all decked out in their finest. With them stood ninety-four nobles and captains, including Nothelm, Captain of the King's Guard, who kept an alert eye on everything around him. Behind and around them thronged three hundred priests in their white robes, and on the other side of the temple, facing Bledla's back, six hundred apprentices in their yellow robes waited.

All the congregants fit within the temple's inner circle, which large marble columns ringed in. On each polished black column a torch sputtered. The curved outer walls of the four apses behind the columns also held sconces with torches.

Solemn and still it was. All waited for the ritual to begin. From the large, round window above, the direct ray of the sun's light bathed Bledla, shadowing his deep-set eyes and gleaming on his white hair, beard, and robe. Motes of dust danced and spiraled around him. Noon on the Day of Edan. Bledla nearly gasped when the ecstasy of Edan's spirit entered him. *It is time.* Perfect silence reigned as the supreme priest raised his arms aloft. All within the temple fixed their eyes on him.

They cried in unison, "Blessed be the Eternal!"

Bledla looked above into the light. While the rest of the congregants followed his gaze, the supreme priest uttered to his god, "In the beginning, there was only You, Edan. You made the elements, and from them You created the heavenly bodies and the world. In Your infinite wisdom You inhabited it with life, over which You set men to rule. These were the first men, the forebears of all: Orm and Angra, Regnor and Hruga, Bolthar and Glora, Syn and Logan, Halmar and Dyna, and Sithfar the lonely. These were the firstborn, and we are their children. In after ages, demons of the deep took their form and commanded reverence from our ancestors, who worshipped foul spirits in ignorance. But only those who worship You as Your true children obtain Your salvation. Only those are the Eternal. Only those inherit Your kingdom, the Kingdom of Edan."

"Blessed be the Eternal!" rang throughout the temple.

"On this sacred day," Bledla resumed, "the Day of Edan, the day of light set apart for You, we call upon You, mighty one, and ask You to impart Your strength, so we may go forth as Your chosen ones to spread Your salvation. We call upon You and the elements You wrought in the beginning and from which You created all. In calling upon these elements we unite ourselves to You, so Your power may dwell in us."

"Blessed be the Eternal!" echoed to the top of the dome and filled the curves of the temple.

Passion lit Bledla's bright eyes. "Oh, mighty creator. The life that courses through us unites us with You. We, the Eternal, are of one blood. Blood transformed by Your power and free of impurity. Blood of Your true children. Blood that is the sign of Your salvation. All others shall fall away."

"Blessed be the Eternal!" rang out yet again.

"Blessed be the Eternal," repeated the supreme priest, "And the Kingdom of Edan."

When Bledla finished, the High Priests Morcar and Joruman stepped forward. Morcar took up the Book of Aldmund while Joruman moved the oak stand behind the other high priests. Morcar lowered the tome back on the stand, after which the High Priests Arna and Heremod came forward. The older, grey-bearded high priest stood on Bledla's right with a bronze bowl, while the towering, red-haired one stood on the left holding a black handled knife with curved blade.

Bledla raised his arms and closed his eyes. At this signal, the five high priests chanted, "Edan rakhydon toronai," and the second time they sang it, all the priests and apprentices joined in.

The assembly repeated the chant again and again, the males singing the melody in low voices and the females, about one fifth of those present, accompanying in high-pitched harmony. The echoes of the rhythmic chant snaked between the columns and filled the air to the top of the dome. Earconwald and his dukes looked on with dignified countenances, whereas many of the captains and members of the nobility gazed in wide-eyed wonder.

While the assembly repeated its slow chant, the supreme priest of the Way began to sing in the First Tongue, intoning the eldest of the songs of origin:

Agadatha ar hurolin tirion im rathai,
Ingkhatha in varubin dhanion an ghonai!
Hurishway ni danudon brinkhala targon,
Nonghalay di valanon unghuisha bardon!

At once, fire roared up from the iron braziers on Bledla's right and left, and flames leapt from every torch, reddening the entire chamber for a moment. An audible gasp of thousands of voices in unison came from outside the temple, where the pious had gathered and waited for the ritual to begin. They would have seen the large torches on either side of the outer doors burst upwards with gouts of flame. Within the temple, priests and apprentices chanted all the while, "Edan rakhydon toronai!"

Bledla resumed his fervent solo, weaving it into their chant.

Orduno im broghyu ar vardha grondin,
Unwarno an dhagdu im durna hradin!
Gorghunol hringala an kharunon vingwin,
Dianol voldulva im ragashon dondwin!

A deep rumbling answered him from the bowels of the earth, and the ground quivered for a few seconds. Again came the screams tinged with fear and fervor from outside. More than two hundred thousand people, residents of Torrhelm, soldiers ready for war, and pilgrims who swelled the city, shouted their amazement. But within the temple, the priests and apprentices chanted while the king and his nobles looked on: "Edan rakhydon toronai!"

The supreme priest kept his arms aloft and eyes shut while his two high priests, Arna and Heremod, stood by to brace him. Remaining stiff and upright, the great wizard began the next song of origin.

Shorunai parishwu ar ghanyon durgon,
Volunai ombharu mi khardyon rhandon!
Vuishway randillon di balthar nonghala,
Uronay angwillon im shahar bondhala!

The inner temple darkened. From outside came loud cries of wonder. Bledla looked upward to the large window, and those within followed his gaze as, in the blue sky over the temple, a pale vapor formed and curled. The vapor thickened and writhed until it became a swirling mist that turned from white to dark grey as it swelled. Swallowing the sun, a roiling cloud took shape and expanded over the shadowed city. Between darkened sky and temple a bright bolt of lightning flashed, eliciting another collective gasp, and with its booming thunder the newly formed cloud released a hard downpour that pattered on the circular window high above the supreme priest.

The multitudes outside screamed in exhilaration. Those whom the raindrops touched counted themselves blessed for life, and Bledla knew that many would tear off their clothes so that their flesh could receive the drops. Within the temple, the white robed priests and yellow robed apprentices chanted even as the cloud left the inner sanctuary so darkened that it seemed like night: "Edan rakhydon toronai!" They looked to their supreme priest, whose face shone in the ruddy glow from the iron braziers.

He clenched his eyes as he began his final song:

Voromar in dharu khirgan an ulumo,

Dagathar im ghuishu noldan di khurono!

Husharu ingharno an toronu yondalwy,

Indwinu sturono ni bhaladu fandinwy!

When the supreme priest ceased, all others stopped their chant. Silence.

Within the temple, a fresh breeze from nowhere discernible caressed everyone's hair and skin. With no warning, it surged into a terrible, howling wind. The sudden gust tossed the priests' robes and the nobles' finery to and fro and blew out most of the torches. The nobles, including Earconwald, squinted and leaned forward to keep their balance. Outside, Bledla knew, hats were flying and people grasping their neighbors or anything planted in the ground. In the sky, the wind's force tore into shreds the cloud that had formed over the temple. As the last wisps of mist floated away, the gust died down to nothing. For a moment, Torrhelm was still.

Then the people on the streets broke out in wild cheers that reached within the temple as the sun returned above them. Within the temple, light glowed once again. The ray from the window at the top of the dome descended upon Bledla, who opened his eyes and blinked.

The Supreme Priest Bledla allowed himself a slight smile. He turned to the High Priestess Colburga and nodded, at which signal she descended the steps of the tomb and approached one of her white-robed priestesses. When Colburga grasped her by the arm, the young priestess folded her hands in front of her, gazed upward, and cried out with quivering lips. She let her mistress lead her up Aldmund's tomb.

After Colburga brought her before the supreme priest, he took the long knife from Heremod. Eyes wide and lips slightly parted, the young priestess breathed in quick gasps and gazed up at her lord. He looked down at her with a stern frown.

The supreme priest grasped the priestess's white robe with his free hand and brought the blade to her sleeve. His spotted hand tightened on the handle, veins protruding over bones. He looked her in the eyes and grimaced. Downward he slashed, and the congregants all flinched at her cry.

Bledla grasped each side of the rent he had made in her sleeve and ripped it further open, exposing a pale arm. The priestess raised her other arm in the air, tilted her head back with closed eyes, and released her ecstasy in a wavering moan.

"Behold," intoned the supreme priest, "this pure and innocent vessel of the Eternal." He grasped her slender arm in his left hand, and Arna held the bronze bowl beneath it. With a swift sweep of the knife, Bledla slit open the white wrist of the priestess, who cried out and beamed a wide smile. Colburga helped support her shaking body. Her hips swayed and her eyes rolled upward as her blood oozed out over her open palm. While Bledla held and pressed the arm, Arna collected the red trickle dripping from her fingertips into the bowl. When the supreme priest chanted, "Raghyon vinduilae ar tarkhal hurthodan. Vhardyon kholgathae im bhalgal ranghillan," the flow increased and the young priestess panted harder.

Bledla declared, "Blood of the elements. Blood of the Eternal. Sign of our brotherhood, sign of our inheritance in Edan, and sign of our salvation. All who are present, believers in Edan, receive this token of your salvation. As you go forth into the world, let it be the sign you are among the Eternal."

"Blessed be the Eternal!" the congregants cried.

After the priestess's blood filled the bowl, Bledla nodded to Colburga. The high priestess placed a hand over her charge's wrist and mumbled a spell of healing while the supreme priest took the bowl of blood from Arna and raised it to his own lips, saying, "Blessed are you, eternal one." He tipped the bowl and drank.

The young priestess swooned in Colburga's arms. The High Priest Heremod helped Colburga lower her limp body to several other priestesses, who carried their sister away.

Bledla surveyed his audience, declaring in a loud, deep voice, "Come forth, eternal ones."

No one moved until King Earconwald strode to the tomb's edge. Bledla looked down on his sovereign with a face betraying no emotion. Stooping over, he extended the bowl toward Earconwald. Bledla hesitated halfway there, his hands shivering almost imperceptibly before he put the bowl to his sovereign's lips with the words, "Blessed are you, eternal one."

King Earconwald looked at Bledla's face as he kissed the bowl's rim. When it was done, he nodded and turned to walk out the temple. The congregants parted before him while the dukes of Torrhelm took their turn at the tomb to partake of the blood of the Eternal. After the five dukes came the earls and captains, then the high priests, the priests, and last the apprentices.

All but the high priests left the temple after their turn at the bowl, the priests and apprentices exiting without a noise through a door in one of the apses leading to the monastery. The dukes, other nobles, and captains followed King Earconwald out the main entrance on the other side of the temple, where Bledla knew an escort of armed soldiers waited. When they walked in a procession down Torrhelm's streets, the multitudes broke out in deafening cheers that resounded even inside the temple.

ONCE THE LAST OF THE APPRENTICES HAD LEFT THE TEMPLE, BLEDLA instructed the High Priests Joruman, Morcar, and Heremod to store the Book of Aldmund and vessels of the ritual. He sent Colburga to look after the priestess who had sacrificed her blood. The High Priest Arna remained with him, and they descended the stairs of the tomb to the floor of the temple. When the others had departed through the door to the monastery, the two old men remained alone in the vast sanctuary next to Aldmund's black tomb.

I'm tired, thought Bledla. *But the rites went well. A good omen, thanks be to Edan.*

They stood with their hands folded in reverence before the tomb.

The supreme priest turned to Arna with a smile. "Well, old friend, all is ready."

"My lord, today's ritual was sublime. There's never been a more splendid Day of Edan. Edan has blessed you."

Bledla sighed. "Perhaps. But such power brings great duty. It all reverberates to Edan's glory."

"Yes, my lord."

"We must be single-minded in this. My power, your power, all that is. There's only one purpose for it all: to bring glory to Edan. He manifested this power in me at the end of times, and I must strive to be worthy of the burden He has given me. As supreme priest, I am Aldmund's heir in more than just title."

"My lord. The strength of the gift in you — no one since Aldmund has had such power. Who could deny this?"

"The power that gave him insight into Edan's truth will enable me to fulfill Edan's will. It is as the Prophet foretold: Aldmund's life and power have in truth returned in me. Soon all of Eormenlond will see the signs, for what only he wielded I too wield. And I'll use it to spread the Way over all of Eormenlond, thus ushering in the Kingdom of the Eternal. Edan ordained it from the beginning. We shall help to glorify Edan's truth, for His truth is our strength. We are blessed beyond measure to be the vessels of his will. The Kingdom of the Eternal will soon come to be — you and I will witness it. With a vision of His kingdom Edan has blessed me. I have seen it."

Arna smiled and looked up into Bledla's eyes. "My lord, my heart desires nothing more than to see that kingdom."

Bledla put his long hand on Arna's shoulder and nodded. "Yes, my friend. Your devotion to the Way matches my own. I knew it from the first day we met, when we came as young men to this monastery here in Torrhelm to begin our callings. That's why I leave you in command here while I bring Joruman, Heremod, and Morcar south. Colburga will keep her charge over the priestesses, the brides of Edan, and she may assist you as you require."

"Colburga leads the women well. They're as pious as the men, and some show great promise. While you aid Torrlond's army in war, the priests and priestesses will maintain the rites of the temples and care for Torrlond's people. Nothing need concern you, my lord. I'll uphold the Way in Torrlond, and you may call upon me from wherever you may be if there is need."

"I have no doubt of it, my friend." Bledla let his smile slip and glanced around the shadows of the temple. He said in a quieter voice, "But that's not the reason I wish to speak with you. There's something I can discuss only with you for the present."

The supreme priest hesitated while his high priest leaned forward and frowned. "I'm sorry, old friend, but I must share some of my burdens with you. There's no one else I can rely on. It concerns that apostate, the wicked son of a righteous father who pretends to be our king."

"Earconwald?"

"Did you see it? It gave me such grief to let him partake of the blood of the Eternal in this sacred place. He cares nothing for the rites of Edan. In his wickedness, he thinks to use the Way as a mask to hide his iniquities and vulgar aspirations. Our faith is no such tool. He sullies a great name and a great line of kings. To expose the blood of the Eternal to that unbeliever is a sacrilege, and yet I did it in obedience to our cause. Edan is my witness I've tried to turn him from heresy. I don't know where I failed."

"Surely, my lord, it's not your failure, but the king's willfulness."

Bledla shook his head. "From his childhood, when you and I were still young men and I had just taken office as supreme priest, I tried to teach him the path of salvation. For his father's sake, I bore much. But he was so unlike his father even then. So stubborn and malicious. Now he's become a self-serving wretch whose only ambition is to enrich himself and gratify base desires. Even a mighty king is Edan's servant, but Earconwald in his pride thinks to be master. More than for any other, he'll pay dearly for this sin."

Arna looked around as if checking for any lurking presence. "Edan ordains all and holds each fate."

"You speak the truth. I can't save that vile man from his end. However, Edan has spoken: We need Earconwald for a time. He may be damned, but his greed works to our advantage. Torrlond's power will enable us to spread the Way over Eormenlond, and when Edan has accomplished this, there will be no other kingdom than His. Torrlond's people, who do not know their king is a hollow shell, will follow Earconwald anywhere. His soldiers love him. In spite of his wickedness, he inspires them on the right path, and we need this."

"He has a gift with words, at least."

"Yes, he has his gifts, and he comes from a long line of great leaders who believed in the Way. But Edan will use him for His purpose, and then," Bledla leaned forward as his voice fell to a whisper, "he may be discarded."

Arna's brow furrowed. He swallowed and then opened his mouth, but no words came.

Bledla held up his hand. "I do not mean you will need to do anything in my absence. A time may come when, to obey the will of Edan, our true lord, we'll need to remove Earconwald if he becomes an obstacle to the fulfillment of the Kingdom. However, for now we may let things take their course."

"Their course, my lord?"

"See how Edan punishes him for his sacrilege: he is *childless*. That dissolute wretch who can't even pretend to be a queen has not given birth to an heir — but the blame is not Moda's. Earconwald has no bastards, and it's not for lack of trying. He can't produce offspring. It's a sign from Edan that his line and his kingdom will end. There need be no heir — even Torrlond will fall away when the Kingdom of Edan begins. Earconwald will grow less important, and most likely he'll wither away on his own. For now, he'll serve his purpose by rallying the kingdom as we set forth to spread the Way."

Arna's face relaxed. "Each can only serve the purpose Edan sets for him, my lord. The kingdoms of this world are but fleeting. They will seem the dreams of a moment when Edan brings in the Kingdom of the Eternal."

"Yes, your zeal opens your eyes to truth." Bledla's eyes narrowed.

"But there's one thing you must guard against at all costs while I'm away. Be sure Moda doesn't take it into her head to supply an heir on her own. There are many serving men and guards she could tempt. Keep a close watch on her, especially in the first days of the king's absence. And if she somehow succeeds, you must spread word of the offspring's true parentage. Our spies in the king's guard will assist you." A slight smile crossed the supreme priest's face. "You may advance your purpose by ensuring the queen's wine never runs low. That will keep her more pliable to our needs. In any event, we must keep the king weak by the lack of an heir."

Arna nodded. "And I'm sure we do him a service by preserving his throne's virtue."

Bledla smiled at his friend. "I'm glad we understand one another. One other matter: Regarding the conspiracy the traitor Galdor leads, I want you to summon me through the seeing crystal if you hear anything. Our spies in Ellond have reported nothing of late, and I've heard little more of Faldira in Asdralad or Tirgalan in Sundara. As for Urd, I told you what the fool Bagsac reported. I think it likely she fled to Asdralad. Gobban, our priest in the far west of the Mark, saw her in Farwick, where she managed to board a ship bound south."

"And the boy?"

"He did not see the young man who awoke from the elf-sleep, the witch's grandnephew. As you know, we have good reason to believe he was in Wolvendon. The witch wanted us to think he was with her, but *he* is the only explanation for the incident in Wolvendon. Our priest Bertric is a good man, strong in the gift, and he seemed certain. It could be a trifling matter, and the boy nothing to worry about at all, but at this stage we must be sure. Nothing must interfere with our plans."

"No doubt you're correct, my lord. Perhaps it was some sort of accident in Wolvendon. It could have been someone else. Perhaps the boy never even saw an elf. There are many possible explanations. Bagsac could have been mistaken."

Bledla stared for a moment. "I pray to Edan you're right. But what the young man did to Bertric . . . Broke his power, and without even using a song of origin. Bertric is no weakling, but could he have erred?"

"We are all fallible, my lord."

"The boy may be a test. His power comes from the demons, the elves. Mine from Edan. If it is so, I welcome this contest."

"And it may all be some strange coincidence. A misunderstanding that began with Bagsac."

The supreme priest nodded. "Bagsac is an idiot, so that's a strong possibility. I sent him to keep an eye on Urd, thinking he would be effective there since he needed a chance to redeem himself from his past incompetence. Instead, he's turned out the worst sort of bumbler in a place we needed someone strong. But no matter. If my guess is correct, Urd sent the boy to Galdor in Ellond. Our priests are searching for him in the north and in any town with a port."

"A wise precaution, my lord."

"We'll crush this conspiracy, as we'll crush anything that tries to stay the progress of the Way. Just be sure to summon me if you hear any word concerning this boy or the traitor Galdor and his plot. It would be far better that they not have a chance to unite the south and east against us, and I need not tell you it would be against Edan's will for the boy to receive training from the heretic Galdor."

The high priest bowed, turning his gaze to the floor. "My lord, I'll summon you the moment I hear anything concerning Galdor or the boy."

"Very good. I am assured."

Arna stroked his grey beard, and his forehead wrinkled below his bald crown. "I take it the powers we've gathered are ready? Will you have difficulty moving them such a vast distance?"

The supreme priest shook his head. "I've worked out everything with Heremod down to the last detail. The beasts will march apart from the rest of our forces under cover of night. Besides that, we'll pick up more to augment what we have when the companies converge at Hasumere. A disagreeable place, to be sure, but it serves our purposes well. The beasts are wretched to deal with and are considerable trouble. However, our power is more than strong enough to control them, and using them will spare thousands of the Eternal."

"Edan grant that it be so."

"Torrlond's army could do it alone, of course, but this will both ensure swift victory and fulfill the prophecies. As the Prophet says, 'Trust not in the strength of men alone.' And, as you've often pointed out, it's possible that, once the kingdoms of Eormenlond see our power over the beasts, they'll submit without a fight."

Arna looked down at the floor then up again at Bledla's face. "One hopes, my lord, that we'll accomplish Edan's will with the least amount of bloodshed."

"Of course." Bledla put his hand on Arna's shoulder again. "I know you've always sought the most peaceful means to accomplish our goal, and we've had our differences over that. You understand I feel the same as you."

"Yes, my lord."

"But true peace cannot come until all of Eormenlond follows the Way to make clear the path for the Kingdom of the Eternal. Edan's peace will come through war, my friend. 'Through great strife,' declared the Prophet. This world is full of wickedness and heresy, and Edan has appointed us to purge it. Though we may find the task difficult or unpleasant, only blood can expunge the sins and wrongs of the wayward. There is always a price to pay. Edan demands it. And we all must make sacrifices to accomplish Edan's will."

"I'm ready to make my sacrifices."

"I know you are. We'll offer the way of peace to the kingdoms of Eormenlond. We'll extend to them Edan's salvation, and we may hope they'll take it without stubbornness." The supreme priest narrowed his eyes. "But if any should resist after our triumph over Caergilion, then we'll unleash our greatest weapon upon them. No one can withstand Edan's power, and they will learn that when they witness the glory of His strength."

"All will learn that in the end."

Bledla smiled. For a brief moment, his shoulders drooped and he allowed himself to appear an ordinary old man — frail and vulnerable. "I'm glad we're at one on this, as we've always been, Arna. More than on any other, I depend on you. I go forth assured I leave Torrhelm in good hands." *I'm tired. And we are old. Edan give me strength to fulfill Your will. I am Your humble servant, and all I do is for Your glory. Bless Your servant with the fulfillment of Your Kingdom.*

"My lord." Arna bowed his head. "You may count on me."

"Thank you. Now, I bid you to leave me. I must make my prayers at Aldmund's tomb ere I go. Be sure no one enters the sanctuary."

"Yes, my lord." Arna bowed again.

Bledla watched his friend walk toward the door leading into the monastery. Bent over with age, the High Priest Arna disappeared into the shadows and through the door, leaving Bledla alone with Aldmund's tomb in the stillness of the vast sanctuary.

After gazing into the silence surrounding him, Bledla sighed. He approached the tomb of Aldmund and rested his hands on his weary knees as he knelt before it. In this, the most sacred place in all of Eormenlond, Bledla felt his kinship with the Prophet most keenly. An unseen energy flowed from the tomb and bound him to it. No matter where he was, he always sensed it, but here he could almost touch it. So strong was his connection to the tomb that at times, as he eyed his reflection in the black stone, he felt he was looking out from it at himself. The power of the Prophet was surely in him, reborn to work Edan's will.

But now was the time for prayer. "My lord Edan, I come in humility to confess my sins. I beg your forgiveness, and I ask that you give me the strength to accomplish the task you have set before me."

The supreme priest pulled the sleeves of his white robe and tucked his arms inside it. Then his hands reached through the neck of the robe and pulled it down, leaving the robe bunched around his waist. His torso now exposed, he continued to kneel before the tomb. Ribs protruded beneath the pale skin, moles, and veins of his upper body, and coarse white hair covered his chest. Layers of thick scars criss-crossed the stretched, white flesh of Bledla's back.

He reached into the folds of his robe and withdrew a slender rope that was halfway unwound so that nine thin tails emerged from a handle. Interspersed on each tail were small, barbed beads. Bledla smiled grimly at the instrument in his right hand, and then he swung it over his left shoulder with great force. It whistled and snapped when it bit into his back. Some of the beads caught in his flesh, and he tore them loose with a jerk.

Bledla's countenance was like stone. He repeated the motion over his right shoulder, and again he had to rip the beads loose. After a few strokes, blood trickled in red lines down his pale back, and he continued to flagellate himself and mortify his flesh as he prayed.

"Oh mighty Edan, forgive your servant. I have known lust this day."

An image flashed before him: the ecstatic face of the young priestess whose wrist he had slashed open for the rites of Edan while her uneven breaths rocked her body. The seductive feeling of pleasure and power when his blade sliced into her pale arm. The unleashing of something like desire at her vulnerable cry. The whip snapped into Bledla's back, and the beads tore away chunks of his skin.

"Forgive your servant. I have known pride this day."

How the assembled had gazed on him during the ritual! Like sheep they were, their awe and envy written on their gaping faces. His power was greater than any other's, and they loved and feared him for it. But all power comes from Edan and must serve Him, not worldly pride and vanity. Crack! went the whip. Bledla grunted as it peeled away a long strip of skin when he yanked it loose.

"Forgive your servant. I have known fear and doubt this day."

Plots and treason. It was high time the apostate Galdor should die, but his faith in Edan must be stronger. If he believed with enough strength, he need not fear the traitor. Most of all, the boy. The witch Urd's grand-nephew. *Dayraven*. Why did the boy unsettle him so? Could the story of him waking from the elf-sleep be true? Could it be the fulfillment of the prophecies? *Impossible!* his mind screamed. He must not fear. He must not doubt.

The whip whistled and slapped, whistled and slapped. Bledla ground his teeth and struck his back with such violence that his entire body trembled. Droplets of blood scattered with each slap and flew from the whip, forming a red mist around him. Sweat broke out all over his flesh and mingled with the blood. He must have faith. Whistle and slap! The supreme priest's body began to teeter as the strokes grew more vicious. *More faith. More strength.* Whistle, slap! *Only blood can expunge sin.* His eyes clenched closed. Whistle, slap!

Sublimity enveloped the supreme priest, and the whip tumbled from his hand as he stretched his arms outward. Released from the confines of weak and sinful flesh, he was Bledla no longer. His consciousness expanded to take in the sanctuary, the temple, the city, the kingdom, Eormenlond, and the lands beyond the Great Sea. The ages of humankind and its kingdoms flashed before him, and all was one in a timeless present. Edan. He was one with Edan.

Beyond the world of forms he journeyed, and he beheld the Kingdom of the Eternal, tasted it as it burned away his pain, his flesh, his lusts, his pride, his fear, his doubts, and all else. His eyes fluttered open, and he gazed upward in rapture. Bliss unfastened his mouth in a broad smile, and a moan like laughter escaped from his throat.

Bledla's sweat- and blood-drenched body collapsed to the floor, convulsing with ragged breaths as he wept before Aldmund's tomb.

EDAN WAS NOT THE ONLY WITNESS TO BLEDLA'S PENITENCE. FROM the shadows near the door separating the monastery from the sanctuary of the temple, the High Priest Arna watched his old friend and lord. He winced at the blood running onto the white robe, which was all speckled red, and the pulpy, raw meat exposed on his lord's back beneath hanging shreds of skin.

Tears gathered in the high priest's eyes. He did not know why he had turned back. Perhaps it was the sound of the whip. Perhaps it was his guilt. Perhaps it was his way of saying goodbye. Even now, as he gazed at Bledla shaking in a heap before the tomb, a part of him wanted to rush over and confess everything. *I am a traitor, my lord. You should not trust me.*

The tears trickled down Arna's cheeks and followed the ridges of his wrinkled skin until they disappeared in his grey beard. His jaw quivered as he too whispered a prayer of penitence, and all the while his eyes stayed locked on the supreme priest. "Forgive me for my wrongs, Edan. For too many years I lived in doubt. Forgive me for never forgetting Galdor. Forgive me for aiding Bledla in his madness. Forgive me for betraying him. Forgive me for being too weak to stop the murder and the slaughter, all done in Your name. Too foolish and feeble to know what to do. It's out of my hands now. Edan forgive me for all my wrongs. Spare the innocent, and save us all from madness."

15

IN THE COMPANY OF MERCENARIES

While most folk in Etinstone were celebrating the Day of Edan, several hundred silent Dweorgs filled the main street leading through their quarter of the city. They surrounded a white-haired woman sitting on a wooden chair in the middle of the street.

Dayraven peered over the heads of the Dweorgs. Ropes lashed the old Dweorg woman's body to the chair and held her in place. Her eyes were closed and her lips slightly parted as if she were taking a nap — in the way the elderly can nod off anywhere, even in a chair in the middle of a street — but her wrinkled, sagging skin betrayed the bluish-grey hue of death. On the day her people would bid her farewell, the shriveled and fragile Dweorg woman was clad in a beautiful golden gown embroidered with colorful floral patterns as well as golden slippers. On her brow rested a garland of plaited flowers, whose lively pinks and reds contrasted with the deceased woman's wispy, snowy hair. Her old features spoke of well-earned peace and rest after many days of toil and worry.

Dayraven thought back to the previous evening, when the four friends had reached the home of Gnorn and Hlokk's cousin Ilm. He had been surprised to feel the presence of the gift in Ilm. It was not strong in her, but it was manifest in a certain depth and perceptiveness she possessed, and her gaze had lingered on him, leading him to wonder if she felt the gift in him. As far as he knew, Dweorgs did not use the gift. It had been the Andumae who brought knowledge of it to Eormenlond.

He had liked Ilm from the moment they met. The first thing she had told them after introductions was about the death of an old Dweorg woman, Gna. Gnorn had turned to Dayraven and Imharr. "You must come to the funeral."

"Are you sure?" asked Dayraven. "We don't wish to intrude."

"You would honor us with your presence."

"Then we'll come."

A dozen Dweorg men encircled the chair, and among them were Hlokk, Ilm's husband Flegg, and Bur, the weaponsmith. All the men had the same markings on their forearms that Gnorn and Hlokk had.

Gnorn stayed beside Dayraven and Imharr on the outskirts of the crowd. He explained to the two guests, "Those men are the pallbearers. In the old days, all would have been sons or nephews of the deceased, but none of us have enough sons now. There are Gnod and Hronn, Gna's sons, and Iarn and Var, her nephews. Vig, Hloi, and Hval are her grandsons. We have supplied the rest." The dozen men bent down, and then Dayraven noticed the chair rested on a wooden platform. Each Dweorg grasped a handle attached to the platform and lifted it above his shoulders, with six on each side. As soon as they raised the chair with Gna's body above the throng, the hundreds of Dweorgs began chanting in unison.

"Dagraadungool hzeetarnu khaalvoku shorukweenay . . ." went their voices in words that were long and full of sounds strange to Dayraven's ears.

Gnorn turned to him and Imharr. "This is the song of our ancestors. We sing it to guide the spirit of our departed sister back into their arms. According to our customs, her life's journey is incomplete until she returns to the ancestors. In our case, they are far away, so the song is important. And, the fewer of us that remain, the harder we cling to such customs."

Dayraven nodded.

The men bore the chair on its platform down the street, and the crowd followed along as one mass, all the while singing in their native tongue. Dayraven and Imharr stuck by Gnorn, who now chanted with the rest. The haunting voices coming from the somber faces seemed to invoke the spirits of lost ages. Even without understanding the meaning of the strange words, Dayraven heard the sorrow and the deep memories embedded in them.

As the slow procession wound down the street, the singing grew in intensity, and now and then the sharp keen of a woman or anguished cry of a man rose above the chant. Many of the Dweorgs around Dayraven convulsed with weeping, and some tore at their hair or beards as they wailed. Such poignant grief. And what were they grieving? The end of one woman's life? The reminder that such an end awaited each of them? The demise of their people?

Lives begin and end. Kingdoms and peoples come and go. The world takes little notice as it pulses on in an endless cycle.

The susurration of the elf sharpened in his mind. It stretched and stirred with an alien awareness, exerting a volatile pressure that threatened to rupture the confines of his flesh. Through widening cracks the Dweorgs' emotions were beginning to enter his inner thoughts. At the same time, he was growing detached from the scene, distant and impartial. At any moment, the thing in his mind would tear him from his body.

He fought back the elf-state. *I can contain it. It will not take me. I am Dayraven.* He shook his head, and his eyes regained their natural focus. The shard of the elf's presence in his mind receded. It whispered the barest of caresses. *I can feel their pain without that.*

Dayraven returned to the present, to the chanting and wailing of the Dweorgs in Etinstone. The ease with which he suppressed the elf-state and remained inside himself in the midst of this sea of emotion made him want to laugh, but he kept his face somber as he walked behind Gnorn. *I can master it.* The chanting went on, and the mournful procession continued for a quarter mile or so.

The cobbled street became a rutty dirt road, which soon lessened to a path with grassy banks on both sides. A few abandoned and crumbling stone houses like those the Dweorgs inhabited lined the path. These gave way to grass-covered foundations. At length, they left the last of the former dwellings behind and reached a patch of open land abutting the city wall. There was something strange about the green field ahead of them, and even as Dayraven squinted and craned his neck forward, the realization came to him. Thousands of small, grass-covered mounds dotted the field: the burial mounds of the exiled Dweorgs of the Fyrn-howes. Ahead of him, the men carrying the body in the chair stopped, and the crowd began forming a circle around them.

Dayraven approached behind Gnorn and took his place in the circle. A fresh hole yawned in the earth. A mound of dirt waited next to it. The Dweorg men were already lifting Gna's body and her chair off the platform. They eased it down the hole with ropes, and all the while the Dweorgs continued chanting their ancestral song. When the chair rested on the bottom of the shallow hole, Gna's hoary head still showed above ground level. She faced north.

The dozen men took up shovels and began filling the hole with dirt from the mound next to it. Other men, women, and children grasped fistfuls of soil from the mound and, while still chanting and weeping, threw them in the hole. Metal grated on soil as the Dweorg men found a rhythm with their digging. The dark dirt soon filled Gna's lap. Particles of it clung to her quiet, waiting face and her white hair. The chanting became more subdued and fragmented as the old woman's features disappeared beneath the soil.

Dayraven and Imharr stood back and watched when Gnorn approached the mound and filled his hand. Their friend shook as he sang and threw the soil into the hole, which was fast filling. When the Dweorg returned to them, tears had made wet tracks down his cheeks, but he no longer sobbed.

"Another of us has departed. We Dweorgs have no god or gods as your peoples do. Instead, we worship our ancestors, which we all come from and to which we all belong. They dwell in the land, and they are of the land. Gna's spirit will now return to them."

"It seems she was much beloved," said Imharr.

"She was a good woman, and it sorrows me to say farewell to her."

Gnorn paused a while as the three watched the mourners continue to fill in the grave. "So few left. So few."

He looked up at Dayraven, his eyes still glassy. "Every funeral we have now is not only for the departed one. We last survivors mourn for our lost folk as well. It's the little ones I feel for most. The children. What will their future be when they have no people?"

Imharr put his hand on the Dweorg's shoulder.

Dayraven stood in silence. The question gnawed at him. He wanted to give his friend a consoling answer, but he did not have one. What was anyone without a people? *I'll start a new life. Get to Galdor, master the power inside me. Then find Imharr's sister, and seek Ebba.* The presence of the elf sighed and stirred in his mind like a trembling leaf. In the meantime, his heart went out to Gnorn and Hlokk and the Dweorgs of the Fyrnhowes, who lingered on in Etinstone.

"Thank you for allowing us to witness this, my friend," he said. "We will remember."

On the morning of the day Torrlond's companies were to muster, Dayraven awoke in the attic of Gnorn and Hlokk's cousin Ilm's home. The smell of something cooking downstairs, probably eggs and bacon, tugged him from his dream of wandering the Mark's hills alone. Though he had been home in his dream, something about his solitude had disturbed him. It was the disquieting suspicion that no other human beings were alive there.

The dream's discomfort lingered after the vision was gone. He shook his head to dispel it and return to the concerns of the present. A bit stiff in his back from the wooden floor, he sat up from his sleeping pad and rubbed his eyes.

Imharr stood with his arms folded and hands clasped behind his back looking out the room's only window, which was circular and made of thick glass that allowed in just enough sunlight to see by. The window was set in the stone under the peak of the slanted roof, the only part of the room where the two friends could stand upright.

As he rose, Dayraven took care not to bang his head on a roof beam. Negotiating the barrels of stores the Dweorg family kept in the attic, he walked across the creaking floor planks. Still staring out the window, Imharr did not stir. Dayraven put his hand on his shoulder. "Ready for the mustering?"

Imharr turned around. His grin was weak.

"What's wrong?"

Imharr scratched his beard and then ran his fingers through his curly, dark hair. "It's just, well, this journey's bringing up old memories. Memories I . . ." He shook his head and put on a bigger smile, though it still did not reach his eyes. "Doesn't matter. We need to focus on getting you to Galdor in Ellond. The first chance we get, we leave the mercenary company and head north."

Dayraven nodded. "Aye. But those memories you spoke of . . . Do you want to talk about them?"

Imharr stared at the younger man before sighing and sinking onto one of two stools Gnorn's cousin had placed there for them.

Dayraven sat on the other and waited.

Imharr began, "All my life, I've tried not to think about my family — the one I was born into. The memories were too painful. It was always easier to pretend I was one of you."

"You *were* one of us."

Imharr smiled. "I know, Day. I know. But just under the surface were memories of where I came from. To keep from being torn in two, I kept them in the back of my mind. But, no matter how much I tried to forget, they would never go away. So many nights I've seen them in dreams. Last night, I saw it again: the day the soldiers from Caergilion killed my family. The day they . . ." Imharr broke off and raked his fingers through his hair again. He stared at the floor.

Unsure what to say, Dayraven waited.

Imharr looked up at him. "I guess I've been thinking about them more ever since we left the Mark."

"What were they like?"

Imharr's eyes grew distant for a moment, but then he shook his head. "It's hard to remember them. I was only six. I feel like my mother was gentle and kind, my father proud and strong. Likely what most six-year-olds think. They were noble. My father was the younger son of a duke."

Dayraven's mouth hung open for a moment. "You never mentioned that."

Imharr shrugged. "Never seemed important." He winced. "No, that's not true. I never mentioned it because I was trying to forget them. When you spoke of finding my sister . . . Too many years I kept my family far away. Now, I want to see them, and I want it to hurt. They're gone from this world, but I'll seek what remains of them, after we get you sorted out with Galdor. And if my sister lives, I'll find her. If this life's given her sorrow, I'll make it better. I swear it by Orm and Angra."

Dayraven swallowed the lump in his throat and gazed at his friend. He realized the smallness of his exile next to Imharr's losses. *All these years, behind his laughter was this pain.* "And I swear to go with you until we find her. Once Galdor has trained me, we will seek her together."

Imharr nodded and smiled again. "Riall. My sister's name is Riall."

"Pretty name."

THE TWO GOT UP AND WASHED THEIR HANDS AND FACES WITH water from a basin. They opened a trap door and descended wooden stairs that groaned under their feet. The aroma of eggs and bacon filled the room they entered. Gnorn and Hlokk sat at a large, low table along with their cousin Ilm's husband Flegg, who had a reddish brown beard, and father-in-law Kiar, whose beard had turned all white. The wooden table and benches around it stood on a stone floor, and on the other side of the room was the fireplace, in which hot coals glowed. Though some of it hung about the room, most of the smoke from the fire drifted up a stone chimney. Near the fireplace hung blackened pots and pans, and numerous foodstuffs and supplies lined the room's wooden shelves. The four Dweorg men were in the midst of a discussion about Etinstone's politics while Ilm, a short and stout Dweorg woman in her thirties with large, pretty eyes, tended the food she cooked on a grate over the fireplace.

"Cousin Ilm," said Imharr with a broad smile, "my nose tells me you've prepared a culinary marvel that will not fail to please your undeserving guests. And though I'm undeserving, I will partake, lest I offend."

"Uncle Imharr!" squealed two little Dweorg girls as they burst through a curtained doorway from the sleeping room. Hlin and Spregg, six and four years, were the height of most two or three year olds Dayraven knew, and the elder was a little chubbier than the younger. They had large brown eyes and curly dark brown locks that bounced as they ran to Imharr in their white frocks and jumped into his arms. Though they had hidden from the two tall newcomers at first, Imharr had lured them out of their shyness.

Ilm laughed. "You're welcome, Imharr, though I believe those girls will find it dull here once you're gone."

"Ah, yes, my famous charm. It follows me everywhere." Imharr winked at Ilm as he put the two girls down. He and Dayraven took their places at the table next to the Dweorg men.

"Hmmph," said Ilm. "A shame your charm will be wasted where you're going."

"Not to worry," said Hlokk, "The fellows in the mercenary company will appreciate it, no doubt. Great appreciators of charm, they are. Ha!"

Hlokk roared while the other Dweorg men and Dayraven chuckled, and soon Imharr joined them.

Ilm's brow lowered, and she frowned as she gazed at the men, especially Gnorn and Hlokk. "I don't know how you all can jest and laugh when you're going off to your deaths. Isn't even needed. Let the Torrlonders fight their own war. There's no glory in slaying or being slain."

The laughter ceased. A tense silence filled the room. Ilm turned her back to the men to attend to the sizzling food. Flegg and the old man Kiar looked down at the table. Hlin and Spregg stared up at Gnorn and Hlokk with their innocent eyes.

Gnorn cleared his throat. "Now, we've discussed this, and it'll do no good to go over it again. It's all decided. This is the fate we chose. It's the only path of honor left open according to our people's ancient laws."

Ilm spun around. "Your laws be damned!" She looked Gnorn in the eyes. Her face grew flushed. "Those aren't my laws. The inventions of stiff-necked *men* like you. There's no shame in living with your people and sharing their lives till you grow old with them." She turned back to the fireplace, and her back shuddered.

"Enough, dear," said Flegg. He still gazed down at the table in front of him. "They've made their choice. There's no more to say."

"No more to say because nothing gets through their thick skulls!" Her voice wavered and thickened until the last word came out as a sob. She sniffed and took up a pan from the grate. As she served the men their breakfast on trenchers already laid out on the table, she wept tears that left glistening lines on her cheeks. When she finished dumping a large serving of eggs and bacon before each of them, she clanged the pan onto the table and stormed through the curtain leading to the sleeping room. The girls stared at the men for a moment with blinking eyes and open mouths, but then they scurried to join their mother. Dayraven swallowed and looked down at the table. His appetite had diminished. Ilm's sorrow almost seemed his own, a weight lodged in his chest.

The other men appeared to examine their food until Gnorn sighed and began eating. They ate with little relish, pushing the eggs around with their spoons and chewing the bacon far longer than necessary. None of them said a word. Other than their spoons and knives scraping on their trenchers, the only sound was an occasional sob from behind the curtain. When they finished, they washed up and prepared to go.

Dayraven and Imharr returned to the attic to don their full war gear. They wriggled into their clinking byrnies, which they put on over their old kirtles. The supple leather padding inside his bulky chain mail seemed molded for Dayraven's shoulders. The byrny was a pleasant weight on him, and he admired how the shiny links caught the light as he moved. Over their byrnies they wore their new grey kirtles, on which they had sewn the king of Torrlond's ensign on the left shoulder. Dayraven buckled Sweothol's baldric over his left shoulder and paused to look at its blood-red gem, which prodded him with memories of his father and the Mark. He put on his cloak. When he donned his helm and took up his round linden shield, he looked down at himself. He might just pass for a soldier. His mouth slid into a half smile.

Ilm's grief still echoed within him. In addition, he worried about how he and Imharr would free themselves. There had been little choice but to join the mercenary company, and little choice but to stay with it until now. He would not risk harm to the Dweorgs, whom he had come to love in his brief time with them. A chance would come. He and Imharr would just have to be sharp when it did.

Imharr stood in his gear with Wreaker at his side, and his friend's splendid appearance made Dayraven smile, banishing fear for a moment. Dayraven told himself he was ready. He nodded and, following Imharr, descended from the attic.

When it was time to go, Ilm emerged from the sleeping room. She embraced Hlokk first then Gnorn. Tears streamed down her cheeks. Turning to Imharr, who had just kissed the two girls on their brows, she embraced him, though the top of her head hardly came to his chest. She came to Dayraven. After she wrapped her arms around him, he swallowed the tightness in his throat and stooped to murmur, "We'll never be able to repay your kindness."

Her wet, beautiful eyes looked up into his, and her face grew somber. "You can repay me with an oath."

Gnorn held up a hand, and he shook his head. "No, cousin. That is hardly necessary."

Ilm spun toward him. "Will you deny me even this small comfort?" She turned back to Dayraven. "You're unusual among your kind, especially for one so young. You understand honor and kindness. Compassion. Will you swear an oath to me?" The pain of her loss grew in him. He did not know if it was because of the elf-state, or if the power of her grief was too sharp for his defenses, but however it came to be, her sorrow leapt out of her to become his. Along with it came the loneliness of the Dweorgs of the Fyrnhowes, who, like him, had lost their home.

Dayraven swallowed. "What would you have me swear?" His voice trembled.

The Dweorg woman wiped her cheek with the back of her hand and held her chin up. "There will be little solace for my cousins where they have chosen to go. Swear that you will remain true to them, that you will stay by their sides for as long as you can, keeping them from harm and giving them the comfort of your friendship."

Dayraven looked toward Imharr, who watched wide-eyed and gave him a slight shake of the head.

Gnorn stepped forward. "You've no need for an oath, Dayraven. We know you for a true friend."

Ilm did not take her gaze from Dayraven. "Will you swear it?"

He could not find it in himself to deny the fierceness and poignancy of this woman's love, which had somehow become his own. In that moment, nothing – not even his own losses – mattered more. He nodded to her. "I swear it."

Imharr, Gnorn, and Hlokk stood with open mouths.

Ilm gazed at Dayraven for a long moment, and then she nodded with a grim but satisfied smile. "So be it."

Dayraven knew his oath had changed all his plans, but he could not order his mind yet to understand what he would do. *I must still reach Galdor somehow, but later now. At least we needn't worry about how to desert.*

It was a solemn parting as Ilm and her family stood in their stone house's doorway. Dweorgs on the street stopped their business and bowed their heads when Gnorn and Hlokk passed with Dayraven and Imharr. Dayraven felt uneasy being so near the center of attention, especially since the community clearly regarded the departure as a terrible loss. But once the four companions left the Dweorg quarter, he was relieved to find they were no longer worthy of a second look.

It was then that Gnorn put his hand on Dayraven's shoulder. "We will not hold you to that oath."

Dayraven shook his head and smiled. "It was not to you that I swore it." Now he was in truth a soldier.

DAYRAVEN FELT STRANGELY NUMB AS THEY WALKED TOWARD THE mercenary company's compound. He should have been frightened, but he was not. What he had done felt right, and that gave him some peace.

Imharr strode next to him. "You shouldn't have done that." He spoke the words quietly so that Gnorn and Hlokk would not hear.

"But I did."

"I know. And you meant it, didn't you?"

Dayraven nodded.

Imharr's eyes rolled, and he shook his head. "Sometimes you remind me of your father. You know that? Stubborn and full of honor. But it was your mother who had that same eerie way about her."

"What do you mean?"

"Reaching inside a person's head. Not in a bad way, mind. Peaceful like. But still eerie."

Dayraven grinned for a moment, but then his face grew serious. "This just changes the order in which we do things. We'll make our way to Ellond eventually. For now, we're bound for Caergilion. Might be we'll have a chance to look for your sister down there."

"In the middle of a war?"

"Not likely to last long, is it?"

"No telling. And in the meantime, you mean to follow Gnorn and Hlokk until they get themselves killed in a battle?"

"If need be. But what if, in staying by them, we help them see what they have to live for?"

Imharr appeared thoughtful for a moment, and then he grunted. "We'll see." They continued to follow their Dweorg friends through the city.

The people on Etinstone's crowded streets seemed not to care about or even notice the life surrounding them. Individuals bustled about and jostled one another without the slightest look of concern. Their faces seldom budged from bored impassivity. He found it odd how folk grew further apart when there were more of them and less distance between them. Perhaps there was so much going on around them that they shut it all out to get on with daily business. As the four friends made their way on a busy thoroughfare, he thought about how everyone in Kinsford knew one another and never would have passed by without at least a greeting. But something up ahead outside of Etinstone's looming Temple of the Way drove his thoughts away. At first thinking he must be mistaken, he squinted at it. Then his eyes widened, and he shook his head. "No."

A tattered form lay not far from the grand stone steps of the temple, a smaller copy of the one in Torrhelm but still an intimidating building. As they neared the form, it became a child in rags with matted hair. Dayraven recognized one of the many homeless boys who eked out an existence in the city doing the most menial tasks for scraps of food. The poorest girls, Gnorn had told him, usually ended up enslaved in brothels along with a few of the prettier boys.

The child lay on his back just to the side of the street at a place where much traffic flowed. Cracked, leather-like calluses covered the soles his filthy feet, whose little toes pointed skyward. His tangled, greasy hair was stiff and a sickly orange in hue, and it poked in every direction. With small mouth agape and one glassy eye open, his pale face and stillness declared the certainty of his death. There was no obvious trauma to his body, so he had died of some disease or starvation. Stepping around him, passersby did not even blink at the dead child.

Gnorn led them past the body. Dayraven stopped and stared. Streaks of soot and mud stained the boy's hollow cheeks and skeletal arms. Snot crusted his nostrils, and something sticky seeped from the corner of his open eye. Dayraven wondered who the child had been and where those were who should have loved him. *Little one. Had you lived among green hills with a mother's and father's arms to hold you, what might have been? You could have been me. You are me, and your death is my death.* He was unsure where the last thought came from. *Ever since the elf*. . .

Hlokk cleared his throat. "Come, lad. There's naught you can do. Yonder priests are meant to tend the body."

Dayraven came to his senses. This was no place to wander into the elf-state. Many priests were bound to be near, and they might feel the presence of the gift in him. While fate and his oath had forced him to abandon Urd's course for the moment, it was still wiser to avoid undue attention. He turned away and followed Hlokk, glancing back one more time. People were still parting and stepping around the dead boy.

Not one stooped to pick him up or even pause. "It never should've come to that."

Though they left the child's emaciated body behind, Dayraven could not shake the image from his mind. The shard of the elf whispered of shadows and darkness, and with a chill he understood that it regarded one death the same as any other.

After some time, however, nervousness about his first day as a fully equipped soldier in the Mercenary Company of Etinstone crept into his thoughts. He wondered what his father had felt when he joined Torrlond's ranks more than twenty winters before. Edgil had been a year or two older than he was now. Somehow, Dayraven had difficulty imagining his father nervous, but even Edgil had been young and inexperienced once.

In the noise of the streets the companions said little, but soon they reached the quieter side street leading to the Mercenary Company's dilapidated compound. The sun was not quite overhead, so they did not hurry, and a half dozen well-armed men in grey kirtles walked before them. When they passed by the rusted, broken gate, they saw many more men in the courtyard than they had two days before, almost a hundred all told. A familiar voice came from their right.

Thegn Ludecan, the company's lieutenant, held a parchment while he spoke with a short, thickset, bald man with a large pink scar across his face that did not improve his features any. The scar ran from his neck over his large jaw, up his cheek and over his nose, passing just over his right eye. His beard consisted of a thick mustache, a frizzled brown-grey tuft sprouting from his chin, and a few sparse patches on his ruddy cheeks. Like everyone else, the man bore full warrior's gear, but he did not wear the king's ensign or a grey kirtle. Mud caking his heavy black boots, brown breeches, and grey cloak indicated he had traveled from afar. When the stout man turned in an attempt to engage Ludecan again, a green bag slung over his shoulder swung and bumped his broad back. Its embroidered style and shape suggested that it held a harp.

The lieutenant glanced at the four companions and several men who had come in before them. "Wait there a moment."

Turning back to the scarred man, he spoke loud enough for Dayraven to hear: "Sorry, but that's how it is. We've got our hundred men. I suggest you go to one of the regular companies if you're so keen to enlist. Since you're from Ellond, as long as you're a believer in the Way, they'll most-like admit you. Now, you need to leave. I have work to do."

Ludecan walked to the soldiers who preceded the four companions and began checking their names on his list.

With a scowl on his face, the scarred man turned to leave. But on his way out the gate, his eyes widened at Dayraven and Imharr, and then he glanced at Gnorn and Hlokk. He stopped and stared at them. His mouth opened as if he wanted to have a word. But before the scarred man made a move, a gruff voice shouted in the courtyard.

"Damn you, I want it now!"

Soldiers backed up and formed a ring around the source of the shouting. Ludecan pushed aside some men and yelled, "Make way!" They parted for the lieutenant, giving Dayraven a clear view.

Not far away stood the big, ugly fellow with the patch over his eye, the drunk who had shoved him out of the way and fought him when they reported to Ludecan with their gear. Wigstan. The big man was enraged, and the object of his anger was another soldier standing before him.

This second soldier was one of the tallest men Dayraven had ever seen. Even Wigstan looked small next to the towering warrior before him. He had a light blond beard and long, wavy hair of the same color as well as a sharp-featured face with bright blue eyes. His long, muscular arms seemed almost the girth of a normal man's legs, and he rested his hands on his hips, like one in a position of authority. Indeed, three red stripes marked the giant man's kirtle over the king's ensign on his left shoulder, and he wore the scaled corselet of an officer.

"Captain Orvandil," said Ludecan. "Do you want . . ."

"Stand back, Ludecan." The tall captain's voice was deep and calm, and he spoke the Northern Tongue with a sharp accent. His gaze did not shift from the one-eyed soldier leaning too close to his face.

Wigstan, either too drunk or too enraged to allow the man before him to intimidate him, kept shouting, "Where is it, then? I ain't signin' for this fuckin' war for nothin'!"

"Told you," said Captain Orvandil with a slight smile, "pay comes in a fortnight."

"Then I'm leavin' this piece o' shit outfit right now." Wigstan jabbed his finger toward the cobbles and showed his few grey teeth in a snarl.

The smile left Orvandil's face. "Then you hang."

The captain turned around as if that were the end of the matter and began to walk away. Wigstan's face contorted and grew red. Without warning, he lunged toward the officer and unsheathed his sword, raising it for the kill. So swiftly it happened that no one had time even to shout.

But before Wigstan brought his blade down on Orvandil's head, the tall captain unsheathed his own sword with his right hand and swung around in one motion. Swords clanged. Had Dayraven blinked, he would have missed the captain parry the blow and punch his attacker's neck by the collarbone with his left hand. The hand did not move from the neck, and something glistened in it. With an almost bored expression, Orvandil withdrew a long, crimsoned dagger. A spurt of red exited the hole in Wigstan's neck. The captain turned around and walked away.

Wigstan stood with a puzzled look on his face. The one-eyed soldier choked out a gout of blood, which spattered on the cobblestones and dribbled from his beard. Then he fell backwards with a clatter and did not move again.

Captain Orvandil stopped walking. With fierce eyes he gazed around. "Anyone else want his pay now?"

Silence answered him.

Orvandil turned toward his lieutenant. "Cross his name off the list. Line up at noon sharp."

As Orvandil strode back to the building at the end of the courtyard, Ludecan replied, "Yes, Captain."

Thegn Ludecan looked behind him and shouted, "You there!" at the short, bald man with the scar whom he had turned away a moment before. The man, who still waited near the four friends, glanced once more at Dayraven and then walked up to the lieutenant. Ludecan gave him a wry smile. "Seems we have an opening. Welcome to the Mercenary Company of Etinstone."

The man nodded.

"Your first duty is to clean up that." The lieutenant pointed with his thumb at Wigstan's body. A pool of blood collected under it. "Afterwards, report to me over there." He glanced at the sack over the scarred man's shoulder. "If you can play that thing, you'll find yourself even more welcome."

"My lord," replied the scarred man in a sandy voice, "I'm a trained shaper. I'll be glad to lighten the journey with a tale or two."

"Good. More than likely we'll need it." Ludecan looked at two other soldiers standing nearby. "You and you," he said while pointing at them, "Don't just stand about. Help him. And be quick about it."

Dayraven frowned at Wigstan's lifeless body. His brief acquaintance with the one-eyed soldier had not been pleasant, but he supposed someone would grieve. The man had a story, and now it was over. What was more, a voice deep in his mind told him the reason for the wretched man's doomed attack on the formidable captain. *He knew he would fail. He wanted to die. To be free of his misery and his addiction.* He sorrowed as he saw Wigstan's previous attack on him in this new light.

"Come here, you lot." The lieutenant's voice pulled his attention away from Wigstan. After Ludecan checked their names on his list, the four companions walked further into the courtyard. Soldiers in full war gear with grey kirtles milled about and clustered in small groups. Most seemed to be discussing Wigstan's demise, and some were having a laugh over it.

Imharr gazed at the three men struggling to carry away the big man's limp corpse, one at each arm and one at the legs. "There goes your friend. We needn't worry about getting in his way again."

Dayraven nodded, but he was looking at Gnorn and Hlokk, who exchanged tense whispers with each other in Dweorgish. They seemed to be arguing. "What's wrong with you two?"

Gnorn fixed his sad eyes on Dayraven. "Remember what the lieutenant said the other day, that we'd enjoy meeting the captain? Now it's clear. The captain's a Thjoth, one of those who took the Fyrnhowes over our people's slain bodies."

"How do you know?" asked Imharr.

"Didn't you hear him, his manner of speaking the Northern Tongue?" said Gnorn. "But his size and appearance tell it anyway. He's a Thjoth of Grimrik."

Hlokk was growing agitated. "Let's fight him now and get it over with here. Better him than some poor devils from far away who've never harmed us."

"No," said Gnorn. "That is *not* honorable combat. You know the laws."

"What will you do?" said Dayraven.

Gnorn's features calmed into a smile. "We must bear the command of this Thjoth only for a short while. When Hlokk and I are gone, you will be free of your oath, and the pair of you can continue on your former journey. For now, we'd best move over there, where the line's forming. Come, Hlokk."

Hlokk grumbled but followed. The four found themselves next to one another towards the right of the front row of the formation Ludecan set in order opposite the crumbling building. There they waited after the last man found his place as the sun shone directly overhead.

No one said a word as they all sweated under their heavy byrnies in the heat. At length, the tall Thjoth who was their captain emerged from the building. With each step his large boots crunched the loose gravel on the cobblestones. He strode to the front line wearing a stern expression. Starting at the left of the formation, the captain gazed at each man in line as he walked. About a third of the men he greeted by name, and Dayraven reckoned these men must have served under Orvandil's command for some time. Each man he greeted nodded, and others bowed their heads as the captain walked past.

With Hlokk on his left and Imharr on his right, Dayraven watched the captain approach his Dweorg friends. They did not bow.

The Thjoth stopped in front of Gnorn and Hlokk, who stared ahead toward the building, avoiding eye contact with the man towering over them. Captain Orvandil crossed his arms in front of his broad chest and frowned. "Why are you Dweorgs here?"

Gnorn cleared his throat and did not move his eyes. "Same reason you're here: to fight for Torrlond."

The huge man scowled. "You'll take orders from me?"

Hlokk was twitching with the effort to control himself. Without thinking, Dayraven blurted out, "They'll fight as well as any man here."

As what he just did dawned on him, Captain Orvandil turned his head and fixed his bright eyes on him. He added "my lord" to his hasty words.

The Thjoth stepped in front of Dayraven, keeping his arms crossed. "Who are you?"

He looked up into the huge man's eyes. "Their friend, my lord. My name is Dayraven."

The captain's face was steady and unreadable, his gaze like a knife. "'Dayraven'? Your true name?"

Dayraven nodded. "Yes, my lord."

The huge man's eyes narrowed as he studied Dayraven. "First thing you learn in the Mercenary Company is don't speak unless I tell you. Understand?"

"Yes, my lord."

Orvandil said nothing but continued to gaze down at Dayraven. At once, the tall Thjoth reached out in a quick motion with his right hand and grasped the hilt of Dayraven's sword. Before Dayraven could react, Orvandil yanked out Sweothol, which rang as it emerged from its baldric. The captain swung the sword's tip to Dayraven's throat.

He stood and stared into Orvandil's eyes. Without turning, he sensed the tension in Imharr and the two Dweorgs, who were ready to spring.

The shard of the elf's presence awakened from whisper to roar in Dayraven's mind. His body tensed with a stab of panic, and he fought against the foreign entity's resurgence as the vast pair of eyes flashed before him. This time it was too strong to tamp down, and he clutched for some sense of control.

With a spark of memory, he recalled the strange level of perception that opened him to the timeless realm when he freed Rudumanu and Hraedflyht from the priest back in Wolvendon. A new idea sprang to life in him, and though it seemed a fool's path, he let go.

Instead of fighting it, he allowed the shard to burst loose and tear him from his body. The disembodied elf-state took over, and it seemed to him that he heard the triumphant cry of a raven. At the same time, though it was at first dizzying, he found he was able to hold on to himself. As his energy spread above and around him, he remained anchored to a sense of who he was, and this sense gave him sudden courage.

Calm came over Dayraven. Though the sharp tip of his own sword pricked the flesh of his neck, he was not afraid. Instead, he watched as if it were someone else who had a giant Thjoth pointing a sword at his throat. He was still. Not a trace of panic, or any other emotion, came from him.

For a fraction of a moment, the deep blue eyes of the elf surfaced again in his mind, and he perceived everything in front of him with an uncanny clarity. The gazes of the other men in the company reached his consciousness. Their fear and tautness crept around him. Imharr and the two Dweorgs were angry and on the verge of violence. But, at the center of all these emotions, he remained strangely serene. He heard the Thjoth's breathing, beheld his eyes and looked within. Somehow, he knew Orvandil would not harm him. He could not have told why, but in that moment, he knew. *He's testing me. Have I seen him before? In a dream?*

In a subtle balancing act, Dayraven kept the elf-state from severing him from his body, but he allowed enough of it to flow into him to keep sensing the thoughts of the man before him.

The tall captain's eyes widened. Somewhere in the Thjoth's mind, a feeling was born, a dim awareness that the man could never have put into words. *He too feels he knows me, but he doesn't know why.* Dayraven remained in control even as he floated in the elf-state. Never before had he been able to focus the gift in such a way, and he grew confident. *If I can wield it, not only can I hide it, but perhaps I can use it.* In his dissociated yet somehow very connected state, the possibility of such power became intriguing. The presence of the elf pulsed within him, but it seemed to obey his will.

The captain returned Dayraven's stare and kept Sweothol leveled at his neck. "Fine blade, Dayraven. From where?"

"My father," he answered coolly. It sounded like someone else's voice.

Orvandil removed the blade and offered the hilt to Dayraven. When he grasped it, the Thjoth nodded to him. It was over.

Centering his thoughts on his body and his breaths, Dayraven commanded the thing in his mind to diminish. He snapped into his body, and his mundane perceptions returned with a slight queasiness. The elf-state receded back to a bare hush, and he sheathed Sweothol. He had passed more than one test. He stood straighter as triumph suffused him, but he kept his face steady.

The captain said in a loud voice, "Loyal to friends. Good. Be loyal to soldiers in this company, and you'll do well. Second thing you learn."

Imharr breathed a sigh when Captain Orvandil walked back over to the center of the front row. The Thjoth addressed the company. "For we go to war. Only thing to keep you alive is the man next to you. You're the Mercenary Company of Etinstone. Expect to be on the front lines, where death stares you in the face. I promise no glory, for war gives none. I promise no wealth, for those who rule you take that. I promise one thing: Follow me and stay true to each other, and more of you will live.

"Listen! We march to Hasumere. We reach it in five days. Bring nothing you don't need. Supply wagons have provisions. We add what comes in our path. Expect little comfort."

Orvandil scanned the men. "Any questions?"

No one among the company said a word.

"Good. We leave soon, when the supply wagons are ready. March through the city in formation and in time. Once out of the city, walk how you like, as long as you keep up. Now, wagon drivers and standard-bearer, come with me. The rest wait for the order to leave."

After the captain departed, the men relaxed and conversed among themselves. Imharr turned to Dayraven. "Fine way to introduce yourself."

"Friendly fellow, isn't he?" Dayraven smiled.

Gnorn put his hand on Dayraven's shoulder. His sad eyes gleamed when he looked at him. "Thanks, lad. The big bastard's right. You're loyal to friends. Just make sure you take no harm from it."

"Nothing you wouldn't have done for me. And somehow I don't think he would have harmed me. At any rate, Hlokk was close to swinging his axe at his kneecaps, so I had to say something."

"Ha!" said Hlokk, "So you nearly got us all killed before we even arrive at a battle."

The four companions laughed. Dayraven grinned as he recalled how he had controlled the elf-state while facing Orvandil, even used it for his own purpose. Much had changed this day, and he was almost dizzy with it all. He had real hope that he could learn to wield the power within him, and he was a soldier on his way to war.

16

PAST, PRESENT, AND FUTURE

The image came to her at once, unbidden, as her glimpses into the future always were: On a sloping field with jagged mountains looming in the background and a hard rain pouring down, a drenched Imharr in soldier's garb shouted amidst a chaos of screaming men.

Death was everywhere. Bodies, some lifeless and some groaning in agony, lay all around in blood-soaked mud. Soldiers fell with gaping wounds. Men hacked at each other in desperation. And a dozen soldiers clad in red surrounded Imharr, who wore Torrlond's ensign on the left shoulder of his blood-spattered grey kirtle.

With fury in his eyes, Imharr cursed at them in his birth language, Eastern Ondunic. The soldiers, seeing their prey at bay, closed in, but he lashed out with his sword, catching one in the face. The man screamed and held his hands to the red stripe leaking from his cheek and eye.

The others backed off, and Imharr could have tried to flee. But he was protecting something he stood over: the prostrate body of another soldier, from whose crimsoned neck the life flowed out of a deep gash. A line of bright red dribbled out of the young soldier's mouth, contrasting with his pale face and downy beard. Emptiness stared from his blue eyes as rain pelted him. Urd knew the face well, for it was Dayraven's. After the shock of recognition, the soldiers rushed in to slay Imharr just before several other blurred figures shot into view.

She awoke. "What have they done?"

Though she opened her eyes, darkness surrounded Urd, and wood creaked as her body pitched. She put her hand to her chest and winced, trying to slow her breaths. *Curse the young fools. And I can do nothing now. If only I had some way of reaching them. But what then? Gods, there's need for haste.*

With a groan she rose from the sacks of wool that served as her bed and put her feet on wooden planks that would not hold still. The joints of her hips and shoulders and knees popped and cracked as she unfolded her body. She groped her way with her hands in front of her and stumbled over to a source of light above her. The light shone down from a hatch and spilled onto a ladder, which she grasped with both hands. She climbed up into the full light of day, her old limbs shaking from the exertion and from the shock of the true-dream.

She composed herself after she emerged on the deck of a mid-sized merchant ship. Squat and deep bellied, it was large and well built enough to brave the Great Sea's waves, though never far from a known coastline. She squinted in the sunlight as a salty, strong sea breeze tossed a few loose strands of her bound white hair. The ship groaned and kicked up foam as it cut through the waves. The pregnant square sail whipped and rippled, dancing with the wind that urged the ship along. Beyond the vessel, endless grey-blue glistened under the sun.

A dozen or so sailors conversed and shouted in Western Ondunic, and, perhaps still unnerved by the dream, Urd had to shake her head to remind herself where she was and how she had arrived there. *Too many journeys. They begin to blur together. And I'm too damn old.* The ship's home port lay on the isolated western coast of the kingdom of Caergilion. The men on the first vessel from the town of Farwick had brought her from the western edge of the Mark to a small trading port on Caergilion's coast. There, after a couple days, she found a merchant ship full of the famed wool from Caergilion's remote northwestern hills bound for Asdralad.

The merchant who owned the ship had been more than willing to give Urd passage after she healed his youngest and favorite daughter of the fever that took three of his village's children. Since those gifted in magic and healing seldom visited Caergilion's coastal villages, his little girl too likely would have died without her intervention. The poor fellow had not stopped thanking her during the whole voyage.

Avoiding the rigging and the sailors who kept the ship on course, Urd toddled on the starboard side. Never too confident aboard a ship, her advancing age did little to strengthen her sea legs. At least she had been able to keep that morning's gruel down. She tottered and grasped the railing as she made her way toward the merchant, who stood at the bow with his arms crossed before his chest and the big grin that always lit up his face, except when he was yelling at his sailors.

He had the dark hair and bronze skin of the south, and, to judge by his belly, he had done well enough for himself over the years. Though his garb was cleaner, he dressed like his sailors, who were lean and even darker than he from their toil in the sun. All of them wore short breeches reaching their calves and, while half went about bare-chested, the other half wore light tunics. Some, like the merchant, wore cordwain shoes, but most of the sailors went barefoot. In addition, the merchant, who called himself Cormar, sported a baggy felt hat cocked to one side, and his oiled mustache curled up on both ends.

Cormar beamed at Urd and motioned with open arms for her to come near. "You are being below long time. You sleep good?" He spoke with a thick, lilting Ondunic accent in the Northern Tongue. No matter where in Eormenlond, even the humblest merchants, if they had any desire to trade beyond their own shores, needed at least a smattering of the Northern Tongue.

The sailors, who spoke only the Western Ondunic of their native soil, stared from time to time at their master and Urd, whom they feared as most folk everywhere fear a sorceress. They took care to avoid her during the entire voyage, and she obliged them by keeping to herself. But now she was in a hurry, and being cooped up on this ship gnawed at her patience.

"I've slept in less comfortable places." She forced a smile. "How much longer until we reach Asdralad?"

"We make good time. Last evening we are passing between Asdralad's north point and Dirgal, most north of Isles of Yaladir. If this wind is holding, we reach Asdralad's chief city Kiriath with time to find lodgings before supper. And food is excellent in Kiriath." The merchant laughed and grinned as he rubbed his belly.

Urd smiled in return, though food was the last thing on her mind. "Good. Thank you."

"It is I who am owing you thanks." He bowed his head as Urd turned.

She walked aft until, passing by the tiller on the starboard side, she reached the ship's stern, where she was out of the sailors' way. Staring at the ship's wake for some time, she gazed north. Her thoughts reached out, and she pondered where her grandnephew and Imharr had gone.

The two young men occupied her entire mind. She was certain they had turned from the path she set them on and were now in Torrlond, the last place she wanted them to end up. And the gods only knew how much damage Dayraven might do before he met the terrible fate she had seen. All that power on the loose, and no one to guide him. It was hard to catch her breath, and she fought back tears at the idea of losing him like that.

Was it too late? Too late for Dayraven, and too late for Eormenlond. Her thoughts grew desperate, and she wanted to scream out her frustration. *No good, that. Must think what to do.* Could Galdor find them? Little chance of that. *Have I ruined all our hopes? That foolish boy is stubborn like his mother was. I woke ere the true-dream ended. No way to prevent it, but there may be something there. Think. How to find him? Oh, my dear boy. If I've sent you to your death, my own grief shall be greatest.*

A seagull's cry far above the ship broke into her thoughts. She looked up and scanned the blue sky, squinting and shielding her eyes from the bright sun. A spot drifted high in the air. She nodded to herself and chanted, "Tulimmin nidanwi ar duwando shoran. Ardommin vinanwi im farando dhunan."

As she repeated the phrases several times, the seagull circled lower and lower. The distant speck grew, its white wings coasting on the wind. In a gyre it descended until it flew overhead. First hovering over the ship for a moment, it floated just past the mast as it lowered itself and flapped its ruffled feathers. With the sailors all watching, it landed on the railing next to Urd and gazed at her with its beady eyes, waiting for her to speak. The men stopped even pretending to work at their tasks and stared with mouths agape when she whispered to the bird. The witch ignored them as she imparted her message. "Go to Kiriath, to the palace on the hill, and tell the queen. All must be ready when I arrive. There's no time to spare."

The merchant Cormar, who had also been staring, scolded the sailors in Ondunic, "Fabrarth doch gwaeri, don vilot gagleri!" His shouting startled them into returning to keeping the ship on course, though they stole glances at the witch when their master was not looking.

A moment later, the seagull cried once and spread its wings so that the breeze bore it back up into the air behind the ship. The witch, the merchant, and the sailors all watched it flap up into the air currents, which carried it ahead of them due south for a while. Before long it disappeared from view.

THE SEAGULL CONTINUED ITS FLIGHT SOUTH OVER SHIMMERING waters. For miles it flew until the sea far below it changed from dark greyish-blue to a translucent azure like sapphire. Soon after, waves broke in white lines one after another on a sandy beach beneath craggy cliffsides. The seagull kept its course, and before long the coast expanded into land fertile and brown with the southern sun's heat. Olive trees grew on rocky hillsides, and the bird passed over a few small villages of square-shaped homes wrought of the tan limestone predominating in that soil. After some time, its shadow winked across a few trees, and then a green forest of cedars, cypresses and tall firs covered the land. Above the forest the seagull shot through the sky, borne by the strong wind. The wind took it for a while until the forested hills gave way to a city standing nigh a bay. In the bay's clear water floated various fishing vessels and merchant ships.

Among towers and columned buildings wrought of tan stone and smooth streets paved with the same, dark specks of people milled about. Swollen white domes rested atop a few of the larger structures, but red terracotta tiles roofed most buildings. The bird flew over the city's wall, also wrought of the light brown stone, and made its way to a building set above the rest of the city on a rocky hillside.

Slender and carved tan columns supported a roof tiled with some iridescent stone, atop of which rested a curved dome peaking in a spire. Beneath a large porch wrapping around the structure, mosaics made of small, deep-hued stones covered the floor in dazzling patterns. The doors and large windows were all open to welcome the sea's breeze.

Over the dome's top the seagull coasted, and on the other side it alighted on the branch of a hibiscus tree in an enclosed garden. On the borders of the garden stood tall cedars, and further within grew two rows of hibiscus trees with large crimson flowers drooping from their branches. On both sides of the flower-laden trees, luxuriant bushes displayed dark green leaves and slender purple buds. Sundry petals of white, yellow, red, and pink rampaged in a riot of color over other bushes scattered throughout the garden. The keepers of the flowers trimmed them in places and in others left them to wander, letting some climb in vines up the garden's stone walls. Through the bushes of flowers wove paths of white gravel, and each path led to a rectangular pool of clear water in the garden's center. On the pool's bottom was a mosaic of bright stones in intricate patterns zigzagging in and out of each other. Stone benches bordered the pool on each side, and on one of them sat two women conversing.

The elder of the two had long black hair with strands of silver in the middle. Her large, dark eyes gazed at her companion, at whom she directed a gentle smile. Her bronze skin contrasted with the bright blue-green dress draping her tall, slender body. She wore no ornamentation other than a gold ring with a deep-blue gem on her right hand's index finger.

The younger woman wore a dark crimson dress, and the waves of her long, raven-colored hair glistened in the sun. Though not as tall as her companion, she too had a slender build. A keenness dwelled in her dark brown eyes. Listening to her companion, the younger woman stared with intensity and nodded as if drinking in and weighing every word.

The elder woman first noticed the seagull in the hibiscus tree. She went silent and gazed at it.

"What is it, my queen?" asked the younger woman in High Andumaic.

"We have a visitor," replied the elder in a voice like silk. "Let us see what it tells us." She chanted in a tongue far more ancient than even High Andumaic or any other. "Tulimmin nidanwi argellon an kellor. Roninnin beldulwi vindallon ni bindor."

After she sang the song of origin, the seagull leapt from its perch and glided to the bench where the two women sat. It landed and hopped toward the elder woman, who closed her eyes. While she did this, the bird cried several times. When it had been silent a while, she opened her eyes. "Thank you, little one. You may go. Rest your wings in the bay, where fish wait in plenty for you." At that, the seagull flapped its wings and flew over the garden wall, crying out once before it disappeared in the distance.

The younger woman's question showed on her face. "Who sent the message, my lady?"

The elder smiled. "Urd. She arrives shortly in a merchant vessel from Caergilion. Our lesson for today is finished. You will go to the docks to meet her. Her journey has been long, but I sense her impatience. Try to convince her to rest for a while, Sequara. Then bring her to me."

Sequara returned the smile. "With pleasure, my queen."

Rising from the stone bench, she bowed to the elder woman and walked through the garden to a pair of carved doors leading into the palace of Queen Faldira. Along with the queen's personal guards, Karad was waiting within. Now strong and fit, he showed no sign of his terrible wounds after she healed him that day, though his thigh and shoulder would always bear the scars. *I was able to keep him from dying, thanks be to Anghara. But not Aravh.*

The memory of killing Aravh along with the priest of the Way and the Torrlonder soldiers who had attacked her and her men was as strong and fresh as ever. The scene had revisited her in nightmares since. Even now it flashed before her: The bright, terrible *almakhti* she had called forth rent the air. Their cries and the smell of their burnt flesh were as vivid as on the day it happened. Their agony and sudden knowledge of death screamed in her mind. Suppressing a shudder, she reminded herself of her present purpose and walked on.

With a nod, Karad fell in beside Sequara. She turned to him. "We're to meet an old friend at the docks. Urd is arriving."

"Very well, my lady."

They made their way through the spacious and airy hall, passing several light brown pillars with small, colorful stones set in them. On many walls hung silk tapestries of bright and variegated colors, stirring in the sea breeze that ghosted through the palace. The dozen or so palace guards they met all bowed to Sequara. Like Karad, over their white tunics, the guards were clad in light corselets of black leather with small square plates of steel set in them. They wore wide, graceful helms of steel and bronze, and each bore a curved sword sheathed in a black scabbard. The thongs of their shoes crisscrossed up their calves, and they tucked their loose white breeches into these cords. After the manner of men in the east of Eormenlond, they were clean-shaven.

Keeping her face impassive, she nodded to acknowledge the guards and walked on, with Karad keeping pace. Eventually, they came to the building's front doors, which were carved with graceful vines and scrolls. The doors were already open, and four guards bowed as they walked out.

When they emerged from the palace doors, Sequara took a moment to gaze down at the city.

Karad waited next to her. "That's a sight I never tire of, though I've seen it thousands of times."

Sequara allowed a half smile on her face. "It's home." The white domes and red roofs of Kiriath clustered below them. Its tan buildings and streets glistened in the sun, and beyond its walls the translucent blue of the bay shimmered. Her smile disappeared, and a sigh escaped her lips. Such beauty was fragile and vulnerable. It would fall to her one day to keep her city and kingdom from harm. *Torrlond is coming, and we're not ready.* "Let's go."

She and Karad descended the series of wide stone steps meandering down the hillside. Stately cedars interspersed every twenty feet lined both sides of the steps. The sea breeze thick with its salty tang ruffled Sequara's hair, and the warm sun caressed her skin. When they reached the last of the stairs, she changed her countenance into a look of regal detachment. No smile. Chin high. Steady gaze speaking of devotion to duty.

Next to her, Karad gave her a brief grin before putting on a stern frown. Much of his task was to keep people away from her, and he knew the right look to accomplish it.

The stone steps leading down from the palace ended in Kiriath's central thoroughfare. At the foot of the hill, shops and homes occupied both sides of the street. Like the palace, but on a smaller scale, the squarish structures of Kiriath were open and airy, beckoning the winds from the Great Sea to invade them through spacious windows. And though every shop and home was wrought of the same tan limestone, the city was a haven of bright colors, for no other folk was as skillful with or as fond of their textiles as those of Asdralad, who sought to outdo each other in the vibrancy of their garments.

"How is Heera?" Sequara spoke without turning to Karad.

"Well enough to keep me in order," he answered without changing his impassive face.

Knowing how formidable Karad's wife was and how she showed her love and her pride in her husband by scolding and fussing over him, Sequara almost grinned. "What did she have to say about your latest scars?"

The veteran snorted. "Told me a couple more holes would do me no harm, and to be more careful looking after you. Of course, I couldn't tell her where I got them."

"Of course." Sequara frowned, knowing the secrets Karad kept from his wife were yet more sacrifices he made. *We all have our duties.*

The hum of conversations filled the air as citizens gathered in small groups in and around the street. From the inns and eating houses emanated the voices of female singers and their accompanists on lyre and drum as well as the enticing aroma of spices and seafood. Occasional laughter burst out of their open doors and windows. Sequara and Karad made their way down the wide, sunlit avenue by the rows of two and three storied buildings. Over the shops' roofs soared the tall watchtowers that the wealthiest noble houses built out of ancient custom. Peaking in crenellated tops, the towers reminded the citizens of the glory of their ruling houses, in all of which the gift ran strong.

They were also a constant reminder that Sequara did not belong to one of those houses. Those tall towers were still strangers to her. But that did not matter. She had proven herself to Queen Faldira, and she would serve Asdralad as best she could.

The largest number of shops sold fabrics, Asdralad's chief delight and specialty. Many of these shops had existed for generations, and the families of the oldest establishments counted theirs the most prestigious. At the famed textile shops and elsewhere, the merchants and their customers, all dressed in Asdralad's loose-fitting and colorful garb, stopped their business to bow to Sequara as she passed. Karad stayed close by her side, scanning the street and resting his hand on his sword's hilt.

A buzz of recognition followed in their wake, but Sequara was long accustomed to that. Since the day more than a decade ago when Faldira had named her successor in accordance with the ancient custom of the Andumae, the people of Kiriath and all of Asdralad had held Sequara in great honor and esteem. Even if many in the traditional ruling houses still regarded her with coldness behind their courtesy, the common people showed nearly as much love for Sequara as they did for Queen Faldira.

Near the columned temples of Oruma and Anghara they walked. The two squarish temples were among the oldest structures in the city. Simple and elegant, their façades rose fifty feet and stood side by side. Each had porticos with columns carved out of some dark green stone resembling marble. Sequara had often sought guidance from the Father and Mother in their places of worship, though her duties had kept her from visiting the temples for quite some time. Worshippers of every class trickled in and out of the open entranceways to the buildings. Those who noticed Sequara bowed as she went by, a few whispering to their neighbors after they turned their backs to her.

There would be some time before Urd arrived, so she made a quick decision to duck into the Temple of Anghara and observe the rites, which often gave her peace and clarity as well as a chance at brief anonymity of a sort. She turned to Karad. "I'll go inside just for a moment. Wait for me on the steps."

He frowned at her. The veteran did not like leaving her side when they were outside the palace, but she had always insisted that the temples were sacred spaces where she must appear like all others in communion with the Mother and Father. He knew her well enough not to argue. "Very well, my lady."

SEQUARA CLIMBED THE STEPS OF THE TEMPLE'S PORTICO AND SLIPPED off her shoes, leaving them among the dozens of other pairs. Within the wide, open entrance was a shallow, square pool fed by a gentle, gurgling fountain, and along its edges lay numerous clay vessels for any visitor to use. Torches in sconces along the walls reflected in the pool.

A small group of citizens who had preceded her were sitting at the pool's edges and bathing their feet. Sequara joined them. Though they all glanced at her, no one spoke. No one would disturb her in the hushed silence of the temple even to greet her. She took up one of the vessels and, after filling it at the fountain, poured water over her feet. Then she sat at one edge of the pool and let them dangle in the water for a while.

As the water soothed her feet, the rest of her body relaxed as well. All the weight of her duties fell away, at least for a little while, and peace lulled her. When she was ready, she rose from the pool and entered the inner sanctum. The stone floor was cool on the soles of her feet. Past a network of columns she walked, brushing by worshipers who had finished and were returning to the mundane world outside. Torches mounted on the columns provided a little light, but few would recognize her in the dimness of the temple's interior.

She neared the back wall of the temple. A sorceress was chanting up ahead. Even before an infant began to mewl, she recognized the rite of welcoming a child into the world. It was auspicious to come to the temple at such a time. While Sequara would never have a child of her own, she always felt the presence of the Mother was strongest in her place of worship when the birth rites were being performed. She smiled as she approached the holiest portion of the temple, where the ancient representation of the Mother waited.

On the floor rested a circular stone some four feet high and ten feet in diameter. It must have weighed several tons. In the ruddy torchlight, it was impossible to tell the stone's true color, but it appeared dark and wet. Hundreds of years of rituals had worn the stone's surface smooth, and it was hollowed out to form a shallow bowl. Though Sequara had seen the stone thousands of times, mystery and power emanated from it.

In the center of the stone lay the naked newborn on her back, her tiny limbs swiveling in the air. The withered stump of her umbilical cord was still attached to her round belly, for the rite took place on the third day from birth. A shock of dark hair covered the top of her head. Her little eyes were open, and they stared up as if unsure what to make of her dark surroundings. Though she was not crying, she emitted a few whimpers as if exploring the possibility that she might need to. On either side of her atop the stone sat her mother and father, who smiled at her with adoring eyes as the sorceress chanted the words of the rite. The young mother and father stole glances at each other from time to time. From those glances Sequara could guess how happy and in love they must have been.

She watched as an anonymous observer. The sorceress in attendance was too weak in the gift to sense Sequara's presence from that distance, but Sequara could feel the power in the red-robed woman. It was difficult to tell in the dimness, but she thought it might be a noblewoman named Namila.

She found herself gazing at the young mother and wondering what it was like. It was not envy or even regret she felt, exactly. But she was witnessing something holy. Something belonging to a realm she would never explore.

Surrounded by relatives and friends, who stood on the floor all around the sacred stone, the young parents waited for the sorceress to finish chanting the words of the rite in High Andumaic: "In the name of the Mother, we welcome you to this world. In the name of the Mother, we welcome you to this life. May Anghara bless you and witness your parents' vow to protect you, to offer you comfort and joy, to guide you as best they can in the ways of wisdom. And long may Anghara keep you in the company of dear ones . . ."

At a signal from the sorceress, the parents poured a trickle of water over the infant's forehead. The little one decided it was indeed time for a cry. Breaking Sequara's trance, the baby alternated between quick intakes of breath and little feline wails. Sequara recalled her purpose. She turned away and walked back out of the temple, leaving behind all the emotions in the darkness of that sacred space.

AFTER TUGGING ON HER SHOES, SHE SQUINTED AT THE BRIGHT sunlight outside and descended the temple steps. Gazing up at her, Karad waited at the bottom of the steps, conveying his relief at seeing her with a mere nod and the slight raising of one eyebrow, the closest he would come to scolding her or expressing his impatience.

They continued down Kiriath's main thoroughfare. Now coming closer to the docks, they met the more simply dressed farmers selling fruits and vegetables and fishmongers peddling their wares from wooden carts. Their cries and transactions ceased when they noticed Sequara's presence only to resume seconds after she walked by. All who met her bowed, and though some cast a wary glance toward Karad, in their smiles for her was no trace of the practiced deception that marked the grins of their social superiors. She sighed and admitted to herself that she still felt more at ease among such common folk.

A quick nod of approval from Karad told her that he noticed their smiles too. "They're proud of you, my lady." His voice became so low that she hardly heard him. "We're proud of you."

Glancing down and pretending not to hear, Sequara suppressed her emotions – both joy at the praise and anxiety at the weight of expectations – to embrace the equanimity that should be hers at all times.

Soon the plaintive piping of seagulls replaced the din of conversations. The pulse of the waves breaking on the beach rumbled nearby. The street led straight to the docks, which met the bay's lapping water. Not far from the docks, a series of palm trees looked out over the water. With Karad beside her, Sequara made her way toward the shade and solitude beneath the long fronds, where no one would dare disturb her. There she sat down with her back against a tree and waited on the white beach. Karad moved under the shade of the next tree over, standing at attention as he kept scanning the area. His presence meant she could wander in her own thoughts for a time without fear.

As the wind murmured through the leaves, it tossed back her hair and stroked her face. A tiny rivulet of sweat crawled down from her neck and tickled her back. It was a pleasantly hot day. The trees provided a welcome haven to Sequara, who watched the fishing boats and busy dockworkers. After noting her presence from a distance and bowing, the men who labored at the docks continued their tasks of loading and unloading goods from waiting ships.

Over the waves she gazed, and her thoughts reached out. She closed her eyes and let her consciousness expand. Her mind pulsed along with the repetitive hush of the waves, and soon she hearkened to the timeless voice of the island. The sands and stone of her kingdom had witnessed generations of her people come and go. They were part of this island, and it was part of each of them. The waters sundering them from the rest of Andumedan had also molded their character as a folk set apart, devoted to their two gods and their past. It was no accident that the common Andumaic spoken in Asdralad was most like the High Andumaic of old. They were the upholders of the ancient ways and laws handed down from Oruma and Anghara, and they fulfilled their calling with a special sense of and devotion to beauty.

Amidst these meditations something disturbed Sequara and called her back to the troubles of the present. In a savage world, beauty was not much of a defense. Her exquisite home was in danger. This knowledge seldom left her conscious mind, and it allowed her little peace these days.

The people of Asdralad did not yet know it, but across those waters on the mainland of Andumedan, a great army of the northern invaders had formed and was on the verge of swallowing the southern kingdoms, Caergilion and Adanon. True, everyone knew the Torrlonders' intention to invade Caergilion. But few knew the barbarians would use their brutal religion as a pretext for conquering all of Andumedan, thus finishing the process their illiterate ancestors had begun.

After Torrlond finished with the south, the eastern kingdoms would be next. Alone, Asdralad was too small to make a difference, and at length its time too would come. The peace and stillness of the small island offered no defense against such a powerful force. Its loveliness and color, even its lore and strength in sorcery, were small and delicate compared to the consuming, zealous hate driving the mighty Torrlonders and their conquering religion. The Asdralae needed to learn to fight. She would see to it they did.

Thus lost in her thoughts, Sequara did not feel the time passing as she waited for Urd's arrival. Karad, however, cleared his throat, a signal she understood to mean that she should return to the present. She rose from her spot and brushed sand from her dress. A moment later, a dockworker cried out identifying an incoming merchant vessel as hailing from Caergilion. Within a short enough time the ship's sailors reefed the sail, and then they rowed it to one of the docks, which Sequara approached.

As dockworkers tied the vessel with hawsers thrown by the seafarers, she walked closer to look for Urd with Karad trailing her. Before seeing the woman, she sensed the familiar presence of the gift in her, and soon enough her old friend appeared on the ship's deck. The women smiled at each other from a distance, after which Urd spoke to a portly man who appeared to be the ship's owner. He bowed copiously to his passenger as she said farewell. Once Urd walked down the plank with a wary sailor's assistance, the two women embraced.

Urd stroked the younger woman's long dark hair and spoke in fluent High Andumaic: "You've grown more beautiful than ever, my dear Sequara."

"It is not I but you who are beautiful."

"Nonsense."

"Beauty shines from you, Urd. Only a fool could not see it. But you must be weary from your voyage. Shall I ask Karad to find a carriage?"

The old woman shook her head. "No. A walk would do my bones some good after being cooped up like one more sack of wool on that tub." She turned to Karad. "And how do you fare, Karad?"

The veteran gave a bow. "Well enough, my lady."

"Good. And what of Heera? How is her garden?" Always interested in herbs, Urd had spoken with the veteran's wife several times on past visits.

Karad grinned. "As bountiful as ever. I'll fetch some of her flowers for you on the morrow."

Urd smiled. "I'd like that very much."

They left behind the shouts of men and cries of seagulls at the docks and made their way into the city. Hand in hand the two women walked with Karad following close behind. Urd's progress was slow, especially when they reached the steps leading up to the palace, but Sequara was glad of her company. They talked together of small events in the Mark and in Asdralad as if they had no greater burdens in the world.

Eventually, they arrived at the palace's front doors, still wide open to welcome the newly arrived guest. Urd was taking somewhat heavy breaths, but Sequara was impressed with the old woman's stamina. The guards bowed to the two women and nodded to Karad. When they passed inside, Sequara said, "I'll show you to your quarters, where you may rest for a while."

"I wouldn't mind washing up a bit, but I have urgent matters to discuss with your mistress. Rest comes later."

"The queen told me you would be impatient."

"Good. Then she'll be expecting me."

A SHORT TIME LATER, SEQUARA LED URD TO QUEEN FALDIRA IN A private chamber. The room's sparse furniture and decor lent it elegance and airiness. Bright tapestries covered each wall, and a large window's shutters were wide open to let in sunlight and a pleasant breeze that toyed with the edges of the tapestries. A patterned rug covered the stone floor, atop of which a few embroidered cushions surrounded a low and small but richly carved table. Queen Faldira sat on a chair of wine-red wood next to the window, out of which she gazed. When Urd entered, the queen turned toward her, stood up from her seat, and smiled. The two women approached each other and embraced.

"It's good to see you," said the queen in High Andumaic. On her forehead rested a slim golden band with a blue gem identical to the one on her ring.

"And you, your Majesty," said Urd in the same tongue. "We have important matters to discuss."

"Yes, my friend. Sequara tells me you're in haste, as is your wont." The queen's smile lit up the room. "But first I insist you eat a little something with me to tide us over until we sup."

"Very well," said Urd with mock impatience, "if your Majesty insists."

A maidservant brought pomegranates and sundry berries that grew on the island of Asdralad, and the two younger women reclined on the cushions around the table. Urd sat cross-legged on a pillow. While they ate, the women inquired after each other's health with a fondness coming from years of friendship as well as sympathy of the mind.

"Did you try the powder I gave you last time for your aches?"

"Yes, and it did wonders, but I ran out some time ago. Can't find half the ingredients in the Mark. I must have some more."

"Of course. Sequara will make some herself. She's skilled at all the healing arts."

"No need to trouble the heir to the throne on account of my old bones."

"Nonsense," said Sequara. "It will give me pleasure to make it for you."

White-haired and fragile with many years, on the doorstep of old age, and in the full bloom of ripe youth — they brought together a balance of past wisdom, present power, and future promise. Yet something deeper than blood, something larger than each woman, bound them together. It was not only that the gift ran deep in each of them. It was a common vision of the world and their place in it, something each woman was prepared to work and fight for.

They stopped eating. Urd spoke in a new tone, suggesting it was time for deeper matters. "I've traveled from afar, and I'm certain things have moved since I set out. Have you received news, your Majesty?"

Faldira's face became grave. "Sequara has lately returned from Torrlond. She brought the promised song of origin back to Asdralad, but I fear none of us can wield it. That test must come later, though. Other tidings are not good. Bledla and Earconwald captured two of Galdor's men while they waited for Sequara to meet our benefactor in Torrhelm. Fortunately, the messengers did not know our benefactor's name. Galdor has been wise to keep to such secrecy, but the priests appear to have tortured every other piece of information out of the two men. They know we are aware of them and their plans of conquest over the southwest and, eventually, all of Andumedan. And they know we are attempting to unite the southwestern and eastern kingdoms before the hammer falls."

Urd frowned. "Not good. But those are not all ill tidings."

Faldira paused before she resumed. "There is worse. In spite of our efforts, we cannot overcome the hatred between Adanon and Caergilion. The two enemies refuse to see their common danger. King Balch of Adanon, who has an army strong enough to make a difference, refuses to believe Torrlond's ambitions extend beyond Caergilion. He's too gleeful at the prospect of Caergilion's demise to see his own danger. And King Malruan of Caergilion is too proud to ask his old foe for aid. Bledla and Earconwald know this. They know how weak we are, how disunited. Without Adanon to help defend Caergilion's borders, there's too little time to act, and even less hope for the southwest. As for the eastern kingdoms, they will not move until Torrlond threatens their borders."

"What do you plan next?"

The queen sighed, seeming to reconcile herself to a difficult course. "Asdralad can do little in the coming war, at least for the present. We lack the military power. Our strength has never been in arms, but we need to remedy this. In the short term, I have decided to send Sequara one last time to King Balch in Adanon and King Malruan in Caergilion. She will attempt to persuade them to see reason. If she is to replace me someday, there will be no greater testing ground than this. I only wish it had not come in her time."

"My lady," said Sequara, "I'll do my best to serve you."

Queen Faldira smiled at Sequara and continued. "There may be time for one last attempt at uniting Caergilion and Adanon. The armies of Torrlond are even now mustering and making their way to the Marar Mountains. And you know as well as I what horrors the priests of the Way bring with them. Caergilion will fall if it fights alone, but there's a chance we can hold off Torrlond if Adanon comes around. Perhaps then the eastern kingdoms will come to our aid, and even Torrlond could not withstand the rest of Andumedan were it brought together as one."

"Otherwise," whispered Urd, "the cost will be terrible."

The three sat for a moment in silence. It was Urd who spoke again.

"Yet there is a glimmer of hope." She smiled at Faldira and Sequara. "It was under my nose for the longest time, but I was foolish enough not to see it. Perhaps I was afraid. Well, I could not have known what would happen. Only now, I fear with all my heart it's almost lost to us." The old woman sighed.

Sequara asked, "What is this hope?"

Urd's forehead creased as she raised her eyebrows. "A foolish young man who's probably found the quickest way to get himself killed."

"It doesn't sound like much hope, then," said Sequara. "Who is he?"

"In fact, he's my grandnephew. Dayraven." Urd's eyes kindled as she smiled. "What would you say if a mortal survived an encounter with an elf, even came back from the elf-sleep with the gift so augmented in him that you fear to stand next to him?"

Queen Faldira sat up and stared at Urd. "Such a thing has never happened. If it were true, that person must have a deep link to the life that quickens the world, an unknown potential to see behind the veil enfolding our existence. In short, he would have great power. He could be the one we need. And then there is the matter of Aldmund's prophecies. Waking from the elf-sleep might be taken to point to certain statements Aldmund made about the returning of his power."

Urd nodded. "'My power shall be reborn in the one who awakeneth and beholdeth the world anew. It is this one who shall save Eormenlond from destruction, and such will be the true Prophet of Edan.'" She spoke in the Old Northern Tongue.

Sequara gave a puzzled frown.

"From the Book of Aldmund," said the old woman, switching back to High Andumaic. She turned to Queen Faldira. "Yes. If he were trained, Dayraven could wield the song of origin Sequara brought. He could rival and even overcome the Supreme Priest Bledla. None of us has this strength — not I, not you, not Tirgalan of Sundara, not even Galdor."

"Are you certain he's that strong?" asked Faldira.

"If you could see Dayraven now, feel the presence of the gift in him . . . It was so strong I had to muster the courage just to remain in his presence without gawking. He could master Bledla, take away his strength. And Bledla's strength, the strength of the Way, is Torrlond's backbone. If someone could challenge him, take away his control, it would not only eliminate the threat of the priests' beasts. It would destroy Torrlond's arrogance by revealing the supreme priest is not invincible, not Edan's almighty chosen one. It would break them. Give Eormenlond a different Prophet of Edan, and Bledla's cause is lost, and Earconwald's along with it."

"Are you saying your kinsman truly awoke from the elf-sleep, that he came back from the death of Anghara?" asked Sequara. It was hard to believe, and if anyone other than Urd or Faldira had told her of such a thing, she would have dismissed that person as foolish or insane.

Urd closed her eyes and took a deep breath. "I saw it myself. He always had the potential to wield magic, the gift in great measure, but I let him be because of what he desired. For his sake, you understand. He never wanted to be as alone as devotion to the gift demands. Well, it doesn't matter now. His awakening from the elf-sleep changed everything. The moment I saw his body, I knew something was strange. Then, when he awoke and the power blazed forth from him . . . It stole my breath away. For a moment I believed all of us who witnessed it would perish." She shook her head. "Well, as I said, none of it matters now. What matters is we could lose him, which would be our ruin and my own deepest sorrow."

"Why do you fear this?" asked Faldira.

Urd looked at the queen and sighed. "I was afraid. The agents of the Way were coming for us. I did not know how to begin to control Dayraven's power, so I did what I thought best. I sent him to Galdor in Ellond. Kinsford's priest wanted him dead. The fellow was harmless enough himself, but he would have told his master, and Bledla would have known the threat to himself. The supreme priest sees himself as the prophesied heir to Aldmund's power, but he could not fail to see what Dayraven's awakening might mean. The boy's life was at stake, so I sent him to the safest place I knew while I came here, hoping to draw attention away from him. He would have been in danger with me, and only you or Galdor could hope to train the boy. He's too close to me, you see. Too dear."

The queen put a hand on Urd's shoulder. "Then you took the wisest course."

"Perhaps. Perhaps not. Our difficulty is Dayraven did not go to Galdor. I have reason to believe he did the last thing we could have wanted, short of delivering his own head to Bledla. He's joined Torrlond's army."

"Why would he do such a thing?" asked Sequara.

"I don't know. He spoke of it once, but I thought I had convinced him to do otherwise. Perhaps something happened to him on his journey. Perhaps it is because of his father, or because of Imharr."

"As is your wont, you speak in riddles," said the young woman.

Urd looked at Sequara and smiled. "Dayraven told me that once. But you know that folk in the Mark don't look upon Torrlond the same way you do. To them, Torrlond is the land of their kin, a good kingdom that would never undertake a wrongful cause. They see Torrlond's people as they see themselves, as decent and just. And most folk in Torrlond are good enough — not so different from those you'll rule one day here in Asdralad. The truth is, it's easier to see the justice in people you deem to be like you, and far easier to find the wrong in those who differ."

While Sequara took that in, Urd continued. "But those in power can deceive even good people through fear. Earconwald and Bledla have convinced Torrlond's people that their salvation depends on conquest, that their safety lies in war. I hope that people will see these lies for what they are one day, but that will happen only after much destruction if we don't expose them sooner. That's why we must find Dayraven. And there's his companion, Imharr."

"That's an Ondunic name," said Faldira.

"Yes. Imharr was a bondsman in Dayraven's home, but he was born in Adanon. Soldiers from Caergilion murdered his family and enslaved him when he was a boy. You can imagine he has reasons for joining Torrlond's war against its southern neighbor. But he may prove our hope now."

"How do you mean?" asked Sequara.

"Something I saw. And his connection to Adanon may be useful."

"It seems you've devised a plan to recover Dayraven for us," said Faldira.

Urd smiled. "Something occurred to me while you were speaking. It involves some risk, however."

"Go on."

"Someone must find him and bring him to safety. I would draw danger rather than help, as would you, your Majesty. We need someone with power who is less known to Bledla. Also, someone skilled in healing may be required. You are sending Sequara to Adanon and to Caergilion. She'll be close to Dayraven and Imharr."

Faldira's face hardened. "She'll be close to a war."

"I said there'd be risk."

Sequara took a breath. "You want me to seek Dayraven. I'm ready, if what you say of him is true."

Faldira held up her hand. "That decision is mine."

"Your Majesty, I would not ask this of Sequara if she were not willing and if I did not believe it necessary."

Queen Faldira's eyes narrowed. "It's dangerous, and we don't know how she'll approach him. Sequara is the future of Asdralad, my chosen successor, and I would not risk her life lightly." She paused and gave the barest of nods. "However, if what you say of Dayraven is true, he may be the one we need. I've learned to trust your feelings, Urd." The queen turned to the young woman and asked, "Are you resolved to seek him?"

Sequara gazed at her two older companions. "Even for Urd's sake I would do this. How much more, when the future of us all may depend on it?"

Faldira took a deep breath and let it out, never taking her eyes off her heir. "Very well. But do not risk your life without need, and the moment you're in danger, you must return to Asdralad."

Urd's face grew somber. "Even Asdralad will not long remain safe from Torrlond and the Way. We must act." She turned to Sequara. "Come here, my dear. You'll need to know Dayraven and Imharr. Let me show them to you."

Sequara faced Urd. They sat cross-legged in front of one another. The old woman reached up and put her wrinkled hands on the young woman's head. Her gentle touch soothed Sequara. Both closed their eyes. Urd chanted, "Druanil ecthoniae di borolin ar doranae. Varadil ingharonae im govalin ni hurodae."

The room was otherwise silent as Urd repeated the chant again and again in her clear voice. The soft probing of Urd's energy mingled with the edges of Sequara's awareness, and she opened her mind. The older woman stopped chanting. The old woman and the young remained quiet and still. The young sorceress let go, succumbing to this ultimate act of trust between two with the gift.

A strange, tender sensation grew in intensity as more of the women's energy coalesced. Sequara knew Urd well, but the full array of her personhood struck the young sorceress as a thing of intricate and awesome wonder. The woman's beauty, strength, loneliness, devotion, all her emotions, her deepest fears and desires, loves long ago relished and lost — all permeated the young woman, and her soul nearly wept and shook apart at the miracle of another being. What was more, she knew she was laying bare herself in a similar fashion to Urd, and there was a certain beauty in surrendering herself in this way too, as if she were being cleansed.

Images and impressions seeped into Sequara's mind from Urd's. Or rather, their two minds were now one, and it was impossible to tell whose memories Sequara now recalled.

Two young men appeared to her. One was handsome and dark, a man who often smiled but hid great pain beneath the surface. The other had a more serious face. He was light-skinned, like all the northern folk, and slender. He was hardly more man than boy. But there was a depth to him that astonished Sequara, a presence that suggested far more than his years should be able to bear. He was sad and mysterious, perhaps because of a keen awareness of life's fleetingness, which gave it both beauty and tragedy that colored everything he saw and experienced. And though she could not feel the gift in this young man without being in his presence, the extent of Urd's awe and fear over the boy's power was shocking.

Yet, there was something even greater: the love Urd bore these two young men. She cared for them, and her desire to save them stemmed not only from her fear for Eormenlond, but from their dearness to her and her deep affection for them. It was not easy for the old woman to think of using Dayraven as a tool in the coming struggle against Torrlond and the Way.

The old woman's energy began a gentle retreat, and it seemed odd to Sequara to realize she was not Urd, but someone else. The two women separated, each caressing the other with her energy, like wisps of mist floating through one another. As the strands of her own identity returned to their places, Sequara remembered her body was in a room of Queen Faldira's palace. Her sense of herself returned, and she smiled. Peace lingered for a long moment. Both women opened their eyes as if emerging from a calm meditation.

Sequara gazed at Urd. "Your memories of them are soothing. I'll do my best to find them."

"They're both dear to me," said Urd. "In addition to knowing their appearance, you'll feel Dayraven's power if you're close enough to him. It's unmistakable."

Queen Faldira put a hand on each of the other women. "It's settled, then. Let us go over the preparations. You must travel light and swift."

"Yes, my lady," said the young woman.

The three sat for some time discussing the arrangements for Sequara and the messages she would convey to the kings of Adanon and Caergilion. For hours they talked, not ceasing even when servants brought in the evening meal. The three women — past, present, and future — wove their plans as the sunlight shining through the window moved across the room, grew dim, and yielded to darkness.

17

IN THE MONSTER'S CLUTCHES

Wishing he could cast aside his heavy shield and byrny, Dayraven trudged forward, one foot in front of the other, keeping up with the rest of the Mercenary Company only through its collective will and the fear of being seen as weak. Etinstone and the villages along the way where folk cheered them on seemed a lifetime ago, though it was but the fifth day of marching since they had set out.

The dreary trees – cottonwoods, mostly, but a few forlorn, scraggly oaks joined them – seemed about the only thing alive in the forsaken place they walked through, the clinking of their byrnies and their heavy steps the only sounds. Mist obscured the land. The sun was a pale, sickly disk appearing once in a while as it struggled to burn through. The putrid vegetation stank. Worst of all, innumerable insects swarmed them, incessantly biting and producing itchy welts on any unprotected flesh. The supply wagons had become stuck three times that day, and Dayraven was still soaked through from the last time, when he had been knee deep in muddy water while pushing on one of the wheels. The stench of decay seemed part of him now.

With his head drooping down beneath the weight of his helm, his ragged breaths went in and out. One foot in front of the other.

No one spoke. Even Imharr, who marched next to him, was no longer smiling or jesting. His friend had taken on a hard edge that Dayraven suspected had less to do with the marching than with the surfacing memories of his family. While Dayraven did passably well during the grueling training excercises Captain Orvandil put them through every evening after trudging all day, Imharr threw himself into them and had earned respect from the other soldiers. They still called him "Wetnurse," though, the nickname bestowed on him by the unfortunate Wigstan.

Gnorn and Hlokk proved sturdy and enduring during the marches and the combat drills as well, handling their axes with great strength and agility. Dayraven had the feeling they would be formidable in battle, even if they were seeking honorable death. But at the moment, all he could think of was putting one foot in front of the other until someone told him he could stop. His muscles ached, and the blisters on his feet burned, but the worst was the sheer exhaustion permeating his body and muddling his mind. That, and the abiding presence of the elf, which curled along the edge of his awareness during the day and whispered in his dreams at night.

He looked up and blinked. Somehow, without his noticing, the sun had lowered and the gloom descended all around them. The smell of rot never went away, though.

"Still miles from Hasumere's heart." So long had they been silent, the voice surprised Dayraven, though he lacked the energy to be startled. It was old Eafa, not far to his right and speaking, it seemed, to no one in particular. Perhaps too exhausted to care, no one answered him, but he continued anyway. "The aglaks are in there." No one said anything to that either, but it got Dayraven thinking.

Eafa had grown up in those parts and knew a thing or two about Hasumere, a long, shallow body of water surrounded by inhospitable fens. From what Dayraven had heard of aglaks, distant kin of trolls that dwelled in swamps, he had no desire to visit them. Though slightly smaller than their troll cousins, aglaks were said to be cleverer. Eafa also had spoken of strange lights in the fens, soft glows that appeared in the distance and lured unwary travelers deep within until they could never find their way out again. It was not a place where he wished to linger.

Dayraven leaned forward as they climbed a brushy knoll, his free hand resting on his knee as he struggled up. A few flickers of red appeared before him, and, thinking at first of Eafa's marsh lights, he shook his head.

"Aldmund's blessed balls. Thank Edan," said someone among the company.

A moment later, as more and more of the lights appeared, Dayraven realized they were campfires. Thousands of them dotted the landscape like stars in the night sky.

In spite of his weariness, he smiled. The Mercenary Company of Etinstone had reached the vast encampment of Torrlond's army at Hasumere's eastern end. It was situated on a plain just beyond the fenland, and somewhere down there was the spot where he would lie down and sleep. He sighed and trudged on. The campfires gave him enough hope to struggle through the fatigue.

NEWLY MADE CAMPFIRES CAST A RUDDY LIGHT IN THE DARKNESS AND created dancing, elongated shadows. The men of the company stood in formation awaiting their orders to begin their usual combat drills before they could go to sleep. Dayraven's head jerked up after he caught himself nodding off even as he stood there. The exhaustion descending on him was so heavy that he felt as if his blood had all drained away. Even the ache of his muscles and the burning of the blisters on the bottom of his feet and the back of his heels seemed remote. His vision grew blurry as he shook his head and fought to keep his eyelids from closing.

Captain Orvandil loomed before them, showing no sign of fatigue and scowling as if he knew how weak and tired they were. One corner of his mouth quirked up into a half smile. He shook his head. "Enough for today. Dismissed!"

Many of Dayraven's comrades released audible sighs of relief, which made him glad to think he was not the only one barely able to stand.

He stumbled next to Imharr and the Dweorgs to find an unoccupied spot on which to throw down his spare cloak as a bed. Though wet and smelling like the fetid fens he had struggled through all day, he smiled at the idea of drifting off as soon as his body hit the ground. He grunted when he lay down in between Imharr and Gnorn and, after removing his helm, he let his head sink into the small pack that doubled as his pillow.

But before his eyes closed, the plucking and strumming of harp strings made him sit up, resting on his elbows. The Mercenary Company's shaper sat by the fire, which crackled as it cast its red glow on the man's scarred face. Each night, after the long day's march and the training exercises, the shaper had re-created one of the old tales with his six-stringed harp and strong voice, making even some of the rough men of the company grow teary-eyed with his stories. At the moment, he was tuning the instrument while a couple soldiers bellowed out requests for songs.

The shaper just smiled and twisted a peg as he plucked a string, which changed pitch slightly. More than once, Dayraven had taken a good look at the instrument. In the old style, the harp's rectangular body was hollowed out of maple, while the sounding board was of linden wood and the pegs of willow. The company's shaper played it better than anyone else he had ever heard, making him wonder why such a man would waste his talents among a company of castoffs and misfits. Of course, because of the Way, shapers in Torrlond did not receive the same honor they once had. Though Imharr and the Dweorgs did not stir, Dayraven reckoned he could stay awake just a little longer to hear at least the beginning of the tale.

After a brief, satisfied nod, the shaper plucked the gut strings in a blur of his fingers and closed his eyes for a few moments. In those moments, all who hearkened to the interweaving notes entered another world, the ageless realm of tales. Then he leapt into song, letting the rhythm carry the story.

Listen! A song of sadness will the shaper now weave,
A dirge of deeds from the days of yore,
The yearning of years that yielded long ago.
We have heard of the hardships that hounded the maid,
The troubles that tossed her and tore her from kin,

How the sorrowful soul o'er the sea journeyed far,
The bales she abode and her boldness in death.
Famed was her fairness, but fate took Aelfscyn . . .

The shaper was reciting the tale of Wilfar and Aelfscyn, a woman of Ellond who lived ages before. It was one of the most sorrowful and longest stories, requiring several nights to finish, and only a master shaper could recite it with the right effect. Dayraven well knew the bones of the tale.

Raiders from the Wildlands, the barbarous Ilarchae, destroyed Aelfscyn's village in the night and sailed away with her. The tribe's leader made Aelfscyn his wife, and she bore a son. Longing for her home and her former betrothed back in Ellond, she named the boy Wilfar.

In the meantime, the boy's namesake sought Aelfscyn for many years with twelve friends who swore revenge on the raiders. They had nothing but ill luck in the Wildlands, being attacked and forced to live for a time in the dreaded Ironwood. All died but Wilfar and one companion, Deorwin, who escaped and returned to Ellond in sorrow.

Fifteen years after the raid, Wilfar heard a fur trader speak of a woman of surpassing beauty among a tribe of the Wildlands. She had spoken to the trader in the Northern Tongue. Wilfar summoned Deorwin, whose vow bound him.

Pretending to be traders, the two found the tribe of Ilarchae and recognized the chieftain's wife as Aelfscyn, though she did not see through their disguises. At a feast that night Wilfar unsheathed his sword to slay the chieftain, but the boy Wilfar came in between and died instead. A moment later, the chieftain pierced the man Wilfar with his own blade. When Aelfscyn cried out her dead son's name, her dying former lover answered, and she knew then who he was but said nothing.

The Ilarchae broke Wilfar's body and cast it to the wolves. They imprisoned Deorwin with the intention of sacrificing him to their gods. However, Aelfscyn set him free in secret just before going to her son's funeral pyre. From the shadows Deorwin watched as Aelfscyn approached the pyre and snatched her son's blade from the flames. The Ilarchae expected her to slay herself in grief, but instead she pierced her husband, the chieftain, straight through with the hot blade and then threw herself on the flames with her son. Deorwin escaped to Ellond bearing the tale.

Dayraven sighed as he listened, and a tear formed in the corner of one eye. But it was not the ancient sorrow that moved him at that moment, for the tale put him in mind of looking over the hills of home with Ebba on the day before life betrayed him. He had mentioned the tale of Wilfar and Aelfscyn to her that day as they sat by the copse and gazed out over the landscape of the Mark. She had remarked that it was a sad story after he jested about being like Wilfar seeking Aelfscyn.

He would seek Ebba someday. First, he would see about living through the next few weeks. When he would gain his freedom, he and Imharr could seek his friend's sister. Then to Galdor, who would teach him how to master the power within him. Perhaps his own tale might have a happier ending than Aelfscyn and Wilfar's.

At length, as the shaper's interweaving voice and notes grew distant and blurry in his ears, Dayraven eased his body down and let his eyes close. Weariness claimed him, and he willingly surrendered to the oblivion of sleep. His last thought as he drifted off with the elf's sussuration pulsing in his mind was relief that Hasumere was behind him.

"It seems yesterday's stroll was just a little introduction to Hasumere." His hands resting on his hips, Lieutenant Ludecan looked at them all with a grim smile as they stood in formation in the thick mist, whose damp chill seemed to have entered Dayraven's bones. "Our orders today are to wander deep in the fens to find and capture aglaks."

Angry and dismayed mutterings broke out among the men, but when Captain Orvandil strode closer they ceased.

The tall Thjoth scowled. "Those who rule you chose several companies for this mission. I don't pretend to understand, nor do I like it. But orders are orders, and we carry them out. A high priest of the Way comes. Report any sightings to him. Go without byrnies, helms, or shields. Light and swift. Other companies have hunted the aglaks for two days, so the beasts are wary. Our task is to capture them alive. Stay with your group, and follow orders."

Dayraven stood with his mouth open. He was not sure which was worse: going into the fens to find and capture aglaks, or the coming of a high priest of the Way. *A high priest? What if he senses me? Will he let me be if I tell him I just want to be a soldier?* The splinter of the elf pulsed in soft breaths that caressed his mind.

Ludecan counted off the company into four groups of twenty-five and gave each group two nets woven of thick rope. He led one group and Orvandil another, while the captain picked two of the company's sergeants, Bisi and Rhof, to lead the other two. Dayraven, Imharr, and the two Dweorgs found themselves under the captain's command. As the men segregated themselves into their groups behind their leaders, Dayraven scanned in all directions for somewhere to hide. There was nothing but mist around them. And how could he escape without anyone in his company noticing? Captain Orvandil glanced in his direction and met his eyes. Could the Thjoth read it in his face that he wanted to run?

Like a dim ghost, a white-robed figure approached the company through the mist. Dayraven held his breath. The gift in the man was a strong presence. Awareness of it tingled all over Dayraven's body. This man was powerful in magic. Surely the high priest knew he was there. Perhaps if he was far enough away, the man would not feel the monstrosity the elf had inserted in him. He inched backwards.

He positioned himself at the rear of his group and backed up a couple more paces, taking care not to hurry or draw attention. Imharr glanced back at him and then at the white figure materializing from the fog. Gnorn was watching him as well with a puzzled frown. Was it too late to run? *No good. It would only draw attention.* He swallowed and stood frozen, hoping beyond hope the high priest did not sense him.

When the high priest came close enough to emerge distinctly from the mist, he appeared a friendly, middle-aged man with a blond beard. He greeted Captain Orvandil and exchanged a few words with him. Then, with a smile directed at the men, he declared, "I am the High Priest Joruman. I too come from Etinstone in support of our great endeavor. As men of a mercenary company, not all of you follow of the

Way. However, today, you'll do well to follow me. The beasts we hunt are dangerous. But I assure you, through Edan's might, His priests have power over them. Yesterday, I captured a dozen with the One Hundred and Fourth Company of Torrhelm. I'm confident that, with your help, we can do even better today. So, if you discover any sign of an aglak, see that I find out, and do not harm it. They're useful only if they're whole. I will accompany one of your groups, and the groups are to stay not far from each other, so I'll always be in calling distance. Edan go with you."

For an anxious moment, Dayraven feared the high priest would choose his group to accompany. However, when the white-robed man finished speaking, he turned his back and walked toward Sergeant Rhof's men. Dayraven let escape a sigh.

As if he heard the sigh, the high priest spun again in his direction and stared. Dayraven pulled the hood of his cloak over his face and hid behind the men standing before him. *Where do I run? Can't run. Tell the man. Tell him the truth. They can't make me a priest. Tell them what Osfrid said.*

When he dared to look again, the high priest was gone.

"Let's go, men," said Captain Orvandil.

Dayraven fell in and followed his group as they walked through the mist in the direction of the fens.

GIANT, TWISTED FORMS LOOMED ALL AROUND IN THE PALENESS THAT obscured everything. Once, Dayraven had flinched at an aglak with its arms raised above it before it resolved into a rotten tree. Others had laughed at him, but the brittle laughter betrayed their nerves, and he was not the only one startled by half-cloaked trees. The damp mist clung to them and dripped from their hair, and the shadowy clumps of moss-covered trees and shrubs made it difficult going. Imharr, Gnorn, and Hlokk remained close, whispering only once in a while due to the order to stay quiet.

Dayraven was soaked up to his thighs, like all the others, and his boots sank into the mushy soil beneath the dark, putrid water. At times it reached his ankles, other times above his knees. Like everyone else, he kept sweeping his gaze all around him to keep an eye out for any movement, but no one could see much through the mist.

All at once, a big soldier who had been in Dayraven's line of sight disappeared with a quick yelp and a splash. *Bernred,* remembered Dayraven as his mouth gaped in horror. He and others rushed to where the man had been standing. A pale hand poked up from a dark pool that was bubbling with movement. Two others leaned in to grab the arm and, with grunts, began hauling up Bernred.

"Heavy bastard," said one of them between gritted teeth.

Bernred came up dripping and spluttering. He struggled out of the pool on all fours and then stood up, stamping his feet and waving his arms. "Fuck me. Bloody, nasty fens." Dead reeds and weeds hung from his hair, and, as he scowled at everyone, the other men began to chuckle.

"Nice time for a swim, Bernred," said someone.

While Bernred yanked the reeds out of his hair, the others had a good laugh at his expense, though Dayraven could not help but notice the uneasiness in the laughter.

Bernred looked down at his hand, and his face wrinkled in disgust. With his other hand, he pulled at something that was black and several inches long. The end of it stuck to his flesh, and it stretched as he tried to peel it off. "Ugh. Fucking leech." It broke off, and he tossed it into the water.

"There's another on your neck." One of the men who had fished him out pointed near the skin beneath the big man's beard.

Bernred's hand jerked up to his neck and felt around it. "Shit." He winced when he tugged the creature off and then threw it into a pool, where it disappeared with a plop.

"Don't worry, they'll do you no harm." Old Eafa grinned. "Unless they get ahold of your cock. Shrivel it forever, they will."

Bernred's eyes went wide, and his hands shot toward his breeches before he realized he was the object of a jest. He frowned at Eafa and then chuckled while everyone else laughed.

"Enough noise," said Captain Orvandil, and the men went quiet. He gave the signal to follow him, and they resumed their search, their boots sloshing through the water.

Dayraven and his friends fell back a bit to allow the two fellows with the nets to go first. He scratched an itchy welt on his neck and then waved his arms at the cloud of tiny black dots hovering around him.

Imharr too was snatching at their tiny but merciless tormentors. He whispered, "Midges and mosquitoes. What do they want with anything in this shit-hole of misery?"

A few paces away, a stout and friendly man called Bothelm replied through his few grey teeth, "Word from other companies is white-robes'll use the beasts for our side. Mate o' mine from Torrhelm says they got others too — huge trolls, and them slimy little nightgangers. He seen some. Beasts'll be first into battle. They reckon to save some of our skins that way."

"Their concern's touching," said Imharr. "But what if the aglaks kill us first?"

"They've already feasted on quite a few poor bastards the last two days," said Mull, on the other side of Bothelm. The tall man brushed some of the long brown hair sticking to his bony cheeks out of the way. "Some of the men who go out hunting never return from this cursed fen."

"Best stay close together to make sure *we* return," said Gnorn.

A loud splash came from the clump of trees and brush they were approaching. Everyone froze and stared ahead at the dark, tangled mass of plants and mossy trees, dim and grey in the mist. Dayraven waited for the captain's orders.

Orvandil crept closer. With his hand he directed the men to follow him toward the brush, singling out the two who held the nets to come in front. As a group they edged behind their captain. Though they tried to move with no noise, the water gurgled around their ankles with every step. The Thjoth eased his sword out of its scabbard, and the rest followed suit. Some men lingered behind, close to the trees they had just hacked through.

Orvandil crept closer to the brush, peering inside for sign of living creature. Not far behind, Dayraven watched him. The captain stopped and bent when he was only a couple feet from the brush. In a blur of motion, Orvandil grabbed for something in the water and sent droplets flying. Several men jumped back.

The captain stood up and held something that he raised into view. When he opened his fist, a fat bullfrog jumped out of his hand and splashed back into the water. Orvandil grinned. The men who followed him laughed, especially those startled by the sudden movement. Dayraven breathed a sigh and smiled.

Something popped and crunched behind them. At once all the men turned around.

Towering over them at twelve feet, an aglak with legs and arms as thick as tree trunks let loose a deep and vast roar of defiance. Thick tendrils of viscous spittle flew from its huge maw. Every man flinched or cowered at that booming sound. A layer of slime matted with swamp plants stuck to its pale green flesh, and the veins and knotted muscles in its arms, legs, and chest bulged. Yellow eyes narrowed over its two flared nostrils, mere slits in its face with threads of snot stretching across them. Jagged teeth protruded from its gaping mouth as its lips tightened backward in a feral snarl. Between its legs wobbled its thick genitals, declaring its sex. In one hand it held the body of a man from their group, Ingbald, who had lingered near the trees. In the other it held Ingbald's head by his hair. Blood dribbled from the man's neck, and his face still wore a look of shock.

Chaos erupted. Those nearest the creature screamed and fell or ran backwards, splashing dirty water everywhere.

With terrible speed, the aglak hurled Ingbald's head at Utred, one of the two soldiers holding a net. The gruesome missile smacked Utred's face with a crack, sending him reeling and splashing into the water. Man and net sank below the surface. The creature took down Garmund, the other soldier carrying a net, by twirling the headless body in its other hand through the air with equal accuracy. The impact sent Garmund back several feet, and he disappeared in the water with his net beneath the headless body.

Orvandil boomed his orders: "Eorp and Bosa, fetch them from the water and find the nets! Bothelm and Adda, get the priest — with Rhof's group, that way! Be swift! The rest, follow me!"

The huge creature lumbered closer to poor Sebbi, who tried to flee but tripped over a root and fell face forward into the dark water. The little bald man was sputtering and frantically fishing for his sword when the aglak thrust down its long arm and picked him up by the neck. Sebbi's legs dangled beneath him, spinning in the air. His face grew red and his eyes bulged. He made a futile effort to pry the monster's thick fingers from his neck.

The aglak opened its mouth wide and ran its green, slime-dripping tongue along its sharp teeth. Sebbi gurgled in terror. The monster stuffed his head inside its mouth and twisted its jaw with a quick jerk. Blood sprayed from Sebbi's twitching body, which the aglak dropped before it spat out his head.

Sergeant Irling yelled and thrust his sword into the creature's chest with a squishing sound. When Irling tried to pull out his sword, it stuck in the slime. The sergeant let go and ducked, but the creature seized him by the head with its enormous hand and lifted him out of the water.

In the next instant Orvandil reached the monster and, with a blow that would have carved through a young tree, wheeled down his sword on the arm grasping his soldier. Slime and blood splattered. The aglak shrieked and released Irling, who fell in the water onto his knees and gasped for breath.

Orvandil yanked on his buried blade, but it caught in the thick secretion on the creature's arm. Clamping its huge arms around the Thjoth, the aglak forced him towards its gaping mouth. The captain strained as he pressed against its chest. With an oozing sound, his hands sank into the creature's flesh, or the layer of mucus covering it. Even the tall Thjoth seemed a small child next to the aglak as it brought his face closer to its razor teeth.

Splashing and scattering drops, Dayraven sloshed through mud and water toward Orvandil. He strove to hasten, but something besides the mud sucking at his boots slowed his body, and he moved as if in a nightmare. Many fled in the other direction as he, Imharr, and the two Dweorgs approached the creature grasping their captain by the back of the head to devour his face. Hlokk yelled beside him. A blur flew toward the aglak. When Hlokk's axe ripped into the monster's thigh with a wet thud, the aglak quivered and roared, but it kept its relentless grip on Orvandil, whose strong arms could not keep his face from inching closer to mutilation and death.

Then it was that the splinter of the elf's presence quickened in Dayraven. His instinct was to resist it, but he realized Orvandil was about to die. *They'll know me now, but it's the only way.* He let go.

The alien power wrenched him from his body. Dayraven's mind expanded and slipped away, and his fear dissipated even as the terror all around him screamed into his awareness. The elf's eyes flashed in his mind, and he emerged dispassionate and serene while his sharpened perceptions took in everything. The world appeared once again with uncanny clarity. The panicking men, Orvandil's desperate struggle, the enraged aglak: He took it all in at once and understood as if he had witnessed it unfolding for a thousand years. In the realm without time, all evolved before and around him, waiting for him to intervene if he so chose.

Focusing on the aglak, at once he grasped its being. Strong and proud, it was a lord of the fen. A predator to many, but a tender caretaker to its young. It delighted in dark, hidden places, grey mist, soothing mud, and slippery fish and eel. Earth and water were its ancient ancestors, and in its lineage was a special fear of one creature: the human. The human with its sharp, shiny sticks and its cruel flames.

All of this flooded Dayraven's consciousness until he became the aglak. Everything happened from his own viewpoint and at the same time from the creature's. Fear twitched in all its muscles, unfastened its jaw in a roar, and strained its heart. Orvandil's struggling face appeared before him, teeth clenched and the veins in his head and neck protruding with desperate effort. Dayraven was himself no longer, but someone outside this scene, or rather something enmeshed throughout it. His will awakened, and he knew what he must do.

Be still.

The beast's fear increased tenfold, but the fear was no longer in command. Something vast and foreign occupied its mind, and it had no way of resisting this new will. Even as its mind cowered, to the aglak, it felt as if the impulse to cease fighting originated from within it.

At once the beast released its grip on Orvandil, who grasped his sword and pulled it out of the creature's arm. When the sword slurped out with bloody cords of slime stretching from it, the monster winced but made no movement to harm the captain. The aglak stood still and stared at Dayraven. The remaining men all turned toward him with wide eyes and open mouths.

Come to me.

The dripping creature never took its eyes from Dayraven as it walked a few paces toward him through the swamp. Orvandil, Imharr, Gnorn, Hlokk, and the few others who stayed behind gawked where they stood. The aglak plucked Irling's sword out of its chest and Hlokk's axe out of its leg, dropping the weapons in the water while its wounds bled. Dayraven felt the burning pain of the wounds as the blood dripped into the water. The creature walked a few more paces until it stood before him. The anger in its face sagged into sorrow. Its eyes resembled a scolded dog's. Its mouth formed a round shape, and from it came a high-pitched, mournful wail.

All the while, even as he controlled it, Dayraven understood the beast without any need for language. Its thoughts leapt to him without intervening words. It pleaded for its life, terrified of what the men would do. It begged for mercy, to let it stay in its home unmolested. Its children and its mate: They would mostlike die without it. Its hatred stemmed from naked fear, a fear greater and more justified than the men's fear of it and its kind. It was helpless now, and only its despair outmeasured its horror.

Sharp and terrible was its terror. So much anguish. This was the raw and tragic truth of existence. The fear underlying all life. All creatures spend their days finding ways not to feel it, but it screamed at Dayraven with full force.

Deep within the elf-state, the human part of Dayraven recoiled. Trying to shake away the feeling, he retreated from the pain and lost his concentration. Something snapped. The elf-state slipped away, and the world abruptly resumed its normal focus. He crashed back into his body. The connection with the beast ended. Nausea tore at his stomach, and he buckled over. The aglak's sorrowful look mutated back into a snarl, and it raised its gigantic arm to strike him.

"Goronae imdhugadon ulushar im dagodhin! Kharkunae

vinduilanon brinunar ni shulokhin!" The song of origin came from somewhere behind Dayraven.

The aglak froze before its blow fell, its eyes wide.

The High Priest Joruman broke through the brush with Bothelm and Adda trailing him. A few other men who had run away also straggled back behind the high priest. Joruman, whose white robe was spattered with mud and filth, waded through water towards the beast, which remained still. He inspected the aglak. "What happened here?"

The high priest's power pulsed into Dayraven's awareness. He stood up and winced as the nausea spiked and his mouth filled with bitter saliva. Discovery was inevitable. He looked over at Imharr, who stepped forward and then hesitated, looking from Dayraven to the high priest.

At the moment, the white-robed wizard was examining the beast's arm and thigh, from which red blood oozed. "A fine specimen, but the creature's damaged. You must be more gentle. As it is, we've a hard enough time keeping them alive outside the water." Joruman paused and looked about as if listening for something. He turned his head around and gazed at Dayraven. He smiled, and in a quiet voice, he said, "Now, *you* have some explaining to do."

At once, all of Urd's warnings about the Way flooded back to Dayraven. He looked around for a way out. Gnorn and Hlokk peered at him with furrowed brows. Imharr held up one hand and opened his mouth, but no words came out. Captain Orvandil stared at Dayraven with a frown.

Sergeant Irling, the man Orvandil saved from the aglak, spoke up. "Thing killed at least two of us. Would've killed me and the cap'n too, hadn't been for that fellow." Irling pointed at Dayraven.

Orvandil silenced him with a motion of his hand. The sergeant and the few others who witnessed the event looked down, taking a sudden interest in the water around their shins.

Joruman gazed at Orvandil then at Dayraven. He asked with one eyebrow cocked, "What does he mean?"

"He means," answered Orvandil, "that soldier drew away the beast. It was about to kill him in turn. You came with good timing, though we lost two men, and two are hurt."

Joruman stared at the captain. "Your losses are regrettable." He stole a glance at Dayraven. "The incident no doubt warrants a report to the supreme priest himself, who takes great interest in the troops' welfare. You, Captain Orvandil, and this young man here, can give testimony. I suggest the three of us bring the injured to camp and report to the supreme priest before continuing our hunt today."

Unspoken tension weighed thick in the air. Captain Orvandil hesitated. He looked at Dayraven, then at the aglak. "Alright. My two men need help. Perhaps your supreme priest will heal them."

"He has many important duties, my friend, but I promise I'll do what I can."

Dayraven's feet were stuck in the mud, his body rigid. *The supreme priest. But if what Urd said is true . . . Grandmother, how did I end up here?* But there was no way out he could see.

The High Priest Joruman checked Utred and Garmund and after a short time declared they both would live. "I must conserve my power for today's task, but I'll see to their care before I dispose of the aglak at camp." He made a conspicuous motion with his hand in the direction of the two injured men, who lay unconscious in other soldiers' arms. The aglak lumbered toward them, splashing drops with every step. Like a mother bear handling her cubs, the gigantic beast picked up the two drenched men and slung one dripping body over each shoulder.

The captain told the remaining soldiers to continue hunting for aglaks after burying the dead and gathering the men who ran away. He appointed Sergeant Irling as leader and told them to be careful. "Two other high priests, Morcar and Heremod, are nearby, as well as several other priests. Till we're back, report any sightings to them. Find a white-robe before you approach one of the monsters. Don't try anything by yourselves."

"Shall we?" said the High Priest Joruman as he motioned with his open palm for Dayraven to walk before him.

Dayraven looked at Imharr, who reached toward Wreaker at his side. *No, my friend. That's certain death. I'm not ready to give up yet.* He shook his head, and Imharr froze.

"As you say, my lord," he said to the high priest, sounding braver than he felt. He smiled at Imharr, Gnorn, and Hlokk, who stared at their friend as he turned around, and bade farewell to them in his mind.

Waving his hand at the large beast, Joruman commanded the aglak to tread forward, and he fell in next to Dayraven as the monster's huge legs crashed through brush and splashed water ahead of them. Orvandil looked sullen and said nothing. The high priest gazed at Dayraven and wore a grin as they walked. "I'd be interested in hearing more about how you managed to distract the beast. Would you care to indulge me?"

Dayraven glanced at Orvandil before answering to appeal to the tall Thjoth for help. Orvandil did not notice or did not care to intervene. The Thjoth looked ahead and moved brush from his path.

Given at least one priest of the Way wanted him dead, and remembering Urd's words about the Supreme Priest Bledla, Dayraven dreaded what this shrewd high priest now guessed about him. He swallowed and looked ahead at a clump of trees. How much could he afford to tell this man? There could be no doubt the high priest sensed the gift, or whatever it was the elf inserted in him. He had to say something. "I . . . I shouted something at it, my lord."

"What was it you shouted?"

"I don't recall. Whatever came to my mind. I think I told it to stop. It all happened so fast."

"I see. They are perilous beasts, unless one knows how to handle them. For the gifted" — Joruman pressed his hands to breast — "they can be quite useful."

The aglak tore a twisted tree out of the path of the high priest, who smiled as if to say, "*You see?*"

The high priest's stare made Dayraven uneasy. The man was measuring and weighing him behind those clever eyes. He decided it would be best to say little else along the way. For his part, Captain Orvandil said even less. But Joruman compensated for their silence by chattering about the wonderful preparations and irresistible power assembled in the camp. The one thing he did not mention was the enormous strength of the gift lurking in Dayraven. Instead, as he toyed with a gold ring with a dark red jewel on the little finger of his right hand, he said a great deal about the Eternal and the place they would take at the end of times.

"Those who follow Edan will inherit everything: beauty, wealth, knowledge, *power*. They will know bliss, and they will come to understand the world as it was meant to be. Yes, my friend. Those who ally themselves with the Way of Edan have much to gain. Much indeed."

Dayraven had a feeling the high priest wasn't speaking only of gains in the Kingdom of the Eternal, but he said nothing. His imminent meeting with the supreme priest occupied his mind, where the elf-shard whispered of silence and darkness.

WHEN THEY ARRIVED AT CAMP, JORUMAN WAS TRUE TO HIS WORD and commanded the aglak to bring the two wounded soldiers to a tent where someone would attend to them. Garmund was waking up and groaning, but Utred, who had a nasty cut and bruise over his eye and a bloody nose, remained unconscious. After leaving the wounded men, the high priest directed two temple guards in white kirtles to put the aglak in chains and escort it to a holding pen. He also gave orders to a priest to accompany them and heal the aglak. Dayraven wondered why the priest could not have healed Garmund and Utred as well, but he thought it wiser to say nothing. Joruman bade Orvandil and Dayraven to accompany him, and he led them through the bustling camp, where many preparations went on as more companies arrived.

Some soldiers staked tents, and others cooked food, while many more exercised or performed combat drills in groups. Their boots thumping in unison made a powerful, compelling din, and men everywhere rushed to obey the orders their superiors yelled out. It all had a glorious sort of order and tension to it. Torrlond's army transformed the plain into a vast makeshift city, one more populous than the largest in most kingdoms of Eormenlond. Dayraven wondered aloud, "How many men do we need to beat Caergilion?"

Joruman answered, "Your captain here could tell you we'll have some ninety thousand troops when we enter the enemy's land. No force in Eormenlond could match it, and it's only half of Torrlond's military power. In addition, thanks to the might of Edan, we'll have other means of conquest at our disposal. As you witnessed, the aglaks make formidable fighters, and we have much more up our sleeves." The high priest grinned. "It may seem a bit much, perhaps, but we aim for a swift and decisive victory. This will prevent unnecessary loss of life."

Captain Orvandil's lip curled in a subtle smile, and the big man looked ahead.

This high priest's words always mean more than they seem, thought Dayraven.

Soon they entered the camp's heart, and they approached a large, ornate tent that dwarfed all others. Golden fabric bordered the white canvas, and the king's banner stirred and fluttered atop a large, red pole poking up from its center. Numerous helmed and mailed guards stood outside the entrance.

Wearing only his sword and his soaked, muddy breeches and kirtle, Dayraven felt out of place, almost naked, amidst all the splendid finery. Far worse than that, a new presence entered his awareness. Vast power emanated from the tent and pierced his consciousness. Someone inside possessed the gift in greater measure than the High Priest Joruman or Urd. The Supreme Priest Bledla. *So I've come to you after all. Drawn like an insect to honey. Was this what fate had in mind for me?*

Joruman turned to Orvandil and Dayraven and smiled. "Wait here a moment. I'll return shortly." The guards all bowed to Joruman, and one opened the flap over the tent's entrance. The high priest disappeared inside.

They waited outside several yards away from the guards. Orvandil turned to Dayraven. He was glad for the tall captain's presence, not only because he was the only other man in sight who was spattered with mud and soaked. Though he could not have said why, from the first time he encountered Orvandil and saw into the man's mind, he thought of him as an ally.

The Thjoth leaned down and spoke in a quiet voice to Dayraven. "The truth. Why don't you want the priest to know?"

Dayraven hesitated and then looked up at the captain. He felt he could trust him, but there was no time to tell him everything. "I was in some trouble with a priest back in the Mark. He wanted me dead, and

I was exiled. Someone I believe told me to avoid priests of the Way, especially the supreme priest."

Orvandil smiled, though it did not soften his features any. "Strange way to avoid him. But I thank you for saving my life."

"In truth, I don't exactly know what happened back in the fen."

"Well, you're right not to trust the white-robes. Power they have, but only a damn fool or a coward trusts their Way."

"Yet you serve Torrlond."

"Torrlond pays me to kill. I do it well. It has naught to do with beliefs." The Thjoth looked almost angry, but Dayraven was not afraid.

"What *do* you believe in?"

Orvandil held out his large hands. "These — and courage. Naught else."

"And what's courage?"

Orvandil's teeth showed in a grim smile. "Courage is when you fear shame more than death."

Dayraven thought for a moment, and he nodded. He glanced at the tent as he waited to find out his fate. The looming power radiating from it seemed to threaten and beckon at the same time. Strangely enough, now that the moment had come, his fear was gone, and in its place he found bare determination. *No more running. Now I'll see what this supreme priest is all about.*

Orvandil put a hand on Dayraven's shoulder. "I'll do what I can to see you walk out of there."

Dayraven looked at Orvandil and nodded again.

The High Priest Joruman emerged from the tent's entrance. "You may enter now. The Supreme Priest Bledla and King Earconwald are within listening to reports and conferring on our future strategy. They'll sacrifice some of their precious time to hear your tale. It is, I expect you realize, a great honor to you."

The high priest motioned for them to follow and turned around. As a guard held the flap to the entrance, Dayraven and Orvandil entered the tent behind Joruman, the Thjoth ducking to avoid the top of the entranceway. Within, colorful silk cushions and pillows lay atop a sumptuous, patterned rug. A dozen guards arrayed in a line and one old captain in front of them blocked the way. In one corner, a large glass-like orb rested on an iron stand atop a small wooden table. Four of the supreme priest's temple guards in their white kirtles stood in attendance in another corner. One other man clad in a dark cloak stood behind the temple guards, his face hidden under his hood. But the cloaked man walked behind Dayraven and Orvandil and exited the tent with the temple guards as if they had finished their business there.

Orvandil nodded to the old captain. "Captain Nothelm."

"Captain Orvandil." The commander of the king's bodyguard scanned Orvandil and Dayraven. Nothelm motioned to where Orvandil and Dayraven should stand, and the twelve guards parted to reveal the rest of the tent.

Ten paces in front of Dayraven and Orvandil on a splendidly carved chair sat King Earconwald: regal, handsome, and smiling beneath the slim crown resting on his brow. This was a king men would serve and go off to war for.

But by far the most powerful presence was Bledla's. The supreme priest occupied the chair next to the king. Keen and fiery were his blue eyes. The awesome and terrible power Dayraven detected from outside the tent blazed forth from the white-robed wizard, and he blinked in wonder at it. Now that he stood before him, Dayraven could believe that here sat the inheritor of Aldmund's power and glory.

Their eyes locked. For a moment it seemed to Dayraven that they two were the tent's only occupants, and a haze obscured all else. Bledla stroked his long white beard as he beheld Dayraven. Then, for a fleeting moment before the supreme priest turned his gaze from him to Orvandil, Dayraven discerned in the slight widening of his eyes a flicker of something behind all the power and confidence. Had it been dismay?

The Thjoth bowed low before the king, and Dayraven followed suit.

"Captain Orvandil. Good to see you," said the king in a jovial voice. "Forgive the formalities, but Nothelm insists, you know."

"Your Majesty," answered Orvandil, "Captain Nothelm does his job well."

Nothelm bowed his head to acknowledge the compliment.

The king continued. "The High Priest Joruman tells us you just had an encounter with one of the aglaks. Nasty creatures, really. But they have their uses. At any rate, the supreme priest is gathering information about the beasts," and at that moment the king stole a quick glance at Dayraven, "so we may better control them. To employ them to their full potential, it helps to understand their tactics. If you're willing to lend us some assistance, tell us what happened in as much detail as possible."

"Of course, your Majesty."

Orvandil related the events in Hasumere, emphasizing the beast's cunning as it attacked from behind and took out the men with nets first. But when he came to the part when Dayraven commanded the aglak, he said the young soldier shouted something that distracted the beast. "Had the High Priest Joruman come a moment later, this soldier would not be standing here," finished the Thjoth.

"I see," said King Earconwald with a satisfied nod. "Thank you, Captain Orvandil. I'm sure the supreme priest has heard much to our advantage." He turned to Dayraven. "And you, young fellow, did you notice anything else, anything *different*, perhaps?"

"Your Majesty, my account agrees with the captain's." Dayraven stared at the floor.

Glancing up, he noticed Joruman smiling at his lord, the supreme priest, who nodded back at the high priest. He also sensed the stirring of the vast power within Bledla. He saw himself as small before this tall, cold man.

The presence in his mind respired in remote indifference. Could he call upon it to fight the supreme priest? It seemed to come of its own accord in moments of tension. He was not certain he could summon it. His confidence that he could control the elf's power if it did arise disappeared.

Something reached toward him and surrounded him, a force that threatened to smother him. With a chill locking around his heart, he understood the supreme priest was somehow probing his mind. Dayraven was naked and transparent. *He sees through me. Useless to lie to such a man. I can feel it — he senses everything.* Fearing he was capable of prying even into his unconscious thoughts, he dreaded what Bledla would say next. The supreme priest opened his mouth, but before a word came out, someone else spoke first and broke the spell.

"I know that sword." King Earconwald was peering at Sweothol lying in Dayraven's baldric. "Hand the blade to me, young fellow."

Captain Nothelm moved closer, keeping his eyes on Dayraven.

Dayraven obeyed, unsheathing the sword and stepping forward to hand the hilt to the king while keeping his head bowed low.

The king grasped the hilt. "Yes, the very blade. The hilt's unmistakable, as are the runes. It lay in my father's treasury in an honored place when he wasn't using it. An old heirloom. But he gave it away." From his seat King Earconwald looked at Dayraven, and for the briefest moment, Dayraven thought he detected a change in the king's voice as he asked, "How did you come to wear it?"

It would be fruitless to lie, and he also wanted to please the king almost as much as he feared Bledla. "My father gave it to me, your Majesty."

"Yes," said Earconwald. "You're from the Mark, are you not? No need to answer — your accent betrays you. Your father's name?"

Sweat gathered on his hands, and his heart beat faster. "Edgil, son of Conwulf, your Majesty." He glanced at the supreme priest, whose eyes narrowed as he stared back.

Earconwald beamed. "The very man. And may I have the honor of knowing his son's name?"

Feeling a trap closing around him, he looked ahead with defiance at Bledla. "Dayraven, your Majesty." *Courage, the captain said. Might be it's despair I feel, but let it happen now. I'm ready.*

The supreme priest's eyes widened and his mouth opened. He fixed his eyes on Dayraven but said nothing.

Earconwald continued, "Dayraven, son of Edgil of the Mark. You have an interesting name. Do you know why my father gave yours this sword?"

"Your Majesty, I know the tale."

Earconwald looked at Dayraven, still smiling. "Many who were there that day said he saved my father's life. After the previous war with Caergilion, when the scum tried to slay him in the mountains. I recollect your father. He was about my age. You remember the man, don't you, Bledla? Certainly you do, Nothelm. Refused a captaincy, if I recall correctly. What do you think of that, Orvandil?"

Captain Orvandil bowed his head. "Such a man must have courage. His son has some."

Earconwald nodded and gazed at Sweothol. "At any rate, it's a fine blade you inherited. If you inherited your father's prowess as well, then Torrlond is fortunate to have you in its ranks."

The king handed the sword back.

Dayraven bowed low and sheathed it. "I hope to serve Torrlond as my father did." *Is that all? Will they let us leave now?*

"Fine lad. You'll soon have the opportunity. I'll keep my eyes on you." King Earconwald turned to Orvandil. "Very well, Orvandil, you and your soldier may return to your task."

Orvandil nodded. He and Dayraven turned to leave.

A deep, firm voice commanded them: "Wait."

Dayraven took a breath before turning around again.

The Supreme Priest Bledla glared at him. An old man in a plain white robe, yet hard and unbending like steel. And his power. It threatened to strip the flesh from him. Perhaps the worst and most uncanny part of it all was Dayraven felt a strange kinship with him. They were alike somehow. Though Dayraven could not have said how or why, he knew their kinship made it easier for them to understand each other, even to know one another's thoughts. Now examining the young man with his keen eyes, the great wizard seemed to peer into his soul. *There's almost no barrier between our minds.*

Bledla addressed Dayraven without emotion, but there was a weight behind his words that conveyed their importance. "Why have you chosen to join the Mercenary Company of Etinstone? Do you not believe in the Way?"

Dayraven glanced at Orvandil, who clenched his jaw. He looked back at his inquisitor and blinked before Bledla's gaze. "My lord, I joined the Mercenary Company under strange circumstances, and the tale would take too much of your valuable time to tell. But I'm glad to be part of it, not least because of my companions. For my part, I'm no foe of the Way."

"I see," said the supreme priest. A long pause followed, during which Bledla glowered at the young man.

Dayraven could not have said what the stakes were, but he knew a contest of some sort was taking place. The supreme priest was still trying to probe his mind, attempting to peel back layers and examine his deepest hopes and fears. He struggled to shut him out. *What does this old man want? Urd said he might want to train me, or kill me. Not you, supreme priest of the Way. You'll make me no priest of yours.*

Bledla nodded as if he heard Dayraven's thoughts. "You may go. The High Priest Joruman will rejoin your company shortly."

After the Thjoth and the young soldier left the tent, Bledla stared at the entranceway. It was not easy to keep his countenance steady. *Show nothing. Let them see nothing.* Was he trembling? Was it possible? He had witnessed nothing like this before. This boy. This unbeliever. This beacon of power. The prophecies. This changed everything, and the world crumbled beneath Bledla. *How? Why now? It cannot be.*

King Earconwald ordered Captain Nothelm and his guards out, leaving only the High Priest Joruman with them. "Well?" he said to Bledla once the guards had departed. "Found another wizard for your cult?"

Bledla jerked his head toward Earconwald as if a serpent had stung him. He took a deep breath and recovered his wits enough to put on an air of confidence. "Dayraven of the Mark. It seems the bird has flown straight to us. This is the boy Bagsac was supposed to eliminate. The grandnephew of the witch Urd. I don't believe she sent him as a spy. I would have sensed that. No, he's here of his own accord. And he has no idea what power is in him. Could you not feel it, Joruman?"

The high priest nodded. "I sensed it when I first saw him, my lord."

"You did well to bring him," said Bledla. "It cannot be chance. Edan has delivered him to us." The supreme priest stroked his beard. "But for what purpose?"

"His power would serve us well if he were trained," suggested Joruman.

Bledla stared ahead and debated within himself. This might have been the most important decision of his long life dedicated to the service of Edan. *I cannot see the way forward. There are two paths before me, and I don't know which to take. Edan, give your servant a sign.*

Joruman and the king waited for him to speak.

"Perhaps. But did you not hear the lack of zeal when he spoke of the Way? The witch has not trained him, I deem, but she has no doubt corrupted him. I sensed fear and mistrust. He joined this war for his own reasons, perhaps unwillingly, certainly not for love of salvation and truth. He's no believer, and he could be a danger to us. Remember: All those who are not devoted to Edan work against Him. And such power might become a hindrance to the fulfillment of the Kingdom. We must think this over with great care and strive to learn Edan's will."

King Earconwald shrugged. "For my part, I don't care if you kill him. But you can't slay an old war hero's son openly. Do it without anyone knowing. Oh yes, and be sure the sword finds its way back to my treasury." He rose from his seat and stretched. "I'll go exercise with the troops. Good for their morale. As we discussed, the last companies arrive from the north today, and we now have enough of the beasts. We meet again this evening with the dukes to plan tomorrow's departure."

Bledla rose. He and Joruman bowed to the king, who joined Captain Nothelm and his dozen guards waiting outside. After Earconwald departed through the tent flap, Bledla stood still a moment. Joruman waited for him, so he sat and gestured to the other chair to indicate that his high priest should join him.

Joruman obeyed. "My lord?"

"What did you sense, Joruman?"

"Power, my lord. Vast power."

"Yes. And what would you do with it?"

"We could use him . . . to fulfill the Kingdom of the Eternal. Or, if you deem him a threat, we could kill him. Either way, the will of Edan must be done, my lord."

Yes, but for the first time in many years, Edan's will is unclear to me. Bledla gazed at his high priest. "You speak the truth. But did you not sense anything else?"

"My lord?"

"There is something different in the nature of the boy's power. He awakened from the elf-sleep, they say. I did not believe it . . . until now."

A puzzled frown crossed Joruman's face. "I don't understand, my lord."

Bledla could no longer contain his agony. "The prophecies, Joruman. He *awakened*."

The high priest's eyes widened with comprehension. "You don't mean . . ."

"I do. 'My power shall be reborn in the one who awakeneth and beholdeth the world anew.' The power of the Prophet Aldmund reborn."

"But that would change everything. That would threaten *everything* we've worked for. It makes no sense. It cannot be Edan's will."

Bledla's hands gripped the armrests on his chair. His knuckles turned white, and his body trembled. "It cannot be, and yet I doubt. Doubt! What do you think stayed my hand? I could have slain the boy where he stood. Would that I had. But when I felt the power in him, the first thing that sprang to my mind was the words of the Prophet Aldmund. And I wondered . . . Could it be? Doubt. I have never known such doubt. Why? Why now? On the verge of our triumph."

"The power of the Prophet has been reborn — in *you*, my lord."

"Why, then? Why? Who is this boy?"

"It's a test. Yes, my lord. Edan has sent the boy as a test."

"So I believed . . . until the boy stood before me." Bledla closed his eyes and clenched his teeth. *Have I been blind? I have done everything for Edan. Everything in place, and one meeting changes it all. Is this some means of humbling me?*

"It's as you said, my lord. The boy's an unbeliever. How could Edan choose him for His vessel?"

"I don't know. I don't *know*. Edan's ways are mysterious. What if this boy is the one? Would it not be a sacrilege to raise my hand against him?"

"But *you* are the one who wields the song of origin that Aldmund wielded. Only you."

"Think, Joruman. With so much power in him, if the boy learned the song of origin, would he fail to wield it? The only reason he shows no power yet is because he has not learned to control it. But when he does . . ."

Joruman looked around the tent and scratched his head, but then he leaned back in his chair and folded his hands before him as a smile spread across his face. "The prophecies, my lord. We must consider them all. 'Thou shalt know Edan's life in the one that wieldeth the Way by the clear tokens of its glory. It will defy the eldest and greatest powers in Eormenlond.' The elves. What else could the Prophet have meant? You must defy the power of the elves, and it has been sent to you in the form of *this* boy."

The supreme priest sat up straight. "Perhaps . . ."

"It must be."

"Yes . . . But it was so clear in my mind when the boy stood there. Is he the second Prophet? Or must I slay him? Doubt. It gnaws at me, Joruman."

Joruman leaned closer to his master. "Perhaps, my lord, you needn't slay him yourself. The boy is going into battle. Very dangerous. Many will die. If he falls in battle, then it is apparent: He cannot be the second Prophet."

Bledla thought a moment before the idea seized him. "If Edan's will could be thus made clear, then all is well."

"*If* the boy is Edan's chosen one — as I believe in my heart he is not — then He will undoubtedly protect him in the battle."

"Yes. That is certain." Bledla's shoulders relaxed as he took a deep breath and exhaled slowly. It made sense, and it *was* a test of his faith. *Of course. Joruman is right. On the verge of accomplishing everything Edan has tasked me with, I must remain firm. I must have faith in Edan.*

"I will pray to Edan that He will make his will known in this way. If the boy survives his first battle, I will pray for further counsel, and it may be that we will need to train him and teach him the blessings of the Way."

"And if he dies . . ."

"If he does not survive, then Edan has spoken. Until then, we must proceed as Edan has commanded us. I will go now to renew my power over our greatest weapons. You will return to your duty in Hasumere. And keep an eye on the boy."

"Yes, my lord. Blessed be the Eternal."

"And the Kingdom of Edan."

THE HIGH PRIEST JORUMAN LEFT BLEDLA AND THE TENT BEHIND. But, after looking over his shoulder, he did not head back toward Hasumere. Instead, he wove his way deep into the camp. At times he glanced around to be sure no one followed him, and he made an effort to conceal his frustration behind a smile.

The old fool. Prayers and prophecies. Does he think of nothing else? There's too much at stake now. I must inform King Earconwald. He'll not be happy to hear of his supreme priest wavering in his resolve. We still need Bledla, at least until the war is over. After our complete victory, the moment will come. But until then, the old man must still believe he is *the second Prophet. The will of Edan shall become clear to him. I'll make sure of it.*

And yet, even as he made his way through the camp, doubts tugged at Joruman. It was a pity in a way. Had there been the leisure, it would have been interesting to study the boy. There was so much power there. If it was true about the elf, it could have massive repercussions for his research. Such potential lay within him, and he had little idea of it. Besides that, he had nothing against the young man. Perhaps seeing something of his own youthful self in him, he even liked him. *He's no zealot, no crazed fanatic frothing at the mouth to do Edan's will. A potential ally?*

But there was a much more immediate problem. By creating doubts in Bledla, Dayraven was a threat to everything the high priest had been working towards for so many years. Joruman had worked so hard to achieve the delicate balance where he stood now, poised at the verge of embarking on the reform and research that would transform so much, and the boy threatened to upset it all. It would also be impractical to have someone so powerful around — a likely rival whose existence could be more than inconvenient. And what if Bledla exploited the boy for his insane ends? That would be nothing short of disastrous.

And yet, Dayraven had done him no harm. He was naïve but not stupid, and there was something about the young man he kept returning to, something that reminded him of the ideals that had brought him to his youthful resolution. He wished he had more time to think things over.

Joruman stopped walking, clenched his teeth, and sighed. The boy needed to die. It was a damn shame, but one death was a small price if it proved necessary to attain the high priest's ultimate goal, which would benefit uncountable others and lift humanity from the darkness. He would not waver from his path. *I must be relentless. I must harden my heart. No individual life matters in the face of what I can accomplish.* Perhaps there would be a way to examine the boy's power once he was dead. Clearly, he would need to look into the matter of the elves in more depth.

Joruman resumed his walk by many soldiers in grey kirtles, who bowed in deference to him, but soon he arrived at a portion of the camp where the white-kirtled temple guards predominated. The high priest walked by several rows of small tents until he accosted a temple guard. "Where is Crida's tent?"

"My lord. You've nearly reached it. It's four down on the left. He entered it only a few moments ago."

"Very well. You're dismissed."

Joruman approached the tent the man had pointed out. "Crida. It's the High Priest Joruman. Come. I have need of you."

The man in the dark, hooded cloak who had been in King Earconwald's tent when Dayraven and Orvandil arrived emerged from the tent. "My lord. I live to serve."

"Walk with me, Crida."

"Yes, my lord."

Joruman paced for some time between the rows of tents, still wondering if there might be some way after all to spare Dayraven or at least study him. The camp was full of the din of preparations and drills. The high priest sighed, turned to his companion, and took the plunge. "We have need for someone to accomplish an important task in a subtle fashion. That is why I've come to you."

"Tell me what I must do."

"You saw the boy, Dayraven, when he entered the king's tent behind me?"

"Yes."

"Did either of them see you? The boy, or the large captain?"

"No. I wore my hood, and they were looking in front of them."

"Good. The Mercenary Company of Etinstone is short two men. I'll arrange for you to join them."

"Very well."

Joruman swallowed in his throat and forced out his next words, which tasted bitter as they left him. "Dayraven of the Mark must die. He has no control over his power as yet and is therefore no immediate threat. However, his presence has become an obstacle to the fulfillment of Edan's kingdom, an impediment sent to interfere with the supreme priest's calling. It's best to take care of the matter unobtrusively. You have proven your ability and devotion to Edan many times, and it's time to do so again, most loyal of servants."

"Thank you, my lord."

"Men die in combat. The boy wants to be a hero like his father. As a member of his company, you will be close to him when he engages the enemy. Be sure he meets a hero's death in battle. Do you understand me, Crida?"

"It will be done."

"Excellent. I'll make the necessary arrangements on the morrow. Be ready, and dress as a common soldier. One last thing: Tell no one of this mission, not even the supreme priest. He must not know you are aiding him. He has many cares to attend to, so it falls to us to relieve him of this burden. And be sure no one recognizes you. You are doing this as a service to Edan and to the supreme priest, but you must report to me alone. Understood?"

"Yes, my lord. It will be done as you say."

"Good. I must return to Hasumere, but I'll meet you tonight to give you further details. Expect me after dark. You may go."

Joruman watched the man return to his tent, and a grim frown crossed his face. The niggling thought that he was making a mistake would not let go of his mind. What if he could exploit the power in Dayraven? What was more, the young man did not deserve to die. *Who does? Justice doesn't come into it. He's simply a threat to everything I've been planning and hoping for. How many deaths will I avert by sacrificing him? It's unfortunate, and that is all.* He shook his head to banish his remaining doubts. "I'm sorry, Dayraven. You must die. Bledla will have his sign from Edan. Blessed be the Eternal, indeed."

18
CHASING THE IMPOSSIBLE

As the gloaming gave way to the purpling sky of early evening, the distant sound of music floated toward Sequara and Karad. By that and the glow of lights ahead, they knew they were approaching another of the Adanese villages clustering along the River Maranant. The mares they had procured in the coastal village where Sequara's six other men and her ship awaited her were weary after the second full day of riding, and so the sorceress decided the village ahead was a good place to stop. The urgency of her mission gnawed at her patience, but it made no sense to push the horses or herself too hard.

She released a long sigh as she thought of what lay ahead. Convincing Adanon's king to offer help to Caergilion would be next to impossible, she knew. But she must try. If she were to succeed, she would then need to persuade Caergilion's king to accept the aid — also not the likeliest of outcomes. And finding Urd's grandnephew, Dayraven, the one who awoke from the elf-sleep? Perhaps even less in the realm of possibility, considering he was buried deep in the ranks of the enemy. *Then I must find a way to make it possible.*

"That bad, is it, my lady?"

She turned toward Karad, who rode next to her and must have heard her sigh. She considered her faithful bodyguard for a moment.

Almost losing him in Torrhelm had shocked her into the realization that she thought of him as something like a favorite uncle. She was not supposed to have such attachments. The ruler and her heir severed all ties of kinship and friendship alike in order to best serve Asdralad. She wondered if Queen Faldira ever had such difficulties embracing the proper detachment, if she felt affection for her servants or even for Sequara herself. She suspected the queen did, but that she hid it better than Sequara ever could. The alternative was that Sequara was woefully unfit to be the heir to Asdralad's throne.

"Do you ever doubt your purpose, Karad?" she found herself asking the veteran.

Their horses plodded on for a bit before Karad answered. "My purpose is to keep you alive, my lady. Never once have I doubted it. Apart from being with Heera – the Mother only knows how she's put up with me all these years – serving you has been the honor of my life. Now, as to whether or not I'm up to the task is a different question. I reckon having doubts every now and again is a good thing. Keeps me on my toes. But one thing I know for certain: Even if I fail, I'll give my life for it. Maybe that's all that matters. You know why, my lady?" He paused a moment. "Because a life isn't much without a purpose. I'm a lucky man in that mine is simple."

Sequara smiled for a moment, thinking on the wisdom of Karad's words. "I think you might be right."

Above the nearby river's flow came the muffled noises of folk at play, and soon enough the dark shapes of dwellings took form on both sides of the road, some with the glow of fire seeping under doors or through cracks in the window shutters. The music and animated conversations grew louder as they continued through the village, and Sequara directed them aside from the road when they came to the source, the village inn. Thick glass windows emitted the glow of firelight. The building was constructed of cemented bricks stacked between thick wooden beams, and a large sign in Ondunic hung near the door under a lamp. They tied their horses to a nearby post and approached the door with its heavy iron latch. Sequara removed the hood of the dark cloak she wore over her black tunic and trousers while Karad reached for the door. When he opened it, stuffy warmth and the din of music and conversation rushed outward.

Inside were two dozen men sitting at tables, drinking wine and ale, and conversing in the energetic, lilting tones of Ondunic. In one corner, three musicians played a merry tune with pipes, lyre, and voice. And though the tune was merry, there was always something sad about the tones and rhythms of Ondunic music, Sequara found. Perhaps it was the long struggle between Caergilion and Adanon that stamped melancholy on the character of the southwest, but she detected more than a hint of sorrow beneath the vibrancy of its peoples.

The large common room was boisterous with shouting and laughter, and the place had a cozy, well-kept appearance. The heavy scent of frying fish permeated the room. At the nearest table, four well-dressed men, probably merchants, played at one of the many card games the people of the southwest endlessly invented. Several empty wine bottles and a great deal of silver sat on their table, and each merchant stole surreptitious glances at his neighbor's pile of wealth. They looked up when Sequara entered and stared at her until they noticed Karad and went back to their cards. A grey-bearded innkeeper came hobbling from the kitchen wearing a stained apron.

"Looking for lodgings, my lady?" asked the old fellow in the Northern Tongue, meaning he knew her for a foreigner by her dress. He spoke it with a slight Ondunic accent, and the loudness of his voice suggested that, in addition to trying to speak over the noise, he might be hard of hearing. He bowed to Sequara and then nodded to Karad.

Sequara answered in the same language, making sure to speak loud enough. "Two rooms just for the night, thank you. And our horses will need tending."

He beamed back at her, revealing a couple gaps in his teeth and causing a profusion of well worn wrinkles to blossom on the leathery skin around his eyes. The old man's dark brown eyes twinkled beneath bushy white eyebrows. "Such a beautiful young woman. My Dorna would have loved to see you, but she passed away almost a year ago, you see. Been together fifty-two years — you're of an age with my granddaughter. She lives in Palahon. Comes when she can. Anyhow, I'll be right out to stable your horses. Stable boy's taken ill. Stomach isn't so good."

Sequara smiled at the old man. "Don't worry, we'll take care of the horses. Afterwards I'll look at your stable boy if you like. I may be able to help him."

The old man's eyes widened for a moment before he bowed again to her, this time even more deeply. "A healer, then? Bless you. That would take a worry off an old man's back. But aren't you beautiful, and such a pretty smile too." Switching to Ondunic, he shouted at a young woman, though she was serving another guest only six feet away, "Aeri, dae arnal diga bast!" Turning back to Sequara, he grinned. "Rooms will be ready before your man returns from the stable. Plenty to eat too if you're hungry." He glanced at Karad and pointed at the back wall. "There's a torch there next to the fireplace if you like, sir."

"Thank you," said Sequara.

"It's an honor, my lady. If you'll pardon me, I'll get back to dinner before it's burned."

"Of course."

The old fellow bowed once more before he hobbled off to attend to his cooking.

"My lady, I'll tend to the horses," said Karad in Andumaic.

"No. But thank you, Karad. They're tired, and I want to heal them a bit before the morrow. We need to ride them hard. Stay here and find out what these people have to say about King Balch and Queen Rona." She nodded at the table with the merchants and gave the veteran a half smile. "Those four will likely speak the Northern Tongue. I believe you enjoy cards." She slipped a small bag of silver from her cloak and handed it to him. "You've earned a glass or two of that wine as well."

Karad grinned for a moment. "As you wish. But be careful, my lady."

"Not to worry. I won't be out of your sight for long, and I've always found horses easier to manage than people."

Sequara walked to the back of the room and lit a torch in the room's fireplace before going back outside. She untied and led the steeds next door to the stables, where a dozen other horses stood in their stalls chomping on dry hay. After placing the torch in a sconce and finding empty stalls, she unbuckled the saddles and put them aside. She fed and watered both animals and then began to rub down her horse. The grey mare had been faithful and patient. Such a good-tempered beast deserved gentle treatment, but she had ridden it hard. *No choice. I'm driving her as I must drive myself.* Caressing the mare and thanking it in High Andumaic, she spread a blanket on its back. "Good girl. You've had a long journey. I'm sorry to press you so much, but there's great need for haste. If my journey has any success at all, you'll have helped many." Placing her hand on the steed's brow, she chanted beneath her breath and imparted just a bit of her energy to help the mare recover faster from the day's exertion.

When she finished, she repeated the process with Karad's mare, and then, with a sigh, she walked back to the inn.

Sitting at the table with the merchants, Karad made eye contact with her as soon as she walked in the door. He said something to them, and then, with a nod, lay down his cards before moving a small pile of coins over to the man on his right. That man smiled and gave Karad a friendly slap on the shoulder as he left.

Karad nodded to an empty table. Sequara headed there and sat down opposite her bodyguard. The veteran smiled. "I took the liberty of ordering dinner, my lady."

Just then, the young woman named Aeri arrived with two plates of steaming fish and greens. Sequara's stomach greeted the food with a growl. "I suppose I am hungry. I'll see to the stableboy after I eat."

"I've asked Aeri to show us to him once we finish with the food, my lady."

"Good. How did you fare at the cards?" Sequara scooped up a bite of her fish with her spoon and began eating. It was a bit hot still, but with a hint of lemon and pepper, it tasted delicious.

Karad grimaced. "I lost most of the silver, my lady."

She swallowed and nodded. "They are famed for their card games here. And what of the conversation?"

"That went somewhat better, I'm pleased to report."

"Oh? What did you find out?"

He leaned a bit closer. "In addition to a loose tongue due to a bit too much wine and an enviable streak of luck at cards, the fellow who won all your silver has a cousin whose brother-in-law is a close advisor to King Balch and Queen Rona on matters of commerce. He informs me that the king is gruff and short-tempered, whereas the queen doesn't speak much at court. But he takes counsel from her. In fact, they say she's the real steel in Adanon. So, if you want to win him over, you convince her first, my lady. The trick is you do it while talking to him. He takes it ill if he thinks he's being ignored. They say she's a wise woman, and it's an open secret among the nobility that he heeds her in most matters."

She swallowed another bite of fish and then nodded again. "Thank you, Karad. I'd say that was worth a bit of silver."

WITH RISING NERVES, SEQUARA HAD WATCHED PALAHON COME INTO view. Skirting the meandering River Maranant in the midst of a plain, it was a city of strong stone walls and tall towers. Hardened by constant warring with their neighbor to the north and west, Adanon's people had taken pains to protect their chief city. The local brown-grey stones made up most of the crenellated walls and larger buildings, which included many of the swollen domes found in the east and southwest of Andumedan. Ranging from the squalid to the pompous and clustered in their respective neighborhoods, the homes were largely brick. Like the people in the villages of Adanon, those in its chief city roofed their buildings with red terracotta tiles. The largest city in the southwest, Palahon was nevertheless not quite one-fifth of mighty Torrhelm's size. Still, that made it twice as populous as Asdralad's chief city of Kiriath, and it was impressive enough to Sequara.

A steady flow of farmers, merchants, soldiers, servants, maids, and scatterings of nobles walked and rode in contrary streams in and out of the city's gate. Sequara took a deep breath and, nodding to Karad, led her horse to the six guards standing outside it. After stopping before them, Karad presented Asdralad's seal to the guards while Sequara declared in the Northern Tongue, "I am an emissary from the kingdom of Asdralad. Queen Faldira has sent me to speak with King Balch as soon as may be. Kindly conduct me to the palace."

Clad in the green tunics of Adanon, the guards inspected the seal.

"Please wait here, my lady," said one haltingly in the Northern Tongue, and then he disappeared behind the gate. He returned a moment later with his commanding officer, who also took a look at the seal. "May I know your name, my lady?" asked the officer. He spoke the Northern Tongue with more comfort than his soldier did.

"I am Lady Sequara, chosen by Queen Faldira as heir to Asdralad's throne."

The officer gave a deep bow. "I will lead you to the palace. Please follow me, Lady Sequara."

Through the bustling throngs of people and horses the officer conducted her to the royal palace, a solid and formidable structure with round towers looming over its own high, crenellated walls. A brooding and vast fortress within the city, the royal residence bespoke power and stubborn strength. The officer announced Sequara's arrival to the guards at the castle's gate, and they brought her inside, where servants showed her to a room and brought her food as well as a warm bath. Karad was given his own quarters not far down the hall from her.

Sequara was anxious to see the king, but she was also weary and dusty from the road. By the time she finished bathing, it was dark outside. The matronly servant who last came to see her informed her the king and queen were returning from a journey later that night and would grant her an audience early the next day. She slept little that night as she prepared the arguments she would present to Queen Rona and King Balch.

A LARGE FIREPLACE TOOK UP ONE SIDE OF THE SPLENDID MEETING room in the castle. Busts of Adanon's past kings frowned in royal dignity atop pedestals on the other three sides. The walls and floor were of polished brown stone, while large wooden rafters supported the ceiling. Windows high up on one wall let abundant light shine through, and a colorful rug covered the floor.

After a servant had shown in her in, Sequara had sat at one end of a long, dark table stretching more than half the room's length. King Balch brooded at the head of the other end. The petite and alert Queen Rona sat next to her stout husband, while three dignified sorcerers with long beards and a dozen grave noblemen occupied chairs around the rest of the table. The presence of the gift in the three sorcerers entered Sequara's awareness, and while their power was strong enough, not one on his own could match her.

Based on their past responses to Queen Faldira's messages, Sequara expected much resistance against the proposal to aid Caergilion in its imminent war against the invading Torrlonders. The king's countenance, which appeared as if he were about to shout at someone, reinforced that expectation. Below average height, King Balch nevertheless had a large presence, a large voice, a large belly, and, if rumor held true, a large temper. With his wide nose and forehead, he appeared like a bull in the mood to charge the next unfortunate being in its path. Scowling at Asdralad's emissary beneath his bushy black eyebrows, the king scratched his greying beard. "Welcome to Adanon, Lady Sequara. To what do we owe the honor of this visit?" He spoke in the Northern Tongue, and though the words were courteous, the tone was abrupt.

Sequara took a breath.

"Wael san," she said, a traditional Ondunic greeting. "I apologize, your Majesty, for the need to address you in the Northern Tongue. I know little Ondunic as yet, though I find your language pleasant."

King Balch managed a curt smile. "No matter. I don't understand a damn word of your High Andumaic either, though I daresay you could have a blessed long conversation with our three sorcerers here in that tongue. When their noses aren't in their books, they chatter on with each other about all sorts of nonsense no one else understands. Does no one any good either."

Two sorcerers looked down at the table while the third scratched his head and gazed up at the windows.

The king continued, "At any rate, like everyone else, we conduct our business with foreigners in the Northern Tongue, so you'll find yourself quite understood here."

Sequara was not sure whether the king was infuriated or enthusiastic. "Thank you, your Majesty." She glaced at Queen Rona, but the woman's expression was unreadable, and she looked again at the king. "The Northern Tongue is, as you point out, the language of diplomacy and trade in Andumedan. However, if those who wield power in Torrlond have their way, it will become Andumedan's only language. And with it will come only one faith: the Way of Edan."

Balch grunted.

Sequara did not know if the Adanese king meant to agree with her or not. He might have been expressing displeasure. Since he said nothing more, she continued. "King Earconwald and the Supreme Priest Bledla will soon conquer Caergilion with the avowed purpose of avenging their priests. But, as we have indicated to you and your counselors before, they seek more than that. Queen Faldira sent me to entreat you one last time to consider the consequences if we allow Torrlond to occupy your neighbor to the north and west."

Several of the nobles stirred. Two of them crossed their arms before them. None looked pleased. Eyebrows lowering, King Balch scowled and appeared ready to unleash a diatribe.

Sequara cleared her throat and resumed. "Your borders will be open to a power much greater than Caergilion's, and their ambition is greater than their power. I will not hide the truth. Torrlond's army will not stop with Caergilion. We know this for a certainty. They will attack your kingdom next. They will destroy Oruma and Anghara's shrines and temples, and they will stamp out your ways. They will not stop until they swallow us all. That is why I've come to you: The only hope for the southwest, and indeed for all of Andumedan, is to unite with your old foe to keep the greater danger at bay. The alternative is destruction one by one."

Silence followed. King Balch stared at Sequara with his furious, dark eyes. Most of the noblemen and sorcerers glanced at the king as if they were attempting to gauge his response. Queen Rona sat placidly, not taking her eyes from Sequara.

"If the situation is as grave as you say," said a nobleman with small eyes, curly hair, and a salient nose, "then why doesn't Queen Faldira send an army as well?" The bony little man cocked one of his thin eyebrows and smiled as if speaking to a child.

Sequara looked straight at her inquisitor. *He must be Duke Uwain.* Queen Faldira had warned her the little man was the most vicious and dangerous of the Adanese nobles. "Asdralad's strength is not in arms.

We've never sent soldiers beyond our shores, and we lack the means to do so. Adanon has the military power to make a difference, and you're also much closer. Nevertheless, the queen is even now raising an army to aid the southwest. In the meantime, Asdralad will give what it can. Our lore will be of use in the war, for the priests have enslaved beasts to fight for Torrlond, and only other sorcerers can break their control. We'll do our part, but it will help little if Adanon doesn't aid Caergilion."

The youngest sorcerer, a man with deep-set eyes, little hair on top of his head, and a black beard, said, "With all due respect to your queen, whom we hold in great esteem, no one even in Asdralad could counteract the Supreme Priest Bledla's spells. Power like his comes once in several hundred years. Neither we nor even your queen could wrest control over the beasts from him, if he indeed intends to use them in battle."

Sequara was sure this man was Nalhad, the strongest of Adanon's sorcerers and a potential ally, according to Faldira. "There's one who might," she answered. She had debated whether or not to tell them of Dayraven. But they needed something to give them hope and prod them to action. *They're afraid. These people need to know Torrlond and the Way aren't invincible. They must believe in the possibility of countering Bledla and defeating Torrlond.*

Everyone at the table, especially the three sorcerers, stared at Sequara. King Balch crossed his arms, leaned back in his chair, and narrowed his eyes.

The eldest sorcerer, bald and smiling, declared in a raspy little voice, "Galdor of Ellond has tested his strength against Bledla before. He cannot avail us."

The old man was no doubt Howan. Faldira had said he was a scholar rather than a political man, and he would have little influence over Balch's decision. "I do not speak of Galdor," she answered. *Telling them of Dayraven is unlikely to help. Yet I see nothing else.* "There's a young man from the Mark who came back from the death of Anghara. He awoke from the elf-sleep. The sorceress Urd and Queen Faldira agree this is a sign of power never seen before. The prophecies of Aldmund himself speak of the one who awakens. If he were trained . . ."

"Not yet trained?" interrupted the other elderly sorcerer, who was tall and thin and had a long, hooked nose like a bird's beak between two beady eyes. "What good could he possibly be? It will take months, years more likely, before he could use his power, even if this tale is true. I must say I find it unlikely, if not impossible." He scowled at Sequara as if he found her distasteful.

Sequara looked down at the table and sighed. After biting back her initial response, she gazed straight at the sorcerer. *This would be Arlech.* The queen was right about him: pompous, opinionated, and abrasive. "It's certainly true. You needn't doubt that. It would indeed take time to train him, but that's precisely what we're asking you to do: buy us time by aiding Caergilion. Once other kingdoms see you united, they'll join our cause rather than fall under Torrlond's sway."

A burly nobleman with a large jaw and intelligent eyes spoke up next. "Where's this young sorcerer of yours, then? Is someone training him now?"

Duke Gwalor. Sequara recalled what her queen had told her about him: one of Balch's closest advisors, a fierce warrior — hard but a man of integrity. She had feared his question. *I can't lie to these people if I want them as true allies.* She braced herself and did not waver as she answered. "No. In fact, we believe he's even now marching as a foot soldier in Torrlond's army towards Caergilion."

Arlech, the elderly sorcerer with the hooked nose, squawked, "What? Now you tell us this fellow is at this moment fighting for Torrlond. You think to make a sorcerer out of one of the supposed enemy's common soldiers? The notion's simply preposterous. How unlikely, indeed."

"We have good reason to believe he'll join us," Sequara explained. "But that is not the issue at the moment. Earconwald and Bledla intend to conquer all of us."

"And I suppose," said the sorcerer Arlech, all ruffled and refusing to change the subject, "that you'll simply walk up to King Earconwald and the Supreme Priest Bledla and say, 'Pardon me, but may I borrow one of your soldiers, please? We should very much like to make a wizard out of him.' Ha!"

Sequara's face remained firm. "If I must. I'll journey north from here, bearing tidings to King Malruan of Caergilion. I hope to tell him he'll have aid from Adanon. I'll also seek the young man in question, who's traveling with a companion, a man born here in Adanon who was a bondsman in the Mark." *This is not going well. If only I could show them their self-interest in helping.*

At Sequara's last word, one of the noblemen looked up. Until this point he had seemed inattentive, as if he rolled over in his mind something far away and found the whole matter of the council a distraction. He looked about fifty years old, had curly black hair and a greying beard, and, though his eyes betrayed sadness and care, was still handsome. "The Mark, you say?"

"Yes," answered Sequara. "That's where the young man and his companion come from." She was not sure who this man was. One of the barons? A duke?

"Can you tell me the bondsman's name?" asked the nobleman.

Arlech interrupted, "My lord, it is most unlikely . . ."

Ignoring the interruption, Sequara replied before the sorcerer finished. "Imharr. His name's Imharr, but he's a bondsman no longer."

The nobleman's mouth dropped and he stared at her.

"How old?" he managed to say.

"My age. Around twenty-seven years."

"My lord," protested Arlech, "consider how unlikely it is that this fellow could be your nephew. How many bondsmen are there in the Mark? You've spent much time and grief seeking him. Keeping in mind your latest loss, it would be imprudent to distract your mind just now. Let old ghosts rest." The old sorcerer finished with an air of benevolent concern.

The nobleman ignored him. "That's the right age, and it's not a common name even here in Adanon." He looked Sequara in the eyes. "About twenty years ago, just after Torrlond's last war south of the Marar Mountains, I had word of my nephew Imharr in Caergilion. I learned that slave-dealers sold him to a soldier of Torrlond who was from some remote part of the Mark, though I could not find out exactly where. That was the last I heard of him."

He turned to face Arlech. "It may be *unlikely*, but I must find out nonetheless. Perhaps my soul will have some small measure of rest after all."

Facing Sequara again, he said, "My lady, I am Duke Anarad. My younger brother was named Longarr, and he had a son called Imharr, whom our foes in Caergilion enslaved after murdering his family. I sought my nephew and his sister for many years, and I despaired of ever finding them. But you've rekindled my hope, whether for good or ill. If the king gives me leave, I'll take a few of my soldiers and go with you to Caergilion to seek these two young men of yours. And if your Imharr turns out not to be my nephew, I'll bear you no grudge."

Sequara looked at the nobleman and formed a quick judgement. Duke Anarad. Queen Faldira had mentioned him, but she said he was unlikely to be in attendance since he had withdrawn from politics in the last few years. Still, he would be of great assistance in her quest to find Dayraven and Imharr, and he might even help persuade King Balch to aid Caergilion. *Urd was right about Imharr. At last, this might be a way in.* She nodded at the duke. "I would be glad of your company. But first we must hear your king's will." She looked at Balch but could not help glancing at Rona for a moment. Her face was still unreadable, but she was paying close attention.

Crossing his arms, King Balch waited for all eyes to turn to him. The monarch's frown deepened, his eyes widened, and his face reddened until he let loose. "I don't give a flea's fart what happens to Caergilion!" he boomed as he pounded the table with his fat fist. "In fact, it would be a source of *joy* to see those half-breeds wiped out or enslaved, especially their bastard king. And another thing," he said as he glowered at Anarad, "I'm not the least bit keen on one of my most trusted noblemen traipsing up to Caergilion on a wild, half-baked chase for some damn fellow who may or may not be his nephew, the companion of another damn fellow who may or may not be of use to us."

Arlech preened at his monarch's outburst, and most of the noblemen nodded and murmured in agreement.

Sequara's shoulders drooped, and she chewed on her lip. Her negotiations were a hopeless waste of time. She held her temper in check and prepared to give a final argument. An appeal to the Adanese to see reason. Surely they could grasp their interest in propping up Caergilion instead of holding on to old hatreds that would bring both kingdoms down. Of course, reason and hatred made ill bedfellows, but it was her duty to try. In desperation, she looked once more at the queen, making an unvoiced appeal with her eyes.

Queen Rona, who had not said a word, cleared her throat and raised one eyebrow without removing her gaze from Sequara. Glancing at his wife out of the corner of his eye, King Balch shifted in his chair and scratched his head, and then he looked back at Sequara. He held up a hand to silence his council and continued in a stentorian tone. "However! If Duke Anarad wants to waste his time and probably get himself killed, that's his own business." He glanced at the queen again, who did not look at her husband but raised her eyebrow once more.

Balch swallowed, paused, and then addressed Sequara. "As far as Caergilion is concerned, tell that bastard Malruan that, if he's willing to beg for Adanon's help, I'll consider it. We'll need some incentives, you understand. A treaty recognizing the true boundary between our kingdoms and Adanon's right to settle the border region would be a start. I make no promises, but it might be worth it for the pleasure of seeing Malruan come on his knees. If he is to accompany you, Lady Sequara, Duke Anarad will bear testimony to my wishes and bring Malruan's reply to me."

The noblemen and sorcerers sat straight in their chairs. They looked at each other with pursed lips and frowns. None of them said a word. King Balch glanced one last time at Queen Rona, who smiled and looked in her husband's eyes.

So this is indeed how diplomacy works in Adanon, thought Sequara as she observed the exchange. *Thank the Mother and Father for Karad.* Seizing on this slimmest chance, she looked at the king but glanced at the queen as she replied, "By the time I return, Caergilion may be in ruins, and Torrlond's army on your doorstep. Nevertheless, I'll convey your message to King Malruan. It's possible he'll manage to hold off Torrlond in the Marar Mountains. Then he may see the wisdom of requesting your aid."

King Balch scoffed. "Malruan is less likely to ask for my help than he is to hold off Torrlond. But good luck to you all the same. As my emissary, Anarad will take my seal with him, and he'll aid you in your journey. He's a good man, and I can ill afford to lose him. So you'd better come back with him alive, or don't come back at all. Now, if there's nothing else, pray excuse me, Lady Sequara, for I have other matters to attend to with my council. Anarad, since you've decided to run off looking for your nephew, you can escort Lady Sequara back to her quarters and make arrangements for your departure. Return to me later for instructions."

Sequara rose from her seat and faced King Balch. "Thank you, your Majesty." Turning to Queen Rona, she said, "Thank *you*, your Majesty." The queen smiled and nodded.

After bowing, Sequara and Duke Anarad left the room.

Queen Rona had said nothing during the entire meeting, yet Sequara guessed from her brief yet warm smile how much intelligence and will dwelled behind the still surface. *It's well for Balch he understands this too. Rona must have spoken with him before our meeting about their response. She understands the benefits of helping Caergilion, yet she's managed to keep Adanon uncommitted for now. Not a bad strategy, but too much caution may prove their ruin. I might have done the same in her place. I just hope it's not too late.*

19
STALKING THE ENEMY

"Break camp! Move it, you laggards!"

Lieutenant Ludecan's shouting snapped Dayraven out of his troubled sleep. His eyes blinked and then opened to the grey of early morning. There was not much more to see than the ever present mist and the dark form of Imharr lying beneath his cloak next to him. Overlaying Hasumere's musty stench was the smell of woodsmoke. Shadowy forms began to move in the mist, and more than few of them were cursing and grumbling as they rose. He yawned and stretched to rouse himself.

Feeling he could have slept even on the damp, hard earth for much longer, Dayraven groaned and became aware of how sore and stiff every muscle in his body was. Still, he was one of the lucky ones. The morning after he and his fellow soldiers hunted aglaks in Hasumere, there were two fewer members of the Mercenary Company of Etinstone, both lost during that first encounter, and several more were injured.

His company fared better than others that ventured into the fens — some lost as many as twenty soldiers. Dayraven and his companions survived thanks to Captain Orvandil's leadership. The Thjoth had evaluated the aglaks' tactics and devised ways to trap the beasts with the least trouble and risk for his men. Most of the time it involved hiding and waiting in the stinking fens until a decoy lured out one of the monsters.

Still, it was a day of death and misery. The persistent insects and leeches and the screams of men and aglaks had haunted Dayraven's dreams.

Next to him, Imharr stretched and scratched a large welt from an insect bite on his arm. Shaking the dew from his cloak, he groaned and complained, "They ought to have us round up all the mosquitoes from the swamp too. We could set the bloodsuckers loose on Caergilion's troops in addition to the aglaks."

"Not too loud. They might hear you and send us back in."

Imharr chuckled, but then his face grew serious. He lowered his voice. "Are you sure we needn't worry? That Bledla fellow, the supreme priest, didn't say anything about Bagsac?"

"Not a word. Like I said, Captain Orvandil told me to watch my back after we left. He said look out for anyone showing too much interest. But it seems Bledla decided I'm not worth troubling about." *At least I hope so.*

Imharr still frowned. "Or might be he's just patient. After what you did yesterday, I'd say you're worth troubling about. He's mostlike deciding what to do about you. He'll not leave you be. Just as Urd said: You have a gift, Day."

"Not a gift. A curse."

"Call it what you like. But you can't run from it."

Imharr's words awakened Dayraven's own fears. "You think we made a mistake coming here?"

"Didn't have much choice, did we?" Imharr thought for a moment. "No. We're here for a reason, though we may be thinking of all the wrong reasons. But we've got to get you to that wizard Galdor at the first chance."

"Not until we seek your sister."

Imharr looked at Dayraven, and then he broke his gaze with a smile and a nod.

At that moment, Hlokk appeared from the mist, striding toward them and calling out, "Hey ho, you two sluggards, there's work here!

You better get up before someone packs you and stuffs you in with the rest of the baggage. Ha!"

"Most excellent Dweorg," said Imharr, "you're welcome to carry me on today's march in your pack if you wish."

Hlokk laughed, and Gnorn joined the friends with a bowl of steaming porridge in his hands. He pointed his fat thumb at a growing line of men from their company. "The three of you better hurry if you want any breakfast."

Dayraven and Imharr sprang from the ground, overtaking Hlokk and jostling him as they sprinted for the breakfast line.

After they finished their porridge, the four companions washed up and prepared to leave. As they walked together to pack their few belongings and don their war-gear, many of the men who had been friendly enough before yesterday avoided Dayraven. When he caught them glancing at him, they looked away and pretended not to notice him. They seemed almost afraid, as if he might change into something. He recalled the faces of his people in Kinsford staring at him in the Doomring on the day he began his exile. "What's going on?" he said aloud.

"Seems your fame has spread," said Gnorn. "Some who saw what happened yesterday morning must've talked. They also know you went to the supreme priest. Most folk are suspicious of magic." The Dweorg smiled. "Anything you want to tell us, we're listening."

Hlokk crossed his thick arms and grunted in affirmation.

The presence of the elf skimmed along Dayraven's mind like the morning mist curling over the fens. He looked at Imharr, who nodded, and no one else was within hearing range, so he began, "I'm not sure I understand yet myself. It began in the Southweald, when I met . . . an elf. I should have died, but I awoke. The elf put something in me. A piece of . . . power." He glanced around again to make sure no one was listening. "We meant to go to Ellond. Urd, my great aunt, told me to find a wizard there, Galdor, and to avoid the priests of the Way. She said the supreme priest might want to train me. Or kill me. But on the way to Ellond we ran into you at the crossroads. That's the tale in short. Imharr and I will have to tell you everything else when there are fewer ears around to hear."

Imharr said under his breath, "Speaking of ears around to hear, I could swear that fellow's been watching you ever since the day we mustered in Etinstone."

Imharr made a quick movement with his eyes to his left. Dayraven glanced over at the short, bald man with the pink scar across his face, the shaper whose harp and voice enthralled the men in the evenings. He did not know the man's name. Everyone in the company, including the captain and the lieutenant, called him "Shaper" and seemed content with that as long as he sang for them. A few others in the company went by nicknames, and more than a few, Dayraven suspected, used names they were not born with to hide their past. "Shaper" was one of the best shapers Dayraven had ever heard, if not the best, but there was something odd about him.

Whatever his name was, the man was looking straight at him. Several times over the last six days, Dayraven had noticed the shaper's eyes on him. He thought of Orvandil's warning. *I won't wait for them to come to me.* "Perhaps we should go ask him what he wants."

That proved unnecessary. When Dayraven turned around again, the scarred man had neared the four companions. He carried one of the rolled up canvas tents toward the supply wagons. As if taking a rest, the shaper threw the bundle down only a few feet from Dayraven. Hlokk and Imharr moved their hands closer to their weapons. Without looking at them, the man whispered, "Dayraven of the Mark, do not look at me. Your life's in danger here."

"Who are you, and what do you want?" asked Dayraven as he gazed straight at the man.

"Don't look at me," hissed the scarred man. He stretched his back and looked toward the supply wagons.

Dayraven turned his face toward Imharr and the Dweorgs. Imharr raised his eyebrows and poked his temple, suggesting the man might have lost his wits.

The shaper bent down and pretended to adjust the ropes binding the tent. He still did not look at Dayraven. "It's better if others don't see us speaking. My name's Abon. My master sent me to find you after the message arrived. I wasn't sure it was you until yesterday, when I heard about the aglak. You should not have done that. It's dangerous here for both of us. I don't have long to speak. In the future, don't make contact with me. I'll approach you when the time's right."

"What message? Who's your master?" Dayraven was having trouble remembering to look away from the man.

Abon shook his head. His whisper grew sharper. "Dangerous to say my master's name. But you must trust me, so I'll tell you this: The message came from one you know well. Urd of the Mark. Tell no one of your relation to her."

"Are you from Gal. . ."

"*Don't* say the name," hissed Abon. "You could get us all killed."

Questions raced through Dayraven's mind. "How did you find me?" came out first.

"I told you: My master sent me. I had word of you from the innkeeper at the Crossroads Inn. He told me of someone matching your description traveling with a southerner. Said you were also with two Dweorgs, and the lot of you joined the Mercenary Company of Etinstone. Wasn't hard to track you from there, but I still had to be sure it was you. There are many traps in Torrlond for my master's servants."

Imharr did not hide his suspicion. "But how would you know we went by the Crossroads Inn? It wasn't on our path. We came there by accident."

"There are no accidents," the scarred man replied. "My master told me to look there. He has ways of knowing you and I wouldn't understand. But your friend might." The shaper took a quick glance at Dayraven before he went back to retying a knot on the rope.

Dayraven wanted to curse. Things were growing more complicated, but perhaps Abon was the opportunity he needed. Torn as to whether or not to believe the man, he fidgeted with his sword's hilt as he stole a look at this shaper who knew too much about him. Hlokk anticipated his next question.

"Why should we trust you?" growled the Dweorg. "How do we know you're not laying a trap even now?"

Abon scowled. "Fair question, but there's little time for explanation. Trust me because Dayraven's life depends on it, and much more than that."

"Pardon me."

The voice behind the four friends startled them all. At once the shaper took up his load and scurried off as Dayraven and the others turned to face the newcomer. The man in soldier's gear was tall and had curly brown hair. He was handsome and had a laughing, friendly look in his bright blue eyes. "Do you men belong to the Mercenary Company of Etinstone?"

Gnorn nodded. "Yes, you've found it."

"Good. I'm to join you fellows. I came from Sarham, a village not far to the north, when I heard the army had camped here. I feared I might be too late to join, but when I got here early this morning they told me you lost a couple men yesterday in Hasumere."

"Aye. We did."

"We who dwell near these parts know well Hasumere's a cursed place. Many who go in never come out again. A terrible misfortune. But fate doesn't favor all, does she?"

"No, indeed," answered Gnorn. "I suppose you'll need to speak with Lieutenant Ludecan? He's just over there."

The newcomer looked in the direction Gnorn pointed. "Thanks. He's exactly the man they told me to speak to. My name's Brond, by the way. I'm sure we'll have a chance to get acquainted later."

"No doubt," said Gnorn.

When Brond left, the four companions returned to the matter of the scarred shaper, Abon. "The ugly chap left in a hurry. What was that all about?" asked Hlokk.

"That has everything to do with what happened yesterday, and why my life may be in danger. It's a strange tale, but it all goes back to that elf in the Southweald."

Gnorn and Hlokk both frowned with furrowed brows.

Dayraven sighed. "We'll tell you everything when we can. For now, I must think what to do about Abon."

"You mentioned your great aunt," said Gnorn, "and the fellow whose name we're not to say. You said he was someone your aunt wanted you to meet. Perhaps his servant is someone you can trust?"

"But how do I know he truly serves him?" asked Dayraven. *And even if he does, what then? I still have my oath to Ilm.*

"Might be we'll have to wait for another chance to speak with Abon," said Imharr.

"Form ranks!" thundered the voice of Captain Orvandil in the distance.

A flurry of activity followed. Dayraven and Imharr hurried to put on their packs and gear, and soon they joined the two Dweorgs where the rest of the Mercenary Company was lining up. As they found their places, Dayraven glanced around. Abon was watching him from about a dozen places down the line. He could not shake away the feeling something was wrong. Doubt tugged at the edges of his consciousness. *Galdor's servant. Might be he is. But now we're here, and there's no way out.* He turned the other way. Just past Imharr and the two Dweorgs, the new man Brond met his gaze and smiled.

Captain Orvandil appeared before the company with Lieutenant Ludecan by his side. Like the rest of the company, Dayraven stood rigid and stared forward.

"Alright, men," the tall Thjoth said. "Our holiday at Hasumere is over."

The company broke out in cheers.

Orvandil allowed himself a quick smile before he continued with a stern countenance. "Now the real work begins."

No cheers this time.

Orvandil walked a few paces as he faced the front row. "We go to war. We march through South Torrlond's plains the next five or six days. But you'll have no time to enjoy the scenery like we did here. When we arrive at the Marar Mountains, expect a cold welcome. For all our advantages in numbers and in our friends, the aglaks," and this Orvandil said with a scowl, "our foes know the mountains. So stay awake. They defend their homes. They'll fight hard. Other than numbers, our advantage is discipline. So we train after each day's march."

Though no one groaned aloud, the entire company sagged in response. Dayraven reconciled himself to more long marches followed by grueling combat exercises that could last past sunset. Somehow none of the old stories ever mentioned this part of the path to glory.

Yet he respected the captain's discipline. The training might keep more of them alive.

The tall Thjoth reinforced this point to the entire company. "Toughen up if you want to see more than one battle. You'll find your limits, but the final test comes in the storm of steel. Stand together. The time for deeds is at hand. Mercenary Company of Etinstone, are you ready to go to war?"

Cheers rang out again.

The captain looked around, his frown turning into a fierce grin. For a brief moment, his eyes met Dayraven's. The Thjoth gave a quick nod, and then he turned and spoke to his second in command.

Ludecan yelled, "Mercenary Company! To your left."

As a unit, the men obeyed with a quick pivot.

"March!"

In tight formation, the soldiers of the Mercenary Company marched to the beat of a drum hanging by a leather strap from one of the men's shoulders. With perfect obedience, they stamped their feet in time with the throbbing rhythm. Byrnies clinked with each step, and their helms glistened under the sun.

Dayraven looked at Imharr, Gnorn, and Hlokk. With the rest of the men, they were part of an entire company advancing together over the muddy earth toward a common fate. Surely, this was what it meant to be a soldier.

Leaving behind the dissipating mist, it was not long before the Mercenary Company met another company on its way to the wide plain where the entire army would rally. This second company marched parallel to Dayraven's, and their two drummers merged rhythms so that the din of stamping boots doubled in intensity. An immediate bond took hold as they all submitted their wills to the drums' beat. Pride and thirst for glory marked the resolute faces around Dayraven. Soon a third and fourth and fifth company joined them in lock step, and the marching shook the earth.

Dayraven's breaths quickened as a strange excitement welled up in him, throbbing outward from his chest as his personal fears disappeared from his mind. Sweat ran under his helm and byrny. He was part of a mass observing one will with complete discipline. It was exhilarating. Pouring into the plain, more and more companies joined in the thumping rhythm of thousands upon thousands of feet stomping in time with hundreds of drums. The mightiest thunder could not have vied with their din.

Lost in the vastness, Dayraven's heart too kept time with the drums, and he tasted the ecstasy of merging into the one will. At that moment, he would do whatever his commander told him. He would kill and die for Torrlond without asking why. And he knew every man around him felt the same. As the inexorable flood carried them all, there was no will to question, only to obey. Their own collective force impelled them. All that was needed was some voice — whether an authority or a divinity — to direct them or hurl them like lightning, and they would fly and crash in glory against the enemy. They flowed into the plain, the hundreds of companies of Torrlond's army about to embark on conquest, in perfect conformity with the rhythm bearing them along. Nothing could stop them.

But soon Dayraven ceased marching forward. The press of bodies tightened, a sea of flesh and steel. When the Mercenary Company of Etinstone could go no further because of the many companies in front of it, the men kept time with the drums by marching in place. For several minutes the pounding of feet and drums grew, and Dayraven nearly wept at the intensity of it all.

Just when the throbbing became almost unbearable, drums and feet ceased. Scores of thousands of men, a sea of grey kirtles with spears protruding like the masts of myriad ships, waited in silence on the green plain under a clear sky.

Dayraven looked over the heads of the soldiers in front of him at a knoll rising above the plain. Atop the knoll, like a god surveying his creation, a figure rode a magnificent white steed. And though the distance was not small, Dayraven knew the figure was King Earconwald.

Now he understood whose will the drumbeats called them to obey. With this realization, he perceived the great pride illuminating the determined faces around him. In the eyes of his fellow soldiers glowed a strange joy. They were ready to kill and die, to leap into an abyss to get at the foe. They were waiting for the man on the horse to tell them to do it.

But somewhere inside Dayraven a misgiving held him back from releasing himself to the fervor swarming around him. At that moment, it seemed to him all his life he had wanted a king's approval, to become a soldier and a hero like his father, yet something prevented him from losing himself.

He glanced behind him, and his eyes met Gnorn's. The Dweorg's deep, sad eyes told Dayraven that Gnorn too was not lost in this swelling storm of men abandoning their wills. He was a stubborn rock that refused to move with the tide, a rock there for its own reasons. Dayraven turned back to take in the countless rows of gleaming helms in front of him. He was both relieved and disappointed to be an observer rather than a mindless part of the mass. A faint but distinguishable voice came from the knoll as King Earconwald addressed his army.

"Men of Torrlond!"

Thousands roared as one. Even those too far back to hear the king yelled when those in front let loose. The noise drowned Dayraven. When it subsided, he came up for air.

"Followers of the Way!"

Once again the multitudes on death's doorstep let their voices soar, buffeting Dayraven. He remained silent amidst the unbearable tumult. Alone.

"Eternal of Edan!"

At these words, King Earconwald's steed reared while the monarch waved his sword aloft. Torrlond's frenzied army erupted as the voice of heaven, piercing Dayraven's mind. The explosion of zeal left him disoriented, and the shard of the elf quickened like a gale. He fought the pull of the elf-state as he began to slip away from his body. *Not now. Must stay here. Keep control.*

He pulled himself back, but queasiness snatched at his stomach.

The king resumed his speech. "We go forth for our kin, for Torrlond, for the Way!"

More deafening cheers exploded. The cheers swelled to an impossible crescendo, and then, like water bursting a dam, the elf surged in Dayraven, its eyes burning through him like blue flame.

The shard in his mind impaled him. Its power caught him unprepared, and his fragile control over the elf-state snapped. Whatever force the elf had put inside him pounced, ripping him from his body with sudden and terrible violence. His body jerked forward as his energy rushed outward and upward, removing him from the tumult. To the dwindling human part of him came the thought of how childish he had been for dreaming he could control the power lodged inside him.

With the eyes of the elf he gazed around. He was a force outside everything, as if floating above it all, and he listened to the king's words with detached curiosity.

"We go to war to let peace and justice reign, and for eternal salvation!"

In their ecstasy, many soldiers raised their arms and waved them or beat their shields with their spears or slapped their chests with their fists as they shouted.

The absurdity of it all struck him. The tiny human part of him, the part that called itself Dayraven, felt not zeal but a wistful sort of pity for them all. How ardently they needed to believe in something, something they could submit to. Was their delusion then willful? Perhaps.

Above everything, the force that had been concentrated in Dayraven's body surveyed the mass of men and weapons, and though the assembled numbered in the scores of thousands, they now seemed desperate and small. They could not see the infinite surrounding them, so devoted were they to the momentary mirage they called reality. This mirage was a jar, and they were moths beating against its sides and fluttering in senseless circles, all the while ignorant of the endless expanse stretching outside.

"We'll hunt down the enemy as the hunter stalks the beast, and we will prevail! Strike down Edan's foes, and you obtain salvation! Edan go with you, my people! Follow me to victory!"

At this final word, the king's mount reared once again, and he rode it down the other side of the knoll, disappearing from view. The roaring of the multitudes shook the plain for several minutes.

Disembodied and apart from it all even as it observed and experienced every emotion, the force that included Dayraven like a cloud around a drop of moisture saw all the tumult and struggle for what it was: a mere flicker in the beginningless and endless span of life.

But the mortal consciousness awoke, a faint voice like a raven's call that warned it was time to return. The elf-state dissipated. The faint voice exploded into a roar, and Dayraven crashed back into his body. Sweating and panting with the effort to reunite his energy and his flesh, he looked at the ground until he could orient himself. His stomach twisted on itself, and he heaved as he forced vomit back down his burning throat.

When he thought he could look up without falling over with dizziness, he glanced around to see if anyone had noticed him faltering. No eyes were fixed on him. Consumed with fervor, all were still shouting and looking ahead at the knoll. He had won. He was back. *No one saw. Thank the gods.*

Dayraven closed his eyes and sighed when the shouting subsided and the orders came to march. The elf-state had come on him with greater strength and ferocity than ever. But he had somehow beaten it. *I found my way back. This time.*

He looked around again to see if anyone gazed at him. The shouting was over, and the ecstasy in the soldiers' faces had subsided, though many still beamed. Imharr smiled at Dayraven and nodded. No one seemed to have noticed his struggle with the power of the elf. Its gentle, steady hiss was more ominous than before. He stared forward and waited.

It was long before the men of the Mercenary Company took their first steps due to the enormous number of troops in front of them. Orders came. Men began walking. Once they moved forward and the companies spread out, the marching seemed to never end.

On the fifth day of marching from Hasumere through South Torrlond's gentle, lush landscape, the Mercenary Company of Etinstone and the rest of Torrlond's army stopped earlier than usual in the evening to wait for local companies that would swell their ranks further. Of course, Captain Orvandil and Lieutenant Ludecan were using the extra time to instruct the soldiers with more combat drills, and the latter was droning on about being prepared as the men gathered round. Dayraven found he did not mind. He was beginning to toughen up, and he knew the exercises could prove valuable in the coming days. He took a deep breath and let it out as a long sigh. The westerly wind bore mild air from the Sundering Sea, and he tasted the unfamiliar salt in the breeze, which awoke a longing in him to see the great water beyond the vineyards on the hills rising like waves into the distance.

"I said you, *boy*!" Lieutenant Ludecan's voice came into focus, and Dayraven realized the man was scowling at him.

Dayraven's eyes widened, and he pointed at his chest.

Ludecan's eyes rolled. "No, the *other* fucking idiot called Dayraven. Get over here!"

Dayraven moved to stand by the lieutenant, who was surrounded by the men of the company in a circle.

"And you." Ludecan pointed at the newcomer, Brond, who smirked and sauntered out to stand next to Dayraven.

"Now, you attack." The lieutenant slapped Dayraven on the shoulder. "Get your sword out, then, unless you figure on fighting by blinking at him with your mouth open."

Dayraven closed his mouth and unsheathed Sweothol. He swallowed and steadied his breathing. He was glad to be the one attacking since he had only half paid attention when Ludecan demonstrated the move whereby a soldier might parry a forward blow and then bring his sword to his foe's neck. His opponent would do the parrying and perform the maneuver. Dayraven faced the man and nodded.

Brond was ready with his sword out. He smiled. He could not have seemed friendlier, except perhaps for a hint of mockery in the smile, yet something felt wrong. A blankness in his eyes, perhaps.

"Let's go!" shouted Ludecan.

The soldiers surrounding the two mock combatants in the circle were all staring and waiting. Dayraven shrugged off the uneasy feeling and lunged at the man before him, softening the blow because it was a training exercise.

Swords clanged, and Brond pivoted. In a flash, his blade was at

Dayraven's neck, his face inches away. Cold steel pressed on Dayraven's flesh, and an urgent warning sprang up in his mind. *It's just an exercise*, he told himself. *Nothing to worry about*. But the threat still loomed in his mind as his fellow soldier stared him in the eyes. Brond grinned and removed the blade.

"Well done," said Ludecan. "Now, the two of you switch places. You attack, and *you* parry and pivot."

Dayraven took a deep breath and tightened his grip on Sweothol.

Brond gave him a wry smile, and then the tall man lunged at him with his sword. Steel clanged as Dayraven parried like he was meant to and pivoted. But when he tried to finish the movement by swinging his blade toward Brond's neck, he was surprised to find his opponent was not there.

A hard, blunt object slammed into his lower back. He grunted and shuddered with the sudden pain of a blow that drove the links of his byrny into his flesh. Brond appeared in front of him, and the warrior's arms blurred toward Dayraven. The hilt of Brond's sword pounded into his stomach, buckling him over and knocking the wind out of him. Having crumpled to the ground and dropped Sweothol, Dayraven lay in the grass and clutched at his stomach, trying to suck in air. Some of the other soldiers laughed.

"Too slow," came Brond's voice above him.

Unable to respond, Dayraven coughed and groaned. When he glanced toward the voice, a sword tip appeared in front of his face. He was able to breathe in hoarse gasps, but pain still gripped his stomach.

"What do you think you're doing?" shouted Imharr, who strode toward the pair.

"Teaching him," responded Brond as he lowered his sword. "He's too slow. No foe will wait for him to make the move."

"He was holding back! It's a training exercise!"

"This is war we're going to, not an exercise."

"Stand down, soldiers!" yelled Lieutenant Ludecan.

Imharr froze where he stood.

Brond smiled.

"Perhaps you'd like to give it a try?" said the newcomer to Imharr. He spread his arms wide in invitation.

"Might be I would. That is, if the lieutenant gives us leave."

Ludecan scowled at the two. "Fine by me. But no killing or maiming. Last thing I need is to find more men to replace you."

Wreaker leapt out of its scabbard, and Imharr clenched his jaw as he held his sword.

Brond smirked. "Alright. I'll attack, and you parry."

"Fine." Imharr walked toward Dayraven and held out his hand. The pain in Dayraven's stomach had subsided, and he grasped Imharr's hand as his friend pulled him up.

"Alright?" asked Imharr.

"Yes." Dayraven managed a smile. "Careful. He's quick."

"I noticed."

Dayraven picked up Sweothol and walked toward Gnorn and Hlokk, who stood in the circle of men observing. Gnorn smiled and clapped him on the shoulder, but by now Dayraven was more concerned for Imharr than for his own embarrassment. When he turned around, his friend was facing Brond.

The newcomer was still smiling. "Wetnurse. That's what they call you, isn't it?"

"Make the attack."

"Alright, Wetnurse. Are you ready for me?"

Imharr raised Wreaker in answer and stood poised to defend.

Swift as a striking snake, Brond hurled himself toward Imharr and swung his blade. The swords rang out when they met. Imharr pivoted and grunted as he arced Wreaker with savage speed. His blade met only air.

Brond had ducked low, and now the man thrust at Imharr's chest. Dayraven's friend lost his balance as he jerked his body backwards to avoid the sword's tip. But he regained his footing and parried the next thrust, after which both men backed off.

Brond and Imharr circled one another like predators seeking a weakness in their prey, waiting for the right moment to pounce. The one smiled, and the other gritted his teeth.

The newcomer laughed. "Would you like me to show you how it's done, Wetnurse? Come. Attack."

Imharr yelled and swung Wreaker as he launched himself at Brond.

Instead of parrying the blow up high as he was meant to, the newcomer slid aside from the wild swing with such swiftness and ease that it surprised everyone, especially Imharr. As Dayraven's friend grunted and lost his balance, Brond flicked his foot in Imharr's path and shoved him with his free hand.

Dayraven winced when his friend tripped and toppled face forward into the grass. The former bondsman dropped his sword and rolled.

When he came to a stop, Imharr lunged for Wreaker, which lay in the grass a few feet away. Brond was there at the same time. Imharr grasped his blade's hilt. The newcomer's boot stomped on the sword, pinching Imharr's fingers and trapping him on the ground. Imharr cried out, and Brond's sword swept toward his neck. The blade nicked his flesh, but it stopped short of inflicting a serious wound.

"Do you yield, Wetnurse?" Brond grinned as he twisted his foot and put more weight on the sword crushing Imharr's fingers.

Imharr snarled and tried to rise, but he managed to get only to his knees as he pulled on his trapped fingers with his other hand. His face red with strain, he tried to pry up the sword with his other hand, but it was no use.

"You have a temper, Wetnurse." Brond's foot jerked down, and Imharr gasped. "That's going to land you in some trouble someday. Do you know why?"

A low rumble came from Imharr's throat, and his eyes pinched closed as he tried to tug his hand out from under the sword.

"It makes you *predictable*. That's why."

The boot pressed harder. A thin line of blood trickled down Imharr's neck. The steel's sharp edge still pressed on the soft flesh. Brond laughed at his opponent's helplessness. Other men in the circle began to laugh with him. Imharr growled and strained.

Yield, thought Dayraven. *Come on, Imharr. You must yield.*

"Yield, soldier. It's over," barked Lieutenant Ludecan.

Imharr stopped fighting. He looked at the ground and nodded. "I yield."

Brond smirked and lifted his boot. He stared at Dayraven and chuckled before joining the other men.

After Imharr rose and sheathed Wreaker, Ludecan yelled at the men, "Alright, enough play. The rest of you pair up and practice the move. Let's go!"

Imharr scowled as he approached Dayraven and the two Dweorgs. He was flexing the hand that Brond had crushed.

Dayraven spoke first. "Your hand alright?"

"Fine."

"He cheats *and* he's quick."

Imharr's smile was rueful. "I noticed."

"Expect cheating in battle," said Gnorn. "Men hacking at each other and screaming and dying. It's no tale of valor and prowess for children. Blood and guts and shit. No rules, and few die with glory."

"I'll remember the lesson," said Imharr as he glanced in Brond's direction.

It was then that Dayraven noticed Captain Orvandil's tall form standing behind some of the men. The Thjoth was watching him.

When Gnorn, Hlokk, and Imharr followed Dayraven's gaze, the captain turned away and strode off.

Hlokk spat. "What's the big bastard want?"

"Looking after us, I think," said Dayraven.

"The only thing a Thjoth looks after is his sword. His greatest kindness is to kill a man fast rather than slow."

"Yet you helped to save him in Hasumere. You threw your axe at the aglak."

"I was aiming for the Thjoth."

Dayraven smiled at the Dweorg, who grunted and spat again.

"Let's go, you laggards! The exercise!" Lieutenant Ludecan waved his sword at the four friends, and they paired up.

LIKE MOST OF THE OTHER MEN IN THE COMPANY, DAYRAVEN sniffled as tears formed in his eyes. Night surrounded them along with the rest of Torrlond's encamped army, but they were in their own world. In a miraculous blur, Abon's fingers plucked the harp strings, whose vibrations awakened a deep, terrible longing. The shaper sang next to the fire, and its glow reddened the man's scarred face as he brought the tale of Wilfar and Aelfscyn to its bitter, sorrowful end.

The notes of the instrument interwove with the man's voice to bring to life the tale, which swam before Dayraven's eyes as he listened, like all the others, enraptured and lost in deeds that were centuries old.

. . . Midst weeping and wailing the woman looked on,
Dark was the deed that dwelled in her mind,
As she peered on the pyre of the prince, her son,
The child of the chieftain. Chilled was her heart.
The greedy one gulped, giver of warmth,
Foe of forests, the fire devoured him.
The carcass was kindled, crackled the bones,
The heat then hewed the head asunder.
Burst out the blood from the bite of the sword,
From the gaping gash that grieved the young man,
From the wound it welled. The wind now howled.
The smoke now swirled, soaring on high.
The blaze now burned the body of the youth.
A song of sorrow the assembled all moaned.
Moved then the mother, her mind was fixed,
Forward she followed as fate led her on,
And the will of the woman, to work a new grief.
To the pyre she paced and put forth her hand,
And brought out the blade that bided with the youth.
The harm to her hand she heeded not at all
As the flames all flowed on her frock and her hair —
Not soothing was the sword that seared her palm.
Aelfscyn of Ellond, whom the Ilarchae stole,
What drove you to this doom, to this deed of woe?
Who was fair as a flower is now fierce in her death.
The tribe all trusted she would take her own life,
But the lady laughed, though little was her joy.
Bleak was the bold one, bright were her eyes,
She hurried to her husband, the head of the clan,
In the chest of the chieftain she charged the brand,
Halved was the heart of the heathenish warrior,
And the blade burned in the body of the man,
The sword sizzled and sighed as it drank.

Lifeless was the leader, her love for him was small.
She flew to the flames and flung herself on,
On the pyre of the prince she parted from life.
The fire took the fey one, who followed her Wilfar,
High rose the reek, the roaring consumed her,
In the leaves of Logan she released her soul.
Aelfscyn of Ellond, ended is your pain,
Loaned was your life, not long were you here,
Your grief was great, but you greeted your fate.
Thus finished the fair one, few will not weep . . .

After the harp's last chords died, no one spoke. The fire cracked and spat and sighed. The vast darkness of night waited outside its glow. In silence, the men lay on their spare cloaks and drifted off to sleep.

Dayraven served the first shift on the night watch. As he pondered Aelfscyn's sorrow in the night's stillness, he stood apart from the group of slumbering men and gazed up at the stars. The glimmering lights put him in mind of his encounter in the Southweald. Always now the stars reminded him of the elf and its eyes. Its presence crept around the fringes of his awareness.

Urd's words about wizardry returned, and he thought about what happened with the aglak. He was both excited and frightened, the fear reminding him of one thing: the cold Supreme Priest Bledla with his piercing gaze. What would Urd think about him now, so far from where she had sent him? He hoped the old woman was safe, wherever she was. He felt the need to explain himself to her, as if he had failed her by not finding Galdor.

The first chance I get, I'll seek him. Grandmother, I'm not sure how I got here. I tell myself I had no choice. It seemed that way. Now I must see it through for Imharr's sake, and for Gnorn and Hlokk.

About halfway through Dayraven's watch, most of the men snored in their sleep. Someone went to piss in the bushes. After the trickling ended, the man came shuffling back. As he walked by Dayraven, he stooped and pulled off his boot. When he sat on the grass, he tipped his boot. Something fell out of it. A rock?

"We must escape."

Dayraven recognized Abon's harsh whisper. "How?"

"Can't try yet. They'd catch you and kill you as a deserter. It must be during the chaos of battle. Only chance we'll have. Stay close to me during the battle, and look for my signal. When you're gone, they'll take you for slain."

Dayraven thought of his oath to Ilm, and of Imharr and his Dweorg friends. "I won't abandon my friends. There's no honor in that."

"Honor is for idiots and dead people. There's more at stake here than your honor," hissed Abon. "If they're your friends, each would give his life for you. And if they knew everything, they'd *tell* you to flee. I must go. Look for my signal during the battle."

Abon disappeared into the night, leaving Dayraven more confused. He thought about discussing the matter with Imharr or Gnorn. But the shaper was right: They might counsel him to flee with Abon. If he fled, their lives might well be in danger. Naturally, whoever was looking for him would question them. *I swore to Ilm. I gave my word to look for Imharr's sister. I even swore loyalty to this company. I'll follow this path to its end. Afterwards, I'll find Galdor.*

By the time the next watch took his shift, Dayraven was resolute. Not long after he lay down, he fell into a deep sleep in which even the elf-shard's murmuring receded.

WHEN MORNING'S LIGHT CAME, DAYRAVEN MADE A POINT OF passing by Abon as they formed lines for the march ahead. Looking Abon in the face, he shook his head to indicate his decision.

Abon understood, for the scarred man's eyes widened for an instant, but he was too cautious to let his frustration show for long. In any case, nothing could have changed Dayraven's mind. As the men found their places in line, he gazed at Imharr, Gnorn, Hlokk, and his brothers in arms around him, and he almost smiled to himself.

The day's march would bring Torrlond's army within view of the Marar Mountains jutting out of the earth to the south. Dayraven had never laid eyes on them, but from Imharr's descriptions, he envisaged them in his mind: Thick forests blanketed the foothills and lower portions of the mountains, but higher up the forests petered out in a few scraggly pines clutching to the rocks. Above the tree line the slaggy grey peaks soared, and the largest mountains in the background gleamed white in the sun.

The quickest way through those peaks was Balnor Pass, the place where his father won his greatest glory. Torrlond's army was sure to make its way to Caergilion by the fortified pass, and they would find the first major resistance there. Fate, it seemed, was leading him to Balnor Pass.

"Move out!" cried Lieutenant Ludecan.

In unison with the rest of the Mercenary Company of Etinstone, Dayraven marched ahead, trying not to dwell on the fears still twisting in his gut.

20

AT BAY IN CAERGILION

On his way back from scouting ahead, Duke Anarad's man, the tall one with the scarred cheek called Deg, frowned as he looked to the side of the road, which had dwindled into a well worn path. Deg's gaze lingered on the young forest of birches and the remnants of the village – a few crumbling stone walls overgrown with prying brambles – concealed within it. Sequara did not blame him for fidgeting with the hilt of his sword as he rode closer. Like the rest of the disputed border region between Adanon and Caergilion, the place seemed haunted.

A quick shake of the head from Deg directed at Anarad meant there were none of the living to fear up ahead, and Anarad nodded as his man steered his mount to fall in with the other four the duke had brought with them, all soldiers though not wearing their Adanese colors lest they draw the wrong sort of attention. Alert as ever, Karad rode with them as well, easily falling in with fellow soldiers even if he had to speak with them in the Northern Tongue, which all of them knew to some degree. So far, they had been fortunate in encountering no one.

Few folk wandered this wasteland. Sequara knew that raiders from both Caergilion and Adanon had devastated the villages so often that all inhabitants had fled. Like as not, the gaping cellar holes of the onetime village in the forest would include the same charred remains that littered the other ruins they had come across, an ominous testament to the violence of their end. The beauty of the green, fertile hills added poignancy to the abandonment.

The sound of clopping hooves grew louder when Duke Anarad moved his horse up next to Sequara's. Side by side, they rode at a trot.

"My younger brother, Longarr, tried to resettle a village such as that one. You see the results of such efforts." Anarad spoke while staring ahead.

"The place has seen much sorrow. The land murmurs of blood spilled here." Sequara glanced at him, not wishing to pry but inviting him to keep speaking if he wished.

He nodded and sighed. "For centuries Caergilion and Adanon have torn at each other's throats. So many tales of loss, and now we slay one another out of blind hatred, not even for gain, as most folk do. My brother's death is one of too many."

"Why did he wish to live here?"

Anarad waited a while to respond. "The younger son of a nobleman must make his own way."

"Were there no other lands in Adanon? No other opportunities?"

"I suppose he thought he could bring life back to this place. Longarr had much life in him."

"You remember him with fondness."

"Yes. Of course, we quarreled and competed with each other as any brothers do. He was always trying to find a way to catch up with me. Even when we were grown men."

"He tried to settle this land to be like you?"

The duke nodded, and his eyes seemed to look far away. "When we were children, our father told us our ancestors once dwelled in these lands. It was Longarr's dream to resettle the place. Dreams die hard, especially those sown in our youth. Tales of Adanon's glorious past fired his imagination. He loved our kingdom and wanted to restore it to . . . some vision that grew out of stories and songs."

"And what did you think of his plans?"

"I tried to dissuade him. I offered half our father's inheritance if he would stay in our lands closer to Palahon. He wouldn't hear of it. Said it would reduce the integrity of the dukedom. He was right, of course, but . . . Had I known what would happen, I would have given all our lands just to keep him and his family."

"You could not have known."

Anarad nodded. They said nothing for a while.

"We could have a fire inside there, my lord." Loran, the quietest of the duke's five soldiers, had ridden close to have a word with Duke Anarad. Like the others, he spoke in the Northern Tongue for Sequara's benefit whenever he was in her presence, though his Ondunic accent was thick. He pointed at a tree-covered hillock not far from the old road. The shadows were long and soon enough would fade. Sequara too would have liked the comfort of a fire to provide some warmth and keep the darkness at bay.

"No," said Duke Anarad. "I don't like those horse tracks we saw. Too fresh. Tonight we light no fire. We're in a land of bandits or soldiers who are little better. And, at this point, we're more likely to run across those loyal to Caergilion. Best not announce ourselves. We will shelter in those trees, though. Is that acceptable, Lady Sequara?"

"I'll follow your counsel."

Though Sequara was eager to reach Caergilion's chief city of Iarfaen, she knew they must rest. The hillock, not far ahead on their side of the river, was a logical place to stop. One could hide there and still have a view of the road, and it was wise to keep out of sight. *So far we've been lucky. That luck must hold. I must reach Iarfaen soon.*

A dim rumbling from up ahead broke the stillness, and Sequara and her companions all tensed as they looked toward the hillock. The rumbling grew into the sound of many hooves beating the earth.

"Daer gwan hito arad. They're coming fast — more of them than us," said Deg, switching to the Northern Tongue from Ondunic.

"Those trees are indeed an excellent hiding place. They spotted us from it. Stand your ground," commanded Duke Anarad. "No point in fleeing on weary horses. Do not charge unless on my order. Weapons out."

The six men of Adanon unsheathed their swords and positioned their shields in front of them. Karad too pulled his blade out. Their horses danced a nervous step or two, and one snorted and whickered at the approaching troop's din. At once the rumbling of hooves grew louder as they rode over a rise into view.

Two score or more of horsemen galloped towards Sequara and her party. The setting sun bathed them red and gleamed off their helms as they shouted and urged their powerful steeds forward. A dust cloud plumed in their wake. Dressed for battle, they appeared to be soldiers rather than bandits, but it meant little difference. The tunics the charging soldiers wore over their byrnies were red and white — Caergilion's colors — while their shields were rectangular with spiked bosses. Some waved double-edged swords while others readied spears for casting.

Opening her mind and releasing the gift, Sequara expanded her awareness to include the anger and fear in the Adanese who abode the charge with her. Similar emotions propelled the Caergilese, who rushed toward her on their massive steeds. This was a place where men drew blades first and asked questions later.

Embracing the calm that came with the gift, Sequara left behind her own apprehension and readied herself. *I must take control before they do anything stupid. Nothing must interfere with the mission.* She turned to Anarad and spoke with more authority than she felt. "I will try my way first."

Anarad's eyes narrowed and he frowned in doubt, but then he nodded. "Be ready, but do not attack unless Lady Sequara is in danger," he ordered his men.

Sequara turned to Karad. "Remain here with Duke Anarad's soldiers."

The veteran opened his mouth to protest, but then he closed it and nodded. "Yes, my lady."

While the helmed soldiers of Caergilion sped closer, Sequara moved her steed forward a few paces. Slender and small before the raging tide of muscle and steel dashing toward her, she sat straight and unmoving on her grey mare. She held her palms outward, and then she sang in her clear voice, "Hrondin ar dwinnor ghannash in valir. Innin im gwalor runash in bundir."

Into the minds of the horses she allowed her energy to spread. Muscle and fury, power and speed — these were proud, fiery beasts with tempers and training for battle. But neither temper nor training could withstand the strength of the gift in Sequara. As an irresistible presence in their minds she commanded them. The horses had no choice. It almost seemed they were obeying their own will.

The charging beasts slowed then halted altogether when they were but thirty feet from her. The men atop the steeds shouted and cursed in Western Ondunic, "Darga raeri gagleri! Riawn!" The mounts only neighed and snorted. Some of the Caergilese scowled in anger, but most were wide-eyed in astonishment that their war-trained horses did not obey them.

Sequara could not suppress a momentary smile at the men who, moments before, had made up a formidable and overwhelming charge as they flapped their legs and dug in their heels on frozen steeds. One in front, whose helm boasted a red plume, took out a short whip and raised it above his horse.

She held out her palm and said in the Northern Tongue, "Do not strike. Your horses cannot obey you now."

The soldier lowered his arm as Sequara rode forward, and he said something to the rest of the soldiers. His followers all ceased their efforts to command their mounts. Now close enough to speak without shouting, Sequara took in the details of their byrnies and white and red tunics. Their bright helms came to a sharp point on top and had long nose guards in front as well as neck guards splaying out in back. On their shields they bore Caergilion's ensign: three white mountains on a red background.

She cleared her throat before mustering power and more than a hint of anger in her voice. "I am an emissary of Queen Faldira of Asdralad. Is it your custom to assail all those who travel in these parts?" *I must bring these two parties together, or my mission will fail.*

"My lady," answered the soldier with the plumed helm, "we have no quarrel with Asdralad. Forgive us for our haste, but we seldom see anyone other than raiders and thieves from Adanon. It is our charge to question all those who ride through here and to protect innocent travelers."

"And who protects innocent travelers from you?" shouted one of Anarad's men from behind Sequara.

"Borda hool, Deg," snapped Duke Anarad at his soldier. He made a cutting motion with his hand, but it was too late.

The foremost soldier from Caergilion continued to speak to Sequara in the Northern Tongue, but the edge of a threat cut through his voice. "Those men with you are from Adanon."

"I'm on a mission to King Malruan. *They* are my escort."

"They are our foes. Though you may be a sorceress of Asdralad, if you stand between us, I can't be responsible for what happens to you."

Men on both sides raised their swords.

Sequara held up her hands. "Peace! Stay where you are, all of you."

The men all obeyed, though they kept their swords ready.

Sequara took a deep breath and steeled herself. *Bring them together through their common threat.*

She turned to the lead soldier from Caergilion. "You have a deadlier foe than Adanon now. Torrlond is about to smash your kingdom and change your lives forever, if they spare any of your lives at all. I marvel King Malruan has left any soldiers in the south of his kingdom."

"With enemies on all sides, we must guard all our borders, my lady. You who are from Asdralad are fortunate in dwelling on an island."

Sequara nodded. "Yet none of us will be safe from Torrlond. Not even the vast waters will protect us."

The Caergilese soldier frowned. "But the Torrlonders haven't threatened your kingdom, have they?"

"Torrlond won't stop with Caergilion. All of Andumedan is under threat of conquest if we don't band together to halt their ambition. King Earconwald and the Supreme Priest Bledla covet every kingdom. They plan to swallow Adanon once they finish with Caergilion."

"How do you know this, my lady?"

"Someone high in the counsels of the Torrlonders has revealed this to us."

"Then, forgive my bluntness, but why have you come?"

"Queen Faldira sent me to offer aid. I must reach King Malruan as soon as possible. These men came with me from Adanon to discuss joining forces with Caergilion. Duke Anarad bears the seal of King Balch. When faced with common destruction, even the oldest of foes can come together. You must stop Torrlond together, or you will all fall."

The lead soldier's eyes widened and his mouth opened. He shook his head in disbelief, and then disbelief gave way to laughter. He spoke to his men in Ondunic, and the other soldiers from Caergilion chuckled and jested in their tongue. When the leader stopped laughing, he said to Sequara, "My lady, I am sorry, but this is beyond belief. Adanon will *never* aid Caergilion. What you speak of is impossible. Torrlond's quarrel is with us alone. They want to force their Way down the throats of everyone, but how can they conquer all of Andumedan?"

"They can and they will." Sequara's tone was serious enough to wipe the smile from his face. "Unless we stand together. Torrlond is more powerful than ever, more powerful than King Malruan guesses. With their priests' sorcery, they'll smash your army, formidable as it is. Then they'll smash Adanon, and each kingdom of Andumedan will fall one by one. In the world that will follow, those who don't obey the Way will perish."

The lead soldier gazed at her for a long moment with a deepening frown, and then he nodded his head in a bow. "Forgive me, my lady, for my haste and my rash words. If what you say is true, then we owe you our thanks. May I see confirmation of your mission?"

"Put away your blade, and I will free your horse. You and Duke Anarad will ride to me, and we will show you the seals of Asdralad and Adanon."

The man obeyed, and the three met between the two parties, where Sequara and Anarad presented the seals to the soldier. His face grew thoughtful when he looked on them. He remained silent for some time, and then he said, "I'll let King Malruan judge what to make of this. I'm Captain Aruth of the Twentieth Cavalry Company of Caergilion. It's fortunate you came across us before you met someone else in these parts. Some of my men and I will escort you to Iarfaen."

Sequara nodded. "Thank you, Captain Aruth."

The soldier bowed to her again. "King Malruan may know more

than you think. There are few enough of us remaining to guard the south." He shook his head. "These are evil times."

The captain turned and commanded his soldiers in Western Ondunic. Duke Anarad, who said he understood most of their speech, told Sequara he bade his soldiers to treat the travelers with respect.

The captain and his soldiers escorted Sequara, Anarad, Karad, and the Adanese men to the hillock. There they found another handful of soldiers with horses encamped among the trees, putting away their weapons and gear as if they had been ready to reinforce their comrades if necessary. The Caergilese gazed with threatening looks at the newcomers and murmured among themselves, but since the small party came with their captain's blessing, none said anything aloud.

Captain Aruth made sure his guests were comfortable and fed before bidding them goodnight. After he left, Deg stepped closer to Duke Anarad and Sequara before glancing at their hosts. "I'll take the first watch, my lord."

Anarad shook his head. "No need. He may be an enemy, but the captain's an honorable man, and his soldiers will obey him. No harm will come to us this night. I suggest you sleep well. There might be little enough rest ahead of us."

THE WHITE-PEAKED MOUNTAINS LOOMING IN THE DISTANCE DID NOT relinquish their claim on Sequara's gaze as she rode nearer to them through the hilly landscape. Soon, according to Captain Aruth, they would gain their first view of Iarfaen. She could feel the tension rising in the score of Caergilese horsemen as they drew nearer. Her own muscles were taut with nerves as well, and she had to remind herself again to let her breaths flow naturally.

But the last three days of riding in the company of the Caergilese had delivered some measured optimism. Something like respect had grown between Aruth and Anarad as they rode in each other's company. And if their respective followers had not warmed up to one another quite so much, they at least spoke in quick but courteous exchanges. That morning, even Deg had accepted food and drink from one of the Caergilese with a nod. The sorceress could not help but wonder if there was hope as she glanced over at the captain and the duke conversing while they rode near her at the front of the troop.

"Once we reach Iarfaen, I will escort you myself to King Malruan. That should speed your errand." The captain nodded to the Adanese nobleman.

Duke Anarad returned the nod with a quick, tight smile. "I thank you and accept your escort gladly since you've brought us so far."

They rode up a slope, and when they neared the top of the prominence, Captain Aruth held out one hand. "Behold, Iarfaen." But his proud smile disappeared as his eyes widened and mouth dropped open. When Sequara reined in beside him, she could see the reason for the change in his expression.

"Quite a sight," whispered Karad, who had ridden up next to Sequara.

Rugged hills gazed down upon myriad buildings of grey stone nestled in a wide valley. Smaller than Palahon, Iarfaen was the more beautiful of the two cities, though its beauty was stark. Combining the grace of the southern kingdoms with the solidity of the northern, elegant spires and domes reached up in imitation of the great mountains in the distance behind them. The River Maranant meandered like a grey ribbon by the city's strong outer walls wrought of stones hewn from those mountains. The river continued its course until it disappeared from view among the green foothills' folds and creases. But what gave the travelers more pause than the city and the landscape around it was the thousands of troops filling the valley.

King Malruan's army camped across the valley from the city. Thousands of soldiers milled about while red and white banners fluttered and stirred on white tents, which clustered in the valley like mushrooms. Massive dark clouds swelled and gathered over the mountains, threatening to dwarf the city and lending the entire scene a sense of impending doom. Beneath such a threat, the movements of the tiny troops seemed desperate and futile.

Eyes wide, Duke Anarad did not hide his surprise. "There must be fifteen thousand soldiers down there. Three quarters of Caergilion's army."

Captain Aruth glanced at the nobleman with a wince. His face was grim. "Our oldest foe knows us best. You are, unfortunately, quite right. So, the king's called nearly all of us. The rest are no doubt guarding Balnor Pass. There must be an overwhelming force coming. I've never seen the valley brimming like this. But come. Let's meet the king as soon as we can. If there's any hope you can bring aid, it might be welcome news."

THE SOLDIERS WITHIN THE BUSTLING CAMP WERE CLAD IN THE SAME red and white tunics and splayed helms as Aruth's men, and behind their flat stares, Sequara sensed the anxiety in those that spared her and her companions a glance. Aruth accosted a fellow captain with a red-plumed helm, speaking to him in the Northern Tongue, perhaps for Sequara's sake. "Gwanyn. Where can I find King Malruan?"

Seeming in a hurry, the other captain pivoted in mid-stride and then frowned at their guide. "Aruth. Aren't you supposed to be in the south?"

"I am conducting Lady Sequara, who has come from Asdralad with an urgent message for the king." Aruth nodded toward Sequara.

"I see." Captain Gwanyn turned toward Sequara and bowed. "My lady." He looked at Duke Anarad, narrowing his eyes as his gaze lingered on him, but then, after glancing toward wherever he was bound, he turned back to Aruth. "The king is commanding the preparations of the troops and defenses. His tent is in the center of the camp, that way. You can see his banner above it." The man pointed.

"Thank you," said Aruth, and as he offered no further explanation, Captain Gwanyn hastened on his way.

Captain Aruth turned to his sergeant. "Take the men and remain on the camp's southern perimeter. Tend to all the horses, and see that Lady Sequara's guard and the duke's men are cared for."

The sergeant nodded. "Yes, sir."

The captain then looked at Duke Anarad, and, though he hid it well, Sequara sensed the disquiet beneath his forced smile. "Your steeds and men will be in good hands. I'll lead you and Lady Sequara to the king's tent." He turned to Sequara and gestured toward the camp as he bowed. "My lady, if you will follow me, please."

Sequara fell in behind the duke and the captain. She sensed tension bordering on madness as they wound their way through the camp, where men shouted orders and scurried around as if preparing for the end of times. Even Captain Aruth seemed more and more shaken as he looked around and scratched his beard. Supply wagons laden with spears crossed their path, men with shovels hastened to go dig defensive works, a company of archers waited in line for newly made arrows for their quivers, and raw fear followed wherever they went. Only the discipline of routine kept everything together. Had the men not been war-hardened soldiers, panic would have scattered them in complete disarray.

After some time, they arrived at a plain canvas tent with the king's banner hanging from a pole rising above its center. Captain Aruth spoke in Ondunic to the leader of the eight guards outside. Their conversation began warmly, and the two soldiers appeared to know one another. But then, the leader of the guards looked over with wide eyes at Duke Anarad. An argument ensued, and it grew heated for a moment. The guard made abrupt gestures in Anarad's direction, and Captain Aruth grew angry. Duke Anarad looked at the ground while the debate went on.

In the end, the guards' leader strode into the tent. He emerged in little time and spoke again to Captain Aruth, who nodded at the man then turned to Anarad. "I must bid you to leave your sword with the guards. Forgive me, but old mistrust does not fade easily." He gave a sidelong glance at his fellow Caergilese soldiers.

Anarad smiled and nodded. "I understand. Here's my sword." He unbuckled the belt on which his scabbard hung and handed it to Aruth, who gave it to a guard.

The guards' leader nodded to Duke Anarad and gestured for them to follow him into the tent.

Inside, several men looked up from a map spread out on a table. Five were grey haired, but the sixth was a tall, slender, middle-aged man. Most were dressed for battle. The slender man frowned as he gazed at Duke Anarad and Sequara in turn. *Here's a proud, shrewd one. I must be careful*, thought Sequara.

Though he had the bronze skin of the south, his long hair was chestnut brown and his eyes greyish-blue. He wore a golden circlet around his head, and his steel corselet sported a brass emblem in the shape of Caergilion's ensign on it. Mud spattered the bottom of his long red cloak and his black boots. The distant descendant of Lothen, Duke of Torrlond, King Malruan of Caergilion addressed his captain with the unmistakable voice of authority.

"Aruth, gwand do tarath hinol."

"Your Majesty," returned Captain Aruth, who bowed low and spoke in the Northern Tongue, "Forgive the intrusion. I bring visitors who come to offer counsel and aid. May I present Lady Sequara, emissary from Asdralad, and Duke Anarad of Adanon."

As Sequara and Anarad bowed, King Malruan continued to inspect them with a severe frown. The older men around him did not hide their disgust as they stared and sneered at Anarad.

"The people of Asdralad are welcome at any time to my kingdom, but I wonder what brings a man of Adanon here on such a day as this." The king spoke the Northern Tongue with precision and dignity.

"Your Majesty," answered Sequara, "Duke Anarad accompanied me from Adanon to testify to King Balch's willingness to discuss joining forces with you." Sequara presented the seals of Adanon and Asdralad to King Malruan, who glanced at them as she continued. "Queen Faldira sent me to ask you to consider requesting aid from your old foe. As we told you in our previous messages, Torrlond brings an army larger than any ever assembled to invade these lands. The priests of the Way have enslaved beasts to do their bidding as well. Though you're a proud and strong people, Caergilion cannot meet this force alone."

King Malruan raised an eyebrow at Sequara. "My own scouts tell me how large Torrlond's forces are. Their army must cross the Marar Mountains before they can threaten us. A small contingent can defend Balnor Pass against any force they muster. Even were it not so, why would I stoop to ask my oldest foe for aid? Balch would just as soon slay me himself as dance on my corpse after Torrlond finishes here. Tell me, what could motivate Adanon to help us?"

Duke Anarad bowed again. "Your Majesty, if I may?"

King Malruan nodded.

Anarad folded his hands before him and took a deep breath. He controlled his countenance well, but Sequara sensed the deep emotions – some in conflict with others – beneath the surface. "Our peoples have warred without a thought to the future. I have lost most of those I love to this ancient hatred, as have many of your people. However, though we may not like it, we must recognize it when a common threat should bring us together. Queen Faldira has certain knowledge Torrlond won't stop with your kingdom. My own land will be next. As Lady Sequara has said, we either stand together or fall one by one. Though you speak truly of King Balch, he's also a practical man who, like you, knows when his own interest is at stake. Also, I'll not hide my hope that bringing our peoples together at this time might lead to peace between our kingdoms. This would be in the interest of all. In the interest of future generations from both our kingdoms. All you need do is ask King Balch for aid. He'll want terms, an agreement over our border that is favorable to Adanon. But the offer is genuine. Give the word, and I'll send three of my men in haste to Adanon with a message. Balch will come with an army to fight not against you but by your side."

Sequara breathed a sigh. *Couldn't have said it better myself. Anarad's a good man. I just hope Malruan will see it.*

King Malruan stared at Anarad, seeming to weigh the man standing before him.

Before he spoke, one of the older men stepped forward. "Sire, this is madness!"

Wearing a maroon robe and no battle gear, the man had a long grey beard. Here was one of King Malruan's sorcerers. Sequara sensed the gift running strong in him — he was nearly as powerful as she, and he was angry. His dark eyes flashed as he turned to Sequara. "I've traveled to Asdralad and met your queen, and by Oruma and Anghara, I respect no other more save my own king. But hearken to me now: This is not her affair to meddle in. Caergilion and Adanon will never be allies." He looked at Anarad and said, "Tir dahi luarch han ratorch!"

Duke Anarad remained calm and shook his head. "I've not come to look on your destruction, nor am I a spy. You must see an alliance, even a temporary one, would benefit both kingdoms."

"Even were I otherwise to fall in an abyss, I would not grasp your hand, Adanese!"

King Malruan raised his palm and turned to the sorcerer. "Peace, Dalan. Even if we don't accept this proposal, do not scorn the hand that offers aid with sincerity. This man carries King Balch's seal with him. And I deem he speaks the truth. We owe it to him at least to consider his words."

Just then the leader of the guards posted outside entered the tent again. His eyes were wide and his face pale. Everyone turned to the guards' leader, whose mouth opened to speak, but no words would come. His jaw worked, and his lower lip quivered, but that was all.

The guard was not alone. With him was a disheveled soldier who, to judge by his appearance, had traveled a great distance in terrible haste. The man was still breathing hard, and mud as well as blood spotted his red and white tunic and his face. He took several moments to catch his breath, and when he did, he looked at the king with desperate eyes. He began to bow, but he collapsed to the ground and shivered as he panted and sobbed, "Ael nuan ratarchiae! Ael nuan ratarchiae!"

Everyone in the tent gazed at the convulsing man on the ground. Sequara watched as a terrible realization widened all their eyes, and though she did not understand Ondunic, she knew this man's words were dire.

King Malruan did not appear daunted. His jaw was clenched tight, and he stood erect as he looked at his soldier in a heap. Coming forward to place his hand on the man's shoulder, he commanded, "Balra. Taraetha don falway."

The man rose. At first he stammered in words that tumbled out and halted in turns, as if it were an effort even to speak of what he had witnessed. But he found the courage to tell his tale. He spoke in Western Ondunic, but, talking in a quiet voice next to her, Duke Anarad provided a running translation to Sequara of what he said. As she sensed all the emotions in the tent, she did not need a translation to tell her the tidings the soldier bore were catastrophic. He did not stop weeping and shaking even as he spoke:

"Your Majesty. They're all dead. The army you sent to defend

Balnor Pass. Dead down to the last man. Even the reinforcements. It was after noon when the enemy breached our defenses and swarmed over the fortress. Captain Radui ordered us to flee and bear you the news. I saw the others slaughtered. I alone escaped. Torrlond's taken the pass. The beasts. It was the beasts. They doomed us, Sire. Can't bear to think of the horror. Crushed us from above, and when we were helpless they devoured men whole. In the mountains I've seen a troll now and again. But never more than one. By the Father and Mother, I never beheld anything like this."

King Malruan gazed with a steady face at the soldier. "Tell me everything you remember. Take it slow."

The man trembled as he nodded. "We sat behind our defenses in the pass in the late morning. Torrlond's army was nearing. We thought we were safe behind the walls. No more than a hundred of them could come at once, the pass is so narrow. When the vanguard of Torrlond's army drew up, we laughed. Dared them to attack. But they only sat there, just out of bow range. They said nothing. No one expected . . . but it hit us all at once." He shuddered.

"What hit you?" asked the king in a calm but commanding voice.

The soldier shook his head and stared before him with wide eyes as if seeing the memory take form before him. "The foul beasts must have moved in the darkness of night, crawling over the rocks. Hundreds of trolls and thousands of pucas waited over our heads. Must have slain our scouts . . . we had no warning. Swamp-trolls too, the aglaks, though they came later. Everything began when the trolls started throwing boulders down on us. We thought the mountain was tumbling on our heads. Men screamed . . . rocks battered us. Couldn't even see the boulders coming. Rocks and boulders cracking so loud my ears rang. Screaming. And running. Blood and death everywhere. Naihi, a mate in my company, standing next to me . . . next moment, a huge crack, and he's spattered under a shattered boulder. Nothing but pulp left." He shut his eyes and swallowed.

"Go on," prompted the king.

The man's eyes opened, but he continued to tremble. "While the trolls' rocks battered us, the pucas crawled down the sides of the ravine, and hundreds of aglaks advanced in front of our walls with giant ladders. Our remaining archers on the walls unleashed their arrows at them. But the arrows only lodged in . . . didn't even slow them. The aglaks climbed the ladders, and we faced them. Stuck them with spears and slashed them with swords, and still they ripped men to pieces. Then the pucas snuck in from behind. The aglaks tore men's heads off with one blow . . . bit off limbs. Pucas swarmed us. Little beasts clutched and dug. I saw three slice a man's neck open and tear out his eyes with their teeth and nails. We slew hundreds . . . beasts had no regard for their own lives. But Torrlond's army poured over our walls on the ladders. Aglaks slew all our guards around the main gate and opened it. The Torrlonders rushed inside through the gate. The end was coming. For every one we slew, five more came. But we fought on."

"Under whose command?"

The soldier took a moment to think. "Only officer alive was Captain Radui. In our last stand we followed him. I saw an aglak kill Duke Grallon . . . there's little left of his corpse to bury. They hemmed us in. Captain Radui took six of us aside, ordered us out the back entrance. He commanded us, your Majesty. Said you had to know as soon as possible. Six of us ran as fast as we could. Arrows from above got two. The Torrlonders had the walls. Pucas waiting on the other side leapt on three and tore their flesh. I still hear their screams. I broke through . . . don't know how, but I must be the only one alive from the pass. When I reached the lower camp, I took a horse and rode as fast as I could. Captain Amlan of the lower camp is ordering most of his men back to Iarfaen. He and some scouts will come down when Torrlond's army is near striking distance from here."

"Is that everything?"

"That's all, your Majesty. There's nothing more."

When he finished his tale, the soldier's head drooped and he gazed at the ground. Silence filled the tent. The lords behind the king stared at the soldier with their mouths agape. Not one of them moved or said a word. King Malruan looked grim, but he remained proud and erect. Gazing at Sequara, he broke the silence as he addressed her in the Northern Tongue.

"Lady Sequara, it appears the offer that you and Duke Anarad brought, however well intentioned, is too late."

"Your Majesty," said one of the king's grizzled advisors, "we must evacuate Iarfaen."

The king shook his head. "No. Torrlond will be upon us in the morning, if not before. An organized evacuation will take too long, and the Torrlonders would find our citizens strung out across the valley when they arrive, with us unprepared."

"Then," persisted the old man, "we might take refuge behind Iarfaen's walls."

"And how would we fare in a siege against the beasts this man described?" King Malruan gestured towards the soldier from the pass. He cocked an eyebrow to challenge the advisor to answer, but no answer came. "Our walls are high, but do not doubt the beasts can scale them. Such a siege would end swiftly, and with much bloodshed. No. Instead, you, Duke Travor, will go to Iarfaen and surrender the city to the Torrlonders should we fall. You must negotiate for the lives of the citizens. I will defend my realm, but I will not needlessly endanger my people."

He turned again to Sequara with a brief, sad smile that conveyed a portion of his sorrow and regret. It told Sequara that here was a man staring at his doom. "I had thought to defend the pass for some days at least. I had hoped for weeks. Had we held, your proposal might have worked. Alas, we'll never know. But I will spare my city and meet Torrlond's army here in the valley." He nodded to her. "Go home and prepare as you see fit."

To the unbending king Sequara replied, "Your Majesty, though we failed to bring you aid in time, there's one last task for us. With your permission, we'll stay here in your camp until Torrlond's army descends on this valley."

"As you please," said King Malruan with little emotion. "Captain Aruth will see to your accommodations. And now, if you'll pardon me, I must look to the defense of my realm while I still wield power. May you embrace whatever fate meets you with dignity and courage."

As they left the tent, Sequara admired the king for his equanimity in the face of certain defeat and probable death. She also saw he commanded respect and loyalty from his people, including Captain Aruth, who led them from the tent in grave silence.

While weaving through the camp, she glanced up at the massive mountains and the billowing, dark clouds looming overhead. The waning sunlight branded streaks of orange and pink on the black bands of advancing clouds, which appeared more ominous than ever. She would have to seek Dayraven and Imharr in the midst of the coming battle, hoping to reach them before death did. This task would be a little easier since she would sense Dayraven's presence. However, the priests of the Way, especially Bledla, could sense him too, and probably her. She gritted her teeth. *We failed to help Caergilion. I must not fail to find Dayraven now.*

21
THE WAR OF THE WAY

Gods be good. I just pissed. Didn't I?

Dayraven winced. His bladder exuded a heavy sense of pressure, a writhing in his gut, even though, having heard the veterans' stories, he had relieved himself before lining up. His breaths came shallow and quick, and his frantic heartbeat thrummed in his ears. The organic scent of mud mingled with the acrid odor of the bodies pressing close all around him. Completely soaked, he could not tell how much of it was his sweat.

He stood in the rain among the Mercenary Company of Etinstone. One small part of the largest force ever assembled in Eormenlond, the men of the mercenary company took their position on a slope overlooking the valley in which the city of Iarfaen nestled and thousands of soldiers of Caergilion waited.

Torrlond's invading army vastly outnumbered its foe. In addition, the assembled beasts of battle hunched like dumb, wet boulders on the slopes in front of Torrlond's troops, waiting for their masters, the priests of the Way, to unleash them on the doomed army below. Following King Malruan, the soldiers of Caergilion appeared ready to die before coming under Torrlond's rule. For his part, Dayraven wondered at the courage of these men who embraced certain destruction. He had seen the consequences of this courage in the mountain pass the day before.

With the rain pelting his cheeks and pinging on his helm, he recalled the aftermath of the battle in Balnor Pass, during which he engaged in no action. By the time his mercenary company arrived to march through the fortress, not a single soldier of Caergilion was left standing. But the remains of their struggle were everywhere. Massive trolls and aglaks piled Caergilese corpses in a great heap where the battle was thickest, at the rear of the stronghold. Many bodies lay strewn all over, some missing limbs or heads. Thrown in among the corpses with their blank stares were dead pucas, aglaks, and trolls. Congealing pools of blood and vomit and waste covered the ground. The putrid smell reminded Dayraven of the butcher shops and tanneries in Etinstone, and flies buzzed around gobbets of flesh littering the ground.

In another part of the fortress, a few dozen of Torrlond's dead soldiers lay in neat rows. Imharr had remarked that it didn't appear much like an even fight. Balnor Pass, he reflected, was nothing like what he envisioned when he heard tales of his father's glory. A portion of his breakfast came up in his throat with the memory of the dead, and its bitter taste burned as he swallowed it down. He clenched his eyes closed and suppressed the urge to retch.

When he opened his eyes, the neat ranks of Caergilion's red and white soldiers still stood far below in their rectangular formations of companies. This too was not going to be an even fight. But one difference for him was the Mercenary Company of Etinstone would see its share of combat this time. During the early hours before dawn, King Earconwald and his dukes had arrayed the army on the slopes overlooking the valley. The Mercenary Company of Etinstone was among those on the front line, at the edge of the right flank. Good place to see some action, he reckoned.

Dayraven remembered Captain Orvandil barking orders in the darkness and men shuffling around as the downpour began. They had waited in the rain and murk for what seemed like an eternity, but when grey dawn came he looked off to his left. Torrlond's army curved in an enormous arc like a vast forest on the slopes overlooking Iarfaen. So many thousands of spears, shields, horses, and men all merged into one huge mass. Below them all, brooding and silent, thousands of the gruesome beasts of battle awaited their orders. It would be a grim prospect to face them. *Thank the gods I'm looking at their backs.*

He glanced at Imharr on his right and Gnorn and Hlokk on his left. Just beyond the two Dweorgs stood the scarred man, Abon, his green sack slung over his back. It seemed the shaper was determined to stay close to him even though Dayraven refused to abandon the battle. Beyond the shaper the endless rows of soldiers stretched, disappearing in the distance behind the curtain of rain.

Though a sinking feeling gripped and twisted his stomach as the raindrops fell in earnest and mingled under his kirtle, byrny, and undershirt with his sweat, Dayraven told himself he had made the right choice to stand by his friends. *Courage, they all say. What's courage? Fear of shame, said Captain Orvandil. Forgetting the fear of death. Forgetting oneself. A soldier must let go of his will, surrender to forces around him, or he'll go mad, run away in terror. Never think in battle. A soldier must do, not think.* Dayraven's father had often given such counsel, but now, as it tumbled around in his mind, he was having difficulty making sense of it.

Also tumbling in his mind were the whisperings of the elf-shard. They hissed and stroked his awareness. They spoke of darkness and everlasting sleep. He gritted his teeth and resolved to keep the elf-state in check. A battle was the last place for slipping away into ethereal indifference.

"Ready, men!" Captain Orvandil's deep voice broke his thoughts. The moment drew near. *Damnation. Waiting and thinking. Shit. Oh gods. Fear of death. Fear of not being. Let it begin.* He tried to slow down his breaths.

Orvandil continued, "Stay clear of the trolls and aglaks. Don't let the foe around our flank at any cost. On my word, charge at double time."

The company's drummer stood next to Lieutenant Ludecan, the second in command, awaiting the signal from Orvandil. Time stretched. Dayraven inhaled and tightened his grip on Sweothol. He swallowed his spit to loosen the lump in his throat. His shield seemed to drag down his arm, which already quivered with fatigue. Or was it just fear?

Imharr looked over. Dayraven returned the glance. Under the nose guard of his friend's helm was his familiar smile, which reminded Dayraven of the Mark. *If I live through this, I'll return one day for Ebba.* From somewhere behind him came the command, "Archers! Fit your bows!"

Yew and elm creaked as thousands of archers bent their longbows behind him.

The same voice shouted, "Aim!" A brief pause. "Loose!"

As a gust of wind the swarm of arrows whooshed over the soldiers on the front line. The grey sky darkened to black with the flurry of missiles. His heart soaring with the arrows, Dayraven thought, *the fury of the gods.* The arrows sought the swollen clouds overhead then arced downward, mingling with the raindrops.

In response, Caergilion's soldiers crouched beneath their rectangular shields. This saved most, but a fair number in their ranks cringed to the ground with a cry of agony and a shaft protruding from a limb or shoulder. The Caergilese archers below could not reach Torrlond's troops until they marched forward, but this was a temporary comfort.

Twice more the call came for Torrlond's archers to unleash their deadly storm. Each time the hail of arrows bore down more of Caergilion's troops. Dayraven felt pity for them, though he knew it was the last thing he should be doing when he was about to face them in combat. Shaking his head and clenching his teeth, he tried to remember what soldiers of Caergilion did to Imharr and his family. *We're warriors. Here to do our duty. They'll do theirs, we'll do ours. All one can do. Fate sorts out the rest. Death comes where it will. Death.*

Shit. I shouldn't even be here. He took a deep breath and tried to keep his friends foremost in his mind. He would do his best to look after Imharr, Gnorn, and Hlokk.

Ahead of him, hundreds of huge, hairy trolls, each fourteen or fifteen feet high, arose and lumbered down the slope toward the enemy line. Their charge shook the earth. Rocks tumbled in their wake. Their wrinkled, pale hides showed on their upper arms, thighs, buttocks and faces. Matted brown hair elsewhere on their bodies bounced as they led the charge with hundreds of roaring aglaks and thousands of scrambling pucas behind them.

"At least the aglaks'll enjoy the rain," said Imharr.

A war horn's wail shattered the air. Dayraven's heart teetered and leapt.

Brandishing his sword, Captain Orvandil boomed over the downpour, "Forward!"

A surge of rage, a wave of ecstasy, and the men of the Mercenary Company of Etinstone shouted along with Torrlond's army, shaking the heavens as they followed the drumbeat down the slope toward their foes. In that shout Dayraven lost himself.

AMONG CAERGILION'S RED AND WHITE RANKS, SEQUARA OF Asdralad crouched beneath the storm of arrows that fell three times and brought low several men around her. Some went silent, but most rolled around in agony. She shut out their screams. Anarad and his five unscathed soldiers hid her and Karad behind their shields, which endured several loud thuds when arrowheads bit into them. Rain dripping from her hair, she sat with her eyes closed beneath the cocoon of shields, ignoring the men's breathing and scents to focus on Dayraven.

A dim presence arose somewhere amidst Torrlond's vast army. She sifted out all else. The rage and terror and madness of thousands on the doorstep of death: All of it remained but receded in her awareness. She focused on that one presence, which was familiar to her because of the memories Urd had shared. The presence drew nearer. In spite of Sequara's equanimity as she allowed her heightened perceptions to drift in the realm of origins, a small part of her grew excited that she could sense Dayraven. In a few moments she would know in which direction to seek him.

The men around her stirred. Something urgent was happening. Opening her eyes and standing, she looked down the line to the right, where King Malruan mounted a black steed and, sword extended, ordered his archers to answer Torrlond's. In front and high above, the grey avalanche of Torrlond's myriad soldiers descended the slopes in disciplined formation. Before them the huge trolls and aglaks rushed.

The archers behind her unleashed their arrows upward, and many shafts found their target after plunging earthward. Hundreds of the small, quick pucas in front of the charge went limp and fell. Pounding closer, the bellowing trolls and aglaks that the arrows bit into trod on the smaller creatures and scattered their wiry corpses. The archers had time for two more volleys before the beasts closed in.

Just then, Sequara felt a surge of power near the front lines, drawing her attention there. She caught a glimpse of several figures stepping forward from the shieldwall, raising torches and then extending them forward. *The Caergilese sorcerers.* She knew at least a dozen of them were chanting a song of origin up there, and she could feel which one. *So, they're using fire, but they're exposing themselves too.*

A moment later, flames erupted from the torches the sorcerers bore into a massive wall of fire, and the boiling conflagration washed over the foremost trolls before they hit the front line. The sorceress could make out the dark forms of the massive beasts writhing within the inferno, and their piteous wails carried far as they screamed their agony.

The sorcerers kept up their barrier of fire, and it seemed to hold back the onrushing foe. But then, vast power surged somewhere in the distance. From further up the slope, behind the advancing Torrlonder army, a blinding flash exploded and fragmented the very sky, casting the world into a contrast of pure light and eerie shadow. From this wrathful explosion streaked a massive, jagged bolt of what seemed like lightning toward the Caergilese front line, writhing as it tore asunder the air. The earth exploded, and clods of soil, rocks, and bodies flew backward. The almakhti – for this could be nothing other than wizard's fire cast by the Supreme Priest Bledla – swept across the Caergilese front line even as its sound caught up with it in an ear-shattering boom.

Sequara blinked as her vision returned, and a high-pitched whine cut across her muffled hearing even as the almakhti's echoes rolled and rebounded from the mountains. Smoke from the fire and the almakhti curled up ahead, curtaining the Torrlonder army behind it, and the wind carried the scent of burnt flesh. For a surreal moment, all was silence. But then, as their forms materialized and rushed forward from the smoke, massive trolls snarled and bellowed, renewing their attack.

Several rows in front of Sequara, the front line of regrouping Caergilese soldiers presented a spiky wall of spears and pikes to greet their attackers. Just as the men of Caergilion yelled their battle cry, the first trolls leapt over the defensive ditches and crashed into the foremost soldiers. Bodies flew. Men screamed. Knotted with huge muscles under their thick, leathery flesh and scorched and bedraggled hair, the massive trolls growled and tore apart men like rags. One limp corpse twisted in the air near Sequara and collided with three soldiers, sending them sprawling.

But the spearmen and pikemen on the front line used their long weapons of ash and steel to bring down many of the hirsute giants. Pierced by dozens of spears and covered with streams of dark blood, some trolls tumbled backwards with groans like falling trees and filled the ditches. Then the pucas and aglaks reached the Caergilese. The deft pucas crawled behind the spears and leapt on the soldiers, inhibiting them while the larger beasts crushed them.

The tide of battle shifted back and forth, but Caergilion's soldiers gained the upper hand and pressed forward. Aglaks with numerous weapons protruding from their slimy hides bowed to the earth. Soldiers mowed down the small pucas, whose shrieks tore the air.

Seeing the battle going their way, the Caergilese in the rear ranks moved forward in their eagerness to join the fray. Compelled by those pressing from behind, the soldiers on the front lines leapt into ditches choked with monsters' corpses and their own fallen. Men slashed and stabbed. The beasts gave way.

Sequara, Duke Anarad, and his men moved along with the ranks of Caergilion's soldiers. Anarad shouted, "They're rushing forward too fast! They'll expose themselves over their defensive line!"

A few more experienced soldiers saw the danger, but their cries went unheeded as madness and fury reigned. The Caergilese troops reached the bottom of the slope in disarray just as Torrlond's first soldiers arrived hurling themselves headlong and roaring battle cries.

The front lines clashed like a clap of rolling thunder as steel slapped steel and flesh, and Caergilion's forces swayed backward.

Sequara kept her focus on Dayraven as the smoke dissipated in the rain. His presence grew stronger, somewhere far off to her left. Looking up, she tugged Duke Anarad's sleeve and said, "I sense him. This way."

DAYRAVEN GRIPPED SWEOTHOL AS HE NEARED THE MELEE AT THE slope's bottom, still blinking from the near-blinding flash of lightning. Through the thinning smoke he glimpsed bodies writhing, beasts and men alike growling and screaming with little difference between them. Like the rest of his company, he followed Captain Orvandil, who moved with alarming speed. When he encountered Caergilion's front line, the large captain dodged a blow to his right, parried another with his sword, and blocked yet another with his shield. He crushed one adversary's face with his shield's boss, crunching bone and splattering blood. As if reaping wheat, he swung his sword through the second's neck, from which a rope of blood spewed. Into the third's helm he chopped his large blade down to the man's jaw. The helm crinkled like tin, and teeth spun out of his split face before the body collapsed as if boneless.

Dayraven gawked at Orvandil's grace and cold-blooded efficiency. A shiver shook his shoulders, but he had little time to stop and admire or feel sickened.

The armies collided with a cacophony of yells and grating steel. Shield in front, Dayraven smacked into the line of red and white tunics with spiked shields, jarring the bones of his left arm. Swords lashed out. Some veered nowhere near him, but he ducked under one blade and blocked another with his round shield. The sword rang on the iron boss. Another blade glanced off Dayraven's byrny at the shoulder with a sharp screech, knocking him sideways. Its owner wheezed and cringed when Imharr drove Wreaker point first through the man's byrny at the armpit into his chest. A spearman nearly gored Dayraven's thigh, but he turned aside and yelled as he chopped, shattering the spear shaft with Sweothol.

Dayraven's shoulder felt bruised, but it moved fine, and there was no blood. He thanked the Dweorg Bur in his mind for the strong mail. Adding his recent training under Orvandil and Ludecan to all the sparring over the years with his father and Imharr, he remembered his lessons and defended himself with caution. Imharr, on the other hand, wielded Wreaker with fire in his veins. After so many years, he struck out in wild fury at those who raped and murdered his family. Teeth bared in a mad grin, the former bondsman dodged a soldier's blade and screamed as he shoved his sword's tip into the man's face, which erupted in a red spray.

Another foe came at Imharr from behind. Yelling something incoherent, Dayraven parried the blow meant for his friend's helm. After the swords' clang, Imharr wheeled around and stabbed the attacker's neck. Blood welled from the gash and from the man's spluttering mouth. The body collapsed and disappeared beneath legs and boots. Imharr dove back into the fray, leaving Dayraven slack-jawed at his friend's battle frenzy. He stepped back to catch his breath and ward Imharr's back, thereby gaining a glimpse of his two Dweorg friends.

Hlokk belted out a battle cry in the tongue of his kin: "Hzaatarku Kheendwunok!" Ducking a spear, he swung low with his axe and cut a soldier's leg from under him. After parrying a sword blow, he spun his axe back and, with a rib-shattering thrust, crushed the chest of a soldier who rushed at him from behind. The man fell back groaning. Another soldier cut at Hlokk, who met the blow with his axe in one hand and sliced with his dagger in the other through the soldier's thigh. The man clutched his leg and rolled to the earth as he screamed. Hlokk roared over him.

Gnorn fought nearby. The elder Dweorg wheeled and planted his axe in a foe's face, sending him reeling in a gush of crimson. He stood with his back to his brother. Neither of them saw the soldier who rose behind Hlokk with sword aloft.

Dayraven yelled, "Hlokk! Behind you!"

The soldier's blade crashed down on Hlokk's helm, and the Dweorg went down on his knees with shock widening his large brown eyes. Another soldier of Caergilion swept the Dweorg's neck with his sword.

Blood sprayed onto Hlokk's thick beard. His eyes rolled up as he slumped forward, and he wore a slight smile.

"Hlokk!" screamed Dayraven. Two more soldiers pounced on his stricken friend, and the four soldiers hacked at the Dweorg's body. The elf-shard breathed shadows that seized Dayraven's mind, and his feet stuck to the ground as he strove to silence it.

"Khaalgur Jworeeanu!" Sweeping away one man with his axe, Gnorn cried out while leaping toward the soldiers who clove his brother's unmoving body. The other three Caergilese fell backwards, and the relentless Dweorg pressed his attack over Hlokk's motionless form. The chaos of men thickened, and both Dweorgs disappeared from Dayraven's view.

Caergilion's desperate soldiers pushed forward. A wedge of red and white sundered Dayraven, Imharr, and a few others from the rest of the Mercenary Company of Etinstone. Dayraven caught one last glimpse of Gnorn swinging his axe. Nearby, Abon tried in vain to cut through to him. Brond stabbed a soldier in the face, dodged a thrust, and carved through another foe's neck to punch through the Caergilese line.

"Stay together! Hold the line!" cried Orvandil over the pouring rain as he lopped off a large assailant's leg at the knee, spattering blood and knocking the man down. The tall captain tried to smash through the throng that cut off a dozen of his men from the rest of his company. But more and more enemy soldiers pressed back those few, including Dayraven.

He lost sight of Gnorn and even Orvandil. The Caergilese before him shouted with rage and mindless hatred in their eyes. He retreated before the red and white tunics threatening to envelop him. While dodging a slash at his head, he slipped on the muddy earth. He dropped his shield and fell backwards, landing in the mud on his back and jarring his body. He had less than a moment to move.

Go! A sword's tip dug into the earth near his face as he rolled. He sprang up and, screaming with animal fury and fear, thrust his sword forward as his attacker slashed again. Dayraven ducked, and the foe's blade whistled over his head. The man rushed straight into Sweothol.

The ancient blade sliced through the links of the soldier's byrny and sank deep into his chest.

The nemesis in Dayraven's mind struck. He had less than a moment to panic.

Like blue lightning, the shard of the elf's presence flashed as a pair of vast eyes in his mind and jolted his body. He reeled forward. His free arm flung outward as his back arched and his head jerked toward the heavens, and he seemed to see every drop spiraling toward the earth from the clouds. His mouth and eyes gaped wide. Vast and undeniable, the elf-state exploded from him, and his energy burst outward. So great was the power propelling his mind in every direction, Dayraven was helpless even to think of resisting, and he scattered where it carried him.

He lost awareness of the battle raging around him. Muting the screams and clashing of weapons, his attention lurched and focused on the man dying before him. Remote from his own body, he found that his sword hand still grasped Sweothol. In a mechanical, unconscious motion, he withdrew the blade from the man's chest with a tug. The Caergilese warrior's thick blood gushed out. His eyes, bulging with knowledge of his end, stared into Dayraven's.

But he saw more than the soldier's dark brown eyes. The Caergilese man's essence and emotions leapt out as Dayraven's energy inhabited him. Death. Horror of not being. One's story cut short. The rending agony of never embracing loved ones again. Eternal stillness and darkness. All of it pierced Dayraven and became his own thoughts, took over his mind until he became the man. The soldier of Caergilion reached out blindly and withered to the earth. Dayraven withered with him, sharing the final memories flooding the man's mind as if they were his.

With startling clarity, his young and pretty wife appeared before him. Long black hair and dark, beautiful eyes. He wanted her to smile, but she would not. Never again would he tease her, laugh with her as they lay in bed, or caress the curves of her sleek body as he made love with her. Never again would they make plans for the future of their little farmstead in their beautiful, quiet valley. Anxiety for her future washed over him.

His daughter and son, children of six and three, cried as he left their farmstead to defend the kingdom. Tears in their innocent eyes. Deep affection and unbearable joy. Never again would he play with them, pass on to them the lessons his mother and father taught him, caress their soft hair as they slept, or hold their little bodies in his arms. What would happen to them?

His careworn, grey-haired mother stood erect by his wife with tears tracking her wrinkled cheeks. Never again would he watch her instruct and play with his children, give her secret little smile as she prepared his favorite foods, or braid his wife's long hair. Guilt and worry for leaving her, for leaving them all so soon. *No. I can't go. Not yet. Please!*

Naked terror of death stripped away everything. His mind quivered in his last moment of self-awareness. Then came the rushing, white light of oblivion as his life pumped out into the wet soil of his native land.

Deep within the vast presence of the elf, the kernel of humanity left to Dayraven shivered. With blood running down Sweothol, he stood frozen over the body, not understanding how such clear images had burned into his mind. *Gods. I died with him. What have I done? What have I taken?*

"Day!"

The scream came from another world. The call of a raven echoed beneath it.

"Dayraven!"

Imharr's shout roused his friend just as another Caergilese soldier plunged a sword at his chest.

The elf-state fled. The battle returned with full force. Thrashing with a combination of terror and nausea, he jerked backwards to avoid the stabbing blade and fell to the wet ground. He splashed in a puddle, scattering drops and scraping his back. Filthy water and mud filled his mouth and nose. The rushing soldier fell on top of him with a grunt, his weight nearly knocking the wind out of him.

Dayraven choked and coughed and spat grit from his mouth. Both men had dropped their swords, but the Caergilese soldier on top of him pulled a dagger from his belt and drove it down towards Dayraven's neck. Grinding his teeth at the dizziness assailing him, he caught and grasped the man's wrists. Their arms trembled in their struggle to move the dagger in opposing directions. He pushed up with all his strength, but the shiny dagger's tip inched closer to his flesh.

He strained and wheezed through clenched teeth, emitting a feral growl. The man above him screamed through his contorted grimace. Dayraven had only moments. He shifted his weight and twisted his head to the right as he pulled the dagger down to his left. The dagger sank into the wet soil next to his face. Quicker than his unbalanced attacker, Dayraven threw him off. As both men shot up to their knees, he delivered an uppercut to the man's chin, snapping his head back.

Dayraven's blade gleamed in the mud. While the dazed man shook his head, he lunged on all fours and grabbed Sweothol with his aching hand. He stood up, raised the blade, and screamed. The soldier stared at him, debated a moment, and fled, slipping on the wet ground.

As soon as the man turned his back, nausea clawed Dayraven's stomach. He buckled and retched. Puke spattered on the ground, stung his throat and nose, and stretched from his lower lip in a thick tendril of drool. He winced and wiped his face. Gasping for breath, he turned around to look for Imharr.

The slope behind him was littered with bodies. At least nine men of the Mercenary Company of Etinstone lay dead or writhing alongside a score of Caergilion's lifeless or dying soldiers. He held his breath and scanned the carnage for his friend.

Fat Bothelm sprawled with his head split open. Old Eafa too lay dead, as well as young Giso, Sergeant Bisi, and Hoc. Eorp and Adda, both bleeding and twisting in pain, would soon join them. The former had gathered up his spilled intestines as, reduced to a squalling child in the face of death, he called for his mother. His eyes fluttered as he tried to stuff his guts back in, and they slithered out of his weakening grasp. Adda trembled and clutched his thigh, below which blood pulsed from the meat and bone where the rest of his leg had been. Blood also ran all over his face, and his mouth gaped open in a rictus of agony. There was no helping either of them.

Above Dayraven's dying comrades on the slope, Imharr and Brond fought off four remaining attackers. He sprinted toward his friend.

As he hastened up to Imharr and Brond, Imharr finished off one opponent with a parry and a quick slash to his legs. The man fell hard and rolled down the slope. But another Caergilese tackled Imharr. Both men rolled on the ground as they grasped one another. Dayraven huffed and his head pounded as he rushed closer, dodging bodies and slipping in the mud.

Brond, who was closer to Dayraven, stabbed one foe in the chest, piercing the byrny while blocking another's blow with the remnants of his wooden shield. The shield shattered apart, but, using the momentum from his attacker's blow, Brond pivoted and slashed his face. He finished off the reeling man by stabbing him through the back.

Imharr wrestled with his second attacker, a large man. Both had lost shield and sword. They grappled and growled like desperate beasts. Imharr slid backwards in the mud down the hill as the bigger man pressed down on him. Brond gazed at Imharr's struggle and made no move to intervene, but Dayraven thought little of it as he ran to save his friend.

Just as he passed Brond on the way to Imharr, Dayraven sensed in his peripheral vision a blade arcing down. Nerves screaming, he wheeled around. Steel sang as Sweothol swung up and deflected the blow Brond meant for Dayraven's skull. The two men struggled with swords locked. Dayraven grimaced and yelled over the rain in a ragged, hoarse voice, "What are you doing, Brond?"

The man sneered, and his free hand lunged toward Dayraven's neck with something shiny in it. Dayraven jerked back, but too late. Warmth spilled over his neck's right side. Brond grasped a dagger dripping red from its tip.

Covering the sudden, sharp pain on his neck with his left hand, Dayraven swung Sweothol. When the sword grazed Brond's sword arm on the wrist, the assassin cried out and dropped his weapon. Dayraven stumbled when he tried to follow up, his legs too slow to follow his thoughts. The neck wound burned, but a cold numbness branched from it toward his brain. The numbness seemed to grip round his mind, severing his control over his body. Stumbling backward, he grew dizzy and weak. The shadows the elf whispered of loomed around him.

A snarl twisting his face, Brond swung his fist and connected with Dayraven's jaw.

White flashed. Dayraven reeled back. Somehow he was still standing, though his disconnected legs wobbled. A sharp pain throbbed on his tongue, which he had bitten when the assassin punched him.

Brond picked up his sword from the ground. "The will of Edan be done. Thus end all who interfere with the Way."

Dayraven collapsed to his knees, dropping Sweothol in the mud and clutching his neck while his life flowed between his fingers. He could not speak. Salty blood filled his mouth, and his tongue was thick and clumsy. Brond blurred and swam, merging into the vast shadows of the elf-shard. The battle faded. *I'm sorry, Grandmother. Sorry I couldn't help you, Imharr. Father. Ebba. Oh gods, it's coming.*

A column of darkness, Brond approached to finish his task, raising his sword high over his head.

As he grappled with the soldier of Caergilion, Imharr glimpsed Dayraven running by Brond. The latter raised his sword and brought it down on his friend, who spun and flung his weapon in its path. Steel clashed. A wild fury spiked in Imharr as, in the midst of his own struggle, he lost sight of Dayraven. He growled through gritted teeth and strained to pull his foe's hands off him, but the soldier of Caergilion with whom he wrestled held him tight.

"Glach do!" Cursing in his birth language, Imharr pulled the man's weight onto him instead of pushing and jammed the top of his helm into the man's face. Metal clanged, bone cracked, and small lights danced before Imharr's eyes. Both their helms had fallen off with the impact, and blood spurted from Caergilese man's twisted, purpled nose. Imharr followed up with a punch behind the stunned man's ear that sent him tumbling down the slope.

Leaping for his weapon, he grasped its hilt and sprinted towards Dayraven and Brond, who raised his sword over Imharr's kneeling friend.

Imharr shouted and rocketed toward them. The assassin turned and thrust his blade at him. Twisting to the side, Imharr narrowly missed being gored as he swung Wreaker. Brond side-stepped the wild stroke as Imharr flew by, his blade whistling in the air. The former bondsman slid and gained his footing down the slope, and the two faced each other.

Dayraven collapsed in the mud. Blood washed down the right side of his neck.

"You'll die for this." Imharr glared at Brond. He remembered the man's boot stomping on Wreaker, trapping his fingers. He heard his arrogant snigger.

The assassin grinned. "No, Wetnurse. It's your friend who's dying. The dagger was poisoned. You're too late."

Part of Imharr's mind knew the words were meant to provoke his wrath. Somewhere on the battlefield behind him, another huge burst of lightning flared and cracked, whitening the hillside for an instant. While its thunder rumbled, Imharr yelled as if fury-blinded and scrambled up the slope toward his adversary. All that mattered was that this man should no longer breathe.

Brond smirked as he waited.

Raising his sword too far above his head, Imharr teetered to his right, off balance and exposed.

The assassin lunged with deadly precision at Imharr's unprotected side while his mouth opened to boast, "Predicta . . ."

Imharr had already dodged aside, as he had planned. No longer feigning clumsiness, he moved in to grasp Brond's extended sword arm with his left hand and thrust forward Wreaker with his right. The sword lived up to its name. Shattering the links of Brond's byrny and forcing out a gasp of air, the Dweorg-wrought blade slid through flesh and bone.

Inches away, Brond's wide blue eyes looked into Imharr's.

"Predictable? Thanks for the lesson." Imharr yanked Wreaker out of the assassin's chest. Gore welled from the wound.

Somehow, the man was still wearing a crazed smile. "Edan's martyr," wheezed Brond, blood oozing over his lip. His body crumpled backwards into the mud, twitched once, and lay still.

Imharr turned around to look for Dayraven. His friend had rolled down the slope. A dozen soldiers of Caergilion approached and would reach the body in a moment. Imharr grasped Wreaker and screamed as he plummeted down the slope to defend Dayraven.

Behind the press of soldiers, the shaper Abon searched for Dayraven even as he fought for his life. Like most soldiers on both sides, he had cast aside his shield since many blows had splintered it in pieces. "*Not* my gods-cursed war," he muttered as he parried a sword thrust meant for his face. "Shouldn't even *be* here." His attacker swung at him again, but the weapon slipped out of the man's hand and spun several paces away, landing in the mud with a splat.

Abon and the weaponless man looked at each other. The shaper raised an eyebrow. "Lot of rain and sweat. Slippery." He raised his blade. "Fuck off, stupid!" Whether the Caergilese understood or not, he ran away. "Don't want to kill you bastards. I'm on the wrong rutting side." Abon scanned the area around him. The attackers had thinned, and at last he gained a clear view of Dayraven, about two hundred feet up the sloping field.

The young man was running to help his southern friend, who wrestled with a Caergilese in the mud. Behind him, a group of a dozen soldiers of Caergilion was forming, and one of them pointed in Dayraven's direction. Not good. Another soldier of the Mercenary Company of Etinstone stood between Dayraven and Imharr. It was the one who called himself Brond. Bledla's agent. *Shit.*

Abon shouted, "Dayraven! Stop!" The rain and screams and din of battle drowned out his voice. The shaper could only watch as Brond struck with his blade at Dayraven then slashed him in the neck with a dagger. The young man swung his sword, but then he staggered backwards. He did not even put up his hands when Brond punched his face. "Orm take the fool!"

Abon's view of Dayraven disappeared again as several soldiers of Caergilion rushed towards the shaper. Just behind him, the Dweorg Gnorn knelt by his brother's bloody corpse and a pile of slain enemies. Nearby, Captain Orvandil withdrew his blade from a collapsing man's torso.

Abon shouted at them as he shuffled backwards and fended off a blow, "Help me save Dayraven!"

The Dweorg's head snapped up. "Where?"

"On the slope, there!" returned Abon as he avoided another blade. "Fuck!"

The shaper turned to face two Caergilese who threatened to overwhelm him. Both slashed at him. He ducked low and parried one blade. There was no time to deflect the second weapon. He crouched and winced at the coming pain.

With a sound like a windmill, a large blade sailed over his head and smashed into the sword, ramming it out of its Caergilese owner's hand. Before the man's puzzled gaze turned from his empty hand, his head spun off his neck, which erupted in a spray of red as the huge sword carved through it. The Caergilese soldier's body stood with one hand held up grasping nothing, and then it teetered and fell. The tall Thjoth stood over the man he just mowed down. To his left, Gnorn yanked his axe out of the other attacker's ruined chest.

Orvandil shouted at Ludecan, who was not far away, "Lead the men forward till I return!" He turned back to Abon and Gnorn. "Let's go."

The three sprinted for the slope just as something huge flashed behind them and assaulted the air with an enormous boom.

WHERE THE FIGHTING WAS THICKEST ON THE FIELD OF BATTLE, things fared ill for King Malruan and his troops. With their front line in ruins, the chaotic melee swept them back further and further. Monsters and grey-kirtled soldiers enveloped them, and death waited everywhere. Yet they fought on, and the king himself confronted a troll with several broken spears sticking out of its thick hide.

Malruan was still on horseback, allowing him to swing his sword at the hairy giant's tree-thick forearm. The blade bit into flesh rough like bark, and the troll bellowed. The nostrils on its large, squat nose flared wide, and the amber eyes in its pale, wrinkled face narrowed. The troll kicked the legs of King Malruan's black steed, snapping two and tumbling the screaming horse down into the mud. The king half fell and half leapt from the beast, hoping to clear it before he landed. He grunted when his body slammed into the earth, and a sharp pain lanced up from his ankle.

Even as his lord fell, the sorcerer Dalan, who stood nearby, chanted a song of origin: "Orgoshwu imbrillo ar dilghan andhuniae! Tarkanu fuindillo di firdwan inghoniae!"

Just before the troll's foot came down on King Malruan's head, it froze. A fierce smile crossed the maroon-robed sorcerer's face.

The troll turned around and seized a grey-kirtled Torrlonder by the head. Wielding the wailing man's body like a club, it slammed him into two more of Torrlond's soldiers with a bone-snapping crack, sending their bodies flying and shocking its former allies.

Dalan cackled with grim and frenzied laughter.

HIGH UP ON A SLOPE OVERLOOKING THE BATTLE, TWENTY WHITE-robed figures stood in a row next to Torrlond's king, who surveyed the conflict below. Twelve temple guards waited behind the priests, while a hundred elite bodyguards under Captain Nothelm's command stood like statues in the rain in a wider perimeter around the king and priests. Earconwald gazed down at the plain, grinning at the outcome thus far. His troops were performing well, and the beasts were living up to expectations. Once in a while he stole a glance at the priests chanting near him.

As the wind swept their white robes and the rain soaked them, sixteen priests of the Way, three high priests, and the Supreme Priest Bledla shut their eyes in concentration. Beneath their breath the twenty murmured chants that kept as strong as iron bands their power over the beasts of battle. The twenty voices wove in and out of each other as the wind moaned and the rain rushed all around.

Bledla gasped and opened his eyes. A slight smile came over his face, and he whispered, "It's gone. The boy's power. From afar I sensed it, but it's gone. That can only mean . . ."

The High Priest Morcar's face twitched. "One of their sorcerers wrested a troll from me."

Bledla responded in a calm voice, "I sense him. It's Dalan, their best. I'll deal with him."

The supreme priest looked through the grey curtain of rain down at the battle. He strode forward until he passed the perimeter of guards. "Stand well back," he commanded, and the soldiers hurried to obey. Raising his bass voice above the rain, he chanted, "Alakathon turdoniway an dirion ghandor! Ferdianon yaldunoday im khalion sunnor!"

Around the tall supreme priest a flash of bright blue split the sky. Its crack tore the air, and many of the guards fell to their knees and covered their ears as the light bleached their wincing faces. Hot, jagged bolts of energy sprang to life around Bledla, hissing and writhing like snakes, branching into forked tendrils that sought outward. A huge column of lightning-like wizard's fire erupted from his outstretched hands, plummeting toward the battle raging beneath him.

THE SORCERER DALAN LOOKED UP TO SEE HIS BANE STREAK AT HIM, but no one had time to scream.

A vast flash of energy lit up the battlefield, rendering everything for an instant into a bizarre chiaroscuro of light and shadow. A moment later, soldiers everywhere started at the vast boom that sundered the air and reverberated like a giant, ghostly echo. When the normal world returned, many blinked and shook their heads with hands pressed on their ears. Smoke curled up from dozens of burned bodies lying on the field.

The wizard's fire slew soldiers of Caergilion and Torrlond alike. Among those now prostrate was the blackened and shriveled body of the sorcerer Dalan, whose tattered maroon robe flickered with a few flames as the thunderous echo diminished and died. The rain quenched the fire, and Dalan's charred mouth and eyes gaped wide with momentary agony before death.

The troll he had briefly controlled ceased fighting. Shaking its head as if waking from a nightmare, it broke away from the battle and lumbered toward the mountains with twisted and broken weapons protruding from its body. It swept aside any man in its path, and it never looked behind.

. . .

King Malruan had witnessed his most powerful sorcerer's death. The stench of burnt hair and flesh hung thick in the air. A high-pitched whine rang in his ears after the powerful boom, and red splotches floated across his vision from the flash of sorcerous lightning that scorched and slew so many. It had to have been the Supreme Priest Bledla. Such destructive power could have come from nowhere else.

Grasping his sword from where he had dropped it, he grimaced and hobbled up. When he stood, pain shot from his ankle up his leg, and he unclenched his jaw in a rictus. The ankle was at least sprained, perhaps broken. Next to him, his wounded and frantic steed whipped its head up, screaming its agony as its muscles twitched and fluttered, unable to make it rise. Malruan shook his head and ground his teeth. He lurched forward and thrust his sword into the poor creature's neck. It shuddered. He gave the sword a sharp jerk. The steed's struggle ended in a sigh. Malruan withdrew his blade from the bloody neck and screamed.

Gritting his teeth and growling at each jolt of pain in his ankle, the monarch limped toward the thickest part of the battle. A puca leapt at his face, but the king's sword carved it in half from shoulder to ass before it landed, spraying blood and sending the two halves slumping to the ground.

One among a large group of Torrlond's soldiers pointed at Malruan and shouted. They all ran towards him. Gripping his sword with hands he tried to hold steady through the pain in his ankle, the king awaited them. Before the attackers reached him, a Caergilese captain rushed into the group of Torrlonders, stabbing one through the neck and slicing another across the face. "Caergilion!" the man yelled, though the sound blurred in the king's still ringing ears.

It was Captain Aruth of the Twentieth Cavalry Company of Caergilion, unhorsed and without a single man under his command with him. The Torrlonders turned on him, and several stabbed him at once. He tried to cut at them, but one of them sliced off his arm at the elbow.

Malruan limped toward the melee. The Torrlonders were savaging Aruth's body and had their backs to him. He grunted and chopped his blade down on a neck exposed above a byrny, slicing a red gash in white flesh. The man cried out, crumpled, and jerked his shaking hand over the welling wound.

The other grey-kirtled soldiers swung around, and a big one heaved his blade at the king, who moved to parry. Steel clanged, sending vibrations up Malruan's arm as his sword flew from his weak grasp. The Torrlonders surrounded him. He screamed defiance in a fuzzy and faraway voice. They closed in and thrust their blades, shearing through mail and flesh. Sharp, hot pain entered his body from multiple places, and a gasp rushed from his lungs. His face tilted upward. The grey sky brightened to whiteness for a moment before all went dark.

SEQUARA APPROACHED THE RIGHT FLANK OF TORRLOND'S ARMY, where Dayraven's presence grew stronger. She followed it, stopping now and then to focus while Anarad and his men defended her. At one point Torrlond's soldiers, seeing a group of armed southerners, had attacked them. In this way Anarad lost one man, Gawl, who rushed foremost into the throng of attackers. The rest disengaged when a few Caergilese joined the fray. Gawl's death was a terrible loss. He had been a friendly, capable man. She forced herself to put it out of her mind and tried to steer clear of the fighting, but it was impossible to avoid.

The sorceress of Asdralad halted to concentrate once more near a group of slain pucas. Something was wrong. There had been a sudden and drastic weakening of Dayraven's presence. She made tight balls of her fists and forced a deep breath as she focused on maintaining the necessary balance to use the gift.

Another of Anarad's men cried out and fell backward. Five of the nearby pucas, apparently quite alive, had leapt up and scrambled onto Loran, digging their sharp nails into his eyes and muffling his screams by tearing out his throat with their teeth.

The three other men and Karad ran over with drawn swords and sliced the creatures off their comrade's body. One of the beasts scrambled away limping and shrieking, but the others lay dead, this time for certain. So did Loran. The rain pelted what was left of his face, no more than bloody pulp covered in mud. The tall, strong one with the scarred cheek, Deg, shouted in the Northern Tongue, "We must leave here before we all die!"

Sequara swallowed and tore her gaze from the mutilated man. Glancing up at a nearby slope where soldiers were fighting, she squinted and shook her head. *He's right. We're out of time. I must find Dayraven now.* "I sensed him a moment ago, not far from here, but his presence weakened. I fear what that . . ."

Her words froze in her throat as an enormous flash of light and boom like thunder shattered the battlefield somewhere behind them. All their heads jerked toward the source of the almakhti, the wizard's fire. Masses of bodies churned in the distance, and smoke rose among them.

"Bledla," said Sequara. "It could be no other. I marvel he could summon such power twice in one day. We must hurry."

She turned back toward where she last felt Dayraven's presence. A strange struggle played out on the slope in front of her. Two of Torrlond's grey-kirtled soldiers fought each other near the body of a third, which lay a little way down from them. Twelve soldiers of Caergilion closed in on them. The soldier of Torrlond who was missing his helm carved through the other's chest. He ran for his fallen comrade, whom the Caergilese approached. It was too far to tell for sure, but by his dark hair and bronze skin, the running Torrlonder appeared a southerner.

"There!" shouted Sequara. She bolted ahead.

ON THE SLOPING FIELD WITH THE JAGGED MARAR MOUNTAINS looming in the background and a hard rain pouring down, a drenched Imharr shouted amidst the chaos of screaming men. A dozen soldiers of Caergilion surrounded him. Swinging his sword in wild strokes that whistled through the air, he cursed at the foes of his people, the slayers of his family, in Eastern Ondunic. "Viar or holch, don briolda!"

His helm was gone, and the rain could not wash off the blood spattered on him. Seeing their prey at bay, the soldiers closed in, but Imharr lashed out with Wreaker, catching one in the face. The man screamed and clutched his gashed cheek and bleeding eye. He reeled and fell, and his body shook as he wailed. The others backed off, which gave Imharr a chance to flee.

But he did not run through the gap, for he protected Dayraven's still body with its bleeding neck. A line of bright red dribbled out of his friend's mouth, contrasting with his pale face and downy beard. His empty blue eyes stared up as the rain pelted him.

The soldiers yelled and rushed in as a group with blades pointed at Imharr. At the same time, other figures arrived from two sides behind them.

The twelve Caergilese had no idea what was coming.

Not slowing from his full sprint, Captain Orvandil catapulted into them. Blood splattered in his wake. The Thjoth's huge sword decapitated one, whose head twirled in the air. In the next instant he ripped through another's neck with the long dagger in his left hand. A third he lanced through the chest with his sword, tearing through byrny, flesh, and bone. By then one soldier turned on Orvandil and swung his sword at him. But the Thjoth pulled his weapon out of the corpse and swept it in front of the blade. His sword deflected his foe's and with another swing carved through the man's helm, caving in his forehead and flinging his limp body backwards.

Another Caergilese soldier swerved his sword down toward the Thjoth's head from behind. But the blow never connected because of the axe that crunched into the man's chest while he was in mid-swing. Gnorn followed this up by ducking under another soldier's sword and sweeping off his leg at the knee. The Caergilese clutched his bleeding stump, screamed, and fell as the Dweorg readied his axe for the next attack.

After Orvandil and Gnorn arrived, a southerner wearing battle gear but no ensign or uniform rushed in from the right. Imharr did not know who he was, but the man engaged with the Caergilese. He parried a blow from one of the soldiers, who were now aware of attackers from two sides. The newcomer faked a thrust and, when the Caergilese parried thin air, brought his sword down on his opponent's shoulder, shattering the collarbone through the byrny and sending the man rolling and shrieking down the slope. Yet another Caergilese soldier cut at the newcomer. But a tall southerner with a scarred cheek chopped off the attacker's arm before the blow fell and then pierced him through the chest.

Abon appeared as well. The shaper bled from a cut on his arm, but he sank his blade in under his opponent's chin with an upward thrust, sending a gout of blood gushing from the man's mouth and nose. Another soldier of Caergilion met his end at the hands of two more southerners whom Imharr did not know.

One Caergilese looked around at all his dying comrades. Turning back, he growled and dove at Imharr with his sword pointed forward. The former bondsman dodged aside, tripped him, and drove his blade straight down through the man's back, pinning him to the mud. The Caergilese groaned and went still.

Imharr pulled up Wreaker and pivoted toward Dayraven's body. A southern woman dressed in black knelt over his friend. His eyes gazed upward, and he was motionless.

The battle rage abandoned Imharr. His tense shoulders dropped, his grip on Wreaker relaxed, and his grimace gave way to a frown. The sight of Dayraven hit him like a wave driving his breath out. His legs almost gave way. *What have I done? I should have protected him.*

The strange woman examined his bloody neck, from which a trickle of red still ran, and then she put her cheek over his mouth. The roars of trolls and aglaks and the screeches of pucas punctuated the din of the receding battle, but there was no one besides the dead or dying near the group huddled over Dayraven's still form. Even the rain began to wane.

Abon looked at the woman and said, "Lady Sequara? How did you come here? I'm sorry. I failed. I tried to take him away."

"Don't speak of failure yet, Abon," she answered. "While there's a flicker of life left in him, I have a chance."

Imharr guessed she was a sorceress. She was beautiful too, but he would have welcomed her even if she were the ugliest woman in Eormenlond. He did not know why she was there, but she had arrived with the intention of helping his friend. Perhaps there was a chance she could heal Dayraven. He swallowed and chewed his lip as he stared at her.

Orvandil and Gnorn also gazed at the woman Abon had addressed by name. The Dweorg asked the shaper, "Who is she?"

"She's the boy's only chance to live. Lady Sequara of Asdralad."

Imharr knelt over Dayraven and looked at the woman's face. "Please," said the former bondsman. He choked, and his voice was almost too thick to force words from his tight throat. It came out gravelly and husky, little more than a whisper. "Please help him."

The woman called Sequara looked in Imharr's eyes. "I'll do what I can."

She turned toward Dayraven's still face and put her hand near his neck. "The wound won't be mortal if I can stop the bleeding. But there's something else harming him I don't understand."

Imharr slid his hand along his jawline to his chin, where he pulled on his beard. "An assassin of the Way. Bledla's man, mostlike. The dagger was poisoned."

"That complicates things." She took a deep breath. "I need you all to be silent and stand guard."

The other men all took a step back and looked around for any sign of trouble. Imharr did not take his eyes from Dayraven. *The rage. I let the rage take me, and I failed him.*

Sequara bent over Dayraven's body and began to chant under her breath, closing her eyes and putting her hands over his wound. "Druanil vardunay nanduinae . . ."

The words blurred, and Imharr could not make out what she said. Her hands trembled, and her face was tense. He wondered if what she was doing might be dangerous. *As long as she saves him. Oruma, Anghara. Regnor, Hruga. Edan. If there are any gods, may they give her strength.*

DAYRAVEN HAD A DIM AWARENESS OF PEOPLE GATHERED AROUND HIS body, but they became vague shadows that blurred and faded away as a bright light came for him. The light bathed and soothed him, telling him there was no more striving or suffering. The elf was no longer inside his mind but all around him. At last he understood its whisperings.

Weightless, he let go. Now free, he understood he should follow the light, so he allowed himself to float outward. He remembered he had been to this place once before, when he first met the elf. Yet it was, of course, no place at all. It was a return not to a place but to a state, a state that always was and always would be. It was natural he should return. Or rather, he perceived he had never left it. All that time he had been pretending that he could leave it — pretending that he had left it. But now he knew. The life that had been Dayraven recognized home, and he flew towards the bliss of annihilation.

A sound emerged, and he paused. Strange. Such a thing should not have been in that place. It did not belong there. What had disturbed the perfect, eternal nothingness? It was something foreign, something other. Something *alive*.

Again it came. A woman's voice intruded from the world of materiality he knew so long ago. *Dayraven.* The name was oddly familiar, stirring up vague recollections of a faraway time, a life that belonged to him no longer. As for the voice that called it, he did not think he recognized it. Yet it felt as if he should. It was clear and beautiful, like a running stream. *Dayraven.* It called out the name again and again, and dim beneath it came the mirthful chortle of a raven. He turned from the light to look back.

He sensed her. She was still far away, dim and small in the distance, but he knew her. Though he had not yet met her, he knew her. From the world of flesh and blood a vague sense of the features that came with the voice arose in him. Dark brown eyes and jet hair, high cheekbones and full lips, serious expression: All were more than familiar. They were somehow, in the mystery and wonder of this place beyond the world that contained his life, unbearably dear.

The longing and sense of loss she evoked awakened him with a sharp stab that reminded him of flesh and desire. The light and the woman tugged him in opposing directions. The bliss of annihilation was so near, yet this nameless woman who was so familiar, so painfully precious, called out again and again.

I can't come any nearer, she cried. Her voice wavered, but she came closer nonetheless.

Dayraven, come back with me. She reached out, but he was still too far. *We won't be able to return.*

Hearing desperation in her wavering voice and knowing she wished to return, Dayraven sorrowed. It would be far easier to stay where he was, but he did not wish to gainsay her, or perhaps to lose her.

He extended himself toward her, and he started when they touched. A rush of dizzying energy filled him. They drew closer and coalesced. As they grasped each other in a tight, intimate embrace, their minds and their memories mingled, and their identities slipped until his thoughts and hers were indistinguishable. Together they willed to leave the light. *Back to pain. To beauty, fear, desire.*

CROUCHED NEXT TO HIS FRIEND'S BODY, IMHARR WAITED IN A FOG of despair. His hands were clammy with sweat, and he bit his lip until he tasted blood. His stomach growled and gnawed on itself. The others glanced around for any sign of soldiers from either side, but the battle had moved further away from them and closer to the city. Shouts and clashes resounded in the distance, and horns rallied troops.

Imharr did not care. He was waiting and staring at Dayraven, though sometimes he stole a look at the still sorceress for any sign of a change. She sat on the other side of his friend's body with her eyes closed as if in meditation. *Please. Bring him back. You must bring him back. I didn't protect him as I should have. My family. My little brother. I don't know how I'll live with it, how I'll tell his father. You must bring him back.*

Sequara's eyes snapped open. She fell backwards but caught herself with her outspread arms. Panting and wide-eyed, she gasped. "Never happened before . . . Don't understand . . . how he knew me." She raised her hands. Dried blood stained them reddish-brown. Sweat mingled with raindrops running down her forehead. The sorceress was shaking, and her face appeared drained.

Dayraven was pale and his eyes were now closed. His chest rose a fraction of an inch.

Imharr's mouth dropped open. "He breathes." He jerked forward and looked at his friend's neck, where the blood had congealed. "The wound's closed. What manner of miracle is this?" His throat tightened. Tears forced their way from his eyes, and his chest shuddered.

Kneeling next to his friend, Imharr rested Dayraven's head on his lap and held it in his hands as he wept with his shoulders trembling.

"No miracle," said Sequara weakly. "Had he left, I could have done nothing. I only pulled him in our direction, asking his body to heal itself and giving some of my energy to help. Not a moment too soon. He may still leave us. It will be difficult to move him, but I fear we cannot stay here. Quickly."

She pulled a kerchief from a pocket on her tunic and handed it to Imharr. "Wrap his wound in case it bleeds again. Duke Anarad, lead us back. We need to find something to bear him in. We mustn't rest until we reach safety. All our lives are in danger here. Carry him for now, but use great care."

Imharr's head jolted up. Something the sorceress said niggled at his mind, but his concern for Dayraven pressed away the thought. "Where do you want to take him?"

"Eventually, to Asdralad, where his Great Aunt Urd waits for him. But first to Adanon, I think. We'll be able to rest there, at least a few days. If you're his friends, help us now. Much depends on Dayraven's life."

"You saved him." Imharr took a deep breath. "If you know Urd, I'll come with you."

Orvandil, standing a head above the others, muttered, "I too. I owe him a debt."

Imharr squinted at the Thjoth. "Are you sure?"

"Torrlond has enough killers for its mad religion. Besides," he added with a half-smile, "Ludecan will like commanding the Mercenary Company."

"But the Torrlonders will see you as a deserter. They'll hang you if they catch you. Why would you help us?"

Orvandil frowned at Dayraven's still face as if pondering a puzzle. "Might be for the same reason you and the Dweorg stand by him. And I told you: He saved my life. I owe him."

Imharr gazed at the tall captain and nodded. He glanced at Gnorn.

The Dweorg looked over at the battle, peering at where his brother's body lay in the mud. He turned back to Dayraven and stared at his young friend, whose head rested in Imharr's hands. "Hlokk would wish for me to go with you, lad. He'd understand."

"Then we must hurry," said Sequara. She started to rise but sat down again.

"You need help," said the southern man she had called a duke.

She held up her palm. "No. I'll manage." On her second attempt, Sequara stood on her feet.

Imharr finished wrapping Dayraven's neck with the kerchief. He picked Sweothol out of the mud and wiped it clean on his breeches. After sliding the blade into Dayraven's baldric, he put his hands on his friend's chest. "We must be careful lifting him."

The duke approached and put his hand on his Imharr's shoulder. Tears brimmed in the man's eyes. "Let me help you, son." He murmured in his native tongue, "Longarr. Don baer di regoor gwae."

Recognition flooded Imharr. He looked in his uncle's face for the first time in more than twenty years. Memories of a kind man he once adored and worshipped blossomed inside him. This man had far more grey in his beard, and he was stooped and wrinkled around the eyes, but there could be no doubt. A confusing array of emotions collided with his mind, none seeming to rise above the others to give him clarity. He stared open-mouthed. "I know you."

"Yes," answered Duke Anarad with a sad smile. "But proper greetings will come after we help your friend. May Oruma and Anghara grant him life. This is a day of terrible loss, but I at least have found something I've long sought."

He and Imharr lifted Dayraven's torso together, and Imharr cradled his friend's head in one arm. Anarad's soldier, a man he called Deg, took one of Dayraven's legs in each hand. They carried him with great care down the wet, muddy slope. Imharr kept looking between his friend and his uncle. He dared to hope the one would live. He could not believe the other was next to him.

In the distance, the battle moved closer to Iarfaen, where the desperate remnant of Caergilion's army made a last stand against the overwhelming forces smothering it. Stepping over torn bodies of soldiers in both red and grey as well as ruined corpses of pucas, trolls, and aglaks, the party climbed through the defensive ditch and made their way into the camp Malruan's army had set up in the valley. It was abandoned. Almost.

A few of Torrlond's soldiers had already strayed into the camp, perhaps to loot, perhaps to be sure no soldiers of Caergilion hid there. When the Torrlonders saw the party with Dayraven's body, they ordered them to halt.

Fearing they would have to fight their way out, Imharr looked for a place to put Dayraven down so he could draw his sword. But Captain Orvandil stepped forward. When the soldiers saw the three red stripes over his ensign, they bowed and asked for pardon. The tall Thjoth told them to carry on with their duties.

Thus they passed through, and soon they found among the vacant camp's debris a supply wagon with a horse still attached. They laid Dayraven in back, and they had little trouble gathering horses picketed nearby for the others while Orvandil adjusted the wagon's reins. Imharr refused to part from his friend. He rode in the back of the wagon with Sequara while she looked after Dayraven, as did Gnorn, who would have been uncomfortable on the tall steeds they found.

They met no one else on their way out. As they left the carnage behind, the rain hushed and pattered in puddles, and the wagon's wheels grated on the road. Gnorn intoned a dirge in his deep, rough voice and gazed in the direction where his brother Hlokk lay.

"Dagraadungool hzeetarnu khaalvoku shorukweenay . . ." began the slow, mournful chant, which no one other than its singer understood.

Imharr recognized the Dweorgs' ancestral song of mourning. Gnorn was singing his brother back to their ancestors, causing Imharr to realize the enormous sacrifice of leaving Hlokk unburied. He hoped that, in Gnorn's mind, the song alone could complete the ritual. Mixed with his fragile, desperate hope for Dayraven's survival and his amazement at reuniting with his uncle was grief at Hlokk's passing. The others held their heads low. While the dirge washed over him, Imharr grimaced in disgust and tore off the bloodied grey kirtle he wore with the ensign of Torrlond sewn on it. He cast it on the road and did not look back.

. . .

On a slope overlooking Iarfaen, King Earconwald looked on with a huge grin across his face as his vast forces swept away the tatters of Caergilion's army. He glanced at the city with the same satisfaction he felt when he gazed at his treasury. Turning to the Supreme Priest Bledla, who no longer chanted to keep enemy sorcerers from wresting away his control over the beasts, he noticed his chief advisor was frowning and plucking at his long white beard.

"What's the matter, Bledla? You look like you lost something, when we've gained everything this day." The king did not often smile at Bledla, but he was in a good mood.

The rain diminished to a drizzle. The tall supreme priest took a deep breath and sighed. "I felt a strange presence. One powerful in sorcery exerted himself ere we finished maintaining control over the beasts. I thought we had eliminated all of Caergilion's sorcerers of note. I can't account for this one, and yet whoever it was did not use his power against us. It was, I believe, a healing spell."

"I felt it too, my lord," said the High Priest Joruman. "A healing spell, for certain."

Heremod and Morcar scowled at their fellow high priest for a brief moment, but then they professed to agree as well.

"No matter," said Bledla. "We have important things to deal with now. We must enter the city soon and proclaim we will spare all who submit to the Way. And, of course, they must swear fealty to their new king."

Earconwald laughed while the grave supreme priest smiled. On top of the wind-swept hill they celebrated success, hailing the day as an auspicious beginning to the War of the Way.

22
THE CHOICE

Sitting next to his uncle at one of the longest tables in the inn's common room, Imharr was nursing the last of his ale. Duke Anarad's three men sat with them, as did Karad, Gnorn, Abon, and Orvandil. The latter three, like Imharr, had long before discarded their grey kirtles with Torrlond's ensign in favor of neutral garb, but that did not prevent them from being the object of open curiosity and even hostile gazes. However, their clear association with Duke Anarad was protection enough, not to mention the fact that few would care to get into any sort of disagreement with the huge Thjoth.

All of Adanon was abuzz with the tidings of Caergilion's swift fall to the Torrlonders, and the gossip in this busy inn was no different from what Imharr and his party had been hearing ever since they crossed the border. With heads down over the remnants of their bread and mutton and their ales, he and his companions said little amidst all the excited chatter around them in Ondunic, which Imharr listened to with a growing sense of helpless dread.

"Good enough for 'em," said a woman at a nearby table. "If he turned up right here, I'd shake King Earconwald's hand and thank him for ridding the world of some Caergilese."

"If he shows up here, you'd do better to find somewhere safe to hide," said one of her companions, an older man.

"There you go again, all gloom and doom," said another man with a chuckle. "The Torrlonders just took a big mouthful, and it'll take 'em a good while to chew on it."

"Not as long as you'd like," answered the older man. "And anyway, are you telling me it sits easy with you to have the Torrlonders for neighbors with their god they want everyone bowing to?"

"Better than Caergilese," said the woman with some heat. Imharr supposed that, like many others, she had lost someone to the incessant war between Caergilion and Adanon.

He shook his head and then tipped his mug up to finish the last of his ale, which slid down his throat with a bitter taste. Part of him wanted to scream at the woman and everyone else there that they should flee. That the Torrlonders were coming for them next, and sooner than any of them could have guessed. But they would think him a madman, just like the people at the first couple villages where they stopped. There might be a hint of discomfort beneath their laughter, but they would laugh nonetheless. That is, until the Torrlonders showed up.

Knowing that much of his impatience stemmed from his own guilt and frustration, Imharr released a sigh. He looked at his uncle. "I'm going to check on Day."

Chewing on his food, Duke Anarad nodded at him, and then Imharr nudged his chair back with the sound of wood scraping on wood before standing. He weaved through the tables and the noise of the common room while doing his best to ignore the conversations.

Passing through a doorway down a long hallway, he went by several closed doors on the right and left until he reached one near the end. After a light knock, he pressed the door slowly and gently, peeking through the crack he had made into the dimness.

By the light of a candle on a stool, he took in everything in the small room in a single look. Sitting on another low stool, Sequara's back was turned to him. Beneath her, Dayraven lay on a straw-filled mattress. The sorceress turned to Imharr and nodded, giving him permission to enter. He opened the door further and, after coming inside, closed it without a sound.

Sequara glanced at Imharr and gave him a brief and formal smile before turning back to her charge. "I no longer fear we will lose him. His body battles the last remnants of the poison, but the fever is nearly gone." Dayraven was no longer drenched in sweat, and though he appeared pale and thin with dark circles under his eyes, the anguish had vanished from his face. There was even something peaceful in his bearing as he slept.

Standing in silence above her, Imharr watched Sequara change the dressing on Dayraven's neck by the candle's light. He caught a glimpse of the scar there, which caused him to wonder yet again at the sorcery the woman used each day to speed his healing. Dayraven groaned in his sleep as she finished, and she stroked his head to soothe him. The gesture was affectionate, even tender, revealing a side of Sequara that she had not revealed during the whole journey.

Imharr gazed at this rigid yet beautiful woman who seldom spoke to the men in the party. In the last few days, in the few moments when his worry and grief were not consuming him, he had watched her out of the corner of his eye. Now that Dayraven was growing stronger, he had time to take a longer look at the attractive sorceress. He was used to women noticing him, but Sequara hardly realized he was there. *She regards me no more than she does any other man, or horse or tree for that matter.* He was not certain why that bothered him. Perhaps her indifference and her reticence added to the attraction.

As she stroked Dayraven's hair and whispered, Imharr frowned. His unconscious friend brought out this woman's tenderness without even trying. *Never thought I'd envy him for a woman's attention.* Or perhaps the envy sprang from the fact that she saved his friend when he had failed to keep him from harm. *More than likely both*, he admitted to himself.

And now this mysterious woman intended to take Dayraven far away to transform him into something different from the friend Imharr knew. *They'll make a wizard of him for sure.* This would mean Dayraven could not help but leave him behind. Perhaps he would become like this woman, cold and detached, aloof in his world of sorcery. As he watched them, Imharr felt foreign and separate. In the presence of two whose difference from others bound them together, Imharr stood alone and watched the shadows on the walls shift with the candlelight's flickering. But then he nodded and half smiled at Sequara's back. *Dayraven's meant to be someone I can't even understand. Somehow, I always knew.*

"When you saved Day's life on the battlefield," he said in a gentle voice to break the silence, "you said something after you woke from your . . . trance."

"Did I?" Sequara did not look at Imharr, but she ceased stroking Dayraven's forehead.

"Yes. You said he knew you somehow."

She gazed at Dayraven's face. "Your friend is unique."

"And how *did* you save his life?"

The sorceress turned toward Imharr with no emotion on her face, pausing before she answered. "I entered what you would call his mind, or spirit, the energy that is Dayraven, by uniting with the balance of Oruma and Anghara dwelling in him. Once there, I asked his spirit to remain, asked the energy to stay in the body we know as Dayraven. It was possible only if his body could repair itself. His spirit had drifted far. It was a near thing."

"And if you had failed?"

"Then both our spirits would have been lost."

"You mean . . ."

"We would have died."

Imharr nodded. "It was brave, then."

"I took a risk. I did not wish to fail."

"Why?"

Sequara hesitated and stared at him. "Your friend has great power in him. Urd tried to tell me, but when I sensed it for myself . . . Even now I marvel at it. He may be the key to opposing Bledla. If he can help us to stop Torrlond and the Way from conquest, he will save many thousands of lives and preserve the freedom of many more."

Imharr took in her words. To him, Dayraven was his friend, his little brother. What would be left of the young man he knew after they trained him and set him up against the Supreme Priest Bledla? *He'll still be Dayraven. He'll still be my brother no matter what he becomes. They must know he's a man, not just a wizard or a prophet.* "When you entered his mind, did you see everything? I mean his whole life: his memories, his dreams?"

"'See' is not exactly the right word. But, yes."

"So you'd know him. In an instant, you'd know his life."

"Yes, in a manner of speaking." She swallowed. "There was nothing between our minds, no barrier."

"Is that dangerous?"

Sequara looked at the floor. "Yes, it is. All sorcery is dangerous, but what I did with Dayraven was especially so. Sorcery has driven many to madness, and some to early deaths. They lose the sense of themselves. But that's why we train. That's why a true sorcerer can have no attachments as most people do. And that's why it's important we make sure Dayraven is able to wield the gift that is in him."

"I see."

Sequara stared at him a moment longer as if she wished to say something, but she broke her gaze and looked again at Dayraven. "You fear for him," she said without turning toward Imharr. "That is good of you. But he must be trained."

Imharr wanted to argue with her last statement, to plead with her to see Dayraven's humanity. But he did not have the right words, and something held him back. *She's right,* he realized. He nodded at her back.

KING BALCH WAS PLANTED AT THE SAME END OF THE TABLE IN THE same long chamber he had met Sequara in almost a fortnight before. Anarad had taken his previous place as well, but Imharr was now next to him, while Abon, Gnorn, and Orvandil sat next to Sequara at the other end. All others, including Queen Rona, the three wizards, and the noblemen, brooded in the same chairs they occupied earlier.

A long silence had followed Sequara and Anarad's account of what happened.

With a deep scowl on his face, the king stared at Sequara before breaking the silence. "My scouts in the north preceded you. Torrlond's forces are already moving south towards Adanon. Does it give you satisfaction to know you were right, Lady Sequara?"

Sequara frowned. "No." Queen Faldira's earlier warnings were proving far too accurate. Things did not bode well for King Balch or his kingdom. If Torrlond was already on the move, its army must have been on their heels as they journeyed with Dayraven. This would be a short stay.

"What does that bastard Earconwald think he's *doing*?" demanded the red-faced king. He pounded the table as if it could somehow answer his question, and some of the noblemen and sorcerers flinched.

Everyone in the room other than Balch was as silent as the table. Not wishing to sound as if she were gloating, Sequara refrained from providing the obvious answer to the monarch's question. The noblemen and sorcerers, perhaps not wishing to attract their sovereign's ire, tried to look inconspicuous while Balch attempted to calm himself. He fidgeted with his beard a moment and then looked at Orvandil. Softening his tone to something approaching politeness, the king inquired, "Captain Orvandil, just how large is Torrlond's force?"

"Earconwald began with nigh ninety thousand. Best to assume eighty thousand soldiers remain, likely more. Not counting the beasts."

"A good sorcerer," demanded Balch as he turned his gaze on his sorcerers, "can control these beasts, can he not?"

The three wizards fumbled in their seats and looked at one another, each seeming to hope one of his fellows would be foolish enough to reply first. Sequara spared them the need.

"It's possible to wrest the trolls, aglaks, and pucas from the priests of the Way one at a time. However, the longer they've wielded power over the creatures, the more difficult it is to counter their spells. Before finishing, the battle would be over. Not only this, but the priests of the Way are powerful, especially Bledla. All of Malruan's sorcerers perished while attempting to fight or take possession of the creatures, and the gift was not weak in them."

Nalhad, the youngest of the three sorcerers, swallowed, the knob on his throat bobbing up then down. Old Howan raised his eyebrows and pursed his lips as he fidgeted with the sleeve of his robe. Arlech frowned beneath his hooked nose, licked his lips, and blinked. None of them said a word.

One nobleman whose name Sequara did not know said, "But according to your account, Malruan and his men did away with a large number of the beasts. Perhaps the greater part perished, which will make the fight a little more even for us."

"Caergilion's soldiers slaughtered the beasts in great numbers, but the priests of the Way have more in store, perhaps something worse. You must assume they'll contribute to the battle in some way. You face not only an army with three or four times more soldiers than you have in your entire kingdom, but sorcery that will overwhelm anything you bring against it. I felt Bledla's power while I was there, and I've sensed such depths in only one other: Dayraven of the Mark."

"Who lies dying in one of my chambers," growled Balch. "He'll be of no more use than to expire just before the rest of us."

"Dayraven will not remain here. I'm taking him to Asdralad, where Queen Faldira will train him."

"So you mean to run out on us, then." The king snorted.

Sequara looked Balch in the eyes. She kept her words cool. "Asdralad will aid you when and how it can. Torrlond moved faster than any of us feared. No one guessed its army would now be on your doorstep. We've known of Torrlond's ambitions beyond Caergilion not much longer than you have. It was impossible to organize an effective defense, especially when Caergilion and Adanon were unwilling to help each other. Don't forget," she added, and a hint of anger escaped her voice, "you were not inclined to believe us or offer aid to Caergilion until it was too late."

To Sequara's surprise, King Balch sank and stared down at the table, his countenance showing the sad resignation of a man who realized the truth too late. "Yes, well," he muttered, "that's all true. We're grateful for Asdralad's help. Perhaps we can delay Earconwald until we secure aid from other kingdoms. I rely on you and your gracious queen to act on our behalf in this regard. But I doubt the eastern kingdoms will rush in."

"Queen Faldira has sent emissaries to Sildharan and Golgar. We'll try to persuade them it's in their interest to aid you. Caergilion's quick defeat may be our best argument. What's more, as I told you, Asdralad is preparing a force, and it's already likely Sundara will come to our aid. King Tirgalan at least is sympathetic to our cause. Try to hold off Torrlond as long as possible. Stall. Pretend to capitulate to their demands at least for a while. We'll need time to gather aid."

King Balch frowned and shook his head. "The eastern kingdoms will mostlike be indifferent to our fate. Only when the danger comes to their doorsteps will they act. That's human nature, Lady Sequara. Nevertheless, I wish you luck. We'll keep Torrlond at bay as long as we can."

A knock sounded at the door and echoed in the chamber. One of King Balch's guards opened it and peered in the room. He blinked and stared at them all with an open mouth before fixing his eyes on King Balch. "Forgive me, your Majesty. I thought it best to inform you right away. A party with a messenger from King Earconwald of Torrlond has arrived. The messenger's waiting in the reception hall. What shall I tell him, your Majesty?"

King Balch exploded out of his chair, and spittle flew from his mouth as he shouted, "Tell the damned caitiff to drag his arse in here right now and explain why his prickless king is bringing troops to my border!"

The guard hesitated a moment, squinted, scratched his ear, and then stuttered, "In those words, your Majesty?"

Several around the table winced in anticipation of the inevitable eruption that followed. "Choose what words you wish, dolt! But. Bring. Him. Swiftly!"

The guard disappeared out the door, and Balch sat back in his chair with a scowl across his red face. One of his lowered eyebrows twitched.

It was not long before the flustered guard returned with a soldier who wore Torrlond's ensign on his left shoulder with three red stripes over it. The man held his red-plumed helm in one hand and a rolled up parchment in the other. To judge by his bearing and grey hairs on his head and beard, he was a seasoned warrior. Glancing around, the messenger sized up everyone in the chamber as soon as he entered, pausing for a moment at Orvandil. He gave a polite but shallow bow before looking King Balch in the eyes.

"I am Captain Nothelm of Torrlond. It's my honor to command His Majesty's personal guards. My lord, King Earconwald, sent me to bear the following message to you: We offer peace. If you wish to avoid bloodshed, surrender to King Earconwald, and he'll allow you to live under the following terms: Your realm shall become Torrlond's dukedom, owing Torrlond allegiance as well as yearly tribute. You will remain as King Earconwald's duke and vassal, and you will come to your liege lord's aid when required against his foes. Also, according to Edan's righteous will, you and every member of your realm must follow the one true faith, the Way of Edan. Anyone who refuses to follow the Way will suffer execution, as will anyone who practices the rites of the heathen cult of the demons Oruma and Anghara. You must enforce this law with rigor. If found wanting in its enforcement, you will be stripped of your dukedom and executed as a traitor. If you refuse these terms, King Earconwald will take this kingdom through force of arms and Edan's righteous will."

Fixing his gaze on King Balch, Captain Nothelm of Torrlond waited a moment and then added, "King Earconwald requires your immediate reply. I'll wait outside a moment if you wish to confer with your counsel. But know this: In defeating Caergilion, Torrlond and the Way have shown but a portion of our power. Edan has blessed us with much more strength than you can know."

Balch's face grew dark, his scowl deep. When he opened his mouth, he spoke with deliberate slowness, but his words gathered speed and volume as he progressed. "No need for counsel now. Tell that whore's offspring who poses as your king he can take his peace, his dukedom, and his Way and shove them up his nether way. If he wants to bring his big army and tiny prick into my kingdom, he'll find such a welcome as he's never seen. Do you hear me, you ass-licker of a popinjay! Tell him if he dares enter the combat, I'll cut off that little prick of his and feed it to a sparrow!"

The large chamber went silent. Sequara gazed around. Queen Rona and the other Adanese looked satisfied with Balch's response. Even the sorcerers ceased trembling and held their heads up while the messenger scanned the room.

Captain Nothelm nodded. "That reply will cost your life and much bloodshed. But the end will be the same: The Eternal will inherit all. I'll report your words to my king. They will no doubt amuse him."

He turned to the Thjoth. "Orvandil, your presence here confirms your betrayal. You, of course, know the sentence for deserters. As a former captain, your desertion is particularly base."

"Captain Nothelm," said the Thjoth, "I know the sentence. If you want to try to execute it, I'll follow you outside."

Nothelm hesitated, eyes widening a fraction of an inch before he swallowed. He managed to say, "You're a disgrace, traitor. Your time will come."

"Everyone's time comes. I'll greet my fate."

The messenger turned back to King Balch. "I take my leave, then. I'll bear your reply to King Earconwald."

"No one asked you to stay, slave of a fop!" cried Balch as the door closed. But the king deflated as soon as the man left. After a moment of grim silence, Balch grumbled, "So much for stalling. Who could bear such arrogance? I'd rather meet death than pretend to be Earconwald's duke for even a day."

Sequara sighed but kept her silence.

King Balch looked at her and shook his head. "Torrlond will strike before we even have time to organize a proper defense. Forget the notion of allies coming to our aid. Even if the eastern kingdoms would come, they would find only our graves beneath the hordes of Torrlonders. My army's not much larger than Malruan's was. When the battle comes, we won't last much longer. It appears we're all doomed."

"Mae dwarion hinol." Queen Rona straightened in her chair, and everyone around the table turned to her. "If doom is at hand, then we go to it with pride." She switched to the Northern Tongue and spoke it with a lilting Ondunic accent. "My lord, you said what was needful. Long ago, our ancestors, the Riodarae, fled their homes and died in great numbers rather than submit to outsiders, and they founded Adanon. When those outsiders came again and shattered our kingdom to form Caergilion, our ancestors never gave up fighting. We are no less determined than those who came before us to live according to our own laws, our own traditions, and our own faith. Far better to strive and die as our ancestors did than to be Torrlond's slaves."

Several of the noblemen nodded. Duke Gwalor, whose fierce eyes looked ready for a fight, grunted in affirmation.

The queen continued. "Yes, you have the right of it: Open battle would be certain doom for us. But we will *not* make Malruan's mistake. We must not give the Torrlonders what they want. No. Instead, we'll fight on our terms. This is *our* kingdom, and we know it best. We will not meet the invaders on the open field, where they would overwhelm us. But we'll strike at them from behind and under cover of darkness, when they least expect it. We'll wound them and bleed them. If we must flee and hide, so be it. Those who flee when it is wise will live another day to fight. We'll fight the Torrlonders from wherever we can until they understand the wisdom of leaving our kingdom, or until we breathe our last. My lord, let us prepare for a long war."

Sequara could not help but smile in admiration.

With renewed vigor in his eyes, Balch gazed at his queen. "So be it." Turning to his counsel, he asked, "What do you say, my lords?"

Duke Anarad stood up. "Your people are with you, your Majesty. We'll lay down our lives for our rightful king and queen and for our kingdom." He glanced at Imharr as he continued, "We are of Adanon, and our lives belong to it."

The other nobles and the three sorcerers cheered and made fists. Imharr looked up at his uncle, and though he did not shout with the others, a spark illuminated his eyes and his jaw was clenched tight.

When their cries ceased, Balch gave instructions to his nobles to gather their troops with the greatest speed. An excited discussion of their desperate strategy followed. Sequara listened but said nothing. This would not be her battle, at least not in the near term. As the conversation washed over her, she was already thinking about how she would travel with Dayraven.

IMHARR PACED DOWN A STONE CORRIDOR BY HIS UNCLE'S SIDE. Something momentous was building in him, and he was not certain how it would come out.

Duke Anarad smiled at his nephew as he pounded his palm with his fist. "We'll give the Torrlonders a real fight. They'll learn how stubborn we Adanese are." His smile disappeared as he set his jaw. "It won't be easy, of course. There'll be much hardship." He paused for a moment, seeming to see something far away. "It feels like the end of times, but it's strange . . . I feel more alive than I have in years."

"I know. I feel it too."

The older man stopped and put his hand on the younger's shoulder. "I'll leave this life with some peace, at least." He sighed and shook his head. "I wish I could have found your sister as well. I sought Riall for years. All I learned was that some farmer on the Caergilese coast bought her. But I tell you this: Should I somehow survive the coming war, I will join you in your quest to find her."

Imharr nodded. "Thank you, Uncle."

"You're a son to me, Imharr. If my boys were here, they'd rejoice to see you."

Imharr gazed at his feet. "I remember Aran and Ergal from when I was little. I looked up to them, and I recall they were patient with me."

The duke removed his hand from Imharr's shoulder and resumed walking down the corridor, swallowing before speaking while looking ahead. "They were finer boys than a father deserves. After they died in the skirmish with the Caergilese, their mother couldn't bear to live. It so broke her heart. Her body hung on for two miserable years, but on the day she lost her sons she ceased to live. War and sorrow have consumed my life. Now I'm ready for it. Ready for the end. All a man can do is face what comes with as much heart as he can muster. And I'll face it with the joy of knowing you're alive. Wherever you go, make the best of it, and live with courage."

Imharr scanned the floor as their footsteps echoed down the corridor. He knew. It came to him, and though it was painful, it was also clear. He knew what he must do. When they neared the passageway's end, he stopped. "Uncle, I've decided something."

Duke Anarad waited until Imharr looked him in the eyes, and then he nodded.

The younger man swallowed. "I'll remain here and fight by your side as your son, and as a son of Adanon."

The older man smiled, but it was a sad smile that did not touch his eyes. "I'd be proud to have you, yet I'd never ask it. We go to our doom, and you have a life outside Adanon."

"There is hope for Adanon. There must be. And how could I leave my home so soon after I've found it?"

Anarad wore a thoughtful frown for a long moment, and then he smiled again before nodding. "What of your friend?"

Imharr paused before answering. That, of course, was the hard part. "He'll be with those who can best care for him. I was supposed to guide him somewhere else. It wasn't meant to be like this. But Dayraven will recover, and he'll find his place. I know it. And, at last, I've found mine. I regret they brought us to different paths, but it can't be helped. At least we'll be fighting on the same side, though in our own ways." He was relieved to find he believed the words as he said them.

Anarad looked over the young man and nodded. "So be it, then." The two men embraced and clapped each other on their backs.

"Let me say goodbye to him."

IMHARR LEFT HIS UNCLE AND WALKED DOWN SEVERAL CORRIDORS until he came to a closed door. He paused before it. With a sigh, he pressed the door's latch and nudged it open. The chamber he entered had a window with open shutters opposite the entrance. Dust motes floated in the rectangular column of sunlight that brightened a portion of one wall and illuminated the still room, which held little other than a plain bed and a few pieces of furniture. On the floor next to the bed sat two basins, and against the sunlit wall leaned Dayraven's sword, Sweothol. The hilt's blood-red jewel refracted the sun's ray into crimson splashes on the wall.

On the bed lay Dayraven, blue half circles under his closed, sunken eyes. His illness had gouged deeper shadows into his pale cheeks. Dressed in a clean silver tunic, his arms rested on the blanket covering him, the veined wrists and hands poking out of the sleeves looking thin and fragile. Clean strips of white cloth were wound around his neck. His chest's gentle rising and falling was the only movement in the room, his steady breaths the only sound. However, someone sat on a stool next to the bed gazing at Dayraven's face. Imharr cleared his throat, and Sequara turned.

She asked in a quiet voice, "Made your choice?"

Imharr did not move his eyes from Dayraven's peaceful, emaciated face. "Yes."

Silence followed, and Sequara did not ask Imharr's decision. "He's still very weak, but I fear I must move him on the morrow. We need to leave here, and we'll have to travel with less speed than I'd like."

"Urd will care for him," Imharr said, still looking at his friend. He glanced at Sweothol. "Please see he gets the sword. It was his father's."

"I will."

He scratched his beard, held his eyes closed for a moment, and swallowed as guilt swelled in his chest, making his breathing tight. He was severing himself from something as old as his earliest memories. It felt irrevocable. Wrong. He shook his head. *I'll see him again.* "He'll pull through, right?"

"The poison was deadly, but his will is strong. I deem he'll awaken soon."

He watched Sequara gaze at Dayraven. Her beauty once again struck him. Had circumstances been different, he might have tried to seduce her. His mouth formed a wry smile, and he sighed. It was an absurd thought, of course. He had no chance, even if she had not renounced worldly ties for sorcery or religion or being queen of her island, or whatever it was that made her so rigid.

At the same time, the idea once again came that she and Dayraven were akin. He recognized in her that strange look Dayraven sometimes had when his mind wandered. Though he trusted and even liked her, he could not remember a woman as distant and cold, which fascinated him. Most of all, this woman, so attractive and detached, was taking Dayraven far away.

She wrung out a wet cloth and placed it on Dayraven's forehead, rubbing it in gentle circles. When she finished, she tilted her head to the side as if listening for his breath and caressed his head, one of the few unguarded movements Imharr had seen her make.

"He seems to have brought out some tenderness in you," he said with more suggestion in his voice than he had intended.

Her hand dropped to her side. "My interest in your friend is nothing you'd understand." Her voice was icy.

"Why? Is it impossible for you to feel?"

"I'm not sure what you mean to imply," she said after a long pause. "But if you think I've formed some sort of attachment to Dayraven, I assure you such a thing is impossible. I'm wed to my kingdom. No heir or heiress to Asdralad's throne indulges in friendships, love, or family. According to our traditions, our people's rulers are sorcerers devoted only to the kingdom. A friend or lover or child would be a distraction, a weakness that others could exploit. Such ties interfere with the ability to make clear, detached decisions for the welfare of the kingdom and with insight into the balance of Oruma and Anghara in all things. The ability to unite with this balance is the essence of magic. It's not a matter I can compromise on."

It sounded like an argument she had recited many times before.

"But you're still human. No matter how much you hide them, you have feelings."

"I didn't expect you to understand."

Imharr's face grew sober with a frown. "I'm sorry. I'm . . . Well, forget it. You're right I don't understand your magic, or your willingness to give up so much for it. But I know Dayraven's different . . . that he's meant to be with people like you, and I'm grateful you saved him."

Sequara nodded.

He looked at Dayraven and said, "I only hope he understands why I'm leaving him."

Sequara gazed at Imharr and smiled at him, the warmest expression he had seen on her face. It was subtle, but it was gentle, compassionate, and genuine. "I understand. He will too."

Just then the door opened, and Karad entered the room with Gnorn, Abon, and Orvandil behind him. "Lady Sequara," said the old bodyguard with a slight bow, "we'll be ready to leave at dawn. I spoke to these three as you bade me, and they agreed to help us along the way to Asdralad."

"Good," she answered. "The journey will be swifter."

"Well," muttered Gnorn, whose eyes had grown even sadder after the loss of his brother, "I've come this far with the lad. It's my duty to make sure he's alright. Besides, he'll make a great loremaster, and we have many unfinished lessons."

Imharr put his hand on the Dweorg's shoulder. "I'm glad beyond words you're going with him."

Gnorn's eyebrows lowered as he frowned. "You're not coming with us?"

"My place is here, with my people. We'll take our stand against Torrlond. I leave Dayraven in your hands, hoping our paths will cross again someday."

Turning to Orvandil, Imharr grasped his hand and said, "It was an honor serving with you."

The Thjoth nodded.

After releasing his large hand, Imharr glanced back and forth between the Dweorg and the Thjoth, the one several inches under five feet and the other not far from seven feet. He chuckled.

"Have you gone mad? What are you laughing at?" Gnorn puffed his chest out and stood straighter.

"I laugh because it gives me hope. A Thjoth and a Dweorg of the Fyrnhowes traveling in one another's company." He turned to Sequara and said, "If these two can work together, perhaps you'll have luck uniting the kingdoms of Eormenlond against Torrlond."

Orvandil looked down with his bright blue eyes at Gnorn, who tugged at his beard and peered up at the Thjoth. The stern expressions on the sharp-featured Thjoth and the stout Dweorg changed to grudging smiles at the same time.

"Let's hope you're right," said Sequara. "We leave at dawn. We'll transport Dayraven in a wagon again. There'll be only the six of us, including him, so two additional horses should suffice. When we reach Adanon's coast, there'll be a ship lying in wait for us. We'll journey as inconspicuously as we can, though I'm not certain how possible that will be," she added with a shy grin as she looked at Gnorn, Orvandil, and Abon, none of whom could pass as inconspicuous in Adanon or any other land.

Imharr smiled wide at the three while Gnorn rolled his eyes.

"An unlikely group of travelers, no doubt," said Imharr. "But you leave me with a peaceful heart, knowing Dayraven will be with you."

"Good luck to you," said Abon to Imharr. "Often fate favors those who meet it with courage."

"So I've heard."

A groan came from the bed, and everyone turned to Dayraven.

"Quiet now," whispered Sequara. "Let him sleep. We all have preparations to make."

They left the room. Imharr went last and, after one final glance at his friend, shut the door behind him. In the hallway he closed his eyes and whispered, "Farewell, my brother."

UNAWARE OF WHERE HE WAS OR WHERE HE WOULD BE GOING, Dayraven lay in bed, his body still fighting the last remnants of poison from the assassin's dagger. Sunlight warmed the bed covers over him. He stirred and grimaced. Even as his body strengthened, a vision of corpses on a battlefield and the cries of men amidst death and chaos haunted his sleep. The elf-shard's shadowy breath suffused it all, its eyes looming behind everything.

EPILOGUE

In the desolate border region between Caergilion and Adanon, tens of thousands of footsteps marched by the ruins of long abandoned villages. The earth rumbled beneath the pounding of endless rows of warriors crushing the settlements' remnants into the dirt. When the dust settled, a vast army faced south and waited. Arrayed on both sides of the River Maranant, the companies kept to their disciplined formations. The beasts of battle fanned out in front and slumped to the ground, awaiting further commands from their masters, the priests of the Way. The hulking trolls and aglaks resembled hundreds of mounds in the landscape, while the small pucas squinting in the sun crept under the lee of the larger beasts' shadows.

At the head of this great army, some eighty feet from the front line, Torrlond's king smiled with a gleam in his eyes. A few moments before, he had spoken in his tent with his trusted captain, Nothelm, who returned from his errand to King Balch of Adanon. Changing horses several times, Nothelm had ridden hard to reach his monarch with the tidings. Balch had responded just as King Earconwald desired. Torrlond's king dispatched orders to his dukes, who were telling the captains under their command to ready their companies. Even now his soldiers were dismantling tents and preparing to march south.

As he waited for a guard to fetch his horse, Earconwald looked at his old mentor, the Supreme Priest Bledla, who stood nearby with his three high priests. Bledla stroked his long white beard and gazed southward while Joruman, Morcar, and Heremod conversed among themselves. King Earconwald fleered and said to his chief advisor, "Well, Bledla, all goes according to plan. You see, it's easier than we dared dream. The kingdoms of Eormenlond will never unite against us, just as I said. Your friend Galdor's conspiracy will make no difference whatsoever."

Bledla forced a smile. "Your Majesty knows the heretic Galdor is no friend of mine. But you were correct about the ease of our first victory. One minor matter intrigues me, though. Captain Nothelm mentioned the traitor Orvandil's presence in Balch's court along with other foreigners."

Earconwald shrugged. "Yes, well, Orvandil's a killer and a fine captain, but he doesn't matter. We'll find him and hang him, or something more entertaining."

Bledla bowed to his sovereign. "Of course. He is a minor concern, though we should make an example of him. What matters most is the conquest of Adanon. Balch is an insolent fool. We must teach this fool what it means to defy Torrlond's monarch and Edan."

Earconwald cocked one eyebrow and grinned at his chief advisor. "You have something particular in mind?"

Zeal lit up Bledla's face, his eyes wide and his teeth clenched behind a tight smile. "Your Majesty, it is time. If you will consent, I believe we should unleash our greatest weapons against our foes before the arrival of our main army. Let us give these Adanese a taste of Edan's power. In the darkness of night we'll visit death upon them, and they will learn humility. When our forces arrive in Palahon, the Adanese will beg for forgiveness, and the kingdoms of Eormenlond will tremble when they hear of Adanon's fate."

Earconwald's guard arrived with his white steed and its gilded saddle. Torrlond's king mounted his horse and looked down on the tall supreme priest. "You wish to test your prized pets, Bledla? Very well. They may soften up the Adanese for us. Your beasts served us well in the last battle. If these others prove as effective, I'll reward you well. We ride to victory!" He galloped off to stir up the troops.

As his smile sagged into a scowl, Bledla watched his sovereign ride to the front lines. Loud enough for only the three high priests to hear, he said, "Yes, the beasts served us well, indeed. What you fail to realize is you too are Edan's servant. You too are the Way's instrument. All serve Edan or perish. Your day will come. When we've brought low the heathens, Edan will reign. He will cast aside all kings of flesh and blood. Mortal kingdoms will fall away. Torrlond itself will be no more. Even Eormenlond's name will be forgotten when Edan ushers in the Kingdom of the Eternal."

Bledla turned to Joruman. "You heard Nothelm speak of Captain Orvandil's presence in Palahon."

"Yes, my lord."

"It's not the Thjoth that concerns me, but one who might be with him."

Joruman's mouth twitched into a nervous smile. "Surely, my lord, the boy's dead. We both felt his power disappear during the battle."

"Edan's will seemed clear when I lost awareness of the boy's power. But now . . . The healer I sensed during the battle. Whoever performed the spell of healing was from outside, not a Caergilese — they are dead and accounted for — and certainly not one of ours. Perhaps from Adanon, perhaps elsewhere, but whoever used it is strong in the gift. He might have interfered and saved Dayraven's life, then convinced the Thjoth to help bring the boy to Adanon."

"My lord, it seems unlikely . . ."

"Did we find the body?" asked Bledla in a voice like frost. His brows lowered over his wild eyes.

Heremod and Morcar each took a step back.

Joruman swallowed. "My lord, there was no time. There were so many dead, some beyond recognition. All that matters is we *all* felt the end of the boy's power. His corpse is rotting somewhere on the slopes outside Iarfaen. Edan has spoken."

The crazed look vanished from Bledla's eyes. His face calmed.

Joruman pressed his case. "No one can stop us now. Edan has ordained our triumph."

Bledla's eyes narrowed as he considered his high priest's argument. "Yes. It must be. Now is the time for faith. Edan *has* spoken." Once again the master of his features, he turned to Heremod, Morcar, and Joruman. "Prepare yourselves. You and the priests under your charge must control the aglaks, trolls, and pucas. I'll need my power for our greatest weapons. Not since the blessed Aldmund has anyone wielded them. In the coming battle, through Edan's power, I'll reveal myself as the Prophet's true successor."

"Blessed be the Eternal," said the three high priests, and they bowed to their lord.

As Earconwald rallied his troops, the bellow of Torrlond's army rose to the heavens and broke like a gigantic wave upon Bledla and his high priests. While the soldiers' triumphant cries continued, Bledla sent out the barest thought and allowed a grim smile to creep onto his face. A moment later, a new sound tore through the army's din: the distant but vast shriek of some monstrous beast that morphed into a depthless roar like huge boulders grinding together in an earth-trembling avalanche. Silence seized Torrlond's army while Bledla's smile hardened.

THE END

ABOUT THE AUTHOR

Rather than write about myself in third person, allow me to thank you for reading my book, dear reader, and to introduce myself. A medievalist with special interests in Old English, Old Norse, and various mythological traditions, I teach English composition and literature and run a YouTube channel ("Philip Chase" or "PhilipChaseThe-BestofFantasy") dedicated to the exploration of the fantasy genre. Feel free to visit me there and join the wonderful fantasy literature community that exists on YouTube. I can also be found puttering around on Twitter (philipchase90), and if you would like to hear from me occasionally about writing updates or whatever ponderings I might happen to be tapping out on my keyboard, you could wander over to my website, PhilipChaseAuthor.com. Until next time!